A Trilogy
Desperate Times

Volume I

Brother against Brother

Ukrainian Short Fiction in English

Brother against Brother

Selected Prose Fiction

by

Mykola Chernyavsky
Borys Hrinchenko
Pylyp Kapelhorodsky
Hnat Khotkevych
Mykhaylo Kotsyubynsky
Bohdan Lepky
Yakiv Mamontov
Leonid Pakharevsky
Oleksa Slisarenko

Translated by Roma Franko

Edited by Sonia Morris

Language Lanterns Publications

Toronto 2010

Library and Archives Canada Cataloguing in Publication

 Brother against brother : selected prose fiction / by Mykola Chernyavsky ... [et al.] ; translated by Roma Franko ; edited by Sonia Morris.

(Ukrainian short fiction in English)
Translated from Ukrainian.
ISBN 978-0-9735982-7-8

 1. Short stories, Ukrainian. 2. Short stories, Ukrainian--Translations into English. 3. Ukrainian fiction--20th century. I. Chernyavsky, Mykola II. Franko, Roma Z. III. Morris, Sonia V. IV. Series: Ukrainian short fiction in English

PG3940.B76 2010   891.7'932   C2010-903552-6

Design and Concept: © Roma Franko and Sonia Morris
Translations: © Roma Franko and Sonia Morris
Associate Editor: Paul Cipywnyk
Editorial Assistance: Karen Yarmol-Franko

© 2010 Language Lanterns Publications, Toronto
Web site: www.languagelanterns.com

Printed and bound in Canada by
Hignell Printing Ltd. Winnipeg

Introduction

The trilogy, Desperate Times, with its volumes *Brother against Brother*, *Between the Trenches*, and *Conflict and Chaos*, focuses on stories written during the 1900 to 1930 period that encompasses the slide of the imperial Russian Empire into chaos, the breakup of the Austro-Hungarian Empire, World War I, and the subsequent upheaval in Eastern Europe fomented by the Russian Revolution. Some of these works are not for the faint-hearted, for they depict truly desperate times of revolution, war, and social upheaval, along with enormous human emotional and physical costs.

As of the early 20th century, Ukraine had long been divided by other empires—with Russia controlling eastern Ukraine, and various European powers including Lithuania-Poland, Austria-Hungary, and the Hapsburg Empire dominating western portions. In both regions the Ukrainian language, culture and distinctive Ukrainian forms of Orthodox and Catholic rites were at times severely controlled, or completely banned, and conditions for ethnic Ukrainians were harsh. There was little opportunity for education and advancement for Ukrainians, and the rising revolutionary tide that began sweeping Europe in the 19th century, with its concepts of nationalism, democracy, and freedom, soon found fertile ground in traditional Ukrainian territory.

The stories in this trilogy depict attempts at reform and political activism, peasant uprisings, revolutionary and terrorist acts, and the flowering of the Ukrainian independence movement. This blossoming of culture, language and political idealism was soon trampled however, with empires being rent asunder resulting in the redrawing of borders, the First World War sweeping millions to death, and the brutal consolidation of power by communists in the former Russian Empire.

These stories are written from multiple points of view, as is only fitting, for they are all part of the spectrum of beliefs that drove the variously motivated protagonists of those times. Thus we read about Soviet revolutionary heroes—and disillusionment with the new communist regime. We read about atrocities perpetrated by imperial forces, and the complete collapse of morality in areas controlled by anarchist groups. We experience the power of fiction that enables us to put ourselves into others' shoes, to witness events through their eyes, to feel their emotions. The results often are not pretty, but stories such as these actually happened, time and again, shaping real people.

While it is difficult to divide the stories into precise chronological order, we have attempted to begin with ones dating to the Russian Revolution of 1905 that revealed the rotten state of the empire. At the time, Russia was shocked by repeated defeats in the Russo-Japanese War, and revolutionaries of various political stripes—though mostly socialists and communists—realized that collapse was a matter of time.

The Russian Empire had suppressed ethnic and religious groups, and had attempted to impose the Russian language and church upon all within its territory. As the bureaucracy weakened and military disasters in the Far East undermined discipline and pride, the empire was faced with the steady rise of ethnically based national aspirations in many of its regions. The overwhelming human and economic cost of WWI piled on stresses that the ossified and increasingly fractious empire could not withstand.

For Ukrainians, WWI was really a time of brother against brother, and not by choice. Several of the stories in this trilogy depict the anguish as families were divided between empires, with Ukrainians conscripted into both the Russian army, and opposing Germanic-Austrian forces.

By 1917, an exhausted, demoralized and near-destitute Russian Empire was ripe for revolution, and two of them exploded that year. The first, the February Revolution, saw the abdication of the tsar and the establishment of a provisional government. The second, the October Revolution, saw the Bolsheviks under Lenin sweep into power and begin the consolidation of a new, communist, empire that became the Union of Soviet Socialist Republics, or, more simply, the Soviet Union.

The great tragedy of this revolutionary era is that idealism fell by the wayside, devolving into horrific years of civil war in which combatants of all political stripes plunged into an escalating cycle of atrocities. It didn't matter right wing or left wing, all met in extremism, mass murder, rape, torture, looting—and for extended periods—total anarchy. There was complete social, political and economic collapse, with the only authority being the barrel of a gun.

The modern Western reader has little concept of such chaos, terror, and utter helplessness. We have no sense of such ingrained hatred—hatred of the oppressive aristocracy and bureaucracy—followed by hatred of the perversion of Marxism and Communism into a new, even harsher dictatorship that placed no value on human life and blindly espoused totalitarian ends that justified the foulest means.

Yet we see in these stories that amidst the chaos created by the breakdown of the political and social order there were flickers of humanity, of ethical, moral behaviour. Within that chaos, people still loved, dreamed, and hoped. It is heartening to find that within that chaos some people still adhered to humane and principled codes of behaviour, even sacrificing their own lives to save those of others.

The issues central to these volumes of revolutionary stories are still relevant and some are yet unresolved. The short-lived Ukrainian governments of the confusing revolutionary period planted the seeds of independence, and some partisans fought on for decades against the Soviets. The reverberations from those times still impact the ongoing development of a nascent democracy in a free Ukraine in the face of still widely entrenched authoritarian values and practices in modern Russia and its resurgent imperialistic ambitions.

We have tried to strike a balance in assisting those readers who may be embarking into unfamiliar territory by providing glossaries including some of the main parties, armies, and military and political leaders, without overly interrupting the narrative flow.

* * *

Language Lanterns Publications began its mission of adding to the treasury of Ukrainian literature accessible to the English-reading world in 1998 with the six-volume series Women's Voices in Ukrainian Literature which included translations of selected literary works written by eight Ukrainian female authors between 1880 and 1920. In 2004, two companion volumes were published, *Passion's Bitter Cup* and *Riddles of the Heart,* with stories by Ukrainian male authors in the same period.

To date, Language Lanterns has produced 20 volumes of translations including several by Ukraine's leading man of letters, Ivan Franko, and two volumes called *From Days Gone By* and *Down Country Lanes* that added stories written in the second half of the 19th century and the first decades of the 20th by sixteen Ukrainian male authors.

These diverse stories from the mid-19th to early 20th centuries give modern readers a window into societal, political, religious and economic conditions in Ukrainian ethnic lands, and the gradual revival of the Ukrainian language, culture and political spirit following centuries of external domination.

The volume taken most to heart by the public thus far is *A Hunger Most Cruel* that graphically depicts through short fiction the horrendous impact upon Ukraine of the famine artificially created by Soviet authorities in the 1930s in an attempt to break the Ukrainian peasantry. This terror-famine, or Holodomor, that resulted in the deaths of millions of innocent victims, has come to be internationally recognized as genocide.

* * *

Sonia Morris, my mother and the editor of the Language Lanterns Publications team, passed away in April 2007; however, she and her sister Roma Franko, the translator, had begun work on many of these stories. Therefore Sonia's name remains as editor to recognize her passion for her cultural heritage, her historical knowledge and literary skills.

Roma and I dedicate this trilogy to her memory.

Paul Cipywnyk
Associate Editor

George S. N. Luckyj
Ukrainian Literature Translation Prize
awarded to Roma Franko and Sonia Morris

In 2009, the Canadian Foundation for Ukrainian Studies (CFUS) selected Roma Franko, Ph.D. and her sister, the late Sonia Morris, M. Phil., as the first recipients of the George S. N. Luckyj Ukrainian Literature Translation Prize.

Named in honour of the late Professor George S. N. Luckyj, an eminent Ukrainian-Canadian editor and translator of Ukrainian literature, the prize encourages the translation of Ukrainian literary works into English and other languages.

The citation cites Franko and Morris "for their dedication to and tremendous efforts and achievements in translating Ukrainian literature into English and making it accessible to a wide reading audience... After taking early retirement from their respective academic careers at the University of Saskatchewan in 1996, the sisters embarked on new careers, Roma Franko as translator and Sonia Morris as editor. Together they founded Language Lanterns Publications dedicated to publishing works of Ukrainian literature in English translation... To date, 17 volumes have appeared translated by Roma Franko and edited by Sonia Morris... The names of the recipients will be inscribed on a plaque that will be permanently displayed in the Department of Slavic Languages and Literatures at the University of Toronto."

CFUS is a non-profit charitable organization dedicated to securing funds and other resources that will promote the growth and development of Ukrainian studies in Canada in perpetuity. The work of CFUS is supported by the generosity of individuals through donations, bequests, and endowments.

Contents

Blood
(A Sketch)
(1905)

A command was given to have rifles at the ready, to have cartridges at hand, and to be prepared to leave the barracks at a moment's notice. And the barracks came to life and stirred like an agitated anthill.

They marked time only briefly, and then two companies set out from the barracks.

Where they were going, and why, no one knew for certain, but they all sensed that they were being led to a place where something incomprehensibly dreadful was bound to happen. Shivers ran up and down their spines, and they felt disengaged from their speeding feet that carried them mechanically over the cobblestone street.

Their eyes were fixed straight ahead, and they did not take notice of anything except the grim faces of their officers. They were confident that the officers knew exactly where to lead them and would bear responsibility for everything that happened. They had to submit to their will.

They ran.

Swiftly, swiftly.

* * *

Somewhere far ahead they could hear clamouring and the echoes of shots being fired. It was there that something terrifying and incomprehensible was happening—the something that they dreaded so greatly.

Chills raced over their bodies. Terror gripped their chests, and their hearts, exhausted from running, beat erratically.

Should they turn back?

Flee?

Impossible!

Now the clamouring and the shots were very near, around the corner, on the square.

The street ahead of them was deserted. In a window the pale face of a terrified woman flashed by . . . Beside a closed gate a frightened, whimpering puppy tucked in its tail and barked at them. A gust of wind swooped up trash from the street and flung it in their faces . . .

Then suddenly, a steely command: "Halt!"

They halted.

"First company, left face!"

They turned to face the square.

People waving red flags were scattering, running away from the square. Workers.

"First company, fire!"

* * *

They were shooting, and being shot at . . .

Who was doing the shooting—they did not think about that; they just obeyed the commands: "First company, fire! Second company, fire!"

And by instantly obeying every command to the very last word, they felt a sense of relief: they experienced the satisfaction of well-trained soldiers.

And it was only when everything fell silent, when they were gathering up the dead and the wounded, and when they found Petrenko their flag-bearer lying lifeless with a smashed head, that they regained their senses.

They recalled that during the battle Petrenko had stood in front of them, with his arms folded on his chest, without saying a word. He had not made a move to kill anyone himself, or to incite others to engage in fratricide.

And now, when they saw his calm, pale face, it was as if someone had broken a spell that had enveloped them, and terrible questions arose: "Whom were you killing? And why? Whose bullet hit him? An enemy bullet or one of our own?"

And not one of them could say anything in reply. They could not justify their actions either to themselves or to those at whom they had been shooting. And most certainly not to this human being who had lived among them. Who had served as an example for them. Whose corpse they were now cradling in their arms.

They cradled it like something sacred . . .

*　*　*

Tears swirled in their eyes, and curses erupted in their hearts.

They no longer feared blood. It had already been shed. Like red wine, it went to their heads and inebriated them.

"If that's how things are, then . . . let's have blood. More blood! Someone else's, or our own— it matters not!"

The Heroes Come Home
(An Improvisation)
(1905)

The children were walking ahead of me, when all of a sudden they stopped short, grabbed hold tightly of each other's hands, and stared in horror, shifting their eyes from me to something that they had spotted in a crowd of people.

A second later, the older girl dropped the younger one's hand and rushed up to me.

"Oh!" she shrieked as she struck her hands together in despair and pressed herself closely against me.

"What is it?"

"That man over there . . ."

She did not finish what she was saying, but I had caught sight of him myself.

He was not a man—he was a bird, a one-legged bird. One moment he would be standing like a crane and saying something, and the next moment he would be hopping closer towards us, and the people surrounding him walked silently beside him, stopping whenever he stopped.

He was a soldier who had fought at *Port Arthur.

"For the love of Christ, give alms to a crippled soldier; give alms, O benevolent people of God!" he—that one-legged bird—begged.

He was still young.

His hair was cut short in the military manner, his cheeks were cleanly shaved, and his youthful blond moustache was neatly curled.

He had only one leg—his left one. Nothing at all remained of his right one, and both his arms had been torn off almost at the shoulder, and only scrawny little stumps, no more than a few inches in length, peeked out like corncobs from under his rolled-up sleeves.

A small steel cup was attached with a leather strap to his left little stump, and people tossed coins into it, mostly copper coins, but occasionally silver ones as well.

It was a very warm day, and sweat was rolling down the young man's face, and as he walked he would raise his right little stump, bend his head under it—like a bird tucking its head under its wing—and wipe away the sweat with the sleeve of his shirt.

"Give alms, for the love of Christ!"

Chills raked my spine.

* * *

There he is—our wan, taciturn hero!

O my nation, do you see him?

This is your son.

He has come home from a distant land, from a bloody banquet.

Father, mother, brothers, sisters—draw near to him; let him clasp you to his tender heart with his powerful arms!

He is tormented by thirst; give him some water and a towel, pour water over his hands, let him wash up!

He wants to eat and drink—invite him to your table, let him sit in the place of honour under the icons, and let him have some bread, and let him eat, and let him pour himself some cool water, and let him drink!

Call his comrades to him, and may there be great joy among you—your dear one has come home from a distant land, from a horrible, bloody inferno!

"Give alms, for the love of Christ!"

Father, mother, brothers, sisters, where are you?

Come here, come and rejoice, and may all who are near and dear to you share in your joy!

But they are nowhere to be found . . .

* * *

But perhaps, right here in this crowd, at some distance from him, stands his old mother, and her heart is boiling over with scalding blood, and every sound emitted by the voice of her crippled child pierces her heart like a sword.

And she whispers: "Oh, may you be damned! Oh, may you be damned! What have you done to my child? Why have you made such a mockery of my very own blood? It would have been better if . . ."

"Give alms, for the love of Christ!"

And the man-bird hops farther, and with every movement that he makes, the steel cup strikes him on his side, the side where his heart is beating . . .

Oh, it would have been better if . . . the bomb had ripped that heart right out of his breast!

Spring Flood
(1905)

Part One

I

When Trublayevych walked into the large hall with its high ceiling and small semi-opaque windows where an extraordinary session of the provincial council was being held, he was engulfed by tobacco smoke and the suffocating heat created by more than three hundred deputies and members of the general public. The session had recessed, and the deputies, having risen from their seats, were standing around in small clusters and walking in the narrow aisles among the green morocco leather couches on which they had been sitting. Members of the public, who had been seated on rows of chairs at the back of the main hall and up in the balcony, were also standing and stirring like ants in a disturbed nest.

It was noisy in the hall, like in a large train station when a train is arriving, and it was impossible to make out individual words. Everything that was said flowed together, became entangled, and reverberated from the bas-relief ceiling like the clattering of a torrential mountain stream or of water rushing over a dam damaged by a flood: clack-clack-clack-clack!

As he pushed his way forward, Trublayevych surveyed the deputies. They were old familiar faces—gentlemen who were overly fed, overly pampered, overly neat and clean, and with overly slicked-back hair—and there was not a single democratic figure among them. Uniforms, evening coats, smoking jackets, frockcoats . . . Blindingly white collars, ascots, and cuffs. Ruddy, fleshy faces . . . Resolute, restrained movements, and that inextinguishable uneasiness that is ever present in the eyes of people whose hearts are not at peace. In the middle of the hall, the turquoise beret of a councillor—a high official of the customs house—stood out like a garish blemish against the spine of a couch. All this was very familiar to Trublayevych, right down to the beret of the customs official, and so he turned his eyes upwards to look at the balcony. Up there, as if fearing to lose their places in the front rows, the members of the public—for the most part ladies and young misses, with half of them being Jews—seemed to have sent down roots into the balustrade. Dressed to the hilt, they were gasping in the suffocating heat and fanning their flushed faces with newspapers and whatever else they happened to have at hand. They resembled butterflies that had alighted on the balustrade and were now flapping their varicoloured little wings, ready to take sudden flight and fly away.

And it seemed to Trublayevych, that high up in this hall, in the heated air, something tense and uneasy was fluttering, and that it would burst out at any moment with something unusual and unexpected. And that tense, uneasy mood gradually gained control of him.

As he stood there, he let his eyes wander over the audience, hoping to find a spot near someone that he knew.

"Ivan Mykhaylovych! Ivan Mykhaylovych!" a woman's voice called out to him, but he did not hear it.

"Mr. Trublayevych, the ladies are calling you," one of the men standing near him said, and he pointed to the right at a corner of the hall where some young ladies were winking and nodding to him, indicating that he should join them.

Trublayevych began moving in that direction, making a path for himself through the crowd.

He was being called by an attractive young woman, a brunette with luxuriant hair that was braided in the latest style. His face had been a bit overcast when he walked into the hall but it brightened as soon as he saw who was calling him.

It was his fiancée, Lyuba Hovoretska, who was discreetly signalling with her eyes to a spot next to her. After greeting Hovoretska's young female friends, he remained standing beside her, for there was no room to sit down.

"Trublayevych is standing on guard beside his queen," an elderly and rather unattractive lady with reddish hair whispered softly but emphatically to the woman sitting next to her. "He must be afraid that our Zembulat will snatch her from him," she added as she squinted and peered at Trublayevych through the smoke.

He was standing facing the light, and she could clearly see his youthful face with its long slim nose and fine even eyebrows that widened a bit on the bridge to give him a dignified appearance. His only detracting features were his receding chin with its small French beard and a moustache that was a trifle too heavy. He was tall and lean and stood erect with his chest slightly thrust forward.

"Oh, look, he seems to be getting ready to crow again," the reddish-haired woman whispered maliciously to her neighbour as she exhaled cigarette smoke through yellowed teeth that were flat like a trowel.

But the neighbour did not respond in kind; she simply asked, seemingly quite innocently: "And where is your daughter? I don't seem to see her."

"She's over there, at that end of the hall," the lady responded, and as she spoke her expression involuntarily changed, and she fell silent.

Everyone knew that her daughter, the carrot-topped Solokha, as she was called in the city, had recently been pursuing Trublayevych to no avail.

And sure enough, her daughter Solomiya's reddish head with its curly shoulder-length hair could be seen blazing in the light next to a window.

Just then, Trublayevych glanced in that direction and caught sight of her.

She nodded to him, and he bowed to her.

"Whom are you greeting?" Hovoretska asked.

She had noticed that he was bowing to someone, but from were she was sitting, she could not see who it was.

"Miss Dubrayevska."

A faintly disdainful smile flitted over Hovoretska's face, but she did not say anything.

At that moment a bell rang.

The chairman reconvened the session, and the deputies took their places.

"We have just heard the report of the administration about the measures that, in its view, should be taken by the province in the event that cholera spreads to this region," the chairman of the assembly stated, and he scanned the gathering with his sharp, cunning eyes while bobbing his protruding bald head with its thick aquiline nose that seemed to be sniffing out beforehand who would be saying what. "Would any of the honourable deputies like to express their thoughts about this matter?"

The customary discussion of the matter began, but the audience wasn't listening to it. It was just three weeks ago that the Japanese had broken the back of our army at *Mukden, and groans and curses had spread throughout all of Russia . . .

Among those who had family members in the war, very few knew the answers to their questions: were they still alive, had they been wounded? Were their bodies lying abandoned near the graves of the Emperors of China, and were dogs gnawing on their bones at night?

The people were agitated and irritated, like bees. The red telegrams that messenger boys delivered throughout the city had ruined their nerves, and some people could no longer bear to look at them. And now that an extraordinary session of the provincial council had been called, everyone expected that something would inevitably happen at it, that there would be some kind of demonstration. Everyone was anticipating it.

The chairman was also waiting for something to happen, and he was on guard. From time to time he glanced discreetly but questioningly at the audience in the balcony. There were no police to be seen up there. The police force had decided that it would be better to maintain peace and order out in the street, outside the walls of the assembly; on the inside, there were only secret observers.

Everyone was waiting, but no one knew where and at what moment something would happen.

As Trublayevych listened to the speech of Shpachenko, the garrulous, but empty-headed deputy who was well-known throughout the province for his childish antics at assemblies of this kind, it once again seemed to him that there were wings fluttering up above and that a demonstration of some kind was about to erupt.

"Oh, when will that old crow Shpachenko finally stop cawing!" Hovoretska said angrily. "How can he not realize that he's going on about nothing!"

Just then, the deputy unexpectedly stopped speaking.

"Do you have nothing more to add to what has been said?" the chairman asked, rolling his eyes as he was wont to do, and it was impossible to tell by listening to his voice if he was being slightly sarcastic with respect to the orator, or if, by encouraging the talkative deputy to speak for a few more minutes, he simply wanted to drag out the time in order to avoid placing before the council some of the pointed questions that were supposed to be discussed.

"Excuse me . . . I would like to add . . ." the deputy started up again. "I wanted to say that the council has the right to . . ."

"I wish to speak," a raspy voice called out in the hall, and a rustle spread quickly throughout the audience.

"Lynsky wants to speak! Lynsky wants to speak!"

The invisible wings fluttered even more loudly.

When Lynsky, a short, thickset man got up to speak, the hall grew silent. He was the most senior deputy at the assembly, a renowned community activist. He began speaking quietly, so that not everyone in the hall could hear him at first, but gradually his elderly voice gained in strength, and in a few minutes it rang out clearly, like the voice of a true leader and fighter.

He said that he was very old and ancient, and that this speech of his could well be his last one, and that he would like it to touch the hearts of the deputies. He would not spell out everything in detail, but the deputies would understand what he was getting at without having it all laid out explicitly before them.

"At this time, in this crucial hour," his voice resounded throughout the hall, "our council, as an indivisible part of our country—a country that has been dishonoured and disgraced throughout the world—cannot be so deaf that it does not hear what is being said everywhere, and therefore it cannot remain silent. A time of terrible judgement has arrived for our fatherland—a fatherland that is subjugated and devastated at all levels by impossible circumstances. That tribunal is being held in the Far East, where only recently we appeared as heroes, and where we now flee before the enemy like a pack of scarecrows!"

The hall became hushed as people grew silent and listened intently.

The deputy gave a short historical overview of life in Russia and Ukraine, and said that things could not continue in the present manner. That now, instead of concerning itself with petty matters, the provincial council must strive to make radical changes in the internal order, an order that was abhorrent to all decent people and true patriots. It must topple the immovable stone wall that separated the people from the authorities; to break the chains that bound the nation.

The orator once again turned to history to trace in it the societal currents and the efforts made by individuals to raise the flag of national freedom.

The chairman flushed furiously and looked as if he were sitting on hot coals. It was his worst enemy who was speaking. He wanted to stop him several times, but he did not dare to; being a wise and crafty person, he did not want to reveal himself as a sympathiser of the old order, and yet he wanted to demonstrate that he was utterly loyal.

"Our native land expects us to speak honestly and daringly, and we must do just that. I am confident that we will have enough strength and manliness to say what is on all of our lips at this moment: we do not need to add porches and domes to the rotting structure of our regime—we need a complete *perestroika of the entire building. This is, perhaps, my final word to you at this assembly, and I am sure that the council will respond to it!"

An outburst of applause and shouts shook the building and did not die down for a long time. The chairman rang the bell and, gesturing with his head and his hands, pleaded with the public to settle down, but it took him a long time to regain control of the meeting.

Lynsky did not take his seat; he remained standing, and when it was possible to start speaking again, he said: "Our fatherland is being ripped apart. An internecine civil war is spreading. Dark powers are organizing the so-called *'Black Hundreds,' and these 'activists' are violating the people, terrorizing those segments of society that disagree with their convictions. We must find ways of opposing these Black Hundreds that are popping up to disgrace us before the entire world!"

Unrestrained applause and shouts of "bravo" broke out once again, and feet and chairs thundered on the wooden floor. Hovoretska, her friends, Trublayevych, and all the people around them were clapping enthusiastically.

Dubrayevska leapt up on her chair and, glowing ruddily in the light like a dandelion, clapped her hands demonstratively and shouted something.

The entire hall hailed the orator. But when Trublayevych glanced over the audience, he noticed something that resonated like a dissonant note in the gathering.

A dark, rumpled man with an ashen, enraged face was yelling and flinging himself about. The people around him were trying to restrain him. When the applause started to die down, Trublayevych heard the man shout protests against the orator's speech, saying that the public was being terrorized not by the Black Hundreds, but by Jews and students.

"Take a look over there: who is that strange fellow?" Trublayevych asked those sitting nearest to him.

They all turned to look at the protestor.

"Oh, that's Babakov, an anti-Semite, who recently beat up a student and spent time in prison for it."

Babakov, not finding any support for his views, quickly disappeared from the hall.

The public, electrified by Lynsky's speech, could not settle down for a long time, and the chairman was forced to keep ringing the bell and pleading for order so that the council could resume its work. Finally, order was restored.

Everyone wanted to see how the assembly would respond to the speech. But they were to be disappointed: only one more speaker said a few energetic and eloquent words for which he was rewarded with applause, but after that everything went back to normal: the deputies sat silently, sipping tea and *Narzan.

Shpachenko continued babbling his nonsense, and the chairman, like an assiduous lackey cleaning up after extremely impolite guests in a nobleman's household, tried to efface and sweep away everything that had transpired.

The session concluded with the council deciding to elect an authorized delegate in the event that someone would be called upon to go "there."

The assembly began to nod off again. A few provincial leaders who had been perturbed by the freethinking speeches once again began to doze in their seats, forcing themselves to raise their heavy eyelids every now and then, and to glance around with reddened eyes. Several of them, fearing repercussions from the authorities for taking part in such an extraordinary, radical assembly, were preparing to flee to their homes.

But just then, a voice rang out from the balcony.

"I wish to speak!"

"We wish to speak!"

"And I wish to ask the public not to disrupt the council, or else, I'll be forced . . ." the chairman responded as he rose from his chair, ". . . to adjourn the session."

But no one was listening to him, and the gathering stirred.

Shouts flew down from the balcony: "Listen, listen! Stay in your places!"

The chairman yelled: "I'm adjourning the session!" And he began making his way out of the hall.

The delegates rose to their feet.

Shpachenko turned to the balcony, and shouted: "Shut up, we don't want to listen to you!"

But up there, an unknown orator—closely surrounded by young people so that it was impossible to see who it was, as they feared that the police might come in and seize him—hastily read a speech in a thin, reedy voice. Only the occasional word could be gleaned from what he was reading.

The speech ended with shouts from the demonstrators and with the thumping and shoving of chairs over the wooden floor.

Young people were demonstrating.

Most of the other people who were present were pleased with the demonstration; those who were somewhat more upstanding treated it ironically: in their view, it was a joke that had erupted, a childish prank.

Some members of the public laughed cheerfully and called out to their acquaintances; others argued, passionately waving their arms as they tried to prove something to one another.

Trublayevych noticed that Bilohrud, who was married to Hovoretska's sister, was among those who were arguing, and a hostile feeling stirred within him.

"This man is going to try to prove that this childish prank was a social act, and that those who created this uproar are heroes," he thought, knowing in advance that he would have to discuss this event at Hovoretska's home and that he would have to argue with Bilohrud and others who had ties with that small group of students.

This realization spoiled his mood, all the more so because he did not know how Lyuba, his fiancée, would view what had happened. Recently he had sensed a change in her, a change that he did not understand. He turned around to look at her.

Lyuba, all flushed and agitated, and with sparks flying from her eyes, was frowning as she argued with Mrs. Dubrayevska, while the latter with the corners of her mouth trembling in anger, smiled a fake, confident smile that revealed her large teeth.

"A demonstration!" the older woman said. "If I had been the chairman of the session, I would have asked that all the windows be opened after this demonstration to get rid of at least some of the stench of onions and garlic that the Jewish demonstrators left in here."

"There weren't only Jews up there, there were more *Rusyns."

"How do you know? You weren't up there; you were sitting down here, weren't you?" Dubrayevska asked venomously.

And it seemed to Trublayevych that a secret, ulterior thought flashed through her head.

"In order to know that, it wasn't necessary to be on the balcony: that was quite evident from here," he said calmly and, wishing to put an end to the disagreeable conversation and get it on another track, he asked: "Is Solomiya Frantsivna here? Why is it that we don't see her here?"

"But did not you see her? She's over there, by the window."

"Oh, I truly didn't see her."

"*Soma! Soma!" Dubrayevska shouted across the hall as she rose from her chair. "Come here."

"Ivan Mykhaylovych," Hovoretska turned to speak to Trublayevych as she rose to her feet. "Are you going to stay here, or are you leaving?"

She did not want to meet up with the younger Dubrayevska, because she was a trifle jealous of her when it came to Trublayevych.

He understood this at once, and replied without any hesitation: "I don't think that there will be anything else of interest here. We can leave now."

After greeting the younger Dubrayevska quite coolly, they moved towards the exit door.

"Our liberals have spent all their gunpowder and are going away to have a rest," the older Dubrayevska woman called out after them, offended that they had not formally taken their leave of her. "Have a good trip home!"

"Why are they leaving? There might still be something interesting," Solomiya said as she sat down on one of the chairs and ran her hand through her tousled hair.

"They said that there wouldn't be anything else of interest," her mother said pointedly. "It's you that they wanted to avoid, because look over there—they're talking with Zembulat now."

Solomiya glanced towards the door. Hovoretska and Trublayevych were indeed talking with Zembulat, who had recently started working in the administration of the provincial council. He was rumoured to be a radical and daring man from whom one could expect almost anything. It was thought that he belonged to a political party, but no one knew to which one.

He was tall, handsome, and intelligent, and had a nice voice. But his main attraction lay in his eyes—dark and so variable that it seemed there must be not just one, but at least a dozen men behind them. He had captured the hearts of many young women, not only those who worked in the provincial administration, but also well-off ladies, and some of them, when they sang the well-known song about Khazbulat, substituted his name:

O Zembulat, you daring man,
Your mountain hut is humble

And he actually did come from a family of Caucasian mountaineers.

Lately, he had quite noticeably been paying attention to Hovoretska, and everyone found that interesting. They suspected that something very much like a love triangle might come out of the situation, or perhaps even a drama: Trublayevych was engaged to Hovoretska, but now she was starting up something with Zembulat . . . And no one knew if Trublayevych was aware of it, or not . . .

And no one dared to talk to him about it, because he was a proud and solitary man; he had no friends, and he did not associate closely with anyone. Even though Trublayevych had never harmed anyone, he was not liked, and everyone secretly wished that Hovoretska would betray him, and that he would find her betrayal difficult and painful.

It was only the reddish-haired Solokha—the young Dubrayevska—who did not wish him any harm, because she truly loved him. But even so she wished that Hovoretska would reject him. And now, as she watched Hovoretska, Trublayevych, and Zembulat, it seemed to her that Hovoretska was on the verge of falling in love with Zembulat. She followed their every movement, noticed every trifling detail, and was very displeased when her mother drew her attention to the fact that it was not proper to be staring at one spot for so long.

"It's nobody's business," she snapped at her mother, and she once again turned her eyes towards the door, but Hovoretska and Trublayevych were no longer there.

They had left. Evening was approaching. It became evident that the council session was being adjourned to the next day.

II

In the evening, a group of acquaintances gathered at the Hovoretsky home.

The master of the house, who was the vice-president of a mutual fund bank, had left on a business trip three days ago, and the guests were greeted by Vira Stepanivna, a heavyset woman from a middle-class family. Actually, the guests had come to see her daughter, *Lyubov Mykolayivna, but the mother deemed it her duty, as mistress of the house, to sit and pour the tea.

The group was not a large one: the Hovoretskys' elder daughter Hanna and her husband Bilohrud, Trublayevych, Zembulat, the midwife Zahoryanska, the student Habrylovych, and Balabukha, a young but rather husky village lad who was preparing for an examination to become a village teacher.

The conversation centred on the provincial council. They discussed Lynsky's speech, and Zembulat shot down Lynsky's references to the historical period prior to *Ivan the Terrible. In his opinion, Lynsky did not know enough about history, and from an academic point of view, his speech was not worth very much, but from a public standpoint, it was quite important.

Bilohrud, stroking his long black beard and gently tugging it downwards so that his lower lip flapped slightly, authoritatively supported him.

Trublayevych was irritated by his authoritative tone, by his lip that made almost a champing sound, and by his servile deference to Zembulat—a deference that seemed particularly odious to Trublayevych because it was rooted in a ploy to obtain, through Zembulat's influence, a better position in the provincial council where they both worked.

For some time now, Trublayevych had found it difficult to tolerate this man; nevertheless, he had to come into contact with him fairly often because the Bilohruds, having very limited means, spent a lot of time in the Hovoretsky home, a home to which Trublayevych was drawn by his love for Lyuba.

And now, to add to his disaffection for the man, he had recently found out more about Bilohrud's past.

Bilohrud was a townsperson. After completing his elementary education, he joined the army, and furthered his education there. He returned with qualifications similar to that of a medic, and for some time worked in the provincial hospital. Then he landed a job in the provincial administration as a transcriber of documents. He had a good opinion of himself, and entertained ideas that were very radical. And when he married the elder Hovoretsky daughter, an old maid who was lacking both physically and intellectually, he felt that he had gained immeasurably in stature. He controlled his wife and force-fed her all sorts of illegal literature.

They had a daughter who was three years old, but she was not talking yet. No one knew if she had been born mute, or if she was a slow learner. Some people said that at one point she had started to talk, and that she became so noisy that her father lost control of himself, screamed at her and struck her very hard and, from that moment on, she never said a word. Trublayevych was well aware that this man was a very different person when he was out in company than when he was at home. He also knew that Bilohrud had no use for him, but that he curbed his hatred because he thought of him as a future son-in-law of the Hovoretskys and, because of that connection, a relative of his.

"Yes, yes," Bilohrud agreed with Zembulat. "But I think that it would have been more helpful if Lynsky had not been so vague in his speech, and had simply said what it was that should be done. The police were not present, so he could have come right out and said it. Unfortunately he did not have the courage to do so."

"But do you think," Trublayevych asked him, "if you had been in his place, would you have expounded your ideas to the very last word, knowing full well that the majority of the council members are still firm conservatives—provincial bureaucrats, and that the others are weak and divided? Or, is it possible that you too would have said only half of what you thought?"

"It goes without saying that I would have said it all—because that would have been my obligation as a deputy and a citizen. Why would I care about provincial bureaucrats? I would have spoken to the liberal assembly and to the public."

"And do you think that it would have been tactful and proper, if your motion had been resoundingly defeated?"

"Why would it have been defeated?"

"It would have been defeated because the majority of the council does not agree with you. And even the liberal section would have been afraid to put the matter so acutely. And to state it even more simply, the chairman would not have permitted you to speak, or would have removed your motion from the list of items to be discussed. To put it very bluntly, he would have told you to shut up."

"No, he wouldn't have!" And Bilohrud shook his head and stroked his beard. "But what would you have done?" he asked.

And without waiting for a reply to his question, he said: "You, most certainly, would not have made any motion at all, because it seems to you that even the little that Lynsky did say is already very daring and dangerous. Others don't think that way! Young people don't think that way!" he added in an effort—or at least that's how it seemed to Trublayevych—to needle him about lagging behind younger people.

"I assume you're alluding to the demonstration in the balcony? Well, I consider such demonstrations utterly worthless."

"Why? An open, sincere demonstration by our finest, enlightened youth? That's too much! I didn't expect that from you!" Bilohrud looked around and saw that everyone agreed.

Balabukha leaned forward to say something, but he lost his nerve, and in any event, the student Habrylovych and Zahoryanska beat him to the draw and did not give him a chance to get a word in.

"What kind of convictions does one need, to say something like that!"

"I protest! I protest!" Zahoryanska shouted. "You must take back what you just said! You do not have the right to offend our youth for its honest aspirations."

Trublayevych shrugged. Incensed, but trying to remain calm, he said: "You're not being logical, ladies and gentlemen."

"How so?"

"It remains to be seen, who is not being logical," Zahoryanska flung out indignantly as she turned away from him.

"I'll say it again: you're not being logical. After all, should the ideas that people have be confounded by their actions, by the way they carry out these ideas?

"Nobody is saying that," Bilohrud observed.

"But that's the position of everyone here. You're saying that I'm being disrespectful of the aspirations and convictions of our youth . . . and that's not true. I'm simply saying that I consider such actions as the ones undertaken today by our youth as being worth zero, or better yet, as being negative."

Bilohrud sighed demonstratively.

"Well, you be the judge," Trublayevych said, ignoring the sigh. "They raised a ruckus, shouting so that no one could make out a word they were saying, and no one could understand what it was that they wanted except for the shout: 'Listen!' And then they ended it by yelling a few mundane phrases quite clearly."

"Ah, but that's where you're wrong, my honourable Ivan Mykhaylovych! Those shouts constitute an entire program, you must agree!" Zembulat said with a smile. "You're wrong . . ."

"Perhaps," Trublayevych interrupted him. "But all the same, the speaker, instead of babbling a hundred words, could have said ten words in the same amount of time, but in such a way that they would have contained the essence of the matter, the entire program . . ."

"Too bad they didn't ask you!" Bilohrud snorted.

This was a coarse and harsh provocation.

Trublayevych just clenched his teeth and fell silent.

"Kuzya!" Bilohrud's wife drawled in a reproachful but loving tone.

"I said what I said."

The conversation halted abruptly. Only Habrylovych continued whispering fiercely with Balabukha, and Madam Hovoretska clattered some dishes.

"Gentlemen," her daughter Lyuba said, "it's not proper to act this way. Why are you quarrelling? Everyone is free to have his own convictions, and let him have them! Let's talk about something else." She looked around at everyone with a pleasant smile, and her glance did not come to a stop on anyone—not even when it reached Trublayevych's face.

He noticed this and concluded in his thoughts: "She doesn't love me. She doesn't share my convictions."

"Valeriyan Vasylovych," Lyuba turned to address Zembulat, "after what has happened at Mukden do you think that the war will drag on, or will it end soon?"

"She doesn't love me. She's in love with Zembulat," Trublayevych admitted torturously to himself, and he wanted to get up and walk out.

At the moment, however, he did not feel like extending his hand in farewell to Bilohrud and the others, and because it was awkward to leave without doing so, he stayed.

The conversation turned to events in the Far East. Zembulat, basing his views on newspaper articles and telegrams, criticized the actions of the top generals, and tried to prove that the war would not continue much longer, nor should it.

"Just imagine what will happen next, if our incompetent generals do not withdraw from Kharbin right now . . . They will be chased down like a flock of sheep, and entire divisions of demoralized soldiers will be taken into captivity. It's high time that everyone understood that our 'all-powerful' bureaucracy is completely powerless. It is powerless even in the most trivial matters, and it certainly is not able to lead our nation against such a country as Japan. As long as we are the way that we are, we are completely incapable of fighting. The new order will make new people of us, strong, courageous, zealous . . ."

"The new order will instantly transform our blood, radically change our brains!" Trublayevych commented mockingly.

"I'm not saying that. But I'm confident, and I think that no one will argue that under new circumstances, the progressive forces in our country will have more freedom, and this will undoubtedly make us better and more courageous as a nation."

"No one can argue against that," Lyuba, who had not said much up to now, spoke up. "Indeed, I think that even all those levels of society that cannot be called progressive at this time— who are neither this, nor that—even these levels will join the progressive movement when they see an unencumbered path lying before them."

"That may happen, but then again, maybe it won't," Trublayevych observed. It seemed that a spirit of contrariness was ruling him today, and it would not give him any peace.

"Of course, it will happen! One would have to have a very low opinion of people not to believe that! I give them more credit than that," Lyuba said, and she fell silent.

"She doesn't love me," Trublayevych thought once again. "She's in love with Zembulat, she has adopted his views."

And jealousy stirred in his heart. "If that's the case, if I'm not to your liking, then I have no need of you; go ahead and fuss over your Chechen, but I do not wish to look on as you do so!"

Trublayevych rose to his feet, bid everyone a curt farewell, and walked out of the Hovoretsky home.

He was aware that he was behaving improperly, that he should not be acting in this manner, and that by doing so he was offending the Hovoretskys, but an inner voice was whispering in exasperation: "That's fine . . . so be it! I spit on them! Let them play at being liberals. I'm in their way. I can imagine how delighted they must be now that I've abandoned my post! Like geese that have chased away an enemy . . . or when an enemy, without taking notice of them, simply goes away."

At the moment he hated all of them and their convictions, but, at the same time, he sorrowfully acknowledged that he was in the wrong—that intellectually he espoused the same ideas, and nurtured the same hopes in his heart. But some kind of irrepressible, passionate emotion forced him to argue with them, to see falseness in their words and in their deeds.

This emotion was—jealousy.

He understood that they were younger than he, both in years and in spirit; they had not experienced much of what he had suffered and lived through. In their souls they did not have the bitter dregs, the mire that he felt within himself, and even if they did have some, there was much less of it.

And they believed in life. They saw before them the goal that had not been created by them but by past generations, and they assumed that they could reach it in a few steps. They thought that people who were ten years older were archival scraps of paper, that those people were not pained by the same kind of thoughts, that their hearts did not beat with the same anger!

He was annoyed most of all by Bilohrud, a man older in years than he was, but who, in all that time, had not actually lived through anything, and who now flung himself into so-called leading ideas with the zeal of a neophyte.

He knew, and remembered, and could never forget that this very same Bilohrud, when he was already a medic, had participated in an all-national census, and, having received a copper medal for his work, pinned it to his chest like a badge whenever he visited acquaintances during the holidays. Trublayevych could not forget this, and it seemed to him that this gesture revealed Bilohrud's true nature, and that this so-called radical could be bought with any shiny bauble—now a liberal bauble, yesterday a bureaucratic bauble, and tomorrow, some other bauble. And this was the kind of person who was defaming him!

As for Zembulat, he hated him because he felt that this man was standing in his way. Even though he knew that Trublayevych was engaged to Hovoretska, Zembulat was making advances to her. It was a dishonourable thing to do.

Zembulat was an energetic and daring man, a wise and enlightened man, but he was a womanizer. And this made him odious to Trublayevych. And now, as he walked through the darkened streets, it seemed to Trublayevych that they would soon come up against one another as enemies. As for the others . . . they did not count! They were just green youngsters, fanatical supporters of radicalism. They claimed that they were intellectuals who had renounced a belief in all faiths, but they did not realize that they blindly believed in social dogmas that they had vaguely heard about third-hand from someone, that they believed in every passing utopia, as long as that utopia held out the promise that human beings would attain happiness in a distant, obscure future.

Class struggle . . . It still remained to be seen what that class struggle was all about, and where it was leading! They assumed a critical stance towards everything around them, but, in this instance, they were devoid of all critical thinking.

They were incensed by oppression and autocracy, but what would be the outcome if, tomorrow, these shallow people felt that all power was in their hands? A fanatic cannot be free, and he cannot respect freedom—he may not bind it in the same shackles that a tyrant has used, but he will find similar ones.

Trublayevych was walking through a square, and he sat down on a bench to rest. It was a calm, frosty evening, and stars twinkled among the treetops above. The square was deserted, and there was only one alley in which the dark figures of solitary women could be seen wandering back and forth. They slowed down when they heard footsteps behind them, or when a man walked towards them. There were also men there.

The pale streetlamps flickered. Beyond the fence that surrounded the square, wheels clattered, for there was no snow. A night watchman whistled somewhere out in the street.

Trublayevych took off his cap to let his head cool off and wiped his forehead. He closed his eyes for a moment as if collecting his thoughts, and at that moment he heard a noise, rather indistinct at first, somewhere near the square. At first he assumed that it was some drunken tradesmen who were fighting, but he quickly figured out that it was members of the intelligentsia who were screaming and calling for help.

"The Black Hundreds must be tormenting their victims," he thought, and he ran towards the spot from where the shouts were emanating. At the entrance of the square, a rather large group of people was milling about. They were beating someone.

"Help! Help! Police!" a terrified young voice was yelling.

"O-o-o-h, o-o-o-h," someone wailed.

And then a woman could be heard crying.

Trublayevych ran up and saw that two or three students were being attacked. Some wretched men were beating them fiercely, but silently. To one side he noticed a figure that looked very much like Babakov.

"What are you wretches doing?" Trublayevych shouted and, without a moment's hesitation, he flung himself into the middle of the pack.

"Police, over here!" he shouted, throwing punches at the bullies as he tried to reach those who were being attacked.

He struck one of the attackers on the neck, and at the same time someone punched him in the face so hard that he saw stars.

The attackers, realizing that an unknown man had joined the fray, and hearing the whistle of night watchmen nearby, fled in all directions. By the time that two constables ran up and a small group of onlookers had gathered, the instigators of the attack were nowhere to be found.

The only ones who remained were two students and a young lady. Trublayevych did not know them. The young men were so terrified by the unexpected assault that they could not utter a word—they just looked around helplessly for their berets. The young lady was sobbing and speaking very rapidly, but he could not understand what she was saying.

After a while all three of them calmed down a bit, and the police began dispersing the "large assembly." The students, fearing to fall once again into the hands of ferocious brutes, hailed a coachman.

Trublayevych headed for home. From far down the street came the sound of horseback riders. They were *kozaks.

"There you have it, a civil war!" he thought. "On one side there are the fanatics—the liberals and radicals, maybe even Bilohrud himself, and on the other side the other fanatics—the Black Hundreds, with their leader Babakov."

And for some reason he recalled the words of an apostle about people who were cold and people who were hot. Not so long ago, he had come across the passage quite by chance: "I know your deeds; that you are neither cold nor hot. If only you were either cold or hot! So because you are only lukewarm, and neither cold nor hot, I will spit you out of my mouth."

And Trublayevych felt that he was exactly like that: neither cold, nor hot. That he could not wholeheartedly embrace a cause; that his conscience nibbled away at his thoughts, gnawed at their roots, like a worm gnaws a plant, and that was why he was powerless.

In the reactionary period, when everything had still been quiet, he had not felt that way. But now, when a new life was seething all around him, he felt as if he was being left behind on the shore—like a splinter cast out by the water—and the current was rushing past him. It was very difficult to feel that way. But he could not renounce being who he was, and so he could not flow with the current.

He arrived home while thinking these thoughts. He unlocked the door and walked into his living quarters, as sad and lonely as he always was. He did not feel like lighting a lamp. It was better to collapse on the bed and lie in the darkness for a long, long time . . . without words, without thoughts, without movement of any kind. But instead of lying down right away, he sat down in an armchair and fell deep into thought.

After a while he moved over onto the bed.

III

It is possible to lie without moving, but not to lie without thinking.

Trublayevych lay down on the bed, placed an arm under his head and, looking up at the ceiling, continued thinking. To him this day had proven to be highly unusual. It stood out from among the rest of the grey, identical days because of the powerful impressions that he had been forced to experience.

When he had left the bank before dinner, he had not had the faintest idea that he would be feeling the way that he was feeling right now, in the evening. And he had set out to the provincial assembly as if he were going to the theatre to see a familiar play, and one that was quite boring at that. The defeat at Mukden presaged that the meeting might differ somewhat from those that had been held over the past dozen years, but Trublayevych did not have any faith in the power of the council, and he had not had any expectations that the assembly, bound like an infant by bureaucratic swaddling, would be capable of any decisive actions.

And that's how things had turned out.

But if he considered everything that he had seen and heard during the day, and everything that he had experienced, he felt that it was at this precise moment that he had arrived at a dangerous juncture in his life, and that it was inevitable that something untoward was about to happen.

He felt troubled, unsure of himself. He sensed that the ground was being knocked out from under him—he who was neither cold nor hot . . . Like the man who was neither cold nor hot, he did not have allies in his political convictions, and he had to stand alone among his acquaintances, to flee from them.

As one who was neither cold nor hot, he had just abandoned his position vis-à-vis his fiancée, and he was losing her. She did not love him. He could see it in her eyes, he perceived it in how she had shaken his hand when he had left her home in such an unusual manner, when he had abandoned her to his adversary.

He raised himself abruptly and sat up in bed. He ought to go back at once, go back there . . . He could say that he had left because he had to take care of an urgent matter in the bank.

But that would mean that he would be deceiving people, justifying himself in front of people whom he did not respect. It was not proper for a decent person to do that. Let them think whatever they wanted to. And let her do whatever she wanted to. He would not beg for her love, plead for her feelings. He was too proud to do anything like that.

He had lived a solitary life to the age of thirty, and he would keep on living that way. It was not worth his while to bind himself in marriage. He ought not to constrain his freedom, his desires with the desires of someone else—desires that could well be totally unsuitable. Everyone should live for himself alone.

Trublayevych once again fell back on the bed and, shutting his eyes, rubbed his forehead. There, under his bony skull, ideas were crowding into his head, and he could not make any sense of them. At moments such as this, he usually picked up the nearest book and began to read. He read until his eyes grew weary and his head grew heavy and he was no longer conscious of what he was reading, or what he had been thinking about earlier, or what had been irritating him.

And so he now lit a lamp and began reading. He read his favourite section in a journal—the book section—and he made a very real effort to understand what the reviewer was saying, but he could not force himself to do so, because other thoughts kept wandering through his mind. He read a review about the poetry of a renowned decadent poet and ran his eyes over the fragments of verses quoted by the reviewer, but he could not focus, and he only heard someone talking to him incessantly in verse form:

At the age of thirty, you're already bankrupt . . .
You—the one who is neither cold, nor hot . . .

Trublayevych read for a long time. He glanced though the entire section, flipped through another one, and put the journal aside. He would have liked to go to sleep, but it was still too early. He rose from the bed and began pacing the room from one corner to the other.

In the vestibule, the doorbell rang hesitantly and then fell silent. A moment later it rang more loudly. Someone had come. Trublayevych went to open the door. On the threshold stood a young lady covered with snow. It was dark, and snowing quite hard, and Trublayevych did not recognize at once who it was.

"May I come in to see you for a minute?"

Trublayevych realized that it was Miss Dubrayevska.

"Of course, do come in!" he said, as he extended his hand to her and stepped back to let her in.

"Excuse me, I'll only be a moment! I just wanted to have a brief word with you!" Dubrayevska said, as if justifying her presence while she blushed and squinted in the light.

"That's fine, that's fine . . . I'm very happy to see you! Perhaps you'd like to take off your coat—it's quite warm in here."

"No, that's quite alright." She sat down on a chair, pulled a handkerchief out of her muff, and wiped her face.

"It's snowing. I'm all covered with snow. It started to snow when I was still on Mykhaylivska Street."

Trublayevych could smell the fresh fragrance of the melting snow, and his nerves grew taut.

"It's nice when it snows. I like . . ."

"I've rushed over to see you, Ivan Mykhaylovych," Dubrayevska interrupted him, "to warn you that homes will be searched tonight. I've been told that your name appears on the list of the people to be searched."

Trublayevych raised his eyebrows. "Are you sure?"

"I'm sure!"

"Well, let them come. Thank you for warning me."

Dubrayevska rose to her feet and extended her hand to bid farewell to Trublayevych.

"Why are you in such a hurry? Stay a while! It will make me happy!" he said, as he retained her warm damp hand in his. "I'll see you home."

He felt grateful to this girl who had come unhesitatingly to his bachelor's quarters at night to warn him.

Dubrayevska paused a moment, as if she did not want to budge, but then she pressed his hand firmly and went to the door. "No, I can't, there's no time; I'm doing this on my own. I still have a few other stops to make."

She stepped out of the dark porch into the darkness of the night in which soft and airy snowy butterflies were swirling and walked swiftly down the sidewalk to the yellow pool of light created by the streetlamp on the corner. Trublayevych went out on the sidewalk and watched her until she disappeared around the corner. Snowflakes were falling on him and melting from his warmth. He went back indoors.

"So, that's how it is—they're going to conduct a search of my home! Well, that's fine; they have the power and the freedom to do so . . . Let them do it!" he was thinking as he once again began pacing the room.

He knew that there was nothing illegal in his living quarters. Whenever anything like that came into his possession, he sent it back to where it had come from. But there were letters that he would not let anyone read. The letters were from Lyuba. Her first avowals of love . . . her first dreams of happiness . . . Except for him, no one must ever read them. They were precious to him, like a part of his soul. They had to be hidden somewhere.

But what meaning did they have now, when his love was gone, carried away like river ice in the springtime? He must destroy them, so that not even a memory of them would remain. He opened a small compartment in his desk and pulled out a packet of letters tied with a pink silk ribbon.

"Such sentimentality! It's as if some young lady had bundled up letters from an immature cavalry ensign," he thought and he tore the ribbon without untying it.

The letters spilled out of the package. He gathered them up, piled them neatly on his desk, and began going through them.

Lyuba's impetuous handwriting . . . Rambling words . . . And that ineffable, charming breath of a youthful, pure, faithful love that drives people mad, that makes heroes of them, turns them into saints.

> *My sweetheart, my darling, my beloved! How could you possibly think that if some misfortune happened to you—like the one that you talked about—that I would leave you? Never! Such a thing will never happen as long as I live. You must believe me—wherever you are, I too will be there. Wherever my dearest, my incomparable one is, I will be there with him. Oh, how little faith you have! Oh, how naughty you are, my darling, my beloved! I will kiss you to death and then resurrect you with my kisses. Do you want me to do that?*

Trublayevych finished reading the letter and set it aside. He picked up another one. He ran his eyes over it and fell into thought. It was ten years now that he had known Lyuba, ten years from the time that he had first seen her. She had still been in high school back then. Slender, lithe, with happy, shining eyes, and thick black hair. She blushed whenever she met him, and he bowed to her. Then she completed high school and went to study in Moscow.

When she returned a year ago, she was a totally different person. Her figure had blossomed and filled out, her swift, jerky walk was now graceful and unhurried, and her eyes seemed to have lost their lustre. But it only seemed that way. It was only because she had learned how to control herself: lightning flashes still resided in her eyes, and Trublayevych soon saw them. She set his heart on fire, a flame also flared up in her heart, and soon they confessed their love for one another.

Trublayevych found it most endearing and precious that when he confessed to her that he loved her, she responded simply, boldly, and decisively: "And I love you." And she laughed. Their love was passionate and genuine. They were to be married in May. But recently something seemed to have come between them. The change was marked by scarcely perceptible trifles, but it was there. Trublayevych sensed it, but he could not find a reason for it.

"A fire blazes and burns itself out," he said to himself. "And that's what has happened to our love. Everything that lives, that has not congealed in frozen forms, has to change. She loves me less now. But why? What is the reason for it?" He did not feel blameworthy before her in any way. And he decided to ask her about it. He had acted on his intention about a week ago.

They had been skating on a river. The ice was clear and slippery over its entire expanse, from one bank to the other. Near the shore stood sailboats surrounded by fishing holes and barges as flat as turtles. On the hill beyond stood the city, moulded in stone, whitened with lime, and flooded with the rosy reflection of the cold red sky. Along the other side of the river, islands could be discerned in the twilight. People were moving here and there over the ice: on foot, in covered wagons, on sleighs, and on skates. They were hauling reeds on sleds, sitting near the ice holes with fishing rods and, like swarms of midges at twilight, circling in cheerful groups on skates in their favourite spots.

"Let's skate over there, down where the islands are," Trublayevych said.

Her cheeks were rosy, and she glanced with flashing eyes at the spot that Trublayevych was pointing at in the grey mist and said: "Let's go."

And, holding hands, they set out into the distance. They skated silently, and there was only the sound of their skates that, cutting amicably into the ice, seemed to be saying: "Tr-tr! Tr-tr!"

The wind whistled softly in their ears and pinched their faces, and they soared ever farther and farther towards the gloomy banks, where willows and the smokestacks of sawmills and the outlines of buildings glimmered in the mist.

They were silent.

"Lyuba!"

"What?"

"Is this nice?"

"Yes . . ."

And they fell silent once again.

A strange mood enveloped both of them, as if they wanted to lift off and fly, and in their hearts, something tickled. And it seemed to them that they were capable of everything, that they could do everything, and that nothing would stand in their way.

At least that is how Trublayevych felt.

"Lyuba!"

"What?"

"Do you love me?"

"I love you . . ."

"The same as you loved me before?"

"The same as I loved you before . . ."

"And you don't love anyone else?"

"And I don't love anyone else . . ."

She replied using his words, as if she were in a trance. Trublayevych pressed her hand more firmly and felt her respond with an almost imperceptible pressure. They continued skating.

"I'll remember this evening even on my deathbed," Trublayevych said after a while.

Lyuba did not respond.

A night whistle blared in a factory on the bank, and its hoarse, muffled sound stretched ever so far over the river's expanse and echoed from behind the islands.

"It's four o'clock."

She remained silent.

"Lyuba!"

"What?" she asked, just as she had asked earlier, without turning her head and keeping her eyes focussed on the distance.

"Look at me."

She obediently turned her eyes towards him and smiled, and he felt as if a sunbeam had fallen on the strings of his heart, causing them to tremble.

Trublayevych laughed.

"Why are you laughing?"

"Just because. Because at this moment, I'm happy."

She moved her eyes away from him, and they seemed to darken. "Never ask me about that."

"About what?" he asked. A shadow tinged his fading smile.

"About that . . . about love!"

"But why?"

"There's no need to."

"Is that what you want?"

"Yes."

They fell silent. The island was close by.

They skated up to it and sat down on a log under some willows. The red sky was fading and changing from a reddish pink to a greyish red. The city was far away, and it seemed to be standing under a cloud. Stoves were being lit for the night.

Somewhere close by, the ice cracked by the bank. Trublayevych and Lyuba both shuddered, but they did not say a word. A charcoal-grey crow, heavily flapping its wings, flew from a distant tree to the one under which they were sitting; it looked at them and, shifting from one leg to the other, screeched: "Caw." And then it began cleaning its beak on a branch.

"Let's go back."

They rose to their feet and skated away. They did not speak. And when they reached the city it seemed to Trublayevych that, just as the wind had died down, so too had something precious and beloved died in his heart.

He recalled that evening as his fingers continued going through the dear pages—the dear and familiar pages, because he had read every one a dozen times. Take this pink one, for example—he knew it by heart, and he unfolded it and read:

My dearest! You truly amused me yesterday with your recollections, so much so that I'm still laughing now as I think about them! "Come on, gentlemen democrats, come over here!" Oh, those pedagogues of ours! But do you know what kind of a trick our saintly and holy Trubaylo once played? I didn't tell you about it? Well, then, listen to this.

*When I was completing my high school studies, we had a literary-musical evening during the pre-Lenten period, and I recited *Lermontov's 'Mtsyri'. I'm not bragging, but they said that I recited it splendidly.*

Well, after the applause and the calls for an encore had died down, I went into the corridor, and there was Trubaylo limping towards me. He seized my hand, pulled me to the end of the corridor, and showered me with so many compliments, that I could hardly believe my ears.

Finally he said: "You know what, let's leave everything behind and go to the Caucusus."

"Why?"

"I'll be the king of the Lezhins, and you'll be the queen."

I looked at him, and there was a yellow droplet hanging from his nose, and his ears, like those of a donkey, stuck out higher than his bald head. And I think he had a pinch of snuff wadded between his fingers.

I burst out laughing and ran away from him. Some king he is!

Trublayevych smiled. Everyone was attracted to her. And now, there was Zembulat. And the smile vanished from his face. He recalled Dubrayevska's warning, and gathered the letters together. He must burn them! But he regretted having to do that. What if he was mistaken? What if Lyuba still loved him, just as she used to love him . . . And of what concern was his private intimate correspondence to anyone else? Who had the right to poke around in his heart? He would not let anyone enter his living quarters.

And Trublayevych resolved that if the searchers did show up, he would not let any of them come in.

It was very late, and he felt that he might be able to fall asleep. He undressed, extinguished the lamp, and got into bed. It was quiet in his room, and the only sound came from the old acacia tree as its branches scraped against the metal roof.

Trublayevych was dozing off when he heard a small bell ring softly, and someone knocked on the front door.

He leapt up. The searchers!

But he would not let them come in. He listened intently. It was quiet. And then someone came up to the window and knocked on the windowpane.

"Who is it?" Trublayevych called out, and he too walked up to the window.

"Open up! There's a telegram for you!" a voice shouted.

From whom could it be? And it occurred to Trublayevych that it might be from his sister telling him about his mother who had recently fallen ill. The telegram could also be from his brother in Manchuria who had been in the front lines at Mukden, and thus far no one knew if he was still alive.

"Right away!" Trublayevych called out and, throwing a quilt over his shoulders, he went to unlock the door.

He turned the key in the lock and pulled the door slightly ajar, but at that moment something crashed against the door, there was the sound of steel clanging, and several men rushed into the vestibule.

All of them were armed and dressed in army greatcoats.

IV

The next day Trublayevych was late arriving at the bank. The uninvited night visitors had not let him get his sleep, and he could not fall asleep even after he had seen them out.

"Forgive us for troubling you for no good reason," the officer had said as he left, but he had not returned Lyuba's letters to Trublayevych, despite all his pleas.

Broken in body and spirit, Trublayevych walked into the bank, slowly made his way up the stairs, and gave the porter his hat and coat. He combed his hair in front of a mirror, stepped into the gloomy green corridor with its tall, bas-relief ceiling, took one look at the clients, and a thought flashed through his head: to turn around and walk away from the bank—to go anyplace at all, it did not matter where.

But he did not turn around; he walked down the corridor and entered a round green room with overhead lighting where clients were sitting and walking around. He went behind a partition of frosted opaque glass that encircled the area next to the windows like a horseshoe. In this partition there were small wickets, and above them there were black signs indicating what service was provided there. The employees sat behind the partition.

"Ah, Ivan Mykhaylovych! You're still alive and at liberty, and here we were all thinking that you wouldn't be in today!" a squat, grey-haired man with a large head, closely cropped hair, a cleanly shaved chin, and long whiskers called out to him.

It was Donda, the bank's accountant, or, as he was called in the bank: "our Bulba," because his appearance evoked the paintings depicting *Hohol's Taras Bulba. But he was no warrior. His fame lay in the fact that in his sixtieth year he began making violins, with a penknife at first, and then with proper tools, and now he made very fine violins indeed and musicians often used them when they performed in concerts.

"And here we all thought that you wouldn't be coming in . . . ha-ha-ha!" Donda laughed as he peered at Trublayevych through his spectacles; his eyes filled with tears and reddened, as if he was about to cry, and his whiskers quivered on his chest like skeins of spun yarn.

"Well, as you can see, I'm here."

"But you know, half the town was searched last night! There was a search at the Hovoretskys."

"Really?" Trublayevych asked with a shudder.

"They found some kind of a book there, and took Lyuba Mykolayivna away. Ha-ha-ha!" Donda roared with laughter once again. But Trublayevych was not offended, because he knew that this man laughed even when he was weeping.

"They took her! Ha-ha-ha! And her father Mykola Petrovych isn't home just now."

"What they did is wrong. Is there a lot of work just now?"

"Well, there is a bit. Karpo Stepanovych, how much work do you have?" Donda called out to a fellow employee. "Well, fine, I'll do it all myself. You can go."

Donda knew—without being given any hints—that Trublayevych wanted to go to the Hovoretsky home.

Trublayevych silently shook Donda's plump hand and walked out of the bank.

The Hovoretsky's living quarters were quite close by, and a short while later he was ringing the doorbell. No one came right away to answer the door. And then, in response to his question whether the mistress was at home, the servant said that she was in, but she was not feeling well.

He walked into the living room. The room was a shambles. Books and music were scattered all over the window ledges and the floor, the wallpaper was torn in a couple of spots, and the upholstery on the armchairs was ripped.

Trublayevych gritted his teeth. He wanted to sit down, because he felt enervated, but it seemed offensive to do so, and so he stood by a window. It seemed to him as if a great misfortune had taken place in this apartment—as if someone had died a sudden death.

Madam Hovoretska finally emerged, wiping her eyes with a handkerchief. Trublayevych silently kissed her hand that was damp with tears, and she sank heavily into a torn armchair.

"Lyuba is done for! They've taken her away!"

Trublayevych began comforting her, saying that it was not such a great problem: if they took her away, they would have to let her go. Nowadays many people were taken away, because these were dangerous times. He too had been searched, and others as well, and some had been taken away.

But Hovoretska did not want to listen to any comforting words of reason. She talked about her daughter as if she would never be brought back. "O God, what a scandal! In prison, with pickpockets, with thieves. What will her father say when he comes back and finds out everything? What will the entire city say? Nothing like this has ever happened in our family—to be put into prison! And she's a girl—and to be among bandits!"

She wept bitterly.

"And for what? They found some kind of a book, and she wouldn't give up her letters!"

"What kind of letters?" Trublayevych asked.

"She had a packet of some kind of greenish letters . . ."

"So she didn't give them up?"

"No, she didn't. She said that she preferred to go to jail than to have them crawl into her soul. And so they took her away with those letters."

Trublayevych's heart was engulfed in blood: the proud girl had decided that it would be preferable to go to jail than to give up the secret in her heart. And it was all in vain—for he had given away her secret to those very same dishonourable people. They knew her. It could well be that even now they were reading her tender, sacred confessions.

"Oh, may I be damned, why didn't I burn those letters! Why didn't I swallow them and choke on them!" he shouted despairingly in his heart and, clasping his head in his hands, he tore at his hair.

"And her father isn't here, and there's no one to defend her, to make any efforts on her behalf! Maybe they just might let her come back . . . maybe something should be given or promised to someone." The mother once again dissolved in tears.

Trublayevych went up to her. "Vira Stepanivna, I'll go there at once, and I'll do everything that I can to get to see Lyuba."

He bid his farewells and walked out.

He would go there, see her, comfort her, and demand that she be released. He rounded the corner and walked up an incline towards the outskirts of the city where the prison was located. He wanted to hire a coachman, but then he thought better of it: he needed time to collect his thoughts, to figure out how to attain his goal. And so he continued walking.

He had never been in the prison and he had seen it only from a distance. He had seen the guards standing near it with their rifles, and he had felt intimidated by the cluster of stone buildings with their small windows and tall walls. It seemed to him that there were no living people in them—only corpses. And the white stone turrets on the corners looked like sentinels that watched over that lifeless, stony stillness.

How was one to approach a place like that?

Now he sensed with his entire being that there, in that stony coffin, there were live people, that the person who was dearest to him in this world was in there, and that was why he had to go and make every effort to have that person released. As to what he would do, what he would say—he did not think about that.

At the prison he was told that in order to see a prisoner, he had to have permission from the procurator. And so he went back into the city, hired a coachman, and drove around the city for a long time, trying to find the procurator, because he did not catch him at home.

He finally found him on the street and he had to spend a fair bit of time begging and pleading before the procurator gave him permission to go into the prison. From the procurator he found out that, on that night, Zembulat and several others had also been arrested.

With the permission slip from the procurator, Trublayevych gained easy access to the prison. He was taken through a rather large yard and led into the prison itself. Once inside, he went up to the second floor by walking up some broken stairs paved with stones and going through some low-ceilinged passageways— like those in the Monastery of the Caves in Kyiv. And then he was led into a small room where he had to wait.

He waited for a long time. It was as quiet in the prison as in a burial vault. He sat there for quite a while, and then he stood up to read the "regulations" hanging on the walls, and by the time that Lyuba walked in he was standing by the window with his back to the door.

She appeared to be the same as usual, but her eyes seemed to be flashing more, and there were sallow circles under them.

They greeted each other silently, and the guard took up a position by the door. They both felt awkward, and neither one of them was capable of initiating a conversation.

"Vira Stepanivna has sent me . . ." Trublayevych finally began speaking. "That is, she didn't actually send me, I took it upon myself to come and see you, because she's very troubled and concerned . . ."

"There's no reason for her to be concerned!" Lyuba observed coldly.

The conversation stalled without ever having taken off.

Lyuba stared into a corner.

The guard stood by the door and watched them.

"Perhaps you need something?"

Lyuba did not respond immediately.

"A pillow, and some bed linens," she said unwillingly.

Silence descended once again.

"They didn't come to see you?"

"Yes, they did."

"Did they take anything?"

Trublayevych frowned. "The letters, they took your letters."

"What?" Lyuba cried. "You gave them my letters?"

"Yes."

Tears trembled on her eyelashes, and her lips twitched lightly, convulsively. But then she quickly regained her composure and, turning her head determinedly, said firmly: "Fine!"

In that word Trublayevych felt something hostile and unswerving directed at him.

"What other homes did they search?"

"They were at many homes, but as to which ones—I really don't know. They took Zembulat . . ."

Lyuba's eyelids fluttered slightly. And then they both fell silent once again.

The guard shifted from one foot to another. His action reminded Trublayevych that the time allotted for the conversation might end at any moment, and so he broke the silence.

"We'll make every effort to gain your release on bail. In two days Mykola Petrovych will return, and we'll ask him to go and see the governor."

"That's not necessary. They'll release me soon now in any event," Lyuba said decisively, as if she had weighed her options. "There's nothing to hide now. They've already read them . . ."

Trublayevych caught on that she was referring to the letters, and he felt distressed and ashamed of himself, of what he had done. He wanted to justify himself, but Lyuba, as if she had read his mind, gestured dismissively.

"There's nothing more to be said or done! Tell my mother not to worry." She rose from the bench.

"Good-bye. Thank you for not forgetting about me," she said coldly as she walked to the door.

Trublayevych wanted to stop her, to tell her everything, but he did not have the nerve to do it. And what could he have said to her, when he sensed that the abyss that had recently begun to appear between them had suddenly widened, and he was left standing on one bank, while she was on the other one. He felt that the final threads that had held them together were disintegrating as if they had been charred . . . And he walked out of the prison feeling enervated and disconsolate.

A cold wind was blowing in from the steppe, from the cemetery, and it was driving the snow into the city. He turned to walk with the wind. And when he looked down at the grey wavelets of snow mixed with dirt that were rippling ahead of him, it seemed to him that fate was carrying away to places unknown everything that was dear to him, everything that was most precious to him—it was carrying away his recent past. And he felt regret but, much to his own surprise, he remained calm, probably because he did not feel that he was to blame for what had happened, and he knew that what had happened could not be undone. But there was a great void in his heart.

"Well, so what? If that's how it's to be, that's how it will be!" he said out loud as he pressed his walking stick into the frozen ground, and that pressure resonated painfully in his heart.

He walked through familiar streets, met and greeted people whom he knew, but he was not aware of anything that he was doing. It seemed to him that he was surrounded by a wasteland, and that the biggest wasteland of all lay within him.

"A high-priority telegram from General Lynevych! Thousands of Japanese have been taken prisoner!" the telegram carriers shouted, trying to force their telegrams on passersby.

He went to the Hovoretsky home, told Lyuba's mother about everything except the letters, and she asked him to get her permission to go and see her daughter the next day in order to pass her a few items. He promised to do so. After finding out that he had not eaten anything since morning, Madam Hovoretska invited him to have a bite, but he refused, for it seemed to him that he could not swallow even a bit of bread in this home.

Upon leaving the Hovoretsky living quarters, he set off for his own home, but then he turned around and walked towards the river. He felt a need for wide-open spaces, for being apart from other people, for being alone, all by himself with his grief, with the emptiness in his heart.

He was not deceiving himself. Even though the final word had not yet been spoken, he sensed that it was all over between Lyuba and him. Her heart had been given to another man, to the man who was incarcerated with her. He knew this from the way her eyelids had fluttered when she heard that Zembulat had also been imprisoned . . .

Well, all that remained now for him to do was to tear out by the roots all the feelings that he had for her, to chase away all memories of her out of his mind, to forget about her. But was it possible to do that? When he could still see her standing before him in his mind's eye, when she silently reproached him! For what? He was not guilty of anything. She was guilty; she was the traitor! She had deceived him. She had never loved him! Never! It had all been nothing more than a deception!

A deception? No! He knew that it had not been a deception. He knew that it had all been true, that she had loved him, only him—the one who had no friends, no colleagues with whom to share his thoughts, his convictions; the one who was neither cold, nor hot!

At this thought, anger welled within Trublayevych's heart. "It is because you are neither cold nor hot that she has cast you out of her heart!" he thought. "Because she is passionate, and she needs someone who is equally passionate."

He laughed. Indecent thoughts, emerging involuntarily from the dark corners of his heart, arose before him and taunted him. And Trublayevych felt pained, and disgusted, and ashamed, but he did not chase the thoughts away. He wanted to humiliate himself to the nth degree, to indulge in something loathsome because he hated himself. He imagined Lyuba and Zembulat in impossibly shameful poses, mentally forced them to engage in the most repugnant acts; he sneered at them, but all the while he sensed that he was jeering at himself . . .

He was at the river now, out on the ice. The wind drove the snowy waves over the slippery surface, scattered them, and then gathered them together once again. Trublayevych walked along a road that had been beaten down by wheels and horses' hooves, because it was too slippery to walk elsewhere. Along this road covered wagons groaned and people strained mightily as they pulled sleds piled with reeds from the islands. He passed by them and continued walking until he crossed the river.

The path went on down a stream among the islands. On the banks on both sides, willows and reeds rustled in the wind. But Trublayevych did not listen to the rustling.

He was seeking isolation . . . he was seeking oblivion . . . To the left he noticed a small creek and he turned towards it. He walked for a long time without any thoughts, without any desires, and then, with a heavy heart, sat down on the bank.

Now he could hear the bulrushes rustling, even though he did not focus on the sound. His mind seemed frozen, solidified in his head, and he grew immobile. All around him there was rustling, and whirring, and whistling, and whizzing, and shrill notes of solitary weeping. The wind vivified the inert bulrushes, and they came alive with a dreamy, ephemeral life. And in that life there was much that gave one pause to think. At first Trublayevych sat without thinking about anything, and without hearing anything. But then, in the vast sea of sounds surrounding him, he involuntarily began noticing individual notes and listening to them.

Everything was alive, everything was rustling. Everyone in the world had his own place and his own fate. And everyone had the right to his fate . . . to his own fate, regardless of what it was! No one could blame him for what he was, for it was not he who had made him what he was—it was life that had done it.

Was the broken reed over there to blame that it groaned so bitterly, wailed so lustily when the wind blew more strongly? Was it to blame that it was grieving instead of whispering cheerfully like a young girl, or champing its lips in satisfaction like a toothless old granny? It was broken, crushed, crippled. But it wanted to live and it had a right to do so, and there was a place for it among these bulrushes, just as there had to be.

And it was the same with a man. No matter who he was, what thoughts and convictions he had, he had a right to them, and no one had the authority to tear them from him. And no one had the right to punish him for them, to foist his own thoughts, his own desires, his own laws on him. No one had that right.

Everyone lived for himself alone, and they all lived together. Like these bulrushes. There were ever so many dissonances, ever so much that seemed superfluous, unnecessary, among the individual sounds, but when they were taken all together they created a harmony—an expansive and grandiose harmony like nature itself. Like mother nature. There was room in nature for everyone, there was a warm ray of sunshine for everyone—in the earth, and on the earth, and in the water, and way up there, in the azure heavens.

Trublayevych glanced upwards. Up there, right above him, the clouds parted momentarily, and the blue infinity of the sky gazed down upon him. "It's the eye of eternity," he thought. He sat for a while longer, and then rose to his feet.

He wanted to leave, but then he heard the sound of voices coming from the far end of the stream.

He waited for a moment. It was a man and a woman, each pulling a sled piled high with reeds. It was difficult to pull the sleds over the slippery ice.

They came up to Trublayevych and greeted him.

"Here, let me help you," Trublayevych said, and he took hold of the woman's rope.

"Don't bother, don't bother! I'll do it myself . . ."

"It's no bother. I'm going that way in any event."

They pulled the sled together. The woman was old, and she was breathing heavily from the strain.

"Why are you hauling reeds by yourselves? Don't you have anyone younger to do it for you?" Trublayevych asked.

"We have a son, but he's not home now."

"Where is he?"

"He's gone off to the war. We've been left all alone. Maybe he was killed some time ago . . . They say a lot of people have been killed, ever so many! He wrote to us last fall, but we haven't heard from him since then."

"They say that there will be a truce soon," the old man said, and he waved his arms and beat his chest and shoulders like a fisherman out in the cold. "It sure is a chilly one today!"

"Are you a fisherman?" Trublayevych asked.

"A fisherman, and a shoemaker, and at times I work in a sawmill. You have to make a living one way or another! But I have no strength left. And the children don't help us. They're all doing their best to look out for themselves . . . If only I had a bit of land, I could either rent it outright, or lease it to a sharecropper, and then I'd at least have some grain. But as it is, I don't have anything. And so we cut down reeds to heat the house, because otherwise we'd not only be hungry, we'd freeze to death!"

"They say that the Jews have given Port Arthur to the Japanese. Is that true?" the old man asked after a moment of silence. "They're such repulsive ruffians, villains! Half of them should be strung up!"

"For what?"

"Eh! They're to blame for everything. It's because of them that we have nothing to eat!"

The old man was talkative but ignorant. He blamed all his troubles on the Jews. When Trublayevych tried to convince him otherwise, he simply gestured dismissively.

"We know what they're like! Why, just recently, on the Feast of the Elevation of the Cross, the archbishop said that they had even crucified the Son of God."

Trublayevych pulled the old woman's sled out onto the wider stream and then, turning towards the city, left the old couple.

"There you have them—the ignorant masses that spend their entire lives struggling to earn a scrap of bread!" Trublayevych thought as he walked over the ice. "There you have the dry, broken reeds that rustled back there in the bulrush patches. They rustle, and then they vanish with their deeds, their thoughts, their worries. And in the spring, new reeds will grow to replace them, new reeds that will drone their own songs. And as for these old ones—let them live out their lives until they are consumed by fire or swept away by a spring flood."

From the bulrushes came the sound of human voices, and up ahead there were shouts and merry laughter. Young people— youths and young ladies—were skating towards him in a cheerful group.

Among them he spotted Dubrayevska. They exchanged greetings.

"Let's go back!" she shouted. "We'll accompany Ivan Mykhaylovych so that wolves don't devour him!"

"Where in the world would any wolves come from? There aren't even any rabbits here!" Trublayevych laughed.

"Oh, but there are timid rabbits here. If only you knew how badly the gendarmes scared some people yesterday!"

All rosy and fresh from the wind and the frost, she laughed as she looked at Trublayevych, and at the moment she seemed rather attractive to him. Her carroty-red hair undulated in the wind, her short jacket hugged her slender figure tightly, and her rather delicate legs, clad in leggings, moved agilely this way and that way as she fluttered around Trublayevych like a butterfly.

He knew that she had fallen in love with him a long time ago, and now this knowledge warmed his heart: there was a person who loved him, who loved him notwithstanding the fact that he had never paid any attention to her.

He wanted to say something nice, affectionate to her, but he could not. A thought about Lyuba suddenly pierced his brain and echoed painfully in his heart. He restrained himself.

"Why are you standing still?" Dubrayevska asked him as she skated around him in circles and arcs. "Let's go out farther– the ice is better there."

"Solomiya Frantsivna, tell me truthfully: do you feel sorry for Lyuba Mykolayivna?"

Dubrayevska came to a standstill and raised her eyebrows in surprise as if she did not understand what he was asking her; then she tossed her hair and burst out laughing as she spun around like a top in one spot.

"I feel very sorry!" she laughed. "But then . . . not really."

"Why so?"

"She . . . she isn't alone in there!"

"What do you mean?"

"Just that! Let's go."

And she skated off, glancing back at him, as if luring him onwards. Even though Trublayevych knew what she was hinting at, he felt a painful need to have her state frankly what she was thinking—to hear her say the same thing that he was thinking. It seemed to him that if his painful wound were scratched, it would ache less severely.

He asked her again, but she fled without responding, and then she flitted back like a bee and wove patterns around him.

Trublayevych returned home when twilight was falling; he felt crushed and exhausted, but composed. The long walk, the fresh air, the people—all of that had soothed his nerves, calmed his thoughts.

It was only somewhere deep inside, under his heart, that he seemed to feel a deep wound from which blood was oozing—gently, slowly . . .

Gently, slowly . . . like time itself.

V

The next day Trublayevych arrived at the bank at a very early hour and found only Donda there. Wearing a vest without a suit coat, Donda, looking cheerful and pleased with himself, was humming something under his breath as he walked through all the rooms in the bank.

Catching sight of Trublayevych, he smiled happily and hurriedly walked up to him: "You know, ha-ha-ha . . . yesterday I finished my sixty-fourth violin! I'm telling you, it's a fine violin! There isn't another one like it anywhere near here!"

He was truly happy with what he had accomplished.

Trublayevych glanced at him and smiled as well: how little a person needs at times to feel fortunate. This old chubby man-child had a good apartment given to him by the bank. He had been taking home a good wage for, perhaps, forty years.

There had never been any misadventures in his family, not a single drop of his tranquil blood had ever been squandered on public concerns. He was always amiable, serene. And when a superfluous ray of the sun accidentally broke into his life, when he saw himself—and others acknowledged him—as a master violinmaker, his cup of life was filled to the brim. And now every drop that fell into it—every new violin—made the entire surface of that brimming cup shudder joyfully.

Trublayevych smiled and, to increase Donda's pleasure, asked: "Come on, show me the sixty-fourth!"

"Ha-ha-ha-ha!" Donda laughed, and he winked and ran down swiftly to his apartment on the lower level to get it.

A moment later he came back with the violin and a bow. He was carrying them gingerly, as if they were sacred objects.

"Here, just try it, listen to its tone!" he shouted while he was still in the corridor. "Why would you need . . . ha-ha-ha . . . a Stradivarius."

"Well, I've known for quite some time now that you've surpassed Stradivarius," Trublayevych replied in the same tone as he took the violin and tried it out. The violin was very good, and Donda's joy knew no bounds.

Trublayevych thanked him for the favour he had done him yesterday, but Donda just waved his hand dismissively: he would be happy to do his work for him every day, so long as all his violins turned out as well as this one.

"Oh my, what a violin I'll make now . . . out of wood from beyond our borders. I have a small fir tree that's like pure gold: it has the finest veins! Even now it rings like crystal."

He raised his eyes that were filled with admiration, as if he were gazing at a charming woman, at his beloved. Jealousy stirred in Trublayevych's heart: how fortunate Donda was!

"But did you hear . . . ha-ha-ha . . . what happened at the county meeting yesterday?" Donda suddenly asked him.

"What?"

"You didn't hear? Ha-ha-ha!"

Donda was laughing so hard that he was shaking, and he sat down. "It was ever so strange! My son Shurka came home in the evening and told me about it: the councillors were beaten up! Ha-ha-ha!" Donda laughed even harder, as if he had said something unusually amusing and entertaining.

"What are you saying? That can't have happened!"

"But it did! It did, my dear one! The meeting ended, the councillors went off to get the Governor who was to officially close the assembly, and we were waiting: 'Wait up a moment, something will come of this—something is bound to happen!' Well, the Governor came, closed the meeting, and drove away. The councillors whispered among themselves and began to leave. And we began to exit as well. We started coming down from the balcony when one of the councillors ran back indoors—his hat had been knocked off, and blood was streaming from his nose. 'They're beating us up out there!' he shouted."

Trublayevych wanted to stop Donda and say that it was just a fabrication, but then he recalled that there had been students in the square the day before yesterday, and he thought that such an unheard of event could truly have occurred in times like these.

"The councillors put on their coats and moved outdoors in a solid formation. Zhygmont was in the lead . . . You know, he's the big, heavyset gentleman with a full moustache. Well, ha-ha-ha-ha-ha . . . they stepped outside, only to be confronted by a group of thugs who instantly flung themselves at Zhygmont and the others. The councillors shouted: 'Police! Police!' But the police were nowhere to be seen. Rumour has it that the police chief said: 'The police were not admitted to the session, and so they won't go near the assembly hall.' What a great fellow!"

"No, that was an abominable thing to do."

"Why? Phew! The times are such that it's impossible to understand what's going on. Well, and then the kozaks appeared out of nowhere; they began to lash out with their whips to the right and the left, and they chased everyone away. Apparently they really let the thugs have it, and some of the councillors got hit, and our boys as well. They tore Brundzykevych's lip wide open. But my Shurka managed to slip away unscathed. That's how it was! They say that Babakov is directing it all. Well, how do you like all that, huh?"

"I don't like it at all, Zakhar Mytrovych. What's to be made of it all? Out there, in the east, there's a war going on, and the Japanese are beating us, and here at home we're creating our own internal dissension!"

"Truthfully speaking, I'm not able to understand why all this is happening," Donda said with a shrug. "We were living peacefully, in harmony, and that's how we should have gone on living. But no, all sorts of gatherings are called together, associations are formed, conferences are organized! Why, even I was called to a conference of accountants. Well, of course, I didn't go to it. I've had my fill of conferences."

And truly, he did not understand what was happening around him. Trublayevych considered it pointless to explain things to him: he would not understand in any event.

The employees were beginning to show up, and a few clients appeared as well. Donda put on his suit coat. The working day began. Someone knocked softly on one of the wickets of the partition.

"Is it possible to see the secretary?"

The client was inquiring about Trublayevych, and so he went to his wicket and began his customary tasks.

It was routine work for him, but now it all seemed strange, petty, and of little consequence. Some kind of discounts, receipts, debits, credits, at a time when every nerve of life was shuddering, and life itself was agitated and tossing about like an infuriated sea. Mercantile money matters at a time when the fate of Russia—a Russia that only recently had still been somnolent—was being decided throughout its own cities and villages, as well as on the Manchurian steppe and mountains. But he knew that all these discounts, receipts, debits, credits, and all sorts of other transactions could not be dispensed with, and so he kept on writing, signing white documents decorated with colourful flourishes, and passing them on to others.

Tea was served to the employees. Then the mail arrived, and a letter was brought to Trublayevych. He glanced at it and recognized his sister's handwriting. It was the second letter that he had received from her this week. Alarm stirred in his heart, but he unhesitatingly picked up the letter and tore open the envelope: no matter what information it contained, he had to know what it was.

He feared that the letter would say that his brother had been killed or injured at Mukden, or that his mother was on her deathbed and that he had to go and see her. And he was not far off the mark. His sister had written that he had to come home. There was no news about their brother. Their mother insisted that she go through all their newspapers and those of their neighbours to read all the reports that listed which officers had been injured or killed. She was sure that her son had been killed; she dreamed about him, and was wasting away. She could no longer walk on her own, and she just sat in an armchair.

And all around them peasants were rising up in rebellion. They were felling trees in the lords' forests, and taking away grain and straw from the barnyards. Yesterday they had cut down two pear trees and an apple tree in their orchard. Their manservant was threatening to set their farmstead on fire.

Trublayevych read the letter, carefully refolded, and placed it in his side pocket.

It was imperative for him to leave at once. He had not seen his mother for four years, and even back then she had been ailing for some time. When he imagined her sitting in an armchair, weeping and listening to the lists of those who had been killed, he felt achingly sorry for her. He, the miserable and egotistical man that he was, had seemingly forgotten all about her these past few years: his mother was living on a farmstead, was not demanding money, and that meant she was not in need of anything. He was used to feeling alone and independent, but now he realized that he had family members whom he should help.

But how, in what way?

It was not difficult to get there, but what would he do once he arrived? How would he comfort his mother, what would he say to the servant who was threatening to burn down the farmstead, to the peasants who had felled the trees in the orchard?

Banking clients constantly interrupted his thoughts. And he talked with them, wrote out documents and signed them, all the while thinking about what he should do.

He angrily admitted that he and all of his acquaintances, so-called liberals, found it easy to sit around in warm living quarters and solve, by talking, all sorts of problems, both social and political. They argued, debated theoretical issues, but never had to take a hard, realistic stand on anything. And in their way of thinking, people were divided into two levels: on the one hand—the common people, democracy, the proletariat, and on the other hand—the lords, the bureaucracy, and the bourgeois. The former were pure, undefiled angels, while the latter were viewed as odious snakes, deserving to be destroyed. And now the angels were beating up the councillors, robbing the lords, destroying forests and orchards, and preparing to set fire to an inconsequential farmstead along with an elderly person who possibly was already on her way to God.

So where was the justice in all this, and how was one to figure out the tangled mess?

Trublayevych thought about it and could not conclude anything from his thoughts. He did feel, however, that there was some gross misunderstanding in all of this.

He decided to ask for a leave of absence to visit his mother.

He rose to his feet to go and see Donda to consult with him how to handle the leave, when he heard a woman's shrill voice.

She was screeching like a crow: "Ivan Mykhaylovych! Ivan Mykhaylovych! A moment of your time! Come over here."

Trublayevych turned back unwillingly. Madam Valeryanova was calling him. As soon as he saw her, it seemed to him that he could smell a pharmacy, because the odour of pharmaceutical products always wafted from her, and her name reminded one of medicinal remedies. She gulped them down, was saturated with their odour, and was extremely high-strung. She spoke rapidly, as if scattering peas, with all manner of winks and nods, and she considered herself to be very attractive. It seemed to her that all men ought to fall under her spell. She was addicted to morphine.

"I've come to you with a petition . . . or rather, with a protest. I hope you'll assist me in gathering signatures at the bank. As you can see, I've already gathered about a hundred signatures, and I want to gather a thousand; we'll send the protest to the Governor and a copy of it to the newspaper *The Son of the Fatherland*. For God's sake, is it possible to live this way any longer? The rabble is beating up the intelligentsia and attacking provincial councillors, and the police are looking the other way. If things continue this way, we'll ruin all of Russia!"

She spoke passionately and at length.

Trublayevych took the protest from her and read through it. He glanced at the signatures and found many familiar names among them. "So, you want my signature? Well, here it is."

He picked up his pen and signed the protest.

"I need not only your signature, but those of your associates as well . . . But here I have still another . . . message . . ." She dug around in her voluminous purse. "I'm assuming that you'll sign it! It's absolutely incredible and unheard of! Do you know what the Dubrayevsky women are up to—both the mother and the daughter?"

And, without giving Trublayevych an opportunity to say a single word, she rattled on: "Just think how loathsome it is: the elder Dubrayevska works with the secret police, and she reported on all of our people!"

Valeryanova, with widely staring eyes and raised eyebrows, lowered her voice to a whisper and continued speaking: "You know, there were searches everywhere! They took away our dear Lyuba Hovoretska, Zembulat, Palyvoda, Chabanenko, and others. Everyone on her list was searched. And you know, last night, because of that, every single window in her house was smashed! And do you know who did it?"

Valeryanova stuck her head through the wicket and spoke even more softly, as if she did not want anyone to hear her, but her face was beaming with a pleased smile.

"It's our young people who did that! That should teach her a lesson! And now we want to send her a 'message of condolence'! Bilohrud wrote it. Read it and sign it."

"I will neither read nor sign that message," Trublayevych replied tersely.

"Why?"

"Because such a deed is not worthy of decent people."

Valeryanova jumped away from the wicket as if she had been scalded. "How so?"

"In the first place, where is the proof that Dubrayevska is a spy? It's all rumours. And then again, even if she is what you say she is, it's not proper to use violence against her. You just had me sign a protest against the violence of the rabble against the intelligentsia, and now you're doing the same thing, and to top it all off, you're hiding under a veil of hypocrisy by composing a 'message of condolence!'"

"You won't sign it?" Valeryanova asked curtly with a glowering look.

"No."

"Others will sign it!"

"That would be too bad."

Hastily gathering up her papers and her purse, Valeryanova went off to see the other bank employees. A few of them signed both documents, but the majority, after running a cursory glance over them, did not sign either one.

When Valeryanova approached Donda, he gesticulated irritably: "God be with them, all those protests and petitions! I've never signed one in my life, and I won't sign them now."

"Why is that?"

Donda just shouted: "Ah!" and he waved his hand dismissively. "I've grown sick and tired of signing even banking documents!"

The last bit of information that Dubrayevska's windows had been smashed deeply troubled Trublayevych. It seemed to him that there must be some misunderstanding in this instance. The elder Dubrayevska had a vicious tongue, and she had made enemies of half of the city's inhabitants, but he could not give credence to the possibility that she had done what she was now being accused of doing.

He asked some of the other banking staff about the incident, and found out that it had happened because the younger Dubrayevska had warned some of her acquaintances on the evening before the search had taken place. They said that she still had a kind heart, and that after finding out about her mother's intention and reading her list, she had secretly informed a few people about the impending search.

Upon hearing this, Trublayevych concluded that in this instance "no one knew who was doing what." He was aware of the Dubrayevskys' convictions, and surmised how the information about the searches had reached them. In a place from where people left to work the night shift, there was a certain man who could have warned them and who had warned them earlier. And instead of thanking them, their own people had smashed their windows and composed a loathsome "message" for them.

When Trublayevych left the bank, he went to the Dubrayevsky home and found only the mother there. She was infuriated like a wasp, and her anger consumed her. She raged both at those who had brought this shame down upon her and at her kind-hearted daughter who had gone about town warning people without telling her that she was doing so.

"May they all be done away with; there would be little regret if they were!" she said and she sifted so resolutely through all her acquaintances who might have been associated with what had happened to her that Trublayevych was alarmed. And it occurred to him that if they did indeed send her the "message of condolence," her anger might cause her to overstep the bounds of civility and do something that was truly despicable.

Assuring her that there was some misunderstanding, that everything would be explained and take a turn for the better, he left her and went to see Bilohrud. He spoke and argued with him for a long time, until he finally succeeded in convincing him to destroy the message that Valeryanova was circulating through the city and leave the matter as it was with the expectation that things would gradually sort themselves out.

At dusk, when Trublayevych was napping after dinner, he was awakened. Mykola Petrovych, Lyuba's father, wanted to see him. He had just returned home and found out about Lyuba's misadventure. He was greatly distressed, and it seemed that during his trip he had lost his energy, his capacity to think, and all that remained was his habit of maintaining a proud and dignified bearing. He had become hardened in this mould long ago, and it was impossible for him to instantly break out of it.

"What's going on? Tell me, what's going on, now it's not only from Jewish nooks and crannies that they're snatching all sorts of . . . well, who knows what kind of riff-raff . . . but now they've even taken . . . my daughter!" he flung himself at Trublayevych.

Trublayevych tried to quiet him down. He expended much energy trying to explain to him how matters stood. But Mykola Petrovych simply could not comprehend that now people were landing in prison not only for thievery, that not only a person from "Jewish nooks and crannies" could land there, but even someone from the house of the vice-president of a bank . . . He argued and tried to prove that even though "Jews" and "all sorts of riff-raff" might be dissatisfied with the current situation, what did all that have to do with his daughter? Had he ever refused her anything? Had she ever wanted for anything?

"What more did she need? Unless it was some bird's milk! And she did not give any thought to the shame that she would bring down on her father, her mother. O children, children!"

After Mykola Petrovych calmed down slightly, he explained that he had come to see Trublayevych so that they could go together the next day to look in on Lyuba. The mother had not been in a position to go and see her and had not yet passed her anything in the way of linens, a pillow, or even tea and sugar.

Trublayevych told him what to do and how to do it; he himself would have liked to have avoided making a second trip to the prison. It put him in an awkward position to see Lyuba once again, but he did not have the strength to tell Mykola Petrovych everything just now, and to cast still another brick at his troubled head. It was difficult to tell him that it was all over between Lyuba and him, because in the depths of his soul there still remained hidden a glimmer of hope that he was mistaken, that everything could once again be as it had been. And so he agreed to go with Mykola Petrovych. As soon as the older man heard this, he instantly calmed down considerably.

"The poor fellow was afraid to go to the prison himself, he didn't know how to go about it," Trublayevych thought.

And a bitter feeling came over him: how grand and elegant these sleek gentlemen looked when they sat in their directors' chairs and signed documents composed and written by their employees, and how wretched they were when they had to face up to an unforeseen event beyond the walls of the bank, beyond the walls of their own residences. After seeing his guest to the door, Trublayevych pondered what he was to do.

The final word had not yet been said, but it had to be said. If she did not love him, he had to know that, he must hear it directly from her lips, and not guess at it through hints. In his heart he was half reconciled to what had happened.

He loved Lyuba dearly, but his love was not blind. His mind was always standing on guard and, like a functionary at an auction sale, it pounded on his consciousness with a hammer: "You must do this, you must not do that . . ."

Lyuba was of an entirely different nature. She was fiery and impetuous. Her feelings often knocked her mind off central stage and, in its stead, assumed a dictatorial position. She unhesitatingly sewed things together, and then, without giving matters much thought, ripped them apart again, and cut them up. And strangely enough, this was what appealed most about her to the staid Trublayevych.

Now he decided to write her a letter in order to put the question bluntly to her: were things to continue between them as they had been, or were they to part consciously, calmly, without any animosity. And so he wrote a letter that he could hand to her. Then he paced the room, reread the letter, and ripped it up. The letter sounded prosaic and cold, like an "office memorandum."

He set about writing another letter. He wrote for a long time. He recalled the unfolding of their love. He referred to the current circumstances, opened his soul to her, told her of his lack of faith, and pleaded with her to sit in judgment on him: given recent events, could she, or could she not unite her fate with the fate of such a person? If not, then that's how it would be: "Just as streamlets flow together and then part once again, so too have we come together, and so too will we part," he wrote in conclusion. "I will always remember you as the most wonderful woman that I had the opportunity of meeting in my youthful days, and I shall bless fate for this opportunity."

He informed her that he was taking a leave of absence from his work, and he gave her the address where he would be. It was late when he put out the light.

VI

On this day Trublayevych got up early and splashed cold water around for a long time as he washed himself. He placed his head under the tap, let the water stream over his head, and shuddered with pleasure as he felt the cold current make its way through his hair to his scalp, flow over his forehead, course past his ears and then, coming together again after filtering through his moustache, run into the sink in a single trickle.

His head was refreshed after being bathed in this way, and he felt energized and invigorated, ready to work, even though his conscience, racing about like a phantom deep within him, seemed to be clipping the sprouts of this vigour. The remnants of his troubled sleep still bothered him. He had suffered greatly in his dreams this past night and had awoken several times with a sinking feeling that his heart was dying.

Even now he felt uneasy and was in a heightened, agitated state. He dreaded meeting Lyuba. He dreaded it because he did not expect anything good to come of it. He did not want to reread the letter he had written the previous evening, for he did not want to destroy it after looking at it with a fresh mind. Let it be as he had written it.

At the bank Trublayevych had to wait for quite some time for all the directors to arrive so that he could ask for a leave of absence. He did not feel up to doing any work, and today Donda, who was in a foul mood, was finding fault with the junior employees. When he was in that kind of a mood it was difficult to remain in the same room with him. He cursed, was erratic in his demands, unfair to those around him and, falling into a fit of anger, was capable of going to the directors and telling them many loathsome and untrue things about his coworkers. At times like this, everyone in the bank detested him.

"How many years have you been working in the bank, and yet you still don't know how to balance the books!" Donda thundered at his assistant as he threw a batch of papers at him. "There's a whole day's work gone to naught!" The sheets of paper flew in all directions. The assistant silently gathered up the papers; his teeth were clenched and his cheeks tensed visibly. Donda had served in the bank for forty years, and because the entire operation of the bank devolved on him, he felt that he was the master who was in control. The directors listened to him, and the employees feared him.

"If only I can get away from here as quickly as possible," Trublayevych thought. "To go to my native parts, to get away from the unending telegrams, conversations, arguments, petty gossip; to get away from newspapers, from politics, from protests and declarations. It's all become so loathsome! This bank has become loathsome, and so has this bureaucracy, this Donda!"

When the directors met, Trublayevych asked them to grant him a leave of absence, and they approved his request. Donda became more incensed: his workload would increase, and he had not been asked if such a leave could be granted to Trublayevych.

"I need a leave as well; my nerves are also shot," he grumbled, and he snorted and kept adjusting his pince-nez on his reddened nose. The pince-nez kept slipping off.

Trublayevych was getting ready to leave the bank.

"Will you drop in here again before you leave?" Donda asked curtly as he turned to glower at him without his pince-nez from under his grey eyebrows.

"Yes, I will! I'll take care of everything."

"Sure, sure!"

Trublayevych was curious as to what had aggravated Donda so badly, but he did not have the nerve to ask him, nor did he have the time: Mykola Petrovych had asked him to get a pass for both of them to go and see Lyuba.

He drove off to see the procurator. When he arrived, he was asked to wait in the reception room, because the procurator was seeing someone. An officer was sitting in the reception room. It seemed to Trublayevych that he was a gendarme, but he could not be sure, because the man was sitting with his back towards him. When he finally turned around, Trublayevych recognized him: he was the one who had taken away Lyuba's letters when his living quarters had been searched.

They exchanged glances and nodded to one another almost imperceptibly. They both felt awkward, and they sat silently for a few minutes, as if they did not see one another. They were both hoping that the procurator would come in soon and put an end to the uncomfortable situation in which they found themselves. From an inner room came the sound of two voices going on and on without a break. The discussion was proceeding passionately, but it was impossible to hear what was being said. The officer rose to his feet. It seemed as if he wanted to stretch his legs, but then he unexpectedly turned around, came up to Trublayevych, and extended his hand to him.

"We've met before . . . Forgive me: I feel guilty for what I did! Those letters . . . you had the right not to give them to us. And I regret that I took them. But it was my duty . . ."

Trublayevych looked up at him and did not know what to say. "Well, it's over and done with . . . you can't undo the past! You didn't take me at my word."

"I didn't have the right to do so, according to the law."

"And according to your conscience?" Trublayevych asked.

The officer looked at him silently, and in his eyes Trublayevych saw a plea for forgiveness. "You know, in life you sometimes have to . . ." And he just gestured helplessly and did not finish what he was saying. "It's my job!" he said bitterly.

"So why did you take that job?"

The officer smiled. "It sometimes happens that life chases a man into such a blind alley that the only way out for him is to fire a bullet into his head, or do whatever else he can . . . Do you think that we gendarmes aren't human—that we have neither a heart nor a soul? Do you think it's easy to read letters like the ones that we took from you, or the ones that were confiscated from your fiancée? Do you think that all of us do not understand what is happening everywhere around us? That we aren't aware that the blood of our brothers is being spilled in Manchuria? That they're in prisons? Oh, if only it was like that!"

This unexpected confession of a person from an entirely different stratum of society, the dark abyss of this soul that suddenly opened up before him, both amazed Trublayevych and alarmed him. He wanted to shout. "Then why don't you quit that job?' But he refrained from saying anything.

"You know," the officer continued, "we haven't slept for a week now, and we don't have any idea when we'll finally be allowed to sleep. We've crammed the prisons with people but we know that by doing so we haven't done anything to weaken those against whom we are fighting. Even now the colonel is trying to get the procurator to agree to let us search a hundred more houses. By telling you about this I'm committing an offence against my profession, I'm breaking my vow, but . . . it doesn't matter! You can't turn back the clock—only the colonel believes that it's possible to do so."

Trublayevych knew the colonel. He was old, corpulent, and bald. He had a long carroty beard shot through with grey streaks, a toothless mouth that was slightly skewed, thick, protruding frog-like lips that were always gaping, and dark glassy eyes. He was a very pious man, and he had two grown daughters, as kind and meek as young novices in a nunnery. Trublayevych did not consider the colonel to be an evil man—perhaps because of the impression created by his daughters.

"I hope that you'll understand me, and not judge me without some compassion . . ."

Trublayevych silently shook his hand. Still another broken human being in a place he least expected to find such a person.

At that moment the colonel and the procurator appeared in the doorway. The colonel was glancing anxiously all around and wiping his balding head with a handkerchief. His face was as red as a large pepper. "In that case, I'm absolving myself of any responsibility!" he said.

It occurred to Trublayevych that this man was also unfortunate to some degree, bound by orders and instructions, by the routine of the rotten structure of life.

"Don't be concerned, everything will be fine," the procurator said as he bid him farewell.

A few minutes later Trublayevych left the procurator's office with permission in hand to go and see Lyuba. He drove to the bank to pick up Mykola Petrovych, and then, after stopping by the Hovoretsky house to pick up the things that Vira Stepanivna had gathered together for her daughter, they drove to the prison.

They rode in silence. The wheels of the carriage were bouncing about on the potholes in the paved roads, and the rumbling noise filled the ears of both men. In front of the prison they ran into a group of detainees who were being led into the city. Hovoretsky glanced at them and then turned away. It occured to him that Lyuba too might be led through the city in this manner to the derision of all their acquaintances. While they were drawing near the prison he glanced around: was there anyone who could see him going there? But they were in the midst of open fields, and it was only in the distance that a funeral procession was wending its way to a cemetery, and fragments of a hymn drifted in: *O Holy Immortal One . . .* The procession was already passing through the stone gate of the cemetery, and only a few of the accompanying carriages could still be seen.

The coachman turned off the main road towards the prison.

The father's heart cramped, and when he felt the soft earth under the wheels instead of the hard, cobblestone road, it seemed possible to him the ground might cave in under the carriage. He gripped the carriage tightly.

After going through passageways that were already familiar to Trublayevych, they ended up in the same room in which he had been on his first visit. It was the prison's reception room. And once again they had to wait for quite some time for Lyuba to appear.

She walked in looking calm and reserved, and just a tiny hint of a smile flitted over her pale, and now sallow, face as she responded to her father's greeting: "Hello, father!"

She greeted Trublayevych silently. He walked away to a corner of the room to let the father and daughter speak freely. There was no guard in the room this time. He was now stationed outside the door.

"My dearest Lyuba, what has happened to you? What have you done?" Mykola Petrovych addressed his daughter, and for the first time, Trublayevych detected a note of sincerity in the old man's voice.

"Nothing, daddy," Lyuba replied.

"What do you mean—nothing? Why have they brought you here?" Hovoretsky took his daughter by the hand. She did not remove it, but neither did she reply to the pressure from her father's hand.

"For the same reason that they've brought others here. Do you suppose that there aren't a lot of us here?" she asked.

"What do I care about the others! It may well be that I myself would have hanged half of the villains who are in here, but as for you . . . you . . . my daughter? You got the idea of rebelling, you had some odious books in my home? What is the meaning of all this? What were you lacking? Can you recall even a single instance when you were denied something that you wanted?"

"That's just the point: some have everything, while others have nothing. Some are drowning in luxury, while others are swelling with hunger!" Lyuba said sharply, and the corners of her mouth trembled.

"So what? Not everyone can be rich. Someone has to be poor. That's the way the world is."

"And that kind of system has to be changed."

"Oh, sweetheart, that will never happen!"

"Yes it will!"

Mykola Petrovych shook his head. "Do you remember the late Paraska Pankrativna, do you recall how she used to say: 'There can never be equality among people. If all the wealth in the world was gathered together and apportioned equally among all the people, by tomorrow there once again would be those who are wealthy, and those who are poor. Because one person works and earns money, while the next one drinks and does nothing.'"

Hovoretsky expected to convince Lyuba with this argument. But she just smiled. "This was said by a person who in her entire life never raised a finger to do any work, and who lived off the interest on her money. It's the philosophy of sleek, secure people. If there is no such equality, then it must be created. Because it is impossible to go on living as people are living now."

"Well, if so, then let those who desire this equality fight for it, what's it to you?"

"I also desire it."

"Why do you want it?"

"Because without it, a morsel of bread sticks in my throat!"

Hovoretsky fell silent. He realized that he was not saying what he should be saying, and that it was neither the time nor the place to try to convince Lyuba, and that he would never be able to convince her because his Lyuba was not at all the kind of person that he had taken her for. And sorrow, mixed with anger and moral injury, struck his heart.

"Here, your mother has sent you . . . what you need," he said sternly.

"Thank you," Lyuba responded without looking at the parcel.

And the conversation broke off once again.

"It's not good for you to be here . . . I'll do what I can to get you out on bail."

"There's no need to do that."

"What do you mean?"

"Just what I said: there's no need to do that!"

"Why, do you like being here so much?" Hovoretsky asked in an exasperated tone.

"There's no need to do that, because I don't want to separate my fate from the fate of the others who are incarcerated here. You can't put up bail for all of them, so there's no need to do so for my sake."

"What do you care about them?" Hovoretsky shouted. "All this riff-raff—are they your brothers, sisters, father, mother?"

"They are my brothers and sisters," Lyuba replied firmly.

"If that's the case, then . . . if . . ." Hovoretsky stopped short. He was about to say something biting and cruel, but he restrained himself and turned beet red.

"Well, then, what do you need?" he asked, regaining a measure of his self-control.

"I don't need anything," Lyuba said, and she emphasized the word I. "Thank you for coming to see me."

She turned to look at Trublayevych. He was standing by the window with his eyes fixed on her. Now their glances crossed for the first time.

"Is it true, Ivan Mykhaylovych, that thugs beat up the deputies and smashed Dubrayevska's windows? There are rumours here . . ."

"Yes, it's true," he replied. "But Dubravyevska's windows were not smashed by thugs. She's considered a spy."

"That's not true," Lyuba said after thinking for a moment. "Pass my regards to Solomiya Frantsivna."

"I'll do that."

Hovoretsky rose to his feet. Lyuba also stood up.

"So, you're saying that you don't want to . . . go home?"

"No, I do want to. But just now . . . that's impossible. Kiss mother and Hanusya for me. Tell them not to worry about me." The father and daughter exchanged kisses silently.

Trublayevych clutched his letter in his hand and also walked up to her. He pressed her hand tightly and held it for a moment in his own. Feeling the letter in her hand, Lyuba shuddered and tried to avoid taking it, but Trublayevych squeezed her hand even more tightly and said distinctly: "Farewell! I'm going away on a leave of absence."

She looked up at him. Their eyes met, and the familiar sparks flashed between them. And it seemed to them they understood one another without saying a single word.

Trublayevych turned around . . . Lyuba picked up her parcel and walked out of the room. Hovoretsky followed her.

They remained silent as they drove away.

Hovoretsky was as cold as ice, and he was breathing heavily. Trublayevych also seemed to be petrified.

They travelled down several streets in this manner.

Couriers rushed up to them at a crossroads with the latest telegrams: "A royal manifesto! A royal manifesto!"

One lad almost leapt into the carriage as he shoved the telegram at Hovoretsky.

Hovoretsky angrily pushed it away. "Get away from me! You're forever crawling underfoot like dogs with your warmongering."

"Buy it! It's interesting!"

Hovoretsky aimed his cane at him.

"Ha-ha-ha! Well, have you found yourself a buyer?" The lad's friends mocked him.

"Oh, get out of here! An interesting telegram!" he yelled, and catching sight of a gentleman with a long moustache, he rushed across the road.

"Ivan Mykhaylovych! Ivan Mykhalovych!" the man with the long moustache called out and waved at Trublayevych.

It was Donda. Trublayevych descended from the carriage, bade farewell to Hovoretsky, and walked away with Donda.

Donda appeared to still be very agitated, but his anger had abated. "Do you know what happened to me?" he asked.

"What?"

"They've arrested my Shurka!"

"When?"

"Last night."

Now Trublayevych realized why Donda had been so upset this morning.

"I don't know what's going on . . . They're beating people, smashing windows, taking away whomever they come across! What's going on?" Donda waved wildly and blinked rapidly.

"Well, they won't take you!"

"Who knows? It's the times we're living in. Over there, every night they scatter leaflets calling on us to beat up the Jews. But they're not beating the Jews, you see, they're beating the councillors and the students. Let them beat the Jews, or whatever; let them vent their anger on them!"

Trublayevych shuddered. "What are you saying? Aren't the Jews also people?"

"Oh, the devil take it! If they're to beat anyone, let it be the Jews. It's all their fault." Donda lowered his voice. "Just take a look how the Jews bustle about and run things in our bank. Our Rusyns are left far behind!"

"But who is to blame that wise ones among Jews end up there, while our silent fools prefer to lie abed."

"Well, that may be, but nevertheless . . . Now they've organized some kind of self-defence. They say that a cache of bombs, revolvers, and whips was found in Dr. Zelman's home."

"Well what are they to do, if everywhere in Ukraine our Christian folk murder them first here and then there."

"And they'll get what's coming to them from us as well."

Donda had forgotten all about his misadventure when the conversation turned to the Jews. He hated them with his entire being, but at the same time, no one curried favour from them in the bank as much as he did. Trublayevych recalled this fact and he felt disgusted as he listened to Donda.

He came up with a reason for parting company with him and bade him farewell at a crossroads. He promised that he would drop in at the bank the next day.

"And I'm on my way to see Vernyshapka to see what can be done about Shurka," Donda said in farewell.

Trublayevych smiled inwardly: so much ignorance and misunderstanding resided in that grey, rounded head. And how much of more of that could be found in the heads of the people whom he knew in this city!

VII

Trublayevych was on his way home. For the first fifty *versts the wheels of a public stagecoach had groaned over the frozen ground, but now the wheels of a train clacked on rails, and his thoughts swarmed in keeping with the clacking.

Everything that he had seen and heard recently, in the past few days, emerged like fragments out of the darkness, rose up before him, and then vanished again into parts unknown. It was as if a boisterous wind was flinging tattered patches of fog out of a dark abyss and then, with renewed force, was breaking up the agitated, inconstant fragments, ripping them apart, and blowing them away.

The wheels were rumbling, and his heart was beating evenly: click-clack . . . Everything was as it should be. Incomparable in its cruelty, that unfortunate war—the war on two fronts, both in the Far East and at home, all the misunderstandings, all the superfluous, unnecessary victims—it all had to be the way it was.

Life cannot stand still, but it had been forced to mark time in the same spot for forty years . . . like an elephant in a Moscow zoo. It had been lulled to sleep, shackled, but sooner or later it had to tear asunder all its chains. And so now it was shattering them!

And now it no longer was as it had been forty years ago, that . . .

. . . *the great chain of serfdom
Was broken, and it struck
The lord with one end
And the peasant with the other . . .

Hundreds of chains were cracking and breaking daily, and flailing randomly, striking the righteous, striking the guilty, striking out blindly.

Life had become agitated, and it surged in waves like a darkened, enraged sea, and here and there, menacing billows emerged from it. They arose, gathered momentum, and roared. And then they vanished, only to turn up somewhere else: Kyshyniv . . . Zhytomyr . . . Petersburg . . . Katerynoslav . . . Baku . . . Kursk . . . and so on, and so forth, without end.

Everywhere, life was awakening angrily, with a jolt . . . And the stormy petrels were screeching and groaning, foretelling something terrible . . .

The workers . . . The peasants . . . Confusion was swirling!

The stormy petrels were screeching and divining the wrath of life, and in the dark east not a speck of light was to be seen, not a single ray . . .

Hey, will you break through this darkness, O light of day?

The wheels rumbled. The passenger cars thundered. The train was flying forward.

And the heart says: yes-yes!

But was it yes?

And Trublayevych came to with a start, only to sink once again into a reverie, just as Mount Elbrus sinks into the clouds in the evening.

The stormy petrels were screeching, and other birds picked up their cry. Crows cawed, hawks shrilled, and sparrows chirped agitatedly. Even staid hens were clucking irritably and were ready to dig their claws into anyone who dared to touch them.

There would be a storm!

The hundreds of chains that were breaking here, there, and everywhere, were striking everyone, wounding everyone. And there was no end to the people who were being beaten. And there were wounds everywhere, and blood and tears everywhere. And he, also wounded, was going to where his afflicted mother was dying, where his sister was suffering, where . . .

"Oh, there's no end to this suffering!" a scream erupted in Trublayevych's mind, and his thoughts awakened him.

It was gloomy in the day coach. Everything looked grey: the walls, the people, and even the light emanating from the lamp.

A cloud of tobacco smoke hung over everyone. And the people were sitting lifelessly, as if totally crushed, and some were sleeping, and some were dozing. And nearby only the red glow of a cigarette continued to flare from moment to moment. And over there in the shadows, two people were conversing softly.

"What are they talking about?" Trublayevych wondered, and then his own thoughts enveloped him once again.

He was not a stormy petrel, he was not a fighter; he was a staid, honest worker. He believed that human progress was to be attained not by the militant cries of stormy petrels, but by the hands and minds of common workers, by their dogged, endless work, and, if necessary, by their blood. Progress was achieved by human masses that evolved very slowly, very deliberately, but with certainty, without regressing.

"Human masses . . . But hey, what's that?"

The window next to him had turned red. There was a fire someplace. He glanced through the frosted glass and saw that the conflagration was close by. He stepped into the vestibule of the car.

The train was running alongside a village that was situated in a swampy area. Trublayevych could see only the outlying cottages and the domes of a church.

Large stacks of sheaves were burning at the edge of the village. There were several of them, but so far only two were blazing, the ones that were in the wind. They would all burn. There was no one in sight.

"It's arson," said someone in the group of passengers who, like Trublayevych, had stepped out of the coach.

"The lord's wealth is burning . . ."

"Just as it should!"

"If we can't have it, then you can't have it either!"

Trublayevych looked around and saw peasant faces that were flooded with the red light.

They were laughing.

"But might it not have been possible to act in such a way that both he and you could have had some?" he asked.

"Apparently it isn't possible!"

"And if someone who was poorer than you did something like this to you, what would you say?" Trublayevych asked.

"There's no one poorer than we are."

"But maybe there is . . . Think about it."

"Oh, what's the point of talking about it: the times are now such that it's impossible to figure anything out!" someone called out from the group, and they all fell silent.

The train kept rushing onwards.

Trublayevych went back into the car. The red tongues of the flames still blazed in his eyes, and he could not shake the impression made upon him by the reflected brilliance of that fire in the eyes of the people who had stood with him on the lip of the passenger car.

A lack of understanding, an incapacity to understand . . .

A terrible misunderstanding.

He sat down again and lost himself in his thoughts, and the wheels of the passenger car kept on rumbling: "Mis-understanding! Mis-under-standing!" And it continued without end.

"When will we all understand one another?" Trublayevych asked himself.

There was no response.

"An uncultured, ignorant nation, ignorant from top to bottom! You slept in ignorance until the thundering of cannons awakened you, and the blood flowed from hundreds of thousands of your sons! And now you're beginning to stir, and you're grabbing hold of whatever you can, and you're beating up and trampling both your enemies and your friends!

"Now you're launching *Nero's fiery banquets and laying waste to the wealth accumulated by the sweat of your brow! And in the springtime your cattle will starve to death and you'll have nothing with which to plough furrows on your meagre field! When will knowledge enlighten your minds? When will you learn to value both the attainments of culture and your own labour?"

Trublayevych was unable to find answers to these questions.

Part Two

I

Hemmed in on both sides by thick, cavity-ridden willows, the broad road that stretched from Kyiv to Moscow through fields and meadows, hills and swamps, forests and glades hid for a moment in a small grove, and then rushed out of it and kept on running ever farther northwards into the distance through still more fields and meadows.

An unobservant traveller would scarcely have noticed that this was no ordinary, uninhabited grove, and that there was a small manor tucked away in it. Just off to one side of the road, behind some young pines and birch trees, a rather small grey manor house stood sheltered by some old birches.

The house had settled and, tilting to one side, it took on the appearance an old, feeble, worried person. Next to it, also among the trees, there were rundown stables, outbuildings, barns, and a few cowsheds. All the buildings were hidden among the trees, and if a stranger had looked at this scene he would have thought that it was an abandoned manor yard that was being overgrown by the forest, just like something that is no longer needed is overgrown by weeds and grass.

Everything around the manor stretched upwards towards the sky, and only the buildings dropped their gaze downwards to the ground. Next to the well, a tall crane, bent over under its own weight like a fishing line, also looked upwards, and only occasionally bent its scrawny neck to get a bucket of water for the inhabitants of the manor.

This was the ancestral home of the Trublayevych family. There were very few people in it. This past winter, when the old birch trees had hummed and creaked in the wind at night and grazed the roof of the manor house with frozen, drooping branches that resembled bony fingers, only the old lady and her daughter had heard them. And on nights like that, it seemed to them that some unknown, evil giants had wandered in from somewhere and were trying to force their way inside.

At such times, lamps burned all night long in all three of the main seigniorial rooms: large pink, red, and blue votive lamps flamed in front of old icons darkened by age. The wicks in the lamps crackled softly and the flames leapt upward, creating pink, red, and blue streaks that raced over the walls.

Usually, only the red lamp burned every night in the larger room—the living room—but on turbulent nights, all three lamps were lit. And on those nights the old lady and her daughter were rarely able to sleep and so they brought their servant, the widow Petrivna, from the bakehouse into their quarters. Only the manservant Tereshko was left in the bakehouse. But Petrivna was of little help to them: she would instantly fall asleep and begin to snore loudly and spasmodically. But even at that, her snoring indicated that there was someone in the house, and it was not as scary as when they were all alone.

On such nights even old Kudlay was uneasy, and he barked and ran in circles around the manor house. And when he stopped doing that, he sat under a gable window, pointed his snout into the wind, and howled mournfully. He howled, and the mother and daughter listened and fainted with fear and a foreboding that something unknown and terrible was about to happen.

"Shura," the mother said, "wake up Petrivna."

Shura tugged at the servant's shoulder or head.

"Huh? What is it?" Petrivna woke up with a start, sat bolt upright on her bed—a wool blanket spread by the hearth—and set about scratching herself noisily and for a long time.

"Why is Kudlay howling?" the lady asked.

"Huh?"

"I'm asking, why is Kudlay howling like that?"

"Who knows why?" Petrivna replied. She momentarily stopped scratching, as if listening carefully to Kudlay.

"Do you hear him?"

"Yes, I hear him. There are probably wolves wandering around near Kordubivka."

"Are all of our buildings locked up?"

"Yes."

Petrivna sat dozing for an hour or so as she leaned against the fireplace, and then, sighing heavily, she once again lay down on her makeshift bed and instantly fell asleep.

And Kudlay kept on howling and howling . . .

"A-oo-oo-oo! A-oo-oo-oo!" he cried, starting on a high note and lowering his voice until the sound expired like a yawn.

"Oh, may you drop dead!" Petrivna grumbled in her sleep as she turned over.

It was always depressing and daunting to live in the manor. But after the war began, it became even more depressing and daunting after disturbances flared up all over, and after the nearby sugar factory was burned down, and the smoke from the conflagration spread along the river valley to Trublayevych's grove and settled on it, covering the sky and darkening the sun, it seemed that this smoke would never go away.

The smoke weighed heavily on the hearts of the old lady and her daughter: if they burned down the sugar factory, they'll soon be burning down the lords' manors. Khoma Haydun, or perhaps the peasant who delivered their coal, would come in from the village of Kordubivka, grab a bunch of straw, wedge it under the thatched roof of any one of the cowsheds, and set it on fire. And what could you do about it?

And Haydun was capable of doing just that.

"Why did I insist that he haul that stack of sheaves that was nearest to Kordubivka closer to my yard?" the lady could not help thinking at night. "I knew that he had taken the best sheaves to that stack, and I knew that they were the biggest sheaves that he tied . . . well, I should just have just let him take them! He has a large family, and I wouldn't have become any poorer. But there you have it . . . it's as if I'd been tempted to fall into sin! 'Well, I'll make sure that you remember me!' he said, and then he cursed me so vilely, as only an angry peasant can."

The lady feared that this very same Haydun would burn down her manor. He would go to a barn where the cows were and set it on fire. And when Kudlay was howling at the other end of the residence, she often begged him in her thoughts: "Run over to the cowshed and look beyond it to see if Haydun is lurking there. And it would be even better if you would take a quick look throughout the entire grove: maybe he's hiding somewhere out there among the trees."

These were some of her thoughts; the rest of them centred on Andryk.

The lad had just become an officer when that cursed war began . . . For more than half a year the mother had been worried that at any minute she would receive a letter from Andryk telling her that he was being sent away to the war. Several times he had written to her saying that he had drawn lots, but that each time luck had been on his side; and then in the fall he had informed her, this time from Moscow already, that he was going to the war as a volunteer—"for it will be better that way."

At first the news had struck the mother like a thunderbolt: her boy had gone to the war as a volunteer—her Andryk who was so quick to respond to anger or kindness?

He was going to kill, and he would be killed . . . For what reason, why? And she thought for a long time, for days and nights about what had made him do this. And the words: "It will be better this way"—bored into her mind like a drill, and every turn of the drill echoed painfully in her heart.

"It will be better this way."

For whom?

For him, for Andryk?

And how, exactly, would it be better? There was no answer.

What had torn him from peaceful Brest-Litovsk and flung him way over there on the *Sha River, in some kind of Syao-kishin-pu? A desire for glory? But it had been evident from the very beginning of the war that there would be no "glorious heroes" on our side, and moreover, what kind of "glory" could be attained by a second lieutenant in the infantry who was nothing more than cannon fodder! All he could attain was mutilation, a lifelong illness, or death . . . He might manage to earn a little cross or a badge. But what good were they to him?

No, that was not why Andryk had gone to the banks of the Sha. Perhaps he went to war out of a sense of shame, so as not to be seen as freeloading at the public trough?

But were there not many freeloaders who occupied high positions in all kinds of bureaucratic nooks and crannies? First of all it was the generals and admirals, colonels and captains who should be forced to do their jobs, but as for second lieutenants—they did not feast much at the public trough.

No, it was something else, something different that had driven Andryk to go to war.

And her mother's heart, her woman's heart, told her that it must be love, an unhappy, unreciprocated love . . .

That's what it was. It was not without reason that he had been so anxious to go to Kyiv from Brest, it was not without reason that he had written such joyous letters from Kyiv, when he had the opportunity to spend three days there.

Love! Unrequited love!

And the mother cursed that unknown girl in Kyiv who had barred the world for Andryk. But there was nothing that could be done about it. Andryk was already on the Sha: he had been in the trenches on the front lines for twenty-one days, and in the reserves for twenty-one days.

She had begged him to write her everything, everything that he experienced, and he obeyed her and wrote to her.

And at times those letters were like deathbed confessions.

The mother understood and . . . she wept, she wept bitterly over those letters written in pencil; every day she reread all of them, from the very first one to the last one. And through those letters she experienced with him all that he had gone through, and her heart was with him in all his postings.

His letter from Lin-chin-pu, dated the third of February, in which he described his march to the front lines, was dearest to her heart. It read in part:

I wrote to you not long ago, but I'm writing again because I'm sitting in the trenches, there's nothing to do, and it's impossible to sleep. When you write, the time goes by more quickly, and you don't feel so sad.

On the first of February we came here for the second time, to the front lines, for another twenty-one days. I can't say that I was unenthusiastic about coming here. On the contrary, I had rested up in the bivouac and was beginning to feel depressed about sitting around with nothing to do. Here, there once again is a nervous, dangerous existence, the proximity of the enemy, and the feeling that you yourself are the enemy of those people who are sitting across from you in their trenches. Abnormal as this may seem, it excites all of us, forces us to be on guard, because both we and they have come here for the precise reason of attacking with all our might and coming out of the battle as victors or to lay down our lives in the effort.

We will not retreat; we've fallen back plenty of times already. I, at least, will not turn my back to the enemy. These trenches will be my grave, and I've already come to like them.

I'll probably never forget my first march to this place, to this posting. It was, as I wrote to you, on the twelfth of December.

On that day our regiment was to occupy the trenches in order to relieve our second brigade. We were ordered to set out at eight o'clock in the evening from our bivouac that was about four versts from the front lines. At seven we had our supper, doused the fires, got dressed, and prepared ourselves for the march. We left at eight. The regiment stretched for almost a verst. It was dark and cold. At first we talked a bit, laughed as we smoked our cigarettes and pipes, and groaned under the two-*pood weight of our equipment.

It was quiet . . . There were no shots to be heard. There was only the sound of boots thumping on the frozen ground and the clinking of the cauldrons. Conversations gradually ceased, the glowing embers of our cigarettes and pipes died away—we sensed the nearness of the position. We went on for another two-and-a-half versts and halted. The leader of the column had come up to the "communication trench". The communication trench led secretly to our position . . .

The dull sounds of shots in the distance began to reach us. The moon rose, and we could see, but it was foggy. The weary soldiers sat down on the ground to rest. It was quiet. All that could be heard was the occasional stifled coughing of those who had colds. Finally we started out again and we stepped into the trench one at a time. The ditch was narrow, and the heavily laden soldiers were forced to walk sideways.

The shots now sounded closer and closer . . . Peals of moderate salvos echoed. The fog lifted.

And now something whizzed by quite near us, and then something whistled by even more closely. Someone groaned . . . A hostile bullet had found its victim. The wounded man was pulled out of the trench, placed on a stretcher, and the medical orderlies carried him away. We kept on going. The shots were clearer now, the bullets screamed ever more frequently.

The soldiers were hunched over in the trenches, keeping their heads out of sight. It was quiet; there was no sound of thumping feet, only the tinkling of metal cooking pots as they bumped against the walls of the trench, and the whistling of a growing number of bullets, each one with its own distinctive sound, each one in its own manner. One sounds just like an infant that is crying, another buzzes by like a drone, a third one whistles past you sharply and curtly, and still another, slamming unexpectedly into the embankment with a crashing noise, makes you shudder all over.

The soldiers squatted in the trench. Most of them were terrified. It was fearsome . . . Finally the shots sounded very close. They rang out in front of us and from both sides. We had come to our position. We entered the trench one at a time. It was deeper and wider.

The moon was shining; the air was frosty. Pressing against the front wall of the trench stood shadowy figures swathed in fantastic attire. Above them there were luminous spots, and in those spots flashed long fingers. And then suddenly: cr-r-ash!—right above our ears, to the left, to the right . . . And a resounding echo rolled beyond the trenches in thundering salvos.

*This is what our position is like. The fantastic figures are soldiers wrapped in quilts to ward off the cold; the luminous spots—the loopholes; the flashing fingers in them—the rifles, and the thunder—the salvo and the echo beyond the trenches over the Sha river, where we are now standing and where, like our ancestors who once stood on the *Kayala River, we are becoming intoxicated by the blood that is flowing like red wine all around us.*

Here, even in more peaceful periods, a day rarely goes by without someone being killed.

So there you have it, the front lines—the realm of death! Here, death holds sway over everything. The shadowy figures—they are death's sentence on people of another colour, another nation! Here, everything belongs to death! Here, death reigns supreme, and everything emits the odour of death!

* * *

When the mother finished reading the letter to this point, a hail of tears fell from her eyes.

Dropping her head to the table, she clasped it in her hands and, weeping loudly, shouted terrible curses at those who had called forth this misfortune and summoned the terrible tsarytsya of death from her accursed lair . . .

When the initial acuity of her pain, grief, and anger abated, she continued reading.

There is the stench of corpses in the trench, because it has been dug in the very spot known for the fighting on the Sha River.

There are countless corpses here: some are buried haphazardly in the frozen ground, but many have not been buried at all . . .

In many places in the trenches, you can see a leg in a torn boot protruding from the ground, or a petrified arm in a soldier's grey greatcoat . . .

Not long ago, in the very spot where soldiers were brewing some tea and heating up their dinner, an unburied corpse was found. They found out about it only because the corpse began to rot when the fire warmed the ground.

* * *

At this point tears choked the grieving mother, and, with renewed strength, she shouted angrily, despairingly: "Oh, may you be damned! Why has the ground not swallowed you?"

"The poor lad, the poor lad!" she said after a while as she shook her head and held the letter that was damp from her tears, and it was difficult to say whom she was pitying—her son, or the soldier on whose corpse they had lit a fire to brew some tea. Her daughter tried to comfort her, but she did not listen to those words of solace. And when the horrible battle of Mukden began, when the Japanese captured the trenches from which Andryk had vowed not to retreat, the mother's grief and tears knew no bounds.

Every day now, Tereshko rode the seven versts to the post office in the village of Stepanivka to fetch letters and newspapers. The newspapers kept coming, but there were no letters. And the newspapers seemed to focus only on the rout at Mukden . . . But then, the old lady did not read anything except for reports about the war.

She searched painstakingly for news about the tenth *Novoingermanlandski regiment, but there was nothing written about it. And she did not know if all the soldiers in the regiment had been killed, or if they had been captured, or had escaped beyond *Telin. She could scarcely walk through the manor house now, and she never ventured outside at all. She just sat by a window and waited until dusk to catch a glimpse of Tereshko among the birch trees, to find out if he had finally brought either a letter or a telegram from Andryk.

But Tereshko was in no hurry to return to the manor. He was disgusted with living there, and so he tarried in Stepanivka, and in Kordubivka, and indulged in lengthy conversations with people that he met on the road. He brought back a lot of news that he relayed to Petrivna in the bakehouse, and she passed it on to the manor. But this news did not cheer up the ladies.

Everywhere, in all the villages, people were discussing what would be happening in the springtime with respect to the lords and their land: should they rent the land, or should they simply take it and chase the lords away to the city or some other place, or what? If they rented it from them, what should they pay? If they took the land, how were they to divide it among themselves?

This news and other bits of information weighed heavily on the old lady's heart, and one morning she could not get out of bed on her own: her right arm and leg were numb. And after that

happened, the manor grew even more depressing and daunting.
One time after this event, Tereshko returned home drunk from
Stepanivka; he sang, cursed, and threatened that he would burn
down the entire manor, so that nothing at all would remain;
he would burn the "old dames," and then he would go away to
destroy sugar refineries.

That was when Shura had written to her brother that he
should come home. She knew that letters reached *Ivas only on
the fourth day, and she figured out when he might be arriving.
And so, towards evening on the day when she thought he might
be coming, she told her mother that she was going outside to
take a stroll in the yard and then set out in the direction from
which he would be approaching. She wanted to see him first
in order to have a talk with him, so that he would be apprised
of what was happening in their home, and to warn him to be
careful when dealing with their mother.

Shura left the house, walked out onto the road, followed
it out of the grove, and halted; her eyes were gazing into the
distance where the evening was expiring. The reddish rays of
the evening sun illuminated her thin, dusky face, and the biting
frost gave her wasted appearance a fresh new youthfulness,
and at that moment of heightened expectation she looked quite
attractive, even though she was almost thirty and had lost all
hope for any improvement in her spinster status. She resembled
her older brother Ivas: she had the same aquiline nose, heavy
eyebrows running together on the bridge of her nose, and an
insignificant chin.

She stood there, looking and listening. It was deserted all
around, with not a single person in sight. The road showed
up darkly against the white, snow-covered field. The snowfall
had been heavy, and in the course of the winter it had settled
onto the road into a hard, blackened crust of ice. In Kordubivka
cottages were heated at night and smoke was rising from a dozen
chimneys. The evening rays tinged those plumes of smoke with
a reddish hue, and it was pleasant to watch the skeins from these
plumes stretch into the distance like the melody of a sad, drawn-
out song.

Shura felt sad and apprehensive. Her heart was pounding
in anticipation of something unknown, something that might

happen soon, or perhaps not at all. Her spirits had dropped over this past winter, and she had begun having attacks—rarely at first, and then with increasing frequency—that she had never had before: if anything troubled her, a lump would rise in her throat, choke her, and make her cry and laugh. Afterwards, she felt unhinged! And she feared that lump and kept a close watch on herself, to detect it if it should begin to rise. And now it seemed to her that this terrible lump was stirring in her chest, and so she averted her eyes from the smoke.

Behind her, from the other end of the grove, came the sound of male voices. Shura could hear several men approaching.

She darted back into the grove like a wild goat, and hid in a thick stand of young pine trees. She was all ears, because she recognized Haydun's voice.

"Why wait to see what others think," he was saying irritably, "if they don't want to, we'll do it ourselves!"

"You're saying that you'll do it here!" a stranger observed in disbelief.

"Of course we'll do it! If the peasants from Amosenko's manor don't want to, we'll plan something with the ones from Stepanivka—they're in need of land as well."

"They have a lot of their own!"

"They have as much as we have, and Polupayenko is tearing their hide off for it!" Shura once again heard Haydun's voice.

"It would be best if the entire neck of the woods agreed to take all the lords into its clutches!" a third voice rumbled. "All of them, all of the wealthy ones should be under our fist: Amosenko, Polupayenko, Shram, Bordonis . . . and this old lady as well . . ."

Shura realized that they were talking about her mother.

"We'll say: if you want to live and go on eating, then give us your land at such and such a price, because if you don't, then you'll have only yourselves to blame."

"There's no doubt about that! But if only everyone would agree . . ."

"We'll agree. There's no turning back now."

"It would be ever so wonderful!" the third voice rumbled once again and then laughed hoarsely.

The peasants walked on.

These men were from Kordubivka, and it seemed to Shura that she knew the man who had laughed hoarsely: he had shaggy hair and a large beard, and he walked like a bear. But it was dark already in the grove and she could not see him all that well.

But all the same: no matter who it had been that had said it, it seemed that what Tereshko had told Petrivna was true—the peasants were planning to take the land away from the lords.

"And what are we to do—die of hunger?" she mentally asked the rabble that was moving down the road, and anger seethed in her heart.

"Damn you!" she shouted after them, and she felt that the lump was already rolling into her throat.

And she wept and burst out laughing . . . By the time she calmed down, it was dark already. There was no one to be seen or heard on the road. Her brother had not arrived.

II

Trublayevych came home the next day.

Shura did not manage to go out and meet him. After getting out of the sleigh and fending off Kudlay who did not recognize him at first, he walked into the main room. Quickly shedding his overcoat, he walked into the parlour.

His mother was sitting in an armchair by the table and, upon seeing him, cried out softly and leaned forward to greet him, but she could not turn her head and reach out to him with her hand.

"Glory to God! You've come after all!" she said, pressing her son's head to her withered breast and kissing his forehead and hair. "Glory to God! You can see what I've become . . ."

And she started to cry.

Trublayevych kissed his mother, raised her healthy hand, and pressed it to his lips.

"What's happened to you, mother? What is it?" he murmured, struggling to hold back his tears and not quite able to do so. For he felt that something had been ripped apart in his chest. He had not seen his mother for a few years, rarely thought about her, had not spoken of her for months at a stretch, and now he was seeing her in her present condition.

"My dearest mother! What's happened to you?"

"I'm getting ready to die, my dear son . . ."

And both of them began weeping in the parlour, and Shura, upon hearing their sobbing, ran into her bedroom and buried her face in the pillows to stifle her wailing and her accursed, absurd laughter. After a while she calmed down. Dusk was falling. Petrivna lit the lamp.

Shura, her face and hands damp from her tears, walked into the parlour.

"We were expecting you to come last year, when Andryk came home," the mother said to her son as she held his hand.

"I intended to come . . . but it just didn't work out," Trublayevych replied, and he heard a sharp reproach in his mother's words, and a falseness in his own: he had never even thought about going to see his mother after she had asked him to come, because there, in the big city with its stone buildings, in his circle of acquaintances, among his friends and enemies, his mother's desire to see her son, her desire to have her entire family at her side and to live together for a few days, had seemed to him as nothing more than an amusing sentimentality.

Now he felt a heavy reproach in his heart: how cruel and egotistical he was. And wishing to appease his guilt at least partially, he once again kissed his mother's hand.

"Andryk was very sorry then that he didn't get to see you," his mother said, freeing her hand and stroking her son's hair.

"'Who knows,' he said, 'if we'll ever see each other again.'"

"Well, the war will end soon, and he'll come home."

"Oh, if only! But for some reason we haven't heard from him," the mother suddenly grew troubled. "He wrote letters, promised that if he remained alive after the battle, he would send a telegram. But . . . it still hasn't come! My heart is filled with foreboding . . ."

The mother once again seemed on the verge of tears. The son and daughter comforted her. But how were they to convince her when they themselves were plagued by doubts.

"We'll contact the bureau in charge of war prisoners; maybe he's been captured," Trublayevych said.

"Oh, if only God would grant that!" the mother latched on to this thought like a drowning man reaching for a straw.

The son promised to write to the bureau the very next day.

"I've even subscribed to the newsletter of the Red Cross; there are lists in it of the wounded, the ill, and the dead, but the lists printed in it are from the previous months, and there's nothing about those who fell at Mukden. Bring the past issues here, Shura, and let Ivas look through them."

Trublayevych refused to do so.

"What for, mother? If you didn't see Andryk's name in them, then I won't see it either. May God grant that he's still alive, and that he'll soon send us news about himself."

And they all fell silent. The votive lamp sputtered softly and flickered under the icons. Petrivna brought in the samovar.

Trublayevych rose to his feet and began pacing the room. His trip had left him feeling chilled, and shivers were still running up and down his spine. His mother followed him with her eyes.

"First it's Andryk, and now it's the peasants!" she said. "They're coming up with ideas that have never been heard of since the beginning of time. They want to take the land away from the lords."

"Well, mother, that can't happen," her son said as he came to a halt in front of her. "If they buy the land from the lords, then it will be theirs, or if the country buys it from those who now own it, it will be crown land. That would be better. That would be the so-called nationalization of the land."

"No, they just want to chase the lords into the city, and divide the land up among themselves," the mother said, and she tipped her head to one side and shook it worriedly.

"And yesterday I heard that peasants from Kordubivka were conspiring with those from Amosenko and Stepanivka, and with others as well, to set their own price for renting the land."

"That may well be. It's only the peasants who work the land. If they refuse to plough and sow, then the land will remain fallow. And so, if they truly do band together, they can either refuse to rent land from the lords, or set their own price for doing so."

"May they never live to see that day!" the mother shouted, flaring up in anger. "That has never been, and it never will be! They'll swell from hunger!"

Shura signalled Ivas to stop talking. He realized that he had recklessly started this conversation, and that his mother, even though she was old and sick, had retained her fiery nature and her old-fashioned ideas.

"Well, of course that will not happen; I'm just saying that's what they want," Trublayevych tried to smooth over the conversation.

"What they want! There's not much that they don't want! As far as I'm concerned they can devour my land and me as well: I'm about to die anyway! They're already started chopping down the orchard . . . This week they stole turkeys out of the coops . . . Let them gobble them up—may they choke on them! Why didn't God take me to Him sooner, so that I wouldn't have to see what is happening everywhere now."

The ailing woman's anger dissolved into tears.

"Let them take everything! They've already taken my son, they won't bring him back . . ."

"Mother! Mother!" her daughter cried pleadingly. "Calm down!"

"Why are you carrying on: 'Mother! Mother!' I know that I'm your mother. Strangers have torn out my heart, and you're finishing me off, wailing over my head. You'd do better to go and see what's being done in the bakehouse!"

Shura got up and walked meekly out of the room so as not to aggravate her mother even further.

Trublayevych did not know how to handle his mother. He had never been around sick people, and he had no idea how to approach them or comfort them.

"This is what I want to say to you, my son, while I'm still alive," the mother turned decisively to face him. "Those peasants will chase our family out of here; they'll drive me into my grave! And you'll have to take that crybaby away with you. Sell the land for whatever you can get for it, sell it either to these villains or some other villains; cut down the grove and sell the wood, all of it, to the very last tree! And then burn down the manor house and everything in it, so that not a trace will be left here of the Trublayevych family. Because that's exactly what these blackguards will do, and they'll burn you up alive as well!"

The son tried to calm the mother down, saying that nothing like that could ever happen, that in time everything would settle down, take a turn for the better; but the mother did not want to listen to what he was saying, and so, in order to calm her down, he finally had to say that he would do as she wished.

"So that not a trace will be left! The Trublayevyches lived, planted the grove, and worked honestly, and then they're gone, as if they had never existed. Let those peasants be left here by themselves, let them devour each other, let them graze their own cattle on their own fields, let them cut down their own orchards, let them burn down their own houses!"

Trublayevych listened to his mother's words and ruminated about the discord that holds sway over people, the misunderstandings. They had been building up for entire centuries out of droplets, out of bagatelles; they were made up of great injustices, legalized in written and unwritten codices, and they had resulted in people becoming enemies of their own brothers, justifying the savage Latin proverb: *Homo homini lupus est*—a man is a wolf to another man . . .

And this wolf does not stop to think about whom he is ripping apart—a righteous man or a guilty one, a healthy man or an ailing one, an old man or an infant. He is consumed by anger, and he has teeth, and so he slashes indiscriminately . . .

And this wolf dwells not only in those unenlightened peasants—he inhabits the hearts of enlightened lords, he is lodged in the heart of his dying mother.

The class struggle.

"But mother, after all, there is God. You believe in God, don't you? Do you suppose that He will allow things to come to that, to be as you're saying?"

The son uttered these words as a generality, without putting undue weight on them, but his words dropped on his mother's heart like water on a fire. She calmed down at once and began crying again, but now she was weeping softly, humbly.

"No, God won't let things come to that. No, He won't!"

The mother wept, but the son remained silent, stern and thoughtful.

Kudlay was barking and racing around madly under the windows.

* * *

The winter night fell quickly. In the manor house they usually went to bed early, and after tea and a bite of supper, they extinguished the lights. Only the votive lamps were left burning. Trublayevych undressed and lay down on the bed, but he could not fall asleep: he lay there and listened to the sounds of the hushed house and examined the memories and the impressions of recent days and times.

On his way home, all he had heard were conversations about the war and the ubiquitous riots, and no one was happy about that war or about those disturbances; and everyone asked why it was necessary to fight, since the war was entirely superfluous and was taking such a terrible toll in human lives. Why were riots erupting all over, since they benefitted no one, neither the victims, nor the ones who perpetrated the beatings, the robberies, and the killings? What purpose did it all serve? And everyone felt that there was a single reason behind all of it, but how could it be set aside?

And now, lying in bed, Trublayevych felt that just by using the word "misunderstandings"—a word that had often crossed his mind in recent times—you could not solve such a complicated and immense question that had been put forth by the times.

And the immensity and the complexity of the problem terrified him. There was no doubt that his native land was going through a process that was profound and not well understood as yet. All of the old structure's hinges were creaking; plaster, boards, and bricks were breaking away and crushing everything on which they fell. But what would be built to replace that structure, and how would it be built? He could not reach any conclusion about that.

Trublayevych bitterly thought about how simple a task it had seemed to him and to his acquaintances to restructure the entire empire. It had seemed that it would suffice to come up with a sensible basic law and release it in a suitable manifesto, and everything under the sun and the moon would be renewed, and everyone would be happy and content. But now he could see that it was not at all as simple as it had seemed, and that the new order of life would have to step over many corpses, first of all, over the corpse of his very own mother, of his sister . . . For they were, after all . . . yes, they were . . . parasites!

Those were his thoughts. He would have liked not to think about anything, to fall asleep. But sleep would not come. He recalled that when the train had been going past the conflagration, his neighbour, a squat, corpulent merchant who had been awakened by the other passengers, simply blinked when he looked at the reddened window and then dropped off again, snoring with his head resting on his chest. As long as he was not on fire, what did that blaze matter to him!

"May that merchant be damned! It's because of people like him, people who tear the hides off others, that everything that is happening now has come about," he thought.

And was not he, Ivan Trublayevych, also to blame in all that was going on? Had he not cast many a stone under the chariot of the glorious god of brotherhood, equality, and harmony?

Trublayevych groaned.

"Are you sleeping, Ivas?"

"No."

"Then come to me."

Trublayevych threw on some clothes and went to see his mother. In the rosy light of the votive lamp, he saw his mother sitting slumped over on some pillows in an armchair; and she looked so feeble, so crippled by life, by illness, and by her thoughts, that his filial heart was suffused with searing blood.

He wanted to say something nice and noble, to warm her heart with the fire of hope, to press her to his bosom. But he was incapable of doing that. He just pulled up a small chair, sat down quietly at her feet, and huddled closely at her knees.

"I'm not pressing too hard on you like this, am I?"

"No."

They remained silent for a few minutes.

"Ivas!" the mother spoke up softly and kindly.

"What is it, mother?"

"Why don't you tell me something about yourself?" she asked, and she reached out gently for his forehead with her warm hand.

"What am I to tell you? So far I'm living quite normally, and I'm not complaining about my fate . . ."

"Well, that's good to hear."

They were silent again.

"And you have no plans to get married?"

Ivas shuddered. "No, mother."

"That's too bad, that's too bad . . . time is slipping by."

"I know, mother, but such is my fate! I have to wait a while longer."

"Get married, my dear Ivas; find yourself a good girl with a kind heart. Love her and watch over her like the apple of your eye. And she will love you in return, and take care of you."

The mother stopped speaking for a moment.

"I'd so love to see your children! It seems to me that if I saw them, it would be easier for me to die."

Another silence.

"And as for Andryk, my poor luckless son, it looks as if he did not meet . . . his fate. It seems to me . . . I feel in my heart. that it was because of unrequited love that he went off to war."

"Who can say, mother! Things happen. Perhaps it's better that way," he said, thinking about Lyuba.

"What's better?"

"Just that, the way things happen in life."

"God only knows!"

The lamp was flickering. It was quiet in the house. Trublayevych wanted to tell his mother everything, to quietly tell her everything, as if at confession. But he restrained himself. Why burden her already broken heart with new wounds? She had enough of them as it was.

"Mother," he asked after a while, "do you ever have a doctor come to see you?"

"The doctor from Stepanivka came a couple of times, but I didn't send for him again."

"Why not?"

"Oh, I'm going to die anyway!"

"How can you say that, mother? That's not right; you must try to find some treatments, and then you'll get better. While I'm here with you, have him come. It well may be that you don't even need that much in the way of medicines."

"You know what?" he asked, after a pause. "When you get better, I'll take you and Shura away with me. I'll rent a nice apartment, and we'll set up our household and live together. When you're with me, you'll be able to rest."

"I'll rest in my grave! And what about the manor? If you go away for even only as much one day, there will be nothing left here, not so much as a sliver. They'll drag everything away in all directions!"

The housewifely instinct awoke once again in the old mistress. She could not even entertain the thought that the ancient, long-occupied nest of the Trublayevyches might be left without adequate supervision. And in her mind's eye she saw the peasants tearing down the outbuildings, the barns, and breaking into the house . . . Haydun was tearing up the floorboards with a pickaxe . . . And over there, they were destroying the orchard, cutting down the birch trees, the pine trees, and even the three fir trees that she had recently planted and that were now growing quite nicely. No, the manor could not be abandoned.

"Then sell it."

"And it would be a pity to sell it. Shura won't live with you forever . . . Maybe she'll still be able to find a decent man. They could settle in the manor, and run the farm. No, it can't be sold. Who knows what will happen next. But here, regardless of how things are, there still is a place to call one's own."

They sat, and talked, and pondered as to what should be done. And Trublayevych decided that he would most certainly call the doctor and try to cure both his mother, and his sister— because his sister was also unwell. She had wasted away to nothing. Both of the women had to have their nerves settled.

He would have to talk with the peasants who had rented the land for many years, and reach an understanding with them, give them some privileges, and appease them as well as his mother and sister. He had to find out about his brother, to get information from the bureau of captives, or from the regimental staff.

He resolved to write a letter the next day to both places, take them himself to the post office in Stepanivka, step in to see the doctor, inquire about his mother's illness, and ask him to stop by and see her more frequently and to prescribe a course of medication.

And when he thought of the post office, hope stirred in his heart that he might find there a letter from Lyuba . . . But no, that was not possible: too little time had gone by. Even if Lyuba had written a letter, it could not arrive in Stepanivka by tomorrow.

He figured out when a letter could be expected to arrive, and the thought about the letter and about Lyuba stayed with him when he said goodnight to his mother and went to sleep. He thought about Lyuba and felt that he still loved her as he always had, if not more. And he wanted to believe that everything that had transpired in the last while would pass away, be forgotten, and that when he returned from his leave of absence, Lyuba would be out of prison, and their relationship would be the same as it had been until recently. He would marry her and, as his mother said, he would look after her like the apple of his eye. For he loved her, he adored her, he could not live without her . . .

How happy he would be when everything went back to the way it was! He fell asleep thinking about Lyuba.

III

Snow. What was likely the last snowfall of the year was drifting gently to the ground from the darkened sky. It was falling in large, fluffy tufts, and it quickly spread a white coverlet over the earth, and the groves, and the icy path where the Kaydanka River flowed. It also clung to Trublayevych who was walking along the Kaydanka to the spot where it flowed into the Uday River. It was not very far—only about three versts, and Trublayevych felt an urge to go and see some familiar places.

He wanted to inhale the fresh air, to feel unfettered, to be alone. He wanted to rid himself, for at least a little while, of the problems and worries that assailed him from all directions and weighed heavily on his mind. He longed to resurrect the past, his carefree childhood, those distant, precious hours that had slipped by so quickly.

He walked over the icy surface of the river that wound through the meadows and the forest, bent itself into an arc and then straightened out only to bend once again in the opposite direction, and so on without end. These twists and turns made the path much longer to the Uday, where Trublayevych wanted to go, but he did not regret the fact that he had not gone by a more direct route. It felt good to give in to the caprices of the little river, to trust it, and to follow it to the spot where it was going. It seemed to him that the closer that it got to the Uday, the more the Kaydanka River wanted to avoid reaching it, and so it meandered and kept changing its course, hiding behind hillocks and concealing itself under trees.

"The little river doesn't want to bow to its fate, to be blended with the Uday," Trublayevych thought. "Its own individuality, its uniqueness is precious and dear to it. For when it flows into the Uday, it will cease to exist: there will be only the Uday. But the Kaydanka is also needed."

And Trublayevych took great pleasure in tracking the path that the Kaydanka chose for itself. Over here it pressed closely to the right bank, undermining it, exposing stones, and then it suddenly veered to the left and spread in a rather large tract near a luxuriant old oak. It circled the dominant position that the old giant occupied, and then set out again, describing picturesque curves as it flowed onwards.

"What a beautiful, eccentric little river," Trublayevych thought, "but to replace it Lord Bellamy would certainly dig a ditch as straight as a rod. And in it there would be only enough water to reach a sparrow's knee, while here, as you can see . . ."

He came to a rather large clear tract. Slender pine trees stood on its bank, and one of them, undermined by the water, was leaning so precariously that it would probably topple over in the first spring flood.

"It will die," Trublayevych thought, "but if one were to dig a ditch, would fewer trees be rooted out? Life should not be prescribed by narrow, unbending doctrines. It should not be placed on a *Procrustean bed. An organism should not be bound in chains; it should be helped to develop freely in accordance with its nature. Life is the greatest and most sagacious creator."

That's what he was thinking. But suddenly other thoughts, like shadows of the first ones, rose before Trublayevych. To think like that was not moral. That would permit everyone to do what he himself deemed to be beneficial. It was to justify that regime, that status quo that held back the development of an entire nation, of hundreds of nations, for a long time. It was to grant authority to the strong over the feeble!

No, not like that. There had to be some natural law that directed life.

A law? There was one. Darwin said that it is the struggle for existence; and that was like the Latin *homo homini lupus est.* Trublayevych could not agree with that. And he felt that he was standing at a crossroads. That he could see society divided into two camps—the old one that had gnawed at and destroyed Russia like termites, and the new one that wanted to make it whole again. But what if the leaders of this camp, following the example of Bellamy, began to bind life in new chains?

And once again an old thought resounded with a sharp pain in Trublayevych's mind: "You lack faith, you are a person of little faith, you are neither cold nor hot."

It was true that he was a person of little faith. And he sensed this at every turn. Take even the conversation yesterday with the doctor. What a deep faith in a better life had to reside in that small, dusky, bearded man! He believed that this anarchy—the war and the ubiquitous riots—would end in something good. They had travelled together to the manor yesterday, and they had talked about this.

"Do you know what I'm going to tell you?" the doctor said. "All that's happening now reminds me of a spring flood. The earth was bound for a long time by frost, everything grew numb on it, became insensible, and a lot of muck was accumulated, and that muck was mixed in with the snow, and it took on all sorts of forms. But then spring comes. Slowly and gently it unchains the earth, breaks the ice. Muddy, but lively, murmuring streams appear everywhere . . . everywhere! They gnaw and undermine everything that they meet along the way. They flow into one another . . . And then they roar, burst forth, break everything that happens to stand in their way, and carry everything forward, ever forward! They carry away all that filth. They tear up and carry away the fertile soil as well. But you know that after it's all over, May will come. And both the sky and the earth will be resplendent."

The doctor laughed. "You see, even I have become poetic!"

And Trublayevych laughed in turn and said: "If only it were so! But what if the sky is resplendent, but the earth is covered by fog instead of ice?"

"Well, fog is not all that terrible: the sun will swiftly burn it off!"

At that moment and even now, Trublayevych envied the doctor for his bright outlook on life. What a fortunate person! He resolved to get to know him better while he was at the manor.

He was still walking along the Kaydanka River, but he could already see where it ended, and before him, through the forest's edge, unfolded the panorama of the hilly right bank of the Uday River. There, on the crest of a hill, grew a forest that stretched all the way to the horizon, to the place where the Uday was flowing. The surface of the Uday, and the ground, and the forest were covered with snow. Flakes were swirling in soft single stars.

It was warm and still. A peaceful lyrical mood enveloped Trublayevych. Yes, the spring flood would cleanse everything and renew the earth. The sky and the earth would smile, and those who would be living on it would be happy. And what about those that the spring floods swept away? But why think about them—such is their fate! In life there are neither innocent people, nor guilty ones.

Trublayevych sat down on a steep bank and rested. The walk had warmed him up, and he undid his coat and deeply inhaled the gentle sweet air.

In life there are none who are innocent, and none who are guilty. And Andryk also was neither innocent nor guilty—Andryk, who was now sitting somewhere in a trench and thinking perhaps about his mother, about the manor, and possibly, even about him. But that was unlikely. Their relationship was cold and insincere. And yet, how much warmth and sincerity Andryk possessed!

This morning Trublayevych had read the letters that Andryk had written to his mother. They moved him, touched his heart, and he resolved that if Andryk came home alive from the war, he would come to see him, talk frankly with him, and live with him like a brother, so that they would not be the strangers to each other that they had been up to now.

He recalled how once, long ago, when they were still little, he and Andryk, also walking over the ice and snow, had come to this very same spot, and had sat here for a while. The Uday had not yet frozen over, and the water was dark, as if diluted with soot, and it created a very pleasing contrast with the white banks and hills. It looked like molten lead flowing over the snow.

They sat and talked about what they would be when they grew up. Ivas said that he would be a professor, but Andryk stared at the water, thought for a long time, and finally said that he wanted to be a monk. All black and sternly solemn, he would walk grandly past people . . . past life.

That's what they had imagined. And now one worked in a bank, and the other was in the army. What an irony of life . . .

He sat for a while longer by the Uday and then set out for home. Now he took a direct route, and his mood was different.

The next day he talked with the peasants. Seven householders, long-time renters of Trublayevych land, came from Kordubivka and asked the young lord to come out to see them.

He went out with some apprehension, for he feared that he would not be able to come to an understanding with them. He had never had the occasion to deal with peasants.

The peasants stood in a group by the porch. Kudlay, favouring his left leg, barked angrily at them, but did not come near them. One of the guests had struck him with a walking stick.

They exchanged greetings.

"We've come, you see, to talk about what will be happening with the land in the springtime. Spring will soon be here," one of them began the conversation.

From what he had heard from his mother and sister, Trublayevych guessed that he must be Haydun.

"Well, let's talk," Trublayevych responded.

The peasants remained silent.

"You see, my young lord, or should I say, my lord?" one of the villagers, a scrawny, grey-haired man, smiled and asked diplomatically. "We've been renting the land from your mother for a long time. We ploughed, we sowed . . . We rented it for money, and we rented it for shares. Now the times are such that, you know . . . it's time to give the land over to us completely."

"What do you mean?" Trublayevych asked.

"It's quite simple, give us the land, and that's that!" Haydun shouted.

"Wait a moment, it's not like that," the diplomatic old man turned to him. "This is how it is, you see . . . We ploughed, and sowed. And now the times are such that people everywhere will be taking the land away from the lords, and so this is what we're saying: let the Trublayevyches give us their land as well, first of all, for five years."

"But you've been renting the land for more than twenty years, and you've taken your crop-share, so why wouldn't we give it to you for another five years?"

"Well, you see, we paid money for it, but now, we won't pay you anything for the next five years. It will be ours. We'll plough, and sow, and everything . . ."

"That's not possible! What are my mother and sister to live on? What are they to do—swell with hunger?"

"Why should they swell with hunger . . . After all, can't you help them?"

"I don't figure in any of this. But the land belongs to my mother, and she should benefit from it."

"She's benefitted enough!" Haydun shouted. "We have to benefit from it too, we also have families!"

"But the land is not yours. What would you say if tomorrow some stranger came to you and said: 'You've benefitted from your land all your life, and that's enough. Let us benefit from it for five years.' How would that strike you?"

"That's an entirely different matter. But we have ploughed, sowed . . ."

"Listen, my young lord, to what I'm going to say to you," one of the villagers, who had previously said very little, finally spoke up after the arguing had gone on for quite some time.

"Your land, if it isn't fertilized, will not yield anything. Well, who is going to fertilize land that doesn't belong to him? This year I may not spare any effort, I'll fertilize it, and then in the spring the lady will rent it out to someone else. Well, we, to be sure, hauled very little fertilizer on your land, and there will be little profit from it both for us, and for your mother.

"In my opinion, we should settle things this way, in a holy manner: rent the land to us, to the Kordubivka villagers, and to no one else; we will then spare no effort to fertilize it. We'll plough it ourselves, sow our own grain and reap it, and we'll give your mother every fourth sheaf. And there will be grain both for us and for you. And there will be feed for the cattle. Let it be this way for five years, and then we'll see how things stand. We don't want what doesn't belong to us."

Trublayevych thought about it and agreed. Even though his mother and sister might not be able to eke out a living off the fourth sheaf, he would come to their assistance. At least they would be sure that they would have every fourth sheaf, and that they and the manor would remain unscathed.

The peasants shook hands with Trublayevych, said their farewells, and went home. "We're confident that your word is as good as the word of the old lady, and that there will be no changes in what has been agreed to!"

Trublayevych promised that he would keep his word.

His mother and sister were waiting impatiently for him in the house. Shura had seen through the window that some agreement had been reached, that Ivas had shaken hands with the peasants, but neither she nor her mother had expected that things would turn out as they did.

Terrified by all sorts of fears, they were expecting something unheard of, and when they found out that everything would be fine, that the land would be theirs and that they would have every fourth sheaf, they were very happy. And if the peasants truly would fertilize the land well, then the grain would grow better, yield more, and they would manage to live one way or another.

Evening came and went quietly and peacefully, and the manor seemed to grow more cheerful. They decided to fire Tereshko and find another male servant, someone who did not drink and who was more tractable. In addition, from his discussions with the peasants, Trublayevych found out that Tereshko had lied to them about the Trublayevyches and had told them that the lady had threatened not to give them any land at all in the spring.

The next day Trublayevych again went along the Kaydanka River to the Uday. And now a clear, slightly melancholy mood seized hold of him, and he sang as he walked along:

An unknown power lures me
To these mournful banks . . .

And he truly was drawn to them, and to the forest, and to the river, and to the hills that rose beyond it. The morning was warm and calm, and a gentle, wispy mist enveloped the earth. Trublayevych felt serene and at peace, and today life did not seem so cold, gloomy, and complicated. He had already come to an understanding with the peasants. He walked along and sang. But then a cracking sound and a rustling caught his ear. He halted where he was on the ice and looked at the other bank from where the noise was emanating.

A man appeared there with an oak cudgel freshly broken from a tree. Wearing a cloak flung over a shirt and white pants made out of coarse linen, he was walking barefoot over the snow. The cloak was undone, and his long hair was covered by large patches of snow that had fallen on his bare head when he broke off the cudgel. The man's eyes were angry and penetrating. He walked towards Trublayevych with his cudgel at the ready, as if he wanted to strike him.

Trublayevych knew the demented man who was called "whoa-whoa Soma," and who came from the neighbouring village of Amosivka.

Trublayevych stepped out of his path.

"What a singer!" Soma muttered angrily as he walked past Trublayevych.

And he kept glancing back over his shoulder until he disappeared around a bend in the Kaydanka.

Trublayevych's lyrical mood was shattered.

Things in this world were far different from what they had seemed to him so recently. Not all evil could be avoided, not all problems could be solved.

Take this madman, for example. Children taunted and laughed at him, and when he chased after them and hit them, their parents beat him up. And several times he had almost been beaten to death. But he always recuperated, and then, dressed in the same mantle he would once again walk about barefoot and mutter angrily when he met up with people. Eventually people stopped teasing and beating him, and now, according to Shura, some people even viewed him as a saint. At the moment he lived in the home of two women who agreed to take him in. And sick people, hoping to be cured, came and listened to the mutterings of "whoa-whoa Soma."

There you had it—the other side of life!

Trublayevych returned home feeling sad and dispirited.

IV

A week went by, then a month. Life in the manor plodded on gloomily, monotonously, like slowly dripping drops of water. Instead of Tereshko, they now had another servant: Hordiy. After the meeting with the peasants from Kordubivka, some women came and demanded that they be charged less for the land that they rented for gardens. An agreement was reached, and they went home satisfied that their demands had been met.

Trublayevych made trips to get the mail and fetch the doctor. The doctor came, examined the ill woman, engaged in conversations, and went home. Her health did not improve. All she thought about was Andryk. She was convinced that something had happened to him, and every day she expected to hear about it. The office in charge of war prisoners informed them that Andryk's name was not on any list of captured soldiers.

As the days passed by, Trublayevych began to lose hope that his brother was still among the living. Before giving his mother a newspaper, he looked through it carefully to see if there was any news of Andryk being killed so that he could prepare his mother in some way before she read about it.

He had come to an agreement about this with Shura.

This year the winter was quite long, but after the last snowfall when Trublayevych had gone walking along the Uday, a thaw set in. Day after day, and night after night, the snow softened and melted. The earth was wrapped in fogs and mists, and the manor birch trees, enveloped in this haze, dropped copious tears. It was as if they were grieving for something . . . But for what? For what had already transpired or for what would still happen?

Trublayevych would walk out of the house, sit down on the porch, and gaze at these birch trees. Grief was gnawing at his heart. It entered his heart imperceptibly, as if finding its way there along with the mist that he was inhaling. He read the newspapers daily, following carefully the events by which society was slowly, step by step, winning back its freedom, but he took no joy in it. The steps were very small, and they were taken with great difficulty . . . and they were still so uncertain!

But what worried him most was the fact that he still had not received a letter from Lyuba. Was it possible that she would not reply? Was it possible that she would not tell him in so many words that she was breaking off all ties with him? And the more Trublayevych thought about it, the more convinced he became that he would not lose Lyuba, that she loved him and would become his wife. And he attributed her long silence to her inner struggle, and he waited for that struggle to end.

He sat around and waited for a letter, and the birch trees lowered their long, supple branches over him, swayed above him, and shed their copious tears.

Then came a day when there was a warm heavy rain that washed away the last vestiges of winter. Spring was arriving. At night, frost still bound the earth, and in the morning white hoarfrost covered the trees and last year's grass, but spring was in the air, and the sun shone more cheerfully and more kindly.

One time when Trublayevych did not make his usual trip to the post office, Hordiy brought him a letter.

The letter was from Lyuba. Trublayevych took it, but he did not go into the house to read it, nor did he read it in the yard; he went into the forest, sat down under a birch tree on the bank of the Kaydanka, tore open the letter, and began reading.

Forgive me for not writing to you for such a long time. I deliberated and thought things over at length before I finally got up the nerve to write this letter. When you left our home that evening after the provincial assembly, it seemed to me that it was all over between us. I saw that our convictions were dissimilar, that we would not be able to reconcile two such differing world views. And so I decided to tell you that straightforwardly at our very next meeting.

Things happened a little differently. And what did happen pushed me even further away from you. That incident with my letters . . . Why didn't you burn them?

But now, as I sit in prison, I've had a lot of time to think things over and I can see that you did the right thing, the best possible thing for both of us, when you passed me your letter.

A ray of hope flashed in Trublayevych's mind.

You opened your heart to reveal your thoughts to me, and I must be as frank with you. It will be best that way, and so I'm saying to you: I love you, but I also love another man. And that love is stronger and more powerful. There is nothing strange or unusual about this, and even more so, there is nothing immoral about it. My feelings are pure, honest, and deep . . .

My dear one, I love you and I'll cherish memories of you all my life! I love you as a decent, honest person, like the older brother that I never had. No, I love you more than a brother, and if what happened had not happened, I would have joined my fate to yours, and we would have been happy. I am confident about that.

But another person has come between us. You know who it is. That person has set my heart on fire with the desire to fight, with the desire to devote myself completely to the cause of ensuring that all people, everyone, can enjoy a better life in this world. I was nearsighted and egotistical, I thought only about myself, about my own happiness, but one must not live that way. You yourself know this, even though you are unable to throw caution to the wind and join those people, that camp, to which my heart is drawn.

I believe in those people, I believe that truth is on their side. Oh, why aren't you at our side, and why is it that you can't be with us!

Forgive me—perhaps I've offended you, but it is not my wish to offend you, for you are a part of my past, a part of my soul. With this letter I want to say to you: please try to understand me and to forgive me for the pain that I am unwillingly causing you. If you can, forget about me. It would be best if we did not see one another, but if we should happen to meet, then I beg you: let us be like good old acquaintances. I know what you are like, and I can expect no less from you. Once more, I beg you to forgive me for the pain that I am causing you.

There was no signature, and none was needed.

Well, here it was—the long-awaited letter! Now there was an end to all his dreams. The knot was undone, completely undone. Carefully, even with tenderness, he had been pushed away; he—who was neither cold nor hot; he—who was lukewarm; he—who always took the neutral middle ground! He could not come to a boiling point when life demanded it of him, and life splashed him out like tepid water that is incapable of either warming a person frozen from the cold, or of cooling parched lips in the heat.

Neither cold nor hot—that was his curse! It was the stamp that the period of reaction had branded on his heart and on the hearts of millions.

He had always been an honourable human being, he had always wished the best for others, but he had lived as if he were chained. He feared to cross the line, he feared to stand out among others so as not to evoke punitive measures from the administration, so as not to irritate an oppressed society with his daring. And he had dried up and withered.

And when there came a time that called for truly brave deeds, he was no longer capable of doing them. He knew only how to analyze, seek out shadows, and find fault with the actions of others, and disillusionment settled in his heart. And he was cast like an unbeliever onto that neutral middle ground . . .

"A piece of trash!" he said out loud to himself. "You're worthless!"

He sat and pondered. And an inveterate thought began weaving its inveterate web. He had done nothing to benefit humanity, but it still remained to be seen what Zembulat and his ilk would accomplish. Would they ever actually do anything? It was easy to spout impassioned speeches, but it was far more difficult to put even the most insignificant detail into action.

And a sharp anger flared up in him against Zembulat: the entire reason for his misfortune lay in this upstart who was so capable of brilliantly spouting a cascade of liberal words and who could flirt so insolently with his bulging eyes! Oh, if only he could meet up with him right now!

But at the very same moment, a traitorous thought crept up to him from another direction and pointed out to him that even if he did meet up with Zembulat he would not do anything to harm him in any way. Because he was incapable of carrying out daring, extraordinary acts. Because he feared what people would say. Because he had a thin skin. He sat on the riverbank and kneaded the torn envelope. He shredded it into pieces and threw them one after the other into the water and then watched as the muddy current swirled them and carried them away.

From that day on, even though spring was appearing everywhere, life in the manor house became even gloomier. Trublayevych lost all desire to do anything, and sat for days on end on the porch, or at his mother's side as he laid out games of patience on the table. He sat and did not say anything, and always seemed to be lost in thought.

Both his mother and Shura could see that he was distracted, and they tried doing things to please him, but he only smiled sadly and remained silent as he took note of their kindness. He no longer made trips to the post office, and only skimmed the newspapers that Hordiy brought when he came with the doctor.

One day, as he scanned the lists of the dead and the wounded, he came across the surname Trublayevych. It was Andryk, and it was written that he had been killed at the battle of Mukden.

Surprised that these words did not upset him, he carefully reread them letter by letter, as if trying to convince himself that he had actually read them, and then he put the paper aside and fell into thought.

What was he to do now, how was he to tell his mother and sister? And the matter of how he was to break the news to his mother and sister seemed more important to him than the fact that Andryk was gone, that Andryk, through no fault or guilt of his own, had been killed somewhere over there in a foreign land. For he had long since grown accustomed to the thought that his brother was no longer in this world, that it was a fact, and that he had to reconcile himself to that idea. And he had long since come to terms with it.

But what was he to do with those who could not come to terms with facts? Hiding the paper, he put on his coat and told his mother that this time Hordiy had not brought back any mail. He walked out of the house and inveigled Shura to come with him. They walked along the forest above the Kaydanka River. The ground had dried already.

They walked in silence.

"What do you want to tell me, Ivas?" Shura asked him after they had gone a fair distance from the house.

"I did not have anything in mind to tell you, I just wanted to go for a walk with you. We stay in the house so much, and my leave is ending soon. I'll go back without even having taken a walk with you."

"But it seems to me that there was something that you wanted to tell me . . ."

"What am I to tell you, Shura? I've been worried about Andryk this last while. There hasn't been any news about him," Trublayevych said, turning away from his sister as if he wanted to break off a branch on a birch tree.

The branch on the birch snapped, and for the first time after reading about his brother's death, he felt as if something had broken in his heart as well. He felt that he might break into tears at any moment.

"I think that something must have happened to him," he added and then fell silent.

"I think so too," Shura said thoughtfully. "I see him in my dreams, and he's usually cheerful and ever so friendly. I wake up and I weep."

They did not speak for a few moments.

"What would you do, Shura, if Andryk did die in the war? It could actually happen."

"What could I do? We, God willing, would cry for some time, grieve, and then slowly reconcile ourselves to the idea, but as for mother . . . She would not be able to live through something like that!"

"Is that what you think?"

"I'm sure of it!"

Shura feared the same thing that Trublayevych feared—that meant that their mother truly could not be told.

But as for Shura . . . should he tell her?"

And Trublayevych decided that he must tell her.

They were walking near a moderately high bank.

"Shura, my dear, let's sit down! It's dry over here," Trublayevych said and he dangled his feet over the edge.

Shura also sat down.

"I won't keep it a secret from you any longer . . ."
Shura looked fearfully at her brother.
"You have to know sooner or later."
"What?"
"Andryk is no longer among the living."
"Ivas! What are you saying?"
"It's true. It's in today's newspaper."
"I knew it all along . . . O my God, my God!"
Shura collapsed on the steep slope and wept bitterly.

Hearing her weeping and seeing how distraught she was, Trublayevych could not refrain from bursting into tears himself.

"Shura, my dearest Shura, don't take it so hard! You can't change what has happened," he said, but he himself realized that his words were futile and that logic could never assuage the grief that was looming over their family and that was already crushing him and his sister.

They took a long time coming home, and they decided not to say anything to their mother about Andryk's death because telling her now would be tantamount to killing her. Perhaps after they had prepared her somewhat, they would be able to tell her later on that he had died. They wandered about the yard until evening, coming into the house only briefly so that their mother would not be able to see in their eyes that they were hiding a secret from her. In the evening they went to sleep early.

The next day when the mother noticed that Shura's eyes were red, she asked her why she had been crying. Shura said that she had not been crying, but that her head had ached all night, and that she had not been able to sleep. It seemed to her that her mother believed her. But when Hordiy brought the next day's newspaper, and yesterday's was still nowhere to be found, the mother grew even more concerned: what if they had concealed it from her?

She did not say anything to anyone, but she was agitated all evening and did not sleep at night. In the morning her face looked waxen.

"Ivas, could you go to the post office today and ask if that edition of our newspaper was misplaced somewhere?" she asked.

"Why do you need it? One newspaper was misplaced, and so be it!"

"No, we must find it, or we must get it from the neighbour. There might be news about Andryk in it."

"Well, fine, I'll go."

It seemed to him that his mother calmed down.

But when he came back from the post office, he did not bring the newspaper with him, and she once again started fretting about it. And it seemed to her that both her son and her daughter were hiding something from her. She could see it in Shura's eyes, and in the way that Ivas and Shura silently exchanged glances and walked out of the house.

And the mother decided to look for the newspaper at home: it had to be here, and they were just not showing it to her.

One time, when neither Shura nor Ivas was in the house, she called Petrivna and ordered her to search everywhere for the newspaper.

Petrivna brought her all the newspapers, but the one that she needed was not among them. Then the lady ordered her to look through all of Ivas's pockets, and all his boxes, and all his suitcases.

Petrivna rummaged around for a long time until she finally found a crumpled newspaper in one of his suitcases and brought it to the lady. The lady glanced at the date and number on it and silently ordered Petrivna to leave the room.

The newspaper was the one that had disappeared. Why had it been hidden? It must contain news of some kind!

A terrifying and long-dreaded presentiment overcame the ailing woman, and it seemed to her that her hair was standing on end. She opened the newspaper with her one good hand and searched through it for the list of the dead and the wounded.

The list was there, and it was quite long. She began reading it slowly, because the letters were jumping before her eyes.

She weakly dropped the newspaper for a moment on her knees, and throwing her head backwards, closed her eyes for a moment to calm herself. But only for a moment, and then she began reading again.

She was now searching for the surnames that began with the letter "T".

"Trokhymenko . . . Torubayev . . . Trublayevych! Andriy Trublayevych!"

She had to look back at the heading to see if Andryk had been killed or only wounded.

"He was killed!" she shouted. "O my God, what can this mean, what can it mean?"

The newspaper fell to the floor, and the mother flung herself back in her chair. She could not breathe.

"Petrivna!" she yelled so loudly in a voice so unnatural that the maid heard her in the bakehouse and came running.

"He's been killed!"

"Who?"

"Andryk . . ." The mother could barely talk because her tears were drowning her words.

"O Lord, accept his tender soul!"

"Oh, what have they done, and why did they do it? Where is the justice in this world!" the mother wailed. "O my son, my son, my falcon, what have they done to you? Petrivna!" she turned abruptly to her maid. "Help me make the sign of the cross!"

Petrivna took the sick old woman's right hand, and crossed her with it, just as little children are crossed.

"O Lord, accept the soul of your servant Andriy," the mother said, raising her weeping eyes. "O Lord, let his soul rest in peace! And as for all of you who caused his death, who instigated this war—may you be damned! May you be damned both in this world and in the next one!"

The mother wept grievously, uncontrollably. And it seemed to Petrivna that she even moved her paralyzed leg and arm.

"My dear lady, don't carry on like that! Have some care for yourself!"

"Why should I care for myself when . . . when . . . " she could not finish what she was saying because of her tears. "Call my children to me."

Petrivna ran to fetch Ivas and Shura, but they were not in the yard. She ran into the grove and began shouting.

Ivas responded.

"The young lord has been killed!" Petrivna called out when she saw the brother and sister through the trees.

"What? What young lord?" they asked her in chorus.

"Andriy Mykhaylovych . . . Andryk!"

"What? Who told you?"

"The lady told me. She's calling for you . . ."

The brother and sister exchanged looks.

"How did she find out?" Ivas asked.

"She read it in the newspaper, the one that was in your suitcase."

"So you're the one who gave it to her?" Ivas pounced on her words.

"The lady ordered me to look everywhere and to bring her all the newspapers. She ordered me to look in the suitcases as well. And I found it . . ."

"Oh, so that's what happened . . . We'd better go to her at once!"

They almost ran into the house.

"What's this? So you wanted to conceal it from your mother?" the mother greeted them.

"Mother dearest!"

"My precious mother!"

The mother shook her head.

"It doesn't matter. I found out anyway, you couldn't hide it from me . . . O God, dear God, what am I to do? It would have been better to have choked him with my own hands when he was a little baby, so that I'd at least know that he's buried in the ground, that he isn't lying unburied, that dogs aren't gnawing on his bones. Oh, damn you!"

Evening descended. The votive lamps were lit in the main rooms. The lady ordered that wax candles be lit before the icons and she sat in her armchair, as if at the side of a deceased.

The house was quiet, and all that could be heard were her sighs. Ivas and Shura sat silently in corners and when they suddenly heard their mother's voice, they shuddered.

"You're lying, my dear son, in the steppe, in the frost . . . Your tender white hands have turned numb, your swift, precious legs have stiffened, your sweet, welcoming lips have turned silent!"

She shook her head as if she was bent over her son's corpse.

"You're lying right there, my son, where you fell . . . And there is no one to lift you, to bind your bloody wounds, to staunch the gushing of your warm blood. And it has frozen in the fierce cold . . . The blood of my blood has frozen!"

The mother shuddered violently, as if chilled by the cold.

"It is *Rachael crying over her children," Ivas thought. "It is that biblical mother who is crying and who, all alone, bereft, cannot not be comforted." And he came out of his corner, sat at his mother's feet, kissed her hand, and dampened it with his tears, because his heart had melted, like wax in a fire.

But the mother appeared not to notice either him or his tears. After remaining silent for a moment, she began lamenting again.

"Death has mown down my precious flower, cut him down: do not blossom in the frost! The white snow has no need of you, the cold stone has no need of you! Oh, my son, my son!" Every word fell like a droplet of blood and scalded like molten lead.

"Rachael is weeping over her children and cannot be consoled . . . And everywhere, throughout all of Russia, many Rachaels are weeping. But while Rachael can only weep, her sons ought to be thinking about how to dry those tears forever, so that her children will never again be killed!" Ivas thought.

And the mother's every word evoked anger in the son's heart, anger at himself and at all those who slept safely, saved their skins, and allowed their native land to be destroyed. No, it was not possible to live thus! To remain silent and to sit by meekly—that was equivalent to taking the side of the enemies of the fatherland, and to wound afresh the heart of Rachael.

No, it was imperative to go there, where Lyuba had gone, where Zembulat and others were going. It was better to be dead than to live without freedom. Because a slave's life was not worthy of a human being!

V

The candles burned under the icons. The votive lamps flamed. It was hot and stuffy in the main rooms. And it seemed that grief had entered these modest, low-ceilinged rooms and had settled in, never again to leave. It sat in the corners, looked around, and blinked its indifferent eyes from every shadow, and it felt comfortable and safe in this decaying old house.

It sat and looked with uncaring eyes at the unfortunate old woman who refused to lie down in bed and continued sitting, propped up by pillows, in an armchair. It looked at the weary, fatigued son and daughter of that woman . . . and it blinked, and seemed to be waiting for something.

"Be damned! May you be damned! From all the corners of our land you have taken away sons from their mothers, children from their parents, husbands from their wives, and sent them to their death. You are spattered by their blood! Look: you're covered in blood! You're covered with the blood of your own brothers! And you will never wash it off for all of eternity!"

"Mother!"

She did not listen and, after a moment's silence, began keening again.

"They will arise, they will come to you, wounded, slashed to pieces, with torn off arms and heads, with lacerated sides and backs, they will come to you and they will ask: 'Why have you killed us? Our blood is on you and on your children. You are damned!'"

"Mother, mother dearest!"

The flames in the votive lamps shuddered and leapt, and grief blinked from the darkened corners.

"A mother had a son, but he was sucked into a bloody maelstrom, and now he is no more . . . Oh, woe is me. Oh, woe is me!"

Woe heard that cry, but it did not respond; it only blinked indifferently. Why would it be concerned? It had done what it was supposed to do, and, when the right moment came, it would do so again.

A clock ticks, tapping out the seconds. People do not count them, but woe does count them, and it waits patiently until its time has come, the time for a new victim.

But who would be the next victim? Who of the three would it be, or would it be all three together?

They were all prepared. The mother and the daughter had been ready for a long time now, and as for the son . . . he too had long been ready! He was sitting as if turned to stone. His mother's words were branded on his brain, and he recalled what he had read today in a letter written by the doctor's brother, a letter that arrived from that wretched country after the battle of Mukden:

We've lived through a lot. I can't understand how the hand of death has passed me by, because I haven't even been wounded. From the 22nd to the 28th our entire regiment was engaged in battles. Suffice it to say that between morning and evening on the 22nd of February we went on the attack seven times, and we lost 1,354 soldiers, and out of 54 commissioned officers, only 11 are left, and three of those have lost their minds.

Everyone all around us was dying from bullets, grenades, mortar shells, and machine-gun fire. If I were a believer, I would have said God was protecting me.

A battle—is hell. All around there's groaning, the din of hatred, of anger, of fear, of rejoicing; noise, whistling, wailing, hissing, thunder, the gnashing of teeth, weeping, fits, cursing, pleas, the frenzy of prayer; destruction, disorder, corpses, bloodied bandages, falling down, the final agony of death, croaking, tears of joy, a frenzied fear, a deathly paleness, heroism—at times, more often—panic . . . And blood. Blood all over and everywhere!

I wonder if all of this is just a dream? Because the riddle of life is being solved here. And all of it has its own ethos . . . And when you've seen your own blood spilled, you want to see another man's blood . . . And it was frightening, and horrific, and cheerful, and pleasant.

"Oh, what animals we still are—all of us human beings! What animals we still are, what heartless animals!" Trublayevych thought, and he reckoned that on the twenty-second of February his brother's regiment was supposed to go on leave, to take a rest, but instead, it went into battle.

And who knows if Andryk was killed with one of the first bullets, or if he repulsed all the attacks and was about to retreat, or if, perhaps, in the general panic, he was fated to be wounded, to fall down and die under the feet of his own comrades-in-arms . . . To plead, to stretch out his hands, to grab at the legs of savage, maddened people, and to die with a final curse on his lips. Who could say?

Shura was sitting motionless.

She fixed her eyes on a corner of the room and did not even blink, as if she was charmed by the grief that was staring at her with a thousand eyes out of that corner and through all the cracks. And all those eyes pierced her heart and cooled it off, draining away her strength drop by drop. It seemed to her that all this was a dream, a delusion of some kind, that the door would open in a moment and Andryk would walk in, but he would not walk in alive, only a shadow of his. And she was afraid to look at the door. She was afraid to raise her eyes to the window.

"He'll come in right away! He'll come in right away," a voice whispered.

The door opened and Andryk walked in. He was missing an arm and a shoulder . . .

He looked at her and laughed. "I've come, ha-ha!"

And he instantly collapsed at her feet.

"Oh!" she shrieked in an unworldly voice and, leaping to her feet, she tottered on wooden legs to the adjoining room and tumbled down on the threshold.

The mother also screamed in surprise, jumped up with a start, and fell out of the armchair onto the floor.

"Shura! Mother!"

Trublayevych ran up to his mother, picked her up as if she were a child and, amazed at how light she was, sat her down again in the armchair, while Shura thrashed around spasmodically, crying and laughing.

"Mother, what's wrong? Did Shura frighten you?"

But his mother did not reply; she wanted to say something, but could not. The thought flashed through Trublayevych's mind that his mother must have had another stroke.

"Petrivna! Hordiy!" he yelled from the doorway. "Get the doctor as quickly as you can!"

But no one responded from the bakehouse. They had been asleep for some time now.

Trublayevych rushed in, woke up Hordiy and ordered him to fetch the doctor. Hordiy, breathing heavily, got up and sat down on the bench: he was groggy with sleep and could not fathom what was happening.

"Harness the horses right now and go to Stepanivka to get the doctor!"

"Horidy! Hordiy!" Petrivna poked him in the shoulder. "The young lord is saying: go get the doctor!"

Hordiy finally woke up. "Fine."

"Petrivna, my dear, come with me; mother is sick, and so is Shura . . ." Trublayevych begged Petrivna. "Bring some water!" And he rushed back to that room where a terrible monster—grief—held sway . . .

* * *

Dawn was breaking. The doctor was standing by the sick woman's bed and talking with Trublayevych.

"There's nothing that can be done . . . it's the throes of death—the final struggle between life and death. It's as I feared would happen: another apoplectic fit. Don't touch her, don't move her!" He took a chair, sat down by the bed, and looked silently at the dying woman.

Trublayevych stood at the head of his mother's bed and watched her ragged breathing, and her wheezing wrenched his heart. What would he not give now to bring his mother back to life . . . How he would caress and care for her, he who had seen her once every four years, and who had not thought about her for years at a stretch.

But there was no such power that could revitalize her.

"You know, truthfully speaking there's very little hope that she will recover. The end has to come sooner or later," the doctor said thoughtfully. "This is just one more victim of the spring flood . . . do you recall it?"

Trublayevych agreed, nodding his head. The conversation died down. And how could Trublayevych talk now about some kind of a spring flood, when his mother was dying?

But it was as if the doctor's words had awoken his imagination, and it seemed to him that something great, unknown, and invincible, something truly like a turbulent spring flood was washing over life, smashing everything that happened to lie in its path, and taking it away to parts unknown . . .

Shura walked in, broken and crumpled like a crushed blade of grass. She went up to her mother's bed, looked at her, and shook her head.

"Sit down, Oleksandra Mykhaylivna!" the doctor said, and he moved a chair towards her.

The chair scraped along the floor and startled the stillness for a moment. Then everything fell silent once again, and all that could be heard was the hoarse breathing of the ill woman.

* * *

Three days later, in the grove that stood by the road, a fresh, slightly rounded grave appeared among the old ones, and a funeral dinner was being held in the manor house. At the table were seated a priest, a deacon, a cantor, a few neighbours, and Trublayevych. Shura did not join them at the table; she was serving them.

The clergy ate and drank with gusto, conversed loudly, and clattered the dishes as if they had been invited to a holiday repast. The fumes from the censer mixed with the tobacco smoke, but it seemed to Trublayevych and Shura that the heavy odour of a corpse still lingered in the room.

The guests did not seem to notice it. The deacon had already begun recounting a humorous anecdote, but the priest stopped him and started a conversation centred on current events. He had a subscription to *The World* and was a great patriot.

"What's the situation like with peasants down south where you are?" he asked Trublayevych as he gnawed on a chicken bone. "Are they stirring, or not?"

Trublayevych looked up. "It's like it is everywhere," he said.

"Yes," the priest said, throwing away the bone and wiping his greasy lips.

"Father Ivan, let's have another round," the deacon said.

"Go ahead and pour it. Yes . . . Well, and do you think that there will be uprisings?" he asked Trublayevych.

"It's hard to say what will happen," Trublayevych replied.

"But I know that there will be!" Father Ivan said, smacking his lips. "The willows will be done away with entirely in our kingdom."

The deacon and the cantor laughed uproariously.

"They'll cut them all down when they begin to soundly thrash the rabble-rousers," Father Ivan continued. "If you have any willows along the Kaydanka, guard them well: you'll get good money for them."

"Tee-hee-hee!" the deacon chortled.

"Corporal punishment is forbidden by law, and no one has the right to thrash people," Trublayevych responded sternly; he was scarcely able to contain his wrath.

"The law doesn't mean anything," the deacon said. "Peasants in three villages have already been thrashed at trials: in Sobyntsi, Hnyla, Dmukhanivka. For burning down a sugar refinery . . ."

"That's an illegal act, and it must be punished."

"Oho, an illegal act! And isn't burning down factories illegal, and isn't it illegal to rob the lord's storage rooms and barns?" Father Ivan flared up angrily. "If peasants break the law, then the authorities must also. If you please: there's a war going on in Manchuria, everyone should give their last penny to support it, they should spill their blood for the honour and glory of their native land, but they're rebelling . . . I'd thrash them all to bits!"

"Tee-hee-hee! Roll up your sleeves, Father, and get down to work!" the drunken deacon smirked.

"And so I will!" Father Ivan shouted in exasperation. "And I'll thrash you first of all!"

"You don't say! But your arms are too short!"

"We'll see."

"Why are you so angry?"

"We know why!"

"It would be interesting to find out."

"If you know too much, you'll grow old too soon . . . Have you ever heard that?"

"Yes, I have. So, maybe we'll have another drink?" the deacon tried to smooth things over.

"Go ahead and pour it! The clergy are drinking, so why aren't the lay people following suit? Let's all drink to the repose of Olympiada, the newly deceased servant of God."

They downed their drinks and ate. They had all eaten a lot. Father Ivan stood up in a dignified manner and rattled through a prayer: "Both the living and the dead are in Your care . . ."

"Lord, grant a blessed repose to Your departed servant . . ." the deacon sang in a bass voice as he gulped down the last bit of meat, "and make her memory eternal."

"Eternal memory, eter-r-r-r-nal memory, e-e-e-eternal memory," all the clergy sang in chorus.

The dinner ended. The clergy and the neighbours sat around for a little while longer, talked, smoked, and then departed. Trublayevych opened up all the windows and walked out of the house. Evening was approaching. In the west, spring clouds were taking on a rosy hue and the birch trees, unfurling their long buds, were standing a reddish light. The younger trees were already turning green.

Trublayevych walked out to his mother's grave. It gave him a strange feeling to see the fresh mound of sandy soil and to admit that this was his mother's grave, that all the thoughts, the pain, the suffering of a precious being had come to an end in this pile of raw earth.

He picked up a withered pinecone from the grave and tossed it aside. Then he picked up and tossed away other cones and leaves that were mixed in with the sand. He wanted the grave to be clean and immaculate, so that there would be nothing on it that would remind one of disorder, of untidiness. Then he picked a few cowslips that were not yet blooming and placed them on the grave at the spot where he thought his mother's breast was.

It was quiet and cool, the fresh spring air enveloped everything—the ground, and the plants, and the trees. And it seemed to Trublayevych that it was better that his mother was now resting and lying there, in the ground, in the coolness; it would be more peaceful for her there. Her thoughts would not torment her, her aching heart would not be breaking, her exhausted nerves would calm down. Because there are limits to everything, and everything must come to an end. There ought to be an end to human suffering as well.

And at that moment it seemed to Trublayevych that death was not terrible, and may even be desirable, that death was not evil, but a blessing, like the natural end of existence.

"Eternal memory to you, my dearest mother! Sleep peacefully. We'll join you soon."

He went into the forest and roamed about in it until dusk, and he kept thinking about life and death, about the great riddle that has puzzled people throughout the ages and will remain unsolved by them forever.

VI

When Trublayevych returned from his leave of absence, he felt as if he was crippled both physically and morally. He fled from the manor as soon as he could after his mother's funeral. Shura stayed behind alone for the time being to care for the farm before coming to the city for a rest, or perhaps even to live there. They had not yet made a decision about that.

For Trublayevych his daily routine began again: the bank, reading newspapers and journals, conversations about current events, arguments and quarrels, egotistical insults—all that nervous tension that constitutes the life of an intelligent person.

He lay down to sleep with a heavy head in the evening, and woke up with a heavy head in the morning, and his heart always felt as if it was oppressed by something.

And, as before, his life was turbid and restless, and it fermented like new wine.

It was still impossible to foresee definite perspectives, although it was clear that the end of the reactionary period was drawing near, that the bureaucracy had been caught up in the spring flood, and it was being washed away and pulled apart, and it could no longer hold up against the pressure of the bold and invincible new currents. It was still mustering its strength, it was still striving, it was still engaged in a war that had been lost long ago both here at home, and over there, in the Far East, it had sent its last squadron, had put at risk—in a desperate, hot-headed step—its last gold coin and was hoping that blind luck would take its side. And that squadron, bewailed and buried before the fact in the waters of the ocean by its own people and strangers, by friends and foes alike, was wandering aimlessly somewhere over the distant seas.

And everyone was waiting for a sea battle.

They were waiting in terror.

And in the meantime society was regrouping, programmes were being formulated, partnerships were being struck, both legitimate and illegitimate ones. And all of them had as their aim the freeing of the people from political bondage, the acquiring of civic rights. Against these forces other, antithetical powers were grouping, and here and there bloody fires flared.

The city where Trublayevych lived had long been a peaceful, somnolent place, but now it too awoke, and all the latest currents resonated in it. Even Donda, after what was for him the unexpected arrest of his son, became infuriated with "the bureaucracy" and defamed it no less than the Jews. Even though in his opinion it was the very same Jews who were to blame for everything . . . And he was expecting that at any moment now they would be taken to task.

Trublayevych was once again slowly drawn into that turbulent life, but now he did not analyse every incident, every fact so one-sidedly, nor did he seek out the Achilles heel in progressive movements—he knew that they existed in every case. He told himself once and for all that progress is better than retrogression, that freedom is better than servitude, and that it is necessary to do whatever is required to attain the goal that everyone saw so clearly . . .

He no longer had anyone to worry about or anything to fear: fate had taken away his mother, his brother, and Lyuba. If anything should happen to him now, it would not affect anyone. And so he amazed his former like-minded associates and enemies with his boldness and irrevocability. He got together again with Bilohrud and established ties with youth groups.

He sensed that the spring flood was seizing him wholly, and he abandoned himself to it completely. "What will be, will be," he thought. "Let this long-awaited flood carry me off, but it will bring others a new life, a better life, and those who will come after us will breathe more easily and live more freely."

Lyuba had been released from prison quite some time ago, because no real guilt could be imputed to her. But Trublayevych had not met with her, because she had left the city to go to Odessa, to stay with relatives there.

Trublayevych knew full well that it had been her father who had finally succeeded in his endeavours to part her from her city acquaintances. Her father hoped that in another city, under the watchful eye of her aunt, she would have a change of heart.

Zembulat was still in prison, but rumour had it that he too would be released soon.

Trublayevych tried not to think about Lyuba, he kept chasing away any memories of her, but he was unable to do so. Neither his involvement in the community nor his work at the bank could capture his attention completely. Not a day went by that her image did not flash before him, smiling at him, casting a serious, thoughtful look at him, searing him with an unexpected spark from under her dark eyelashes. And when he was alone—be it in the park, or on the boulevard, or in his home—she was always with him. In his mind, they communicated in half-phrases, with single words, fell silent, and then conversed once again.

Trublayevych's heart ached and pined: there was no way that he could bring her back; she belonged to someone else. And yet he could not renounce her . . .

There were a few times that he wanted to go to Odessa, to see her, to talk with her, and, perhaps, to win her back. But he immediately chased that temptation away: he could never go there while Zembulat was still in prison. Zembulat was dearer to her now than he had ever been. He was a hero for her . . . Her thoughts were always with him. And Trublayevych wished that he too was near and dear to someone.

Once while he was sitting alone in a dark corner of a city park and thinking about Lyuba, Dubrayevska came up to him. She was dressed lightly and attractively, and she looked quite appealing. Her long, nicely cut hair gave her an added air of intelligence, and her delicate gait, given her rather imposing figure, spoke of her physical strength and good health.

Trublayevych rose to greet her, and then they sat down together on the same bench.

"So this is where you are!" Dubrayevska said, looking at Trublayevych. "I like this spot as well. It's pleasant here."

"Yes, there are times when I sit here for a long, long while."

"When . . ." Dubrayevska prompted him, and she raised her eyebrows as she waited for him to finish what he was saying.

"Her eyes are kind and engaging," Trublayevych thought. And then he smiled as he said: "When I feel like it."

"Well, of course! But you were about to say something else. Nevertheless, I understand . . ." she said with a knowing smile. "At one time it used to be pleasant to sit here . . . and not by yourself, but now . . . sweet memories!"

"Why would you say that there are memories?"

"Just because, but then . . . you're in a better position to know."

"I don't understand."

"You don't understand? Well, if you wish, I can tell you a fairy tale . . . So, do you want me to?"

"Go ahead, I'm listening."

Dubrayevska once again assessed him carefully for a long moment as she tried to determine how best to start her story.

"But you won't be angry with me?" she asked.

"No, not if . . . you don't make me angry."

Dubrayevska laughed and leaned back against the bench.

"She's really quite attractive and cheerful," Trublayevych observed, and a strange mood came over him: he wished that Dubrayevska would tell him that she loved him.

"But the devil take that stipulation," he said. "You tell me a fairy tale, and I'll tell you one."

"Fine!" Dubrayevska replied, and she winked in a friendly manner. "Fine. Listen! In a certain city there lived a man . . ."

"Yes: in a certain city, there lived a man . . . But was there only one man?"

"Ivan Mykhaylovych, don't interrupt me, or I'll be angry!"

"And you won't finish telling me your story?"

Dubrayevska laughed. "Well, so there once lived a man. He was young and handsome, but he was lonely and he appeared to be severe, even though he was not like that at heart."

"We'll take note of that: he was not like that at heart."

"Ivan Mykhaylovych, don't interrupt!"

"Or else you'll be angry?"

"Yes, I will be."

"Well then, I won't."

"Fine, just watch yourself. In that city the man had no family, no people to whom he felt close, no friends, and so he lived as if he were in a desert."

"Your story certainly has feeling!"

Dubrayevska did not pay any attention to Trublayevych's interjection and continued talking: "There was no one in that desert to whom he could give his heart, and then he caught sight of a wild turtledove, and he tamed it. He told the wild turtledove about his life, about his sorrows, told her how hard it was for solitary people like himself to live in the desert, and the turtledove, while her wings were still growing, hopped around him, cooed, and gazed into his eyes. And he grew to love this wild turtledove like his own soul. But one day in the tree under which the turtledove was cooing, a wild dove cooed his own song. The turtledove fluttered up to the wild dove and flew far, far away, and did not return to the lonely solitary man. And after that, his life became even lonelier and sadder."

Dubrayevska paused.

"What's next?" Trublayevych asked, and there no longer was even a hint of jocularity in his voice.

"What's next? That man still lives in that city, and he's still grieving, and he'll continue grieving until he forgets about that turtledove."

"Yes."

"Well, now tell me your story."

"I forgot it."

"Oh, no, you must recall it!"

"Well then, listen."

Trublayevych stopped to think.

Dubrayevska had touched upon the most sensitive string in his heart, and it rang out and filled his soul with sadness.

"My story will be about that same man. When the turtledove flew away, that man grieved mightily, and then one night someone left him an instrument of some kind. The instrument was similar to a human heart, and whenever someone touched it, such mournful sounds emanated from it that the man wept. At times, evil people strummed that instrument, while at other times it was strummed by those who were simply curious. And even when only the wind blew on it, sorrowful melodies and sounds were evoked. One time an attractive butterfly flew in and alighted on it. It tenderly touched the strings, and they rang out even more sorrowfully than when they were touched either by evil people or by those who were curious but indifferent . . ."

"Ivan Mykhaylovych! That's enough, don't go on with your story," Dubrayevska said and her face grew sad and troubled.

"Why?"

"Just because. It's very sad."

"It just seems like that to you." He smiled and took her hand. She pressed his hand tightly. "Forgive me . . . I didn't want to . . . I didn't expect that . . ."

"It's nothing, Solomiya Frantsivna, it may well be that when that man forgets about his turtledove, he'll also throw away that instrument."

"May God grant it!"

"Really?" Trublayevych smiled, turning what had happened into a joke.

Dubrayevska flushed and also smiled. She pressed his hand once more and then pulled her hand away.

"May God grant it! The world is wide and cheerful, and instead of that desert-city there are good people and cheerful cities."

"Shall we go and find such a city?" Trublayevych asked, and it was impossible to tell if he was joking or not.

"Let's go!" she replied in the same tone.

"Really?"

"Really."

"And when shall we get ready to go?"

"Whenever you wish!"

He took her hand and pressed it firmly. "We'll wait a while," he said frankly and warmly, in a brotherly manner. "Let that man's wounds heal at least a little bit."

"Fine."

Everything had happened so suddenly and unexpectedly, that after Trublayevych saw Solomiya home and he found himself alone in the street, he had to ask himself: had it really happened? And he had to admit that the rudder on the boat of his life had veered sharply in another direction, and that the boat now had to take another path.

After that day, Trublayevych met more frequently with Dubrayevska, but neither he nor she ever mentioned that conversation in the park. It was as if they had silently agreed not to talk about what only the two of them knew, and this secret drew them closer together.

Dubrayevska had decided to wait patiently until "the wounds of the grieving man had healed."

But the wound was not healing, and she could see that.

She was aware that Trublayevych had travelled to Odessa after their conversation, and she knew for whom he was searching and whom he had hoped to see. But he did not have the good fortune to meet up with Lyuba, and this fact aggravated his wound even more.

He became still sadder, and anyone who looked at him would say he was ill.

And life did not settle down due to the *Tsushima catastrophe. The squadron on which so many hopes had been placed by those who had sent it was destroyed at Tsushima. The armoured ships sank to the bottom of the sea one after the other like broken cast-iron pots, and the ones that remained afloat lowered their flags and surrendered. Now the dead and the drowned were no longer tallied; only the armoured ships and cruisers were counted.

There had not been a more shameful disaster since the war had begun. But now, such an event barely perturbed the community or caused it to worry. Now even the blind could see that the war was lost on all fronts, and that not even a shred of hope remained. And their thoughts turned away from Manchuria and came back to what was happening at home.

Everyone understood that the reason for such unheard of failures was not to be found out there, in the Far East, but right here, at home. There could be no doubt in anyone's mind about that. And once again everything grew agitated and stirred with a newfound strength.

People were waiting for something the likes of which they had never seen before. They went to bed thinking that they might wake up in a totally different situation, in different circumstances. The nervous tension was reaching its zenith.

Trublayevych continued going to the bank, but it seemed to him that anything could happen, that tomorrow or the day after tomorrow, instead of going to the bank, he would have to do something novel, great, and terrifying. And when he thought about it, he wanted to be beside Lyuba, to stand shoulder to shoulder with her. At those times he forgot about Solomiya and regarded the conversation in the park as a mistake.

And Trublayevych once again set out for Odessa.

He travelled at night, on a quiet starry night, and he paced the deck of the steamship until dawn, thinking about Lyuba and carrying on an internal conversation with her. Now he decided that he absolutely had to find her and to discuss the directions that their lives were taking. Now Zembulat was also a free man, and so he could rest easy on that account: their chances were on an equal footing now. If he had been unable to devote himself to social causes back then, now he was able to do so. Now, the thought of making the ultimate sacrifice no longer frightened him.

But an inner voice kept saying that he was making the trip in vain, that his hopes were futile, and his heart was heavy and he felt ashamed of himself.

VII

Trublayevych arrived in Odessa in the morning. On the way to the hotel he heard from the coachman that the bakers in the city had gone on strike, and that some mechanics were planning to sabotage the horse-drawn streetcars. But he ignored what he was hearing, for such events had become commonplace in recent times. He paid for a room, changed, drank some tea, and went out to look for Lyuba.

"You're visiting us again?" the doorman asked as he opened the door of the hotel. "You're not afraid?"

"What is there to be afraid of?"

"Be careful, it's not all that safe in the city. You know, the bakers . . . the tradesmen. We're hoping that nothing happens, a riot of some kind."

"You think it's possible?"

"We all think it's possible, and we're warning our guests."

"Well, that's fine. It doesn't really matter . . . I won't be here long," Trublayevych said, and he walked out into the street.

It was still early, much too early to go to Lyuba's aunt; moreover, he did not know her address. He had to find it. He went to the appropriate bureau where he was able to get the information.

The aunt's apartment was nearby, and he did not have to hurry to get there, but Trublayevych thought that if he arrived too late, he might not find Lyuba at home, and so he set out at a moderate pace to look for the street and the apartment number that he had been given.

Along the way he looked at the crowds of people and saw nothing unusual: they were all rushing somewhere with preoccupied looks on their faces and without paying attention to anyone else, and only the newspaper and telegram vendors approached individuals that they thought might buy from them, reaching out with their freshly printed sheets of paper.

"Today's newspaper! The latest telegrams!"

Trublayevych bought a newspaper and skimmed through it. There were reports, although they were downplayed somewhat, that some tradesmen were on strike and that they were demanding a raise in pay.

Having located the apartment of Lyuba's aunt, Trublayevych rang the doorbell.

"Is Lyuba Mykolayivna Hovoretska at home, and may I see her?" he asked the maid who answered the door.

"No, the young lady isn't in," the girl replied.

"When will she be in?"

"I don't know."

And asking a few more questions and indicating who he was, Trublayevych found out that Lyuba had not been home for two days now, and that no one knew where she was, and that the aunt was very concerned.

"Has this ever happened before?" Trublayevych asked.

"It has happened once before."

Trublayevych shrugged. He promised to come by again in the evening and then went off to walk around the city. He secretly hoped that he might encounter her somewhere.

He walked through the busiest streets, went down to the boulevard that bordered the shore, and looked out at the sea, at the port. It all looked very ordinary; people were rushing about, steamships were whistling, horns were blasting, and the iron pulleys on the steamships were thundering as they seized piles of boxes or cannon balls, lifted them upwards, and then lowered them again. And the entire port was enveloped in smoke.

After sitting for a few minutes on the boulevard, Trublayevych went to a restaurant to have some breakfast. He found a spot in a corner, sat down, and waited for his meal to be served.

"Mr. Trublayevych! Ivan Mykhaylovych!" someone shouted. Trublayevych looked around the room. He did not recognize anyone. And then a man got up from one of the tables and approached him.

Trublayevych realized that it was Dr. Levandovsky, a friend who had moved from his city three years ago and settled in Odessa.

"You don't recognize me?" he asked.

"Yes, I do," Trublayevych replied, as he stood up and extended his hand to greet the doctor. "But I most certainly did not expect to meet up with you here."

"Huh! A mountain may not meet up with another mountain, but people are always gadding about in the same place," the doctor called out cheerfully. "How long do you plan to be here?"

"A couple of days."

"Then I'm inviting you to come to my home this evening. We'll sit and chat for a while."

Trublayevych promised to drop by if he was free. Levandovsky gave him his address. He had already had his breakfast and now, smoothing down his long pitch-black beard, he was preparing to dash off to work.

"So, I'll be waiting for you," he said, as he took his straw hat and walking stick from a lackey.

"If I can, I'll certainly come," Trublayevych assured him.

"You know, we're living in very interesting times!" the doctor added as he bade farewell to Trublayevych.

And he walked out of the dining room, swiftly and agilely, belying his years.

Trublayevych had known him for a long time. He was a lively, passionate person. He responded sensitively to everything that happened, was interested in everything, and wherever he went he brought with him a pleasant aura of excitement. Whenever arguments flared, no one could settle them as quickly and as effectively as Dr. Levandovsky. Trublayevych decided that he would most certainly go to see him.

He wandered through the city all day long, looking intently at every passing face, but he did not run into Lyuba. And, even if she were in the city, it would have been difficult to spot her if she did not want anyone to see her or to keep an eye on her. But then again she could simply have left the city to go to someone's summer cottage. That was the most likely scenario.

In the evening Trublayevych went to visit Levandovsky. "You know, there are more people here from your city. Not so long ago I met up with Zembulat and a young lady," Levandovsky said after they greeted one another and went into his study.

"Zembulat? So you know him?" Trublayevych asked in surprise.

"Of course! He studied at our university. He's a good fellow, and a great leader. I asked him to stop by this evening, and he just might come."

Trublayevych wanted to ask about the young lady who was with Zembulat, but he did not want to do so right away. He feared that Levandovsky might notice that he was interested in that young lady.

But after some time had gone by he asked: "Did you happen notice the young lady who was with Zembulat?"

"She's not someone that I know. I don't think she's a local girl; she's attractive, dark, and quite tall . . . and her hair is luxuriant."

Trublayevych did not respond, but he concluded that it had to be Lyuba. Zembulat had come here to see her, and it was possible that she had run away from her aunt while he was in town. And perhaps that was not the only reason that she had left her aunt's home: a large disturbance was expected in the city and it was possible that she was involved in it.

But Levandovsky did not give him much time to ponder the matter. He asked him how matters stood with the workers in Trublayevych's city. And, after finding out that Trublayevych had recently travelled to his home, he asked how things were in the villages, and then he told him how the situation was unfolding in Odessa.

After the events at Tsushima, events were once again erupting with renewed energy. The various working classes were restless, and some groups and mobs were already on strike, but all the power lay in the port, and it too was beginning to rumble.

"I don't know how it is elsewhere, but here the Tsushima catastrophe will have serious repercussions," Levandovsky said.

"They're all infuriated by it, like wasps. And besides that, many Odessa residents died there."

As he listened to the doctor, it occurred to Trublayevych that Hovoretsky had acted recklessly by sending his daughter here at this time.

"But why are you so sad and apathetic?" Levandovsky suddenly asked him. "Have you lost something, or are you looking for something, or waiting for something?"

"I? I'm just as I always am."

"No, you're not . . ."

But they did not conclude that line of conversation because at that moment a tall, scrawny man, with gangly arms and legs like a colt, burst into the doctor's apartment. He looked as if he were walking on stilts, and his bony arms were continuously waving about.

It was Zolotnytsky, an acquaintance of Levandovsky.

The doctor introduced him to Trublayevych.

"Have you heard about it?" Zolotnytsky shouted as he crossed the threshold.

"Have you read it?" and he pointed at a paper in his hand.

"What is it?" the doctor asked.

"These verses."

"What verses?"

"Latansky's verses . . . The hymn of death."

"No."

"Well, then, listen!"

Zolotnytsky went over to a lamp so that he could see the writing on the paper, stood at attention, and without further ado began reading:

*Morituri te salutant

Morituri te salutant,
O grim phantom of war
Morituri te salutant,
All of us who are dying innocently:
"You—the absurd, angry, wild one
Who stands in a bloody mist.
May you be damned for all ages
Both in the heavens and on the earth!"

Morituri te salutant,
All of us whom you have not yet killed.
Morituri te salutant . . .
"Do you hear the gnashing of their teeth?
Do you hear the wailing and the groaning,
The insane laughter and the yelling?
It is legions of people shouting:
"Be damned, be damned forever!"

Morituri te salutant
And all your accomplices
Morituri te salutant
And along with you all those
Who are strong and powerful,
Who hold sway over the people
And cast into the flames of war
Entire armies of our brethren!

Morituri te salutant!
Their cries rise to the heavens,
Morituri te salutant:
Be damned forever and ever!
Be damned—by our tears
By our blood, by our grain, by this world,
And by the earth, and by the heavens—
Be damned by everything!

Levandovsky and Trublayevych were listening as if they
were mesmerized.
"Well?" Zolotnytsky asked, looking at the two of them and
blinking his eyes as if freeing himself from a hypnotic spell.
"It's superb! It's wonderful!" Levandovsky cried as he
reached out for the poem. "Let me have it."

You—the absurd, angry, wild one
Who stands in a bloody mist.
May you be damned for all ages
Both in the heavens and on the earth!

"It's powerful, wonderfully written! Oh, how many of them greet that frightening monster as they're dying, and how many more there will still be before this human insanity comes to an end!"

"Let me copy those verses," Trublayevych said. "Please, may I?"

"Why not? Of course you may," Zolotnytsky replied. "They're making the rounds everywhere."

Trublayevych copied them. The verses had made a great impression on him, and it seemed to him that they supplemented the letters that his brother had written from the war.

Perhaps Andryk, when he was mortally wounded, had seen the fierce phantom in his dying moments and had uttered these very same curses at it.

"Well, verses are just verses," Zolotnytsky said as he paced the room, "but life is life: if not tomorrow, then the day after, something is about to happen the likes of which we have never seen before."

And he told them what people thought would happen in the city. He repeated what Trublayevych had already heard from the hotel doorman and from Levandovsky. Everyone was saying the same thing. A threatening cloud was rolling in and everything had fallen silent, suspended, as if gathering strength for an onslaught.

As he returned to the hotel later that night, Trublayevych walked guardedly down the hushed streets, as if fearing to shatter the stillness, to awaken something, even though there was no actual silence: the city in all its vast expanse was rumbling and rattling from the thousands of wheels that were rolling through it, and the pounding of hooves—but it was a softer rumbling, as if the city were dreaming. In the port, steamships called out to one another with their hoarse bass voices as if they were conspiring about something . . .

In the morning, Trublayevych again resolved to look for Lyuba—even though he held out little hope that there would be anything in it for him even if he did run into her. He wanted to bring the matter to a close; he wanted to see her, to look at her. And so that day he once again went to see Lyuba's aunt, and from the same servant he found out that Lyuba had come home towards evening, but that she had gone out once again and had not spent the night at home. These days she was visiting a female friend at her summer cottage, but where that cottage was, and what the friend's name was, she could not say.

Trublayevych wanted to ask the aunt about that, but she was not a home. He set out again to wander through the city.

He walked to the outskirts in one direction, and then returned to the city centre. And then he went to the other end of the city, and walked back again. After that he boarded a streetcar and set out without even asking where it would take him.

He found it pleasant to sit, to rest, and to look at the buildings on both sides of the street, to look at the people who walked past them like insects, and not to think about anything, because his head was weary from pondering, and his mind needed a rest.

He rode for a long time to the end of the streetcar line. The city was left behind, and summer cottages came into view. He decided to go down to the sea, and he descended along a road that he knew well. Soon he was on the very shore of the sea.

The brilliant, greenish sea stretched out into the distance from the low carroty-red coast and blended with the sky on the far horizon. It was slightly agitated and in places it took on an azure colour, and sparkled and shimmered with turquoise hues. The waves reached the shore, raced over its smooth expanse to the sea wall and flung themselves against it with a thundering noise as they spilled over it in a profusion of white foam.

And far off in the distance, steamships spread their smoke, as some of them gradually disappeared into the vastness of the sea while others emerged from it. Not far from the shore, boats were rocking—fishermen were catching fish. There were similar boats on the shore, pulled up on the sand. People were milling around them, and barefooted children were running along the shoreline, dashing into the water, and then running up the beach ahead of the waves.

The waves splashed on the shoreline and roared, as if they were calling out: "Oh, oh!"

On the strand above the water, people, walking and sitting on benches singly and in small groups of two or three, were looking out at the sea.

Trublayevych found an empty bench and sat down.

Born and raised in another part of the country, he saw the sea only rarely. But it always impressed him greatly every time that he did see it. He did not like it when it was raging and storming, but it enchanted him when the weather was good—it was so expansive, so free, and so gently caressing. He sat by it and was not even aware as its calmness enveloped him entirely.

He loved it from his student days, when he had been required to spend a year in Odessa in order to complete his university courses. And now he sat and sank into contemplative thoughts that were as expansive and as serene as the water that he was gazing at.

When a short and stout grey-haired old man attired in lightweight white clothing sat down next to him, he only glanced at him and moved over to make room.

"My, but the sea is splendid today!" the old man said, squinting slightly.

Trublayevych did not respond.

"Yes, yes it is. . . It's so nice. Do you see . . . excuse me . . ." he turned to Trublayevych, ". . . that streak way over there? Do you see how blue it is? It's truly splendid!"

Trublayevych glanced at his neighbour. There was something familiar about the old man, both in his figure and his face. And he then recognized Konchak, a former professor of his.

"Nykon Pylypovych?" he addressed him.

"Yes. And who are you?" he turned to Trublayevych. "Are you Portnyansky?"

Trublayevych told him his name, and the old professor recalled who he was. He was very old now, and had been on a pension for some time.

They started to talk.

Their conversation quickly came around to current events. The old professor told him how everyone was talking about "the spring," about that great movement that had arisen everywhere. He looked at everything optimistically and expected that before long everything would change to a better, more desirable order.

"It won't be long now, and I believe that I'll still live to see another regime," he said. "But if there hadn't been a war, nothing would have changed, everything would have stayed the same! Yes . . . Yes . . ."

"Are you saying that it took all the victims of that unfortunate war in order to awaken society?" Trublayevych asked. "Must a better fate for tomorrow be bought with the blood of people today?"

"Ah . . . yes . . . yes . . . That's the law of life, the law of history."

And the professor smiled. "Humanity has attained every step of its progress at the expense of blood," he added, as he looked closely at a young lady and gentleman who, having come up to where he and Trublayevych were sitting just as he was finishing speaking, had now walked slightly ahead and, standing next to a ravine, were looking out at the sea.

Trublayevych also glanced up at the young couple and blood rushed to his temples.

It was Lyuba and Zembulat.

VIII

"Today there's a rumour that the *Potemkin has come into the port from Tendra, and that all is not well on board. Take a look—is that it?" Konchak pointed at a ship that had left the port but was now coming back.

But Trublayevych was not interested in the ship.

"Excuse me, I must leave you for a moment," he said, and he rose to his feet and went up to Lyuba and Zembulat.

"Good day to you, Lyubov Mykolayivna!" he addressed her as he approached her and extended his hand.

She shuddered in surprise and quickly turned around to face him.

"Oh, how you frightened me! Where were you? I didn't see you."

"I was sitting over there, on the bench."

Trublayevych exchanged greetings with Zembulat.

"Ivan Mykhaylovych was in a cap that made him invisible, and now he's taken it off," Zembulat said.

Both Lyuba and Zembulat felt uncomfortable, and Trublayevych noticed this at once. He also noticed that Lyuba, like a little turtledove, was drawn to Zembulat with her entire being, and now he was convinced without any words being spoken that she loved Zembulat passionately and wholly, and that he did not belong here.

He decided not to try to talk about what he had wanted to find out, and the reason why he had come here.

The three of them felt awkward as a silence descended. Zembulat was the first to speak. He also directed their attention to the ship.

But neither Lyuba nor Trublayevych picked up on what he was saying.

"You've changed ever so much in this last while," Lyuba said to Trublayevych. "Did something happen at home?"

"My brother was killed in the war, and my mother died," Trublayevych said, and he felt like adding that it was harder for him to lose her, than to lose his mother and brother.

He looked at her. She seemed to have grown even more attractive. The joy of being in love was making her more beautiful. That joy shone in her eyes, and its brilliance had been so familiar to him until quite recently, but now it was so strange, so hostile.

Trublayevych recalled that all his acquaintances had told him that he had changed, grown old, and he himself was aware of that; every day he noticed more and more grey hairs in his beard, that cursed grey hair, the herald of old age.

"Do you plan to return home soon?" he asked Lyuba when Zembulat walked away from them to look in the direction of the port, at the columns of smoke that had begun to rise above it.

"I don't know. Valeryan Vasylovych is planning to find a position here, and we may stay here for good."

"Look, look what's happening over there," Zembulat shouted, pointing at the smoke. "It's coming from the port. The port is on fire!"

Lyuba and Trublayevych looked in the direction in which Zembulat was pointing. Columns of black and red smoke had spread over half the horizon. Lyuba grew alarmed.

"That's something unusual! Let's go there!"

"Let's go!"

Trublayevych wanted to say: I'll come with you, but he did not say it. He was superfluous.

They quickly bid their farewells and rushed uphill to the streetcar. Trublayevych was left alone. He watched them leave and then turned his eyes once again towards the smoke.

"Do you see what's going on in the port?" a voice beside him said, and Trublayevych started in surprise. It was Konchak.

Trublayevych looked around.

The entire shoreline was filled with people milling around: there, on the hill, men, women, and children were rushing to the city, trying to outrun one another. And on the shore, several men were hauling boats into the water to go out there, where something extraordinary was happening. A few boats had already moved away from the bank and were rocking on the waves as they headed for the port.

"We'd better make our way home as well," Konchak said. "Where are you staying?"

Trublayevych told him the name of his hotel.

"Then we're going in the same direction. Let's go!"

They started climbing upwards. They came to the streetcar stop and waited a long time before a streetcar pulled up. They had almost given up hope that it would ever arrive. The conductor and the coachman looked very troubled and seemed to be hesitating whether or not they should go back into the city. Finally the streetcar moved forward.

At first they passed through quiet streets and there was not much traffic on them. But the closer that they came to the centre of the city, the more evident it became that everyone was walking and running to the port. They were rushing there in large groups. Tradesmen were running, talking loudly and calling out to each other from one side of the street to the other.

"It really is something out of the ordinary," Konchak said.

The streetcar was moving slowly upwards, and when it came to a level spot, it stopped completely.

"What's the matter?"

"We can't go any farther."

"How so?"

"Take a look."

They jumped out of the streetcar. Up ahead along the tracks the road was barricaded with something. They rushed there. An overturned streetcar lay on the road.

"Aha! Now we'll have to walk. We'll stick together," Konchak said, taking hold of Trublayevych's arm.

They walked on the sidewalk. Now they were no longer walking swiftly, they were trotting. Because everyone was running, everyone was getting all tangled up, jamming together and then separating again.

"Slowly! Slowly!" Konchak said, hardly able to breathe, but he maintained his pace.

At a crossroads they came to a sudden stop. The road was blocked by a mob of people looking to the left. Trublayevych raised himself up on tiptoe and saw that a large group was rushing in from a side street, and above this mass of humanity, red kerchiefs, raised on high, were fluttering. The police, both those on horses and those on foot, were vainly trying to block the path of that group.

There was a terrible din, cries, the pounding of hooves . . . People were yelling . . . Somewhere in the distance, there was singing . . . And suddenly all the people who had been standing in front of Trublayevych began retreating and scattering in all directions . . .

Something resounded shrilly, as if dozens of firecrackers were crackling in the air . . .

A man, white as a sheet, fell on Trublayevych, and grabbed hold of his shoulder . . . Blood was gushing over his fingers . . .

And then everyone who had been running into the street from which Trublayevych and Konchak had come began turning back. They rushed around the corner.

"The kozaks!"

A person was knocked down, another was trampled . . . An injured man fell and rolled under the horses' hooves. Bullwhips whistled in the air.

"Move aside!"

And everyone scrambled to get out of the way.

Trublayevych grabbed Konchak by the arm and pulled him along.

The old man could no longer walk. His feet were giving way under him. He was shaking violently. Trublayevych glanced back. The mob that was approaching from the left was catching up to them.

At the head of it, he caught sight of a tall, scrawny man who was waving his arms around madly. He recalled that he had seen this man at Levandovsky's home—it was Zolotnytsky.

At that very moment, Zolotnytsky took a couple of steps forward and then, as if he had run into something, his arms fluttered and he fell to the ground.

He tried to get up . . .

He raised himself slightly, waved, and crying out with a deathly pale face . . . he collapsed . . .

Morituri te salutant

Again whips cracked and swished . . . And a human roar drowned out the noise of the melee, and the buildings seemed to shudder at the sound.

Something seared Trublayevych's spine . . . pushed him forward . . . and he fell to the sidewalk . . .

He wanted to get up, to yell. But something warm and salty gushed out of his throat and kept him from shouting . . . Green circles filled his eyes, and through them flashed Konchak's terrified face as it bent over him.

"Morituri te salutant! That's how it is!" Trublayevych said as he lost consciousness. "The spring flood . . ."

He did not finish what he was saying.

The old professor grabbed his former student and tried to pull him off the road closer to the buildings, but he was unable to do so . . .

Someone younger and stronger lifted the injured man under the arms and pulled him over to the side.

The old man bent over him, shielding him with his body.

And all around them everything was roaring, thundering, and overflowing with hatred and rage, with rancour and terror.

Comrades
(1908)

"Listen, Mykola, if it's not a secret—if you can confide in me, a former comrade—then tell me all about yourself . . . tell me everything, everything that you possibly can."

"But what am I to tell you? First of all, you tell me about yourself . . . How did you end up here?" the other man said in the darkness, responding to the request with a question that was put in the same tone of voice.

"There's nothing to tell, my friend," the first voice spoke up again, and in the corner from which it emanated there was a heartfelt sigh and the sound of someone turning heavily on a bed. "It's a common story, my friend! And not at all interesting."

"But why not? On the contrary, I'm very interested in it. And I've often thought about you."

Both voices fell silent, as if the men to whom they belonged were resurrecting the past in their minds. It was nighttime, and the room was pitch black. On a nearby wall, a clock ticked in a dignified manner, and outside, a cricket chirped softly under the window.

"Unfortunately, my friend, it's a very common story . . ." the first voice, a dry baritone, spoke up sadly once again. "It could have been different, but then, that's how it is! That's how things turned out . . ."

And he sighed once again.

The second voice did not respond.

"You know, I truly longed to go to university, I thought and dreamed about it . . . but you can see for yourself where I ended up . . ."

"That's why I'm interested to know how things turned out the way they did."

"It all happened very simply. I completed my studies, and I said to my father: 'I can't be a priest—I don't have a calling for it. Help me go to university.' Well, as I expected, my father was dead set against that. 'I've spent a lot of money on you as it is,' he said, 'and am I now to pay for you to attend university? I won't give you even a *kopiyka. Do as you wish.'

"I thought about it. What was I to do? I decided to become a teacher. I'd work for one year, for another year, gather together some money, and then take off for Tomsk. Even though I didn't want to make the long trek to that isolated place, I couldn't see any other way out. I didn't even consider going to Warsaw. I had heard how hostile the Poles were towards the likes of us, and I simply cannot abide hostility. And then a position just happened to turn up in a city, in Pavlohrad. I thought I'd live in a city among intelligent people, I'd read and I'd learn. And so, in the autumn, I moved there."

The narrator went on to describe how he lived and taught, and just like droplets of water dripping from a weeping willow—drop by drop—every word of his was filled with sorrow and enervation.

The school was suffocating, both physically and morally. The city and the club . . . both were equally unenlightened pools of mediocrity. Long autumn and winter evenings! Reading and more reading . . . to the point of boredom, to stupefaction. And when morning came—more of the same.

"The year passed by in this way . . . and then another. Five years flowed by. I didn't put any money together, for there was none to be had—there was hardly enough to eke out a living. The dream of going to university faded further and further into the background. I started to put on weight, to lose my hair, and I grew increasingly indifferent and even hostile to everything that was commendable, idealistic. But what else could the regime that reigned in our country at that time have taught me? You must recall the trash that, like an evil spirit, reigned everywhere back then . . ."

"It's true, that was a bad time," the second voice responded gloomily, and then it fell silent again.

"Well, that's how I lived; I lived and felt that I was sinking ever deeper and deeper into the mud. I had to abandon all freedom-loving goals and plans, all thoughts of working for the benefit of the people . . . I could see that I was of no use to myself or to anyone else. I could see that other people, even if they did not lead lives that benefited others, were at least able to benefit from life themselves. But I was just stagnating there, and like a log in a forest I was becoming ever more overgrown with moss. And to make things even worse, my school was situated by a road on which the deceased were carted off to a cemetery. They took them there every day . . . and every day you saw coffins, church banners, and black sacerdotal vestments."

The narrator sighed and coughed, and the clock on the wall began chiming twelve o'clock loudly and confidently.

"And I was overcome by such sorrow, such boredom," the voice continued after waiting until the clock fell silent, "that I must admit I wanted to do away with myself. I lived with this idea in my mind for about a year. And then I said to myself: everyone else is leading a normal life—they're all happy and healthy, they have wives and children, and they don't experience this damned sorrow, this debilitating boredom. Am I the only degenerate who is fated to rot away in this manner? And if I were to live as all the other people are living, would that cause the earth to spin out of its orbit? All my comrades—I did not know about you, where you were or what was going on in your life—all my comrades, I'm saying, had already become priests. No matter which one you met up with they were all healthy, happy. I was the only one who was withering away . . .

"Well, I decided that before I was carried straight from the school to the cemetery, I'd follow the road that others have taken! And so I up and got married, right there in Pavlohrad, and now I'm serving as a priest here. And that's my whole story . . . So, what about you?"

"I also have nothing to brag about," the other voice—higher and clearer—spoke up, and you could hear that this other man was now sitting up and rustling about in the darkness as he talked. "It's hot; I can't lie here any longer . . ."

"Wait a moment, I'll open the door to the main room, and maybe that will help it to cool off a bit," the other voice said, and the man who had spoken could be heard getting out of bed, groping his way along the walls, and padding on bare feet to the door.

He opened the door and then, treading heavily over a well-worn wooden floor, returned to his former spot.

"My wife is probably boarding the train right now," he said as he sat down on the bed and scratched his chest and back. "It really is hot in the house today."

"When does the train arrive at your station?" his comrade asked him.

"At six. I have to send the horses at five."

"Well, I'll have to leave at around four . . . Forgive me Kost, for coming here like this. You must have guessed by now that I'm an 'illegal person.' But I came to your place without anyone seeing me, and furthermore, no one knows me in this village. And I'll leave very early . . ."

"Why are you talking like that, Mykola! Aren't you ashamed to say such things?"

"No, I'm speaking truthfully. I heard that you were living here, and when I left Rutchenkova, I thought I'd drop in and see you. We used to be comrades . . ."

"Well, thank you for not forgetting about me . . . for stopping by. It makes me very happy . . . Would you like some *kvass? A man gets thirsty after supper."

"Do you have any?"

"Yes, I do; my wife made some quite recently. I'll get it right away . . . You know, at first I didn't recognize you. And of course, it was dark already. I listened—and the voice sounded familiar, but I couldn't quite tell who you were. And then I heard you say—Ivanytsky. Well, I recalled you then at once. So, just wait a moment . . ."

Fr. Kost once again made his way into the main room, struck a match, lit a lamp, and took it with him into an adjoining room.

Ivanytsky sat on the chaise lounge and followed his friend with his eyes: how big and stout he had become, but how slender, how trim, and how delicate in every way he had been in his student days.

They had studied together for five years in the seminary, and they had been friends during that entire time, until Ivanytsky left after the fifth year to prepare for university. They both had read and discussed the same books. They both had been equally bored in the seminary and had fervently longed to leave it. In the springtime they both used to make their way into the thickets of the great Potemkin orchard, lie down on the fresh untouched grass that was intertwined with periwinkle and, as they listened to the warbling of the nightingales, talk about how they would live after finishing their studies first in the seminary and then at the university.

Ivanytsky recalled all this very vividly, but now it seemed so distant, so puerile. It was as if none of it had ever happened, as if it had all been just a dream. And now Kost was a stout, unkempt, balding priest, just an ordinary village priest. But what about himself? Had he ever thought that his life would turn out the way that it had?

His train of thought was interrupted by the light from the candle that Fr. Kost brought back with him as he carried in two bottles of kvass.

The host placed the candle on the table, got out a corkscrew and two glasses, and they set about drinking the kvass.

One of them was tall and corpulent, with curly reddish hair. The other one was by nature slight and swarthy, with thick eyebrows and a short, trimmed beard; now he looked scrawny and pallid with jaundiced circles clearly defined under his eyes.

His shirt was old and had not been washed for a long time. His whole figure appeared to be frail, unfinished in some way, and only his large dark eyes shone, radiating wisdom and a powerful will.

"Well, put out the light," he said, when they had finished drinking their kvass. "It will be better that way."

They lay down on their beds once again and continued their conversation. They did not feel like sleeping. Ivanytsky related the story of his life.

It was obvious to his listener that he was not revealing a great many things, that he was skimming quite superficially

154 | Mykola Chernyavsky

over many events, as if he did not trust him. This offended Fr. Kost somewhat, but he did not let on for he was well aware of the great rift that divided them. And he told himself that things had to be that way, for is it possible for a person who has thrown himself into the flames of battle to reveal everything to a village priest whose life is centred on marriages, christenings, and funerals, who has given himself over entirely to a corpulent wife with limited intelligence, to kerchiefs, *palyanytsi, chickens . . .

And so, even though the sting of insult stirred surreptitiously in his breast, Fr. Kost felt that it could not be otherwise, and he listened mostly in silence, responding only infrequently.

"As I said earlier, after I finished university, I began serving as an excise officer," Ivanytsky said. "But neither the shiny buttons nor the smell of whiskey that pervaded everything protected me from the all-seeing eye of the gendarmes. I couldn't sit around quietly without doing anything, nor did I want to. And so I organized a workers' union in a winery. And then one gloomy autumn morning several familiar guests came to visit me . . . They seized me . . . and began dragging me through one prison after another. They recalled and recounted everything that had happened, and much that had never happened . . . and finally I went off to see what a glorious city *Irkutsk was."

"So that's how it was . . . hmm!" Fr. Kost responded.

"But I didn't stay there long. I thought about it and decided: life is short, and as for the work . . . there's no end to the work that should be done, every day is precious; I'm not going to serve the rest of my sentence in this hole; I'll go back home right now. And so I ran away.

"Our people gave me some money and a passport. I managed to make my way to the Urals . . . I had planned to go farther, but as things turned out, I stayed there. I became a worker in a foundry . . . I learned the trade little by little, and I became a caster. And that, my friend, is my profession now."

He smiled.

"So that's how things are!"

"And you know I feel better now than if I were the chief in charge of some excise district. I deal with dedicated people, crucial causes, and have an immeasurably broad field for continuing my work."

After remaining silent for a short while, Ivanytsky began speaking once again: "I don't know what your position is now regarding the idea of socialism. . . ."

He stopped for a moment, as if waiting to get a reaction from Fr. Kost, but the priest did not respond.

And so he continued: "For me, it's the only faith, the only religion in my heart."

"That means that you should be happy, for it is said that the Kingdom of God lies within you," Fr. Kost said, and he realized at once that he had not responded appropriately.

"No, the kingdom of brotherhood and human equality is still far off, and neither we nor our grandchildren will live to see it. But what you've said is true: I'm happy, because I believe in what I'm doing. The work that I do may be insignificant, but I know that it's genuine work, that people will benefit from it."

"What is it exactly that you do?" Fr. Kost asked, and something unkind, unworthy of him, stirred once again in his breast—something like jealousy, or ill-will towards his former comrade; and at the same time, an old wound that had been healed seemed to be slowly reopening—discontentment with his own life.

"What do I do? Everything that I can: over here, I agitate; over there, I organize workers' unions; and in still other places I simply arouse the consciousness of the people."

"Do you organize strikes?"

"I've done that as well."

"Well, what about the police? Don't they try to catch you?"

"What do you think? I'm on the run from them right now, and it may well be that they're on my trail even now."

"So-o-o . . ." Fr. Kost said, and then he fell silent.

His night visitor also remained silent. It seemed to him that something uncertain and unspoken had passed between them and divided them, something stronger than their former friendship, and that one could expect anything from this well-fed priest. He was ashamed, but he sensed that the all too familiar fear of being persecuted was slowly awakening within him and putting him on guard.

The thought even crossed his mind that he should leave this house immediately and continue on the path that lay ahead of him. But he feared that he would not be able to find his way at night, and he did not want to ask Fr. Kost for directions. And so he just lay there without closing his eyes, ready to leap out of bed at any moment.

Fr. Kost also fell silent, and he too did not sleep, and from time to time he turned over noisily on his bed.

It was quiet in the house. The clock ticked intrusively, monotonously. In the distance, dogs barked in the village, and from that direction could be heard the faint pounding of horses' hooves.

The sound gradually drew nearer. It became clear that riders were approaching.

Ivanytsky jumped out of bed and groped his way to the window that was closed from the inside with shutters. Fr. Kost also opened his window a bit.

The galloping was drawing nearer.

"It's the border guards," Fr. Kost said, having spotted them first.

"Yes . . . that's who it is," Ivanytsky said, staring intently at the group of riders.

He wanted to say that they were in pursuit of him, but he refrained from saying anything and began dressing.

"What are you doing? Are you getting dressed already? It's still early!" Fr. Kost said.

"No, it's time."

"Wait a moment, I'll go outside and have a look."

He didn't say why he was going outside and at what he was going to be looking, but Ivanytsky knew the reason without asking. He didn't say a word.

Fr. Kost put on his boots and cassock in the dark and walked out of the house.

Ivanytsky was also ready to go outside.

A familiar nervous tension gained complete control of him. His heart was beating more quickly, and his ears caught even the slightest rustle.

He heard Fr. Kost go behind the house to the fence and come to a stop there.

He even thought that he heard some noise in the immediate neighbourhood. But then everything grew silent.

A short while later Fr. Kost came back indoors.

"Yes, it's the border guards that have come from Rutchenkova!" he said with a smile, and in his voice there was a tinge of curiosity, and something bordering on kindness. "They've stopped at the village office . . ."

"They're looking for me," Ivanytsky said straightforwardly. "I must flee."

"But why? You can stay here for a while."

"No, that wouldn't be right. Someone may have seen me come to your place."

"Well, so what? Don't lots of people come to see me? You came, and you went . . . What business is it of mine?"

"No, it isn't possible . . ."

Fr. Kost took hold of his hand. All of a sudden he felt very sad and very sorry for his comrade.

"My dear friend, we haven't finished talking yet . . . It may well be that we'll never see each other again," he said sincerely, pressing Ivanytsky's fevered hand.

"It can't be helped! That's how life is," Ivanytsky said, and he felt ashamed that only a short while ago he had almost feared his comrade, had not believed in his sincerity. "Farewell! If you can, take me by a back way past the gardens so that I can get on the road to Oleksandrivka."

"How quickly this has all happened . . . You showed up so unexpectedly and now you're going. My dear Mykola! I don't know . . . I feel so sorry. Let me at least light a candle, so that I can take a good look at you."

"Don't do that, Kost. They might spot it."

"Well, as you wish . . . But wait here, just a moment . . . I'll be right back."

Fr. Kost let go of Ivanytsky's hand and went into the next room. He rummaged through a few things there, as if he was searching for something. Then he came back.

"Well, let me at least exchange kisses with you in my house," he said, clasping Ivanytsky to his chest. "Don't judge me, Mykola . . . You can see what I've become. I'm ashamed before you, and ashamed before myself."

"Come now, what are you saying, and why are you saying it? I haven't heard anything bad about you, because if I had, I wouldn't have come to see you!"

"Well, thank you . . . thank you for that! I don't know . . . it's almost as if we're in hostile camps now, but I swear to God that I am not an enemy . . . And I too would like to do things to help our people . . ."

"I believe you, Kost, and I don't consider you to be an enemy."

"If that's the case, you know what? Take this from me . . . my widow's mite . . . from a former comrade . . . for the cause."

He pressed a packet of money into Ivanytsky's hand.

"That's not necessary," Ivanytsky said. "Why are you doing this?"

"What do you mean—why? Take it . . . It's for my sake—not for yours. I'm the one who needs to do this . . . This money belongs to our people."

Ivanytsky took it.

"So then, farewell!"

"Farewell!"

They embraced and exchanged kisses, one man big and stout, the other small and scrawny, and both of them were equally moved.

They walked out of the house.

In the porch, Fr. Kost made Ivanytsky wait while he went into the yard and led into a shed the dog that was tied to a wire that reached from one end of the yard to the other. When he came back the two of them made their way across the yard to the threshing floor. There they clambered over a fence and went down a lane that led them out of the village.

The night was calm and starlit.

The village was sleeping in a silvery mist, and a fog appeared to be spreading through the valley that they were approaching. By the pond there was a clump of willows, but it was not visible. On the hill beyond the valley, coke ovens that looked like the gaping mouths of dragons were burning, and beyond them shone the lights in the mines.

"Now you can find the road yourself," Fr. Kost said as he came to a halt. "Go down into the valley, across a dam under the willows, and then turn to the right. The road goes uphill, above the ravine."

"Good, I'll find it. Once again . . . farewell. Who knows if we'll see each other . . ."

"We will!" Fr. Kost responded confidently.

They embraced and exchanged kisses.

And they both sensed that they were seeing each other for the last time . . . that their paths would never cross again.

Ivanytsky walked away, and Fr. Kost stayed where he was and watched him descend into the valley. Gradually, his figure disappeared in the darkness.

Fr. Kost turned to go home, and at that moment a horse whinnied. Another horse responded.

"It's the guards' horses," he thought. "I wonder if Mykola can hear them?"

And grief constricted his heart—his comrade had always been that way, even in the seminary, always so fervent and sincere, so staunch and straightforward.

What kind of an end awaited him?

January 9th
(1906)

They set out, brimming with faith and hope.

In their calloused, work-hardened labourers' hands they carried the icons before which their great-grandfathers, their grandfathers, and their fathers had bowed down low, and before which they too inclined their heads in reverence.

These icons were to protect them, to speak for them, to tell others that they were going forth in humility and in peace; that they were worn out by their backbreaking labour, by their joyless lives, by the unjust wretchedness that they suffered under the oppression of the mighty and the wicked, and that they were setting out to plead—to plead for the word that would lift the heavy burden from their toil-worn shoulders, from their stooped backs, that would bring light and joy into their dark, gloomy hovels.

So that if not they, at least their children could grow up to be people who were strong, happy, and free.

Because when all is said and done, the man who spins a wheel, who pounds a hammer, who digs the soil—that man also needs light, freedom, and happiness, just like the man who drinks from a golden chalice.

He needs the same from life—with no difference. And so they were walking along with the naïve faith that at least a drop of that good fortune would fall on them.

They were walking without weapons.

They were met with weapons.

Riddled with bullets, the icons of humility toppled to the ground, never to be raised again . . . Never to be raised again in their hearts, or in the hearts of their children, or their grandchildren.

Riddled with bullets, they too fell to the ground—they had been walking in huddled groups, and they toppled over into huddled heaps: strong young workers, old men, mothers, and sisters drained of their strength by wearisome toil, and little children—the flowers of hope of every nation.

And they dyed the white snow richly with their crimson blood . . .

And as for those who remained alive—they remained to keep the memory of this day alive.

So that workers' chests would never again be riddled by heavy bullets.

So that women would not collapse wailing on the corpses of their slain fathers, husbands, sons.

So that children, vivacious and cheerful little children—the flowers of hope of every nation—could chatter merrily.

So that they would grow up to be strong, happy, and free.

So that all this would be achieved firmly, immutably, forever.

It all happened there, where blood dyed the white snow red.

Brother against Brother
(1907)

As soon as Yevhen Koretsky, the schoolteacher from Ladynka, awoke in his cell on November 18, 1905, it occurred to him that it was exactly two months to the day since he had been incarcerated.

He had arrived in Kyiv on August 6, the very day that a manifesto was issued about the convening of the *National Duma. Everyone understood that after all that had happened—the bloody war in Manchuria, a year of intense struggles at home, all the rallies, strikes, uprisings, conflagrations and blood, frenzied pogroms and mass riots—after all that, this proclamation was much too little, much too insignificant. Everyone understood, everyone was aware that this manifesto could not satisfy anyone, that all the countries, all the nations that were still bound tightly by old chains in this huge empire would not be pacified by this inconsequential attainment, and that nothing would change . . . People feverishly read the proclamations in which explanations were given as to why this reform could not and should not satisfy anyone . . .

It was with a proclamation like that in his pocket, a small package of new books on political topics, and some paper, pencils, and textbooks he had purchased for his school, that Koretsky returned from Kyiv; and when he stepped out of the day coach at the train station of a rather small city near the village of Ladynka—he was immediately arrested.

At the interrogation he was told in Russian: "Ah, so you were drawing up constitutional decrees there! National representatives! Ukrainian schools! Control of the bureaucracy! Well, sir—you had better wait up a bit: you were in much too big a hurry!"

It was obvious that the primary reason for his arrest had been the matter of the "constitutional decree." It was a well-known fact that for some time the district police officer had been demanding that the school council relieve Koretsky of his teaching position. His arrest at that time, however, had resonated loudly in the small city. The progressive members of the city intelligentsia had become interested in Koretsky and his village. The matter even made it into the newspapers—well, obviously, all this had to be taken into consideration, and Koretsky had to "wait up a bit," and he had been waiting for two months now . . .

During those two months he was allowed to see his wife only once—for ten minutes in the presence of a gendarme . . . They had not allowed his children to come in, even though his wife Talya had brought both of them with her . . .

At that time, they had not yet dismissed her from the school where she served as his assistant; but that was only thanks to the intervention of Molovsky who had stood up for her at the school council meeting . . . The next time he might not be there, and then . . . How would they support themselves? Perhaps this question was one that could already be asked? How was he to know?

It had been so long since he had received any news from the outside world! At first he had known a bit of what was happening out there, because newly arrested people kept arriving in the prison. He knew that peace had been made with Japan, that there had been all sorts of revolts . . . But no new detainees had been brought into the prison for three weeks now, and they had even taken away the men who had been in the cell with him—there were no newspapers, no people: he knew nothing about what was happening beyond the stone walls of the prison.

He only knew that life was seething out there, people were fighting, trying to achieve something. His heart was on fire, and it longed to be out there with them . . . He wanted to work and to fight, and he missed his village terribly.

He had worked for nine years in the village school. And among his students there were many who flocked around him and Talya to form a single spiritual family. He had read so many books with them, had so many conversations with them! And some knowledge had been imparted to them . . .

He and Talya had given generously of their own personal selves to them, and these students had become like family—how could he not be sad to have had to abandon them? Especially at a time like this, when the entire nation was stirring, striving to attain a better life; when all of them needed so much help—help that he could give them both with words and with deeds . . . To be sure—

A heart once filled with goodness
Will never grow cold!

—nothing could destroy completely the national and political consciousness that the two of them had inculcated in their students, but still, people lived in such terrible darkness that it was easy to lose your way, even for someone who supposedly knew where he was going!

And he so wanted to see all of them . . . especially Petro and Yakiw.

But how would it be possible to see them, when not even Talya could visit him . . . not even his own children! Why hadn't they let the children come to see him? What could those two little ones have possibly done? And where were Talya and the children now? Were they in good health? Never before had he felt so miserable, so achingly sad without them . . . without Talya's serene eyes, without the cheerful chattering of the children . . .

If only he could see them for a moment, a single moment!

Grimy, grey stone walls—cold, befouled, bespattered—pressed in on him from all sides. And it was only up there, through the grates of a small window almost under the ceiling, that it was possible to see a patch of bright blue sky with a wispy trail of a white cloud as transparent as a veil. The autumn day had turned out to be warm and sunny, and to Koretsky, confined in the dirty, gloomy cell, it seemed more like a spring day than an autumn one.

The very thought of spring involuntarily evoked images of cherry trees covered in white blossoms, of fragrant, shiny birch leaves, and of long silvery willow branches leaning out over the fresh murmuring waves of a cheerful river that wound its way through a boundless green meadow sprinkled with yellow flowers. How lovely it all was, how immeasurably beautiful, spring-like . . .

How was one to live without it? Was it actually possible? Was it possible for a fish to live without water? Oh, now he could empathize, he could truly empathize with those unfortunate ones—the ones who were drawn by an irresistible power to get out from these stone walls, who tried to escape without taking heed of anything, who dodged the bullets of guards, suffered from hunger as they wandered through the Siberian taiga, and who remained undeterred, even by the threat of their own death or someone else's, in their attempt to see the expansive blueness of the heavens above them, to feel an unfettered wind blowing upon them, to fall down on the ground, press their weary chests against mother-earth, and kiss her, kiss her with frenzied kisses, while burying their faces in the fragrant young grass! Oh, for just one day like that it was possible to attempt anything, to do anything!

Keys jangled by the door, and the bolt clattered. The daily morning tea was being brought in.

"Here's something to warm you up!" the soldier-guard said, as he placed a tin teapot and a French bun on the table.

Koretsky did not respond. Mechanically, without giving any thought to what he was doing, he busied himself with the tea, downed it quickly, as if doing something that he could not avoid, and then lay down on the bed, closed his eyes, and began daydreaming once again.

But what if he actually attempted to do it? Not all escapes ended disastrously. And there was no way of knowing how long he would be kept here. They might even send him somewhere up north, or to Siberia . . . somewhere among the Yakuts . . . Was the threat of death any less imminent over there? If a coarse despotic jailer wanted to demonstrate his coarseness to a slightly greater degree, and if a prisoner protested against it—well, that situation had all the makings of a Yakutian tragedy . . . But what if one were to escape out there right now—into the green meadows, under the sunny sky! Oh!

He leapt out of bed and paced the stone walls of his cell, examining them carefully. Oh my, they were ever so sturdy! He stopped by the window and gave the matter some thought . . . Of course, if he could saw through the grates, and if he had a strong rope, he could lower himself to the ground . . . But below the window there was the prison yard, and he had to get outside of it. So how could it be done?

Koretsky tried to recall what he had seen as he had walked through the prison yard, calling to mind the way that the yard was laid out, but he simply could not figure out where he would land if he climbed through the window, slid down a rope, and ended up in the yard. He seemed to remember that his window was in the gable end of the building. If that was the case, then, once he hit the ground, he would have to go to the corner of the building, cross the yard to a middle gate, go into another yard, get through another gate, and only then would he be free.

Yes. But a guard walked to and fro directly under his window, and there was another guard by the first gate. And the gate was locked, and the gatekeeper had the key . . . and the same was true of the second gate. Moreover, outside that final gate, there was also a guard . . .

What was he to do about all these guards? First of all, the guard that was stationed under his window.

Koretsky got up and walked to the window . . .

The guard's footsteps were clearly audible. He kept walking around a certain part of the building: he passed by the window, rounded the corner, and then came back past the window and went to the other corner where he met up with the other guard. So, it was necessary to . . .

But wait a minute—what was that racket out there, out in the street, in the free world? It sounded like a market or a bazaar. However—and he knew this to be a fact—there never were markets or bazaars near the prison . . . There was, nonetheless, a loud racket, as if large throngs of people were talking and shouting . . . No . . . It seemed to have quieted down.

So then, he had to take advantage of the time when the guard rounded the corner of the prison and could not see his window. Would he have enough time?

But wait, the hubbub out in the street was not dying down. Individual shouts could be heard now, but they were unintelligible. Ah yes! He finally figured it out: it probably was not out in the street, but in the prison yard. A large group of prisoners was either being brought into the prison or taken out, and they had crowded together in the yard and were creating a racket for some reason or other . . . Maybe they were quarrelling among themselves . . . or maybe they were arguing with the authorities, "proclaiming their innocence," as the guard put it, or maybe they were simply yelling for no reason at all.

Well then, he had to figure out how much time the guard spent out of sight after he rounded the corner of the building. He waited until it seemed to him that the guard had gone around the corner, and then he began to count. One, two, three . . . He counted up to one hundred and thirty-one. So, he would have to have the rope ready, securely fastened . . . He could hit the ground in about 15-20 seconds, just when the guard was behind the corner, and then he could make a dash for the gate . . .

"And run right into the second guard stationed at that gate," he said to himself. "No, it's a nonsensical idea, and nothing will come of it."

Did that mean that his entire plan was ruined, and that there was no way out?"

But what was that? There was more shouting, and it was even louder now . . .

"Hurrah!"

Why were the prisoners cheering? He simply could not figure it out! It had to be some kind of nonsense!

Could he dig his way out? Oh sure—from up on the second floor!

Well, he could always make a hole in the wooden floor and lower himself to the first floor . . . that's where the criminals were imprisoned . . . and they would also have to agree to try to escape . . .

Hmm . . . There was an element of danger when it came to them: even if they agreed with his plan, there was always the possibility that they might slit someone's throat or strangle someone . . . some guard, or what have you . . . But as for him— just the thought of killing someone . . .

No, no—it would be best not to have anything to do with them!

Well then, what other means were there? Simply walk down the corridor?

"But there is no way of avoiding the gates and the guards," he stopped himself again. "No matter how you try to get out of here, you always end up in the prison yard, and it's impossible to avoid the gate and the guard . . . It's impossible," the depressing thought kept repeating itself.

Hopelessness crept into his heart and stuck fast to it, sucking at it like leech.

He lay down on his cot, clasped his hands behind his head, and closed his eyes. He did not want to think, he did not want to feel anything . . . But he did feel it—he felt the leech that was sucking at his heart . . .

How much longer would he have to stay here? A month? Six months? A year? Until the regime fell?

Until the regime fell!

He believed that it would fall, that it was inevitable, but when would it actually happen? Everything comes to an end eventually, but when would this regime end?

But to die in here, or out there in the Siberian tundra, far away from your native home!

The lock on the cell door rattled, and the bolt rumbled as it was shoved aside. Why were they coming in again? Usually they did not come in at this time, but today they would not leave him in peace!

He did not stir and did not even open his eyes when someone walked into the cell.

"You're wanted in the office," a voice said.

Koretsky opened his eyes; one of the guards was standing before him.

"Why?"

"I don't know . . . you're wanted . . . and quickly . . ."

"Maybe the police commander has come?"

"I don't know . . ."

Koretsky rose to his feet lazily, unwillingly, picked up his straw hat and walked out of the cell with the guard hard on his heels. They walked down the corridor and descended into the yard. It was empty. Where, then, were the prisoners who had been making such a racket?

"What was the clamour in the yard about? Was it the prisoners who were shouting?" he asked the guard.

"I don't know," the guard replied with his customary response, and then, after remaining silent for a moment, he added: "It wasn't in the yard . . . it was out there, in the street. The shouting, that is . . ."

"Why were they shouting?"

The guard shrugged. "The people don't know what they're doing . . . They're taking liberties . . ."

He might have said more, but at that moment the senior guard walked up to them, and he stopped talking. The three of them walked up the stairs, and a moment later Koretsky found himself in the office—a rather small, grubby room.

On the walls there were two ancient portraits of tsars and some framed instructions, but flies had spotted them so thoroughly that it was impossible to read them. There was a half-opened cupboard stacked with documents . . . and two desks covered with blue blotters splotched with ink and piled high with papers.

Behind the larger desk sat the prison's chief administrator—a corpulent, flabby man with a somnolent face. He glanced at Koretsky.

"There's a document here regarding you," he said in Russian as he pulled out a piece of paper and looked at it. "You're being released . . ."

"What?" Koretsky asked, not believing what he had heard.

"I said you're being released . . . Sign here to confirm that you have received all your money and your watch . . ." And he thrust a register at Koretsky.

Koretsky didn't bother to read it, signed it with a trembling hand, scooped up the money and shoved it into his pocket along with his watch.

"Take him away—let him gather up his belongings," the administrator ordered the senior guard. "And then let him leave—he is free to go."

When he returned to his cell, Koretsky did not pack his belongings—he flung them into a basket and could hardly wait for the soldier to finish tying it up. And then, instead of walking, he raced so swiftly through the corridor and down the stairs that the soldier carrying the basket had a hard time keeping up with him.

As soon as they were in the second yard, Koretsky could hear a commotion out on the street behind the gate. But he paid no attention to it. He watched impatiently as the sluggish guard unhurriedly and methodically stuck the key into the lock with his chubby fingers, and then slowly turned it to unlock it . . . He finally unlocked it, pulled off the lock, and clanged the bolt as he shoved it aside . . .

While he was doing all that, Koretsky bent down, took hold of the rope binding the basket, picked it up off the ground, and, as soon as the gate swung open, stepped out into the street.

He instantly found himself in the middle of a throng: a mob that was crowding around the gate—men, young ladies . . . He stopped in surprise and stared at them.

"Koretsky!" someone shouted from out of the crowd.

"Hurrah! Koretsky! Hurrah!"

And at that moment someone grabbed the basket from him, and hands, many hands, seized him, and before he knew what was happening, he was swaying above the heads of the large crowd that flooded the entire square in front of the prison. Directly opposite him flew a huge white flag with an inscription written on it in red letters: "Amnesty." Farther on, there were a few more flags—smaller ones—with the same red inscription on them.

"Hurrah!" the shouting thundered even more loudly. "Hurrah, Koretsky! Long live freedom!"

"Gentlemen, what are you doing? Don't tear the man to pieces!" Koretsky heard a familiar voice say. "We need a coachman!"

"A coachman! Let's get a coachman!" a few voices shouted excitedly.

Koretsky was lowered to the ground. The crowd parted, making a passageway, and at the end of it Koretsky saw a phaeton.

"If you please, Yevhen Petrovych," the same familiar voice said, and Koretsky was taken by the arm by a black-bearded man—the lawyer Yakovenko—who was well-known to him.

Walking between the two rows of people comprised of gentlemen, workers, older ladies, and younger ladies, they reached the phaeton. Koretsky seated himself in it along with Yakovenko, and two more men settled in opposite them. They all shook Koretsky's hand, greeted him, and congratulated him on his "release into freedom;" but Koretsky did not know the other two men, and he had no idea as to what was going on.

"To the Duma!" Yakovenko ordered. "Quickly!"

The horses moved forward. But the throng stayed with the phaeton, surrounding it, and the coachman had to proceed at a walking pace.

"Well, God be praised—we got what we wanted!" Yakovenko said. "You know: the procurator and the gendarmes were dead set against releasing you. But I told them . . . I was delegated by the rally . . . I said: it will be better for the authorities if you release him than if you allow the matter to come to an unfortunate conclusion. After all, there is a large crowd before the prison that is prepared to break down the gate at any moment . . . They thought about it for a while . . . And then they agreed. Now we're proceeding directly to the rally . . . Everyone is demanding that you be present at it, they want to see you . . ."

"What kind of rally?" Koretsky was hardly able to speak. "Why is it being held?"

"What do you mean: why?" Yakovenko asked in surprise. "Oh, of course! You don't know anything about it, you poor fellow! You didn't read the telegrams . . . Gentlemen!" he called out to the crowd. "He hasn't read the telegram . . . Give him a telegram! Quickly!"

"A telegram! A telegram!" the words rolled through the crowd, and several hands holding large sheets of paper reached out to the phaeton. Yakovenko took one of them and passed it to Koretsky.

"Here, read it: 'A Most Important Manifesto . . .' It's the Constitution!"

Shaking as if he had a fever, Koretsky began reading. His eyes would not obey him; they kept jumping from word to word, and a fog seemed to be covering the letters . . .

"Read it out loud! Have someone read it out loud!" shouts were heard. "Let someone read it again!"

Yakovenko took another sheet of paper from someone's hand, stood up in the phaeton that was barely crawling through the crowd and, holding on to the coachbox with one hand, he raised the white sheet of paper in his other one and began to read the Russian-language manifesto.

" . . . to grant the population the solid foundations of civic freedom on the principles of true personal immunity, freedom of speech, of assembly, and of unions."

The loud reading reverberated in Koretsky's ears, but it was suddenly drowned out by still louder shouts: "Hurrah! Long live freedom! Long live the Constitution!"

" . . . to establish, as an inalienable right, that no law can come into power without the approval of the State Duma."

"Hurrah! Long live the State Duma!"

But Yakovenko was already reading another telegram. Excerpts from it drifted to Koretsky's ears.

" . . . the news about the signing of the Constitution has spread throughout Petersburg . . . They had just gathered when copies of the manifesto were brought from the printing press. It was proposed to honour the people who had courageously fought for the newly gained freedom."

"Hurrah! Long live the people! Long live freedom! Away with prisons! Amnesty! Amnesty!"

Koretsky was choking with emotion, and he felt that if he did not control himself, he would burst into tears. He shut his eyes and gritted his teeth.

The procession slowly moved forward, and in the meantime Yakovenko informed Koretsky: "We received the manifesto in the editor's office last night, and we at once decided to publish it as a separate poster . . . By ten o'clock it was already distributed throughout the entire city . . . The people poured out into the street—well, quite understandably, it spontaneously turned into a rally . . .

"They started talking. Amnesty—that was the very first word . . . 'Gentlemen,' Dr. Lavrenko said, 'before amnesty is granted by Petersburg—do not forget that in our prison there sits a fighter for freedom—Koretsky. Let us demand that he be released!' Well, understandably, at moments like that a crowd does not spend much time thinking . . . And off they rushed to the prison; they wanted to use physical force, but we convinced them to use legal means . . . And so a delegation of three was elected: I, Dr. Yurkovsky, and Pavlo Semenovych . . ." and he pointed at the two men seated across from them, and it was only then that Koretsky realized who they were.

And Yakovenko continued   talking. Speaking hurriedly, in snatches, he told Koretsky about the events of the past two months: the conference of rural and urban activists, universal rallies, riots in cities and villages and, finally, the huge strike of the iron workers and other labourers that halted and paralyzed the economic bustle of the entire empire . . .

Koretsky heard all this, but at first he understood only part of what he was being told, only bits and pieces . . . Then slowly he started absorbing all that had happened, he began to understand what had transpired and to appreciate the role that he had played in all these recent events.

An unutterable joy enveloped him, and in the depths of his soul something grand, magnificent, and invincible started to unfold . . . And it wanted to burst out freely, to reveal itself in some way—through a shout—any way at all, just so it could reveal itself.

"Stop! Stop!"

The phaeton came to a halt, and Koretsky noticed that the crowd had grown in size.

"Let's get out . . . We've arrived," Yakovenko said.

Koretsky stepped out.

Yakovenko took him by the arm and began to push his way through the crowd.

"Let us through . . . Let us through, gentlemen!" the lawyer said. "Let us get through to the platform—it's very important."

The people reluctantly created a narrow passageway to let them through—it was no more than a crack, and it closed instantly behind them.

It took a long time for Koretsky and Yakovenko to make their way through this passageway and to finally run into something with their feet that resembled stairs.

"Careful . . . careful . . . don't fall! There's a step here," Yakovenko said, and he held on to Koretsky's hand as he pulled him upwards through the massed crowd.

Trying to stay upright, Koretsky groped with his feet and, amid all the other feet, found some boards; looking down constantly and being very careful, he kept climbing up the boards ever higher and higher.

"Well, here we are!" Yakovenko said.

Koretsky raised his head and saw a table that had been placed on a platform of sorts, and seated behind that table there were some gentlemen . . . He recognized Dr. Lavrenko at once, and realized that he must be the chair of the rally. Alongside him at the table were two other men: one was seated, and the other one—a young, swarthy, thin-faced man whom Koretsky did not know—was giving a speech.

And then suddenly, on all sides, shouts erupted, moderately at first, and then ever more loudly: "Koretsky! Koretsky has been brought here! He's been released! He's been freed! Koretsky! Koretsky!"

Lavrenko, the chair of the rally, turned around and saw Koretsky. He quickly got up and shook his hand.

"I'm so happy . . ." But his voice broke, and the shouting all around them was gaining in strength: "Koretsky! Koretsky!"

The swarthy speaker fell silent. Lavrenko waved both hands at the throng, gesturing them to be quiet. When the shouting died down a bit, he called out loudly, for the entire square to hear: "Citizens. Freedom has truly arrived . . . The first day of our life under the Constitution is already fraught with significance: one of the fighters for freedom, for our national good fortune is no longer in prison, he is here, standing before you—Yevhen Petrovych Koretsky."

"Hurrah, Koretsky! Hurrah! Long live freedom! Hurrah, Koretsky!"

Koretsky saw a sea of heads in front of him, and above it—bathing in the golden light, waving and billowing all over the square, he saw red flags with inscriptions on them . . . And over there—a white one, the one that bore the word: "Amnesty". . . and a black one . . . The flags were billowing, the sea of heads was undulating, hands were raised high, waving straw hats, white kerchiefs . . .

And all around, in all the nearby buildings—in the windows, on the porches, and even on the roofs—people were also massed, waving kerchiefs and flags, and the mighty voice of the liberated people thundered to the radiant, joyous, fortunate sky: "Long live freedom!"

Gradually the shouts died down, the hands holding the straw hats and kerchiefs grew weary from waving. Koretsky was given a seat at the table. The swarthy speaker could now finish his speech.

Koretsky looked out over the crowd. It had spilled out over the entire square as well as the ends of the adjacent streets that ran into it. Students' berets, workers' straw hats, women's hats, the expensive hats of lords, even cylindrical hats—they were all mixed into one immense jumble . . . He spotted a few peasant caps—probably those of peasants from nearby villages. And there were three white kerchiefs of Red Cross nurses . . .

And everywhere, everywhere there were red ribbons—in buttonholes, on straw hats, and on ladies' hats . . . There was one little boy without a cap. He had climbed up a light post and was tying a swath of red taffeta around it. And there were two men in officers' uniforms . . . no, they were army doctors . . . and even they had red ribbons in the buttonholes of their coats . . .

As Koretsky gazed out over the crowd, the swarthy speaker talked about the significance of this moment, about the great task of liberating the proletariat, but it seemed that the crowd was not paying much attention to him, and as soon as he fell silent—new shouts burst forth.

"Koretsky! We want Koretsky to speak! Let Koretsky speak!"

Lavrenko turned to Koretsky.

"You must speak."

Koretsky turned pale but, without arguing, rose to his feet. He did not know what he would say, but he sensed that something grand and magnificent was growing and filling his soul and would suddenly burst out and fly forth freely. He stretched out his hand, and the entire square fell silent.

"Citizens!" he began. "You do not need to be told by me about the holy tears and the noble blood with which the path to freedom has been saturated . . . Never before, until now, have so many tears and so much blood been shed, but then, never before have we strived for the kind of response that we are striving for now. It is the first time that we have heard the word that reminds us of what it is that we want. So far, it is only a word, written on paper, and it is up to us to make it a reality . . . And in order to do this we must be prepared to dedicate to freedom all our strength, all our intellect, and all our love."

As he spoke, he suddenly noticed something familiar over there, in the middle of the crowd . . . A blue veil on a simple straw hat, and under it . . . Could it really be she? Could it really be Talya? Yes, yes—it is Talya, it most certainly was! She was looking at him, laughing, nodding to him . . .

An immeasurable joy enveloped him, and he smiled with a wide, joyful smile, and the words flew out of his mouth of their own accord.

"Here, in our city, perhaps in the very same square where we have now gathered to celebrate the dawn of our new life, a *Kozak Council used to gather, a council of a free, of a liberated Ukrainian nation. It was through hard work that our nation gained its freedom, cast off its chains, in order to realize the ideals of public freedom, of equality in its native land. It is true that we lost the struggle back then; the powers of darkness and of subjugation, the powers of harsh despotism were stronger than our young, newly-born freedom—and so they were able to crush it . . . But those ideals for which our nation fought without sparing lives—those ideals could not be crushed in our hearts by any despotism, by any darkness. And the great transformation that is occurring now is no stranger to us: we awaited it, we hoped for it in the dark slavery of serfdom, in the heavy disillusionment after the end of serfdom, we fought for it—and here it is, the one that is dear to us, the one that we have long awaited.

"And if there was a time when our people were at odds with the intelligentsia, that time is now in the past: our nation has matured, our nation has become the conscious creator of its own destiny and that consciousness unites us with the intelligentsia into one large family. And this family of fighters is going forth to meet the golden sun of the liberation of the working masses, the liberation of its own nation and of all the nations still caught in the rusty chains of the old enslavement . . . It is flaming, it is already shining and calling out to us: Forward! Higher! To the heights of a worker's life that is vigorous, happy, and free!"

A storm of applause, shouts: "Bravo! Glory!' thundered across the square, and kerchiefs and flags were waving once again, and joyous eyes were shining from under a straw hat with a blue veil.

II

Evening was descending as Koretsky rode home with his wife. They had stayed in the square until the rally had ended, and then, together with Yakovenko, they had ended up in the editorial office of a newspaper.

Koretsky had worked for this newspaper on occasion, sending in reportages and short articles, and he went there now to a meeting of co-workers: they were to discuss how to handle matters from here on in. It was decided: to take a firm stand that the manifesto of November 17 had introduced freedom of speech, and therefore the newspaper would no longer be sent to the censors before being published.

Koretsky undertook the task of translating the manifesto into Ukrainian and of explaining it, so that it could be printed the next day, sent out together with the newspaper, and, in this manner, circulated among the population. Yakovenko guaranteed that, in accordance with the manifesto, the print shop would not refuse to publish the newspaper—he had even dropped in to the shop on the way to the meeting, and had begun some preliminary discussions to that effect.

It was clear that the press would have a very important role in all future events, even more important than up to now. Koretsky understood this very well, and he gladly agreed to assist in the work. He was confident that before long he would be able to return to his students, and he was really looking forward to that, but at the moment, the newspaper was a matter of the greatest import. In it he was to speak mainly to the people in the villages, and he obtained permission to write in Ukrainian.

After that meeting, Koretsky was invited to attend another gathering, but though it was tempting, he wanted to go home even more. And so now they were travelling home together. The postal coach clattered on the road, and the postmaster's young son alternately cracked the whip and muttered something under his breath.

Talya was telling Koretsky about what had happened at home and in the village while he was in prison. The children

were in good health, and so was she. So far, no other teacher
had been sent to their school, and she was coping as well as she
could with all the work.

It was all for the best: if another teacher had been sent, it
would have been more difficult for Koretsky to return to his
former position. Still, he would not be seeing the pupils the next
day: she had found out about the manifesto at noon and had
told the pupils at once that, in recognition of such an important
event, tomorrow would be a holiday, and then she had dismissed
them and hurried into the city.

How had the children reacted to the arrest of their teacher?
Oh, very positively! He cannot imagine how much awareness
about the current situation had grown in their village.

Does he remember when the doctor's son, a student, was
searched and then arrested a couple of years ago? At that time the
ignorant villagers had said: "He was making counterfeit money."
Now, however, when he, Yevhen, was arrested, everyone in the
village was saying: "It happened because he stood up for the
freedom of the peasants." The youngsters heard this talk, of
course . . . and they loved him greatly . . . The fact that he was
returning would bring them much joy—he would see that for
himself . . .

How was their organization? Oh, it was in wonderful spirits!
There had been a few get-togethers. They had met three times
in the forest where Petro had his apiary. She had not been at all
of the meetings, but that did not matter: Petro was in charge of
everything now. He was the same as ever: he thought a lot, but
did not say much; when he did speak, however, what he said was
always to the point. Oh, he truly knew how to run things—he
had succeeded in bringing all of them even closer together.

And as for Yakiw . . . He was such a talented lad, witty,
but often bitingly sarcastic and not very tactful. But it did not
matter—Petro always knew how to smooth things over. He was
proving to be the best informed and most steadfast of them all.

"You know, Yakiw and Ivan—Petrenko's Ivan . . . they were
interrogated—they were asked about you . . . Why they picked
on them, and none of the others—we couldn't figure out . . . They
conducted themselves honourably, and now they're making fun
of their interrogators . . ."

"And how are the villagers in general?" Koretsky asked, and he bent over Talya and embraced her closely, ever so closely.

"Don't . . . the postman . . ." Talya said, trying to push him away.

"He's dozing," Koretsky replied laughingly as he kissed her eyes. "So, how are the villagers in general?"

"Oh, that's where our strength lies! Our organization doesn't even have three dozen people . . . but it was able to draw in the entire village . . . Only a few rich ones, like Semenyuta, Starostenko, Karpenko—only those remain hostile and stand apart . . . all the poorer ones are with us . . . At the village gatherings, the entire community always follows our lead . . . Oh, I haven't told you yet! How thoughtless of me! Not long ago the entire community decided to demand your release and to have you come back to the school . . . They wrote out a resolution and sent it off . . . The rich men and their associates—the *Black Hundreds—wanted to protest, but the community shouted them down! Their days are over! Our people have come out on top. Oh, *Henya!"

Talya's voice trembled joyfully as she related all of this to him. And she truly was overcome with an immeasurable happiness for a number of reasons: Yevhen was returning home, and then there was the Constitution, and then, on top of it all, everything was going so well in their village.

"Oh, Henya! Do you understand? It's not at all like it used to be! Not at all!"

And she tugged at Yevhen's hand and kept talking and talking, pouring out her emotions, and making him quiver with a joyous trembling. And then, in the midst of her discourse, she suddenly laughed, and interrupted herself.

"No, you have no idea . . . It's nothing short of a miracle! Stepan Valyushny . . . you know who I mean—Stukachiv's son-in-law . . . Well, one time he came up to me . . . 'Give me a socialist-democratic proclamation,' he says. 'I have no socialist-democratic proclamations,' I say. 'That's too bad,' he says, 'you should have one because our party supports a democratic republic.' 'And exactly which party is your party?' I ask. 'What do you mean, which party? Our socialist-democratic Russian party . . . An agitator travelled here and organized it for us.'

"I thought he was lying, the way he always likes to stretch the truth. So I asked him more about it—and it turns out that he wasn't lying. He had served for a month, or possibly two or three, in the city . . . either in a factory, or as a watchman—I really can't say . . . And he came back to the village with some pamphlets, and then, hard on his heels an agitator showed up here twice to organize the villagers . . . At the second gathering, there were a few of our people among them as well . . . but they didn't join that party."

Talya glanced at the postman's son who was dozing on the coachbox and then, cuddling up closely to her husband's chest, she said more softly: "That agitator also came to see me . . . He tried to convince me that we should go over to them . . . Of course, I said that we wouldn't . . . But he kept trying to convince me: all the people are consciously going over to the socialist-democratic movement, and soon, he said, you and your small contingent will be left all alone, 'thrown overboard . . .' 'That's what you think!' I said to myself . . ."

"Are there many people in their group?" Koretsky asked.

"They say that they have more than a hundred . . . But Petro found out definitely that they have only forty-seven."

"Still, that's quite a few in such a short time."

"Oh, they're very active! They rush around, bustle about, call together meetings one after the other, and they have a lot of printed material . . ."

"Do you happen to know who is with them?"

Talya named a few people.

"They're so-so people," Koretsky said. "Well, at least they're making people sit up and think, and that's all to the good."

"Yes, that is good . . . but the bad thing is that they're having altercations with us. And they're very stubborn. Valyushny even stated once: 'We know all about your parliamentarism.' 'What is it that you know?' Petro asked. 'It's a supremacy of the bourgeois,' he said, 'and we will abolish you!'"

Yevhen and Talya both laughed as they conjured up the image of Valyushny with his bulging eyes, with his naïve belief that candles burn on treasure-troves at night—and that therefore he would indeed find a treasure one day—and with his phrases about "parliamentarism" and "the supremacy of the bourgeois."

It was growing dark. Cuddled closely together, they rode through the darkness on the soft, level road. The postman's son, swaying on the coachbox, had been dozing for some time already, and the horses were trotting along the familiar road on their own.

And now the flickering lights in the cottage windows in the village of Ladynka were glimmering ahead of them, and a short time later they rode into the village. The postman's son woke up, whistled at the horses, cracked his whip, and the horses trotted more quickly.

Despite the fact that it was an ordinary weekday, there were a lot of people out in the street, mostly men, and they were all talking animatedly about something. Koretsky realized that this must be the reaction to the events that had transpired that day. He would have loved to stop and talk with them, but he was even more eager to get home. And so, after exchanging greetings with some of the people, they quickly drove past them.

Several of the men recognized Koretsky, and voices could be heard in the darkness: "Look! It's the teacher! He's come back! They've let him out already!"

At long last, they could see the school. The half of the building that housed the classroom was dark, but the other half where they lived was looking out at them with large, well-lit windows. People were waiting for them there.

The horses came to a stop in front of the veranda. Koretsky was the first to race up the stairs and rush into the house. Blinded by the light, he halted for a moment . . . The room was full of people . . . The table was set out in the middle of the room, and there was a samovar steaming on it.

"Yevhen Petrovych has arrived!" their maid, old granny Khymka, cried as she struck her hands together in joy.

"Daddy's here! Daddy's here!" the fair-haired little Lida chattered as she wound herself around her father's knees.

Koretsky scooped her up in his arms and kissed her cheeks, her large grey eyes, her tiny hands . . .

Then he lowered her to the floor, turned to old granny Khymka and exchanged kisses with her; catching sight of the grey-bearded face of Tereshko, the old school watchman, he also exchanged kisses with him.

Suddenly he heard a child's serious voice: "How is it, daddy, that you're greeting everybody, but you haven't noticed me?"

Dark-haired six-year-old Volodko was registering a complaint about the lack of attention being paid to him. Amid the general laughter, the insulted little boy was swooped up into his father's arms, and he hugged his father's neck tightly. Still carrying him with one hand, Koretsky used the other one to shake hands with Petro and Yakiw and to exchange kisses with them.

By this time, Volodko was struggling to free himself: "Come on, let me go: I'm not a little fellow to be carried about in someone's arms."

Laughter filled the room again.

"We've all been waiting here for you for a long time," the guests said.

"But how did you find out that I'd be coming?" Koretsky asked.

"Well, we were at the rally in the city," Yakiw said. "And Ivan Petrenko was with us as well . . . But he stayed behind in the city, while we came home right after the rally. The entire village knows that you've been released."

They had scarcely sat down at the table when there was a thumping in the porch and three more comrades walked in: one of them, like Petro and Yakiw, was Koretsky's former student, but now he was already a young father; the other two were older householders who used to come to listen to the teacher read, and who later joined their group. More greetings were exchanged. Then they all sat down to have some tea . . .

They talked in fragments, jumping from one topic to another, hurrying to tell Koretsky everything that had happened . . . Peter and Yakiw had thoroughly enjoyed the rally.

"Oh, if only we could hold a rally like that here, in Ladynka!" the fiery Yakiw said, and his eyes blazed with sparks of energy and joy. "How good it would be—to inform the people about everything."

And Petro, ever the silent one, was beaming, and his somewhat unattractive face and his deep grey eyes were glowing with excitement.

As usual, his powerful body was slumped over the table, and he said: "We must do it! We truly must do it! The people all want to be informed . . . A few of them who were at a bazaar in the city brought back the news about the manifesto, and some of them went at once to the priest's home to ask him what kind of manifesto about freedom had been proclaimed."

"And what did the priest say?" Talya asked, as she poured some tea.

"I don't know."

"But I know," Panas said. Tall and with a trimmed beard, he was one of the older men present. "Two of them went—Demyd and Korniy . . ."

"Ah, Demyd!" Koretsky interrupted him. "How is his injured arm? Has it healed well? Because I didn't have time to finish looking after it properly . . ."

"Yes, it's healed—he's working already. He says that thanks to your help he's back on the path of becoming a householder once again . . ."

"And does he attend the readings?"

"No, after you were gone, he didn't show up a single time."

"That's too bad . . . But what did the priest say?"

"Well, they went to him, and I tagged along: I'll listen, I thought, and see what the priest has to say. He said: 'It's all a pack of lies; there is no manifesto.'"

"Really?" Koretsky was shocked. "Did he really say that?"

"But don't you know what he's like?"

"Yes, I do know; but to say that there is no manifesto—I never thought that he'd come out with something like that."

"And as for our rich fellows," Panas continued, "they also don't want to admit that there is a manifesto; they say that the lords and the democrats dreamed it all up."

Laughter rocked the house.

"Dreamed it up! Well, they will see soon enough that it isn't a pipe dream!"

Koretsky felt someone scratching at his knees. It was Lida—she was trying to crawl into his lap with her favourite doll. Her father sat her down on his knee.

They started talking again, but the little girl kept squirming and poking her father.

"What is it, Lida? Why are you giving me your doll?"

"So daddy can play with her."

Everyone in the room laughed, but Talya said quite seriously: "She's very happy that her daddy has come home, and she's giving him her doll."

Her father thanked her and promised that he most certainly would play with her doll, but a little later on.

But Volodko, standing opposite his father, leaned against a cupboard and said seriously and a trifle condescendingly: "Daddy can't play with your doll. Men don't play with dolls. I have a book with pictures in it for daddy."

"What kind of a book?" Koretsky asked.

"It's a book that I made; I drew and coloured a lot of pictures for it, so that you would have something to look at. I'll give it to you tomorrow, because today is not the time to do it . . . But not a doll . . ."

And then, eyeing Lida, he added: "Little girls really do like to crawl around on people's knees."

"Well, my big fellow," Koretsky laughed, "it would be good if you also came over here to me."

The big fellow hesitated at first, but then, unable to resist, he climbed up on his father's other knee.

Old granny Khymka brought in another heated samovar, and while she was setting it on the table, something began twining around Koretsky's legs.

"Katay, Katay has come!" Volodko called out happily as he leapt down from his father's knee.

"The dog jumped in: I left the door open!" old granny Khymka cried out.

A huge black dog was happily wagging its tail, shoving its nose at Koretsky's knees, and putting its large thick paws on them.

"Leave him alone, leave him!" Volodko said to Khymka who was ready to chase the dog outside. "He came to say hello to daddy! Mommy, give him a bun . . . After all, daddy has come back home—and Katay should have a bun as well."

"And a slice . . . and a slice of sausage!" Lida jabbered.

There was a lot of noise and confusion. Finally Katay was allowed to stay in the room; they gave him a bun and a slice of sausage, and he lay down at Koretsky's feet and busied himself with his supper.

The door opened, and Ivan Petrovych came in with two friends.

"Do you know what's happening in the city?" he asked after a hasty exchange of greetings.

"What?"

"There are hooligans walking about the city and they're saying that the manifesto isn't genuine, that the democrats dreamed it up . . . And they dreamed it all up because they want to give the land not to the peasants, but to the Jews, because all the democrats are either Jews, or their close associates . . ."

"What a bunch of nonsense!" Yakiw shouted.

"Well, they're saying that in the democratic documents it is written that 'the Jews are to have equal rights,' and that the land is for everyone—and that means it's also for the Jews . . . But do you know how many Jews there are? So now, because of the Jews, the peasants will get only half as much land . . . They were saying this to our villagers who were at the bazaar. 'You know,' they said, 'how many children the Jews have, and if you give them land, they'll have twice as many, and before the peasant even realizes what's happening, they'll take over all the land . . . and the peasant will have to work as a servant for a Jew. The tsar wanted to have all the land given to the peasants, but as for the democrats—they want it to be distributed equally to the Jews as well . . . That's what they're spouting to the villagers, and to the city folk they're saying that the Jews dupe you and interfere with your trade, and that somewhere outside the city, they were shooting at an icon and at a portrait of the tsar . . . And there are policemen, or some kind of authorities with those hooligans, and they're saying: yes, yes, that's how it is . . ."

"They're fabricating the devil knows what kind of lies!"

"The hooligans are saying: 'We have to beat up all the Jews and the democrats . . . and all those who are for the democrats and for the manifesto . . . We have to carry out a pogrom . . .'"

"Oh, no, we won't let them carry out a pogrom," Koretsky said. "We certainly do need to hold a rally in Ladynka to explain everything to the people."

They began conferring when a rally should be held. The next day was a Wednesday, an ordinary working day—and the people would be busy with their various tasks . . . It would be better to

186 | Borys Hrinchenko

hold it on Sunday . . . However, there was always the possibility
that the Black Hundreds might start doing something harmful
before then . . . Well, fine, let's try to hold it tomorrow after
dinner . . . Koretsky would make a quick trip to the editorial
office, stay there an hour or so, and in the meantime, Petro and
Yakiw would inform the villagers about the rally. They began
planning how the meeting should be set up, who would be
talking about what, and in what order they would be speaking. It
was late when the guests finally went home.

Koretsky was left alone in his abode. The lamp on the table
warmly illuminated the cosy room, the shelves laden with books
. . . the portraits of writers on the walls . . . a large framed print
of Raphael's Madonna seated in a chair with the Christ child in
her arms . . . a white bust of *Shevchenko on the desk . . .

Koretsky went into the adjoining room. There was nothing
on the table now; the children were fast asleep, and he could see
only a fair head and a dark one peeking out from under their
bedcovers.

Talya was not there.

He stepped out into the orchard and walked down a path.
The night was fresh, but not cool. The distant stars twinkled
with kindly rays.

Koretsky went all the way to the end of the path to a spot
where there was a bench under some large trees. On that bench,
he saw a dark figure.

"Is it you, Talya?" he asked as he walked up to the bench.

It was she, but she did not reply. He sat down beside her
and took hold of her hands. And suddenly he heard that she was
sobbing.

"Talya!" he said in alarm. "What is it sweetheart? Are you
crying?"

Talya fell against his chest and sobbed even more.

"My dearest Talya, sweetheart! Tell me, why are you
crying?"

"O Lord, can it actually be true . . . can it?" she whispered
through her tears.

"What? Can what be true?" he asked, not understanding.

"Can it actually be true that there won't be any of this
anymore?"

"Of what?"

"Of all this . . . Of prisons . . . people being exiled . . . subjugation . . . torture . . . the gallows. . . blood . . . And that people will live freely, like people, and not like slaves . . . but like brothers . . . And all of those other things will never come back? Never? Have we really lived to see that happen?" And she once again began sobbing and trembling.

He pressed her to his bosom, stroked her head and kissed it and, without realizing that his own tears were falling on Talya's face, said: "No there won't be, sweetheart, there won't be subjugation any more! Its reign has come to an end . . . There will be a new life . . . a life of freedom . . . a brotherly life . . . a happy life filled with good fortune . . ."

And they both wept tears of great joy, the tears of subjugated people who, exhausted by oppression, are set free at last . . .

And above them the stars twinkled with their affable radiance and it seemed that they also were saying: "No, there won't be . . . there won't be any subjugation!"

III

As soon as he got up the next day Koretsky went out into the orchard that belonged to the school. The community had given the school quite a large plot of land—about one and a half *desyatyny, and during his nine-year stay in the school Koretsky, both through his own efforts and by working together with his pupils, had transformed the plot into quite a presentable orchard. For the past three years the young apple trees, pear trees, and cherry trees had borne a lot of fruit, and every year on the Feast of the Transfiguration Koretsky held a little celebration for the pupils who worked in the orchard and divvied up the fruit among them.

He walked down the path among banks of dewy grass until he reached the edge of the orchard.

It was in this place that a few old oaks and a linden tree, growing here from ancient times, had created a pleasant shady spot, and it was here that he had anchored a table and a long bench in the ground.

He recalled that yesterday he had found Talya sobbing here, and all at once that entire day came alive in his mind's eye. The day had been like a fairy tale, magical and wondrous . . . the kind of tale that made even the most fantastical tales that he knew turn pale by comparison. A poor lad who went to a city looking for work and unpredictably became a tsar could not feel half of what he, Koretsky, had felt when, after being unexpectedly released from prison, he had gone to a rally to address a freed nation!

He walked to the edge of the orchard, to the fence. Just past the fence there was a ravine, and on the other side of the ravine, opposite the orchard, stood the half-ruined buildings of an old brick factory.

It was in one of these old sheds that they had taken cover—he, and Talya, and the children—when they had been caught unexpectedly in a downpour. They had been going home from Petro's house when the rain started coming down in sheets, and they had to take cover at once. Cramming themselves into the farthest corner where the rain could not reach them, they had sat there on a pile of old straw, laughing all the while.

The ravine made a turn right here, below the village, below the gardens, and a row of houses—the backs of which could be seen from here—also made a turn, and the street took on the appearance of a huge bow, with the school at one end of it, and with Petro's house—of which only the roof could be seen from here—directly opposite it, quite far away at the other end. Koretsky stood and gazed at the village, and then he strolled through the orchard again. It was warm. He glanced up at the azure blue sky, at the sun that was already at high noon, and he involuntarily began to recite:

> *The blue sky floats on high,
> It's blue, but strangely blue;
> The golden sun beams down,
> But its warmth is not true.

"No, its warmth is true!" he thought, and he smiled with pleasure as the warm rays of the sun permeated his body. "But how could it not be shining warmly—especially now, when freedom is shining brightly on the oppressed?" he added, and he laughed joyously. "Even though nature is indifferent to our human joys and sorrows, at times like this it has to rejoice as well!"

And, still smiling, he took a deep breath, inhaling the cool, fragrant air.

A line from one of *Nekrasov's verses about foreign countries that enjoyed freedom popped into his head: "It's easier to breathe, with three-quarters of your chest . . ."

"But we want to breathe with our whole chests, and we will!" he said out loud to himself, and then he laughed once again.

The sound of a commotion, of barking, reached his ears. He glanced back at the school and saw a trio running down the path towards him: big black Katay was in the lead, Volodko, hanging on with one hand to the dog's back, was hurrying after him, and a little farther back, fair-haired Lida was rapidly pounding along on her stubby little feet. Katay was barking with sheer joy, the children were screaming, and all three of them were rushing straight at Koretsky.

"Mommy's calling you to come and have some tea!" Volodko yelled, trying to drown out Katay's barking.

"Some tea . . . Mommy! Some tea . . . Mommy!" Lida also called out shrilly.

"Bow-wow-wow!" Katay's voice added to the clamour.

Katay jumped up on Koretsky's chest and wiped his grimy paws on him, and then the children flung themselves at their father.

After calming down all three of them, Koretsky set out for home. Talya was already walking towards them—her overly thin face was flushed, and she was trying to shield it from the sun that was beating down on her; her blond hair looked golden in the sun's rays.

When he sat down at the table, Koretsky found a notebook with a painstakingly printed inscription on the first page: "My Gift to Daddy Koretsky!"

It was Volodko's notebook filled with drawings that had captions under them: "Daddy, on his way to school," "Mommy is walking with Lida," and then there was Volodko himself, and old granny Khymka with old man Tereshko, and Katay—and, they all looked very much alike except for one small difference: when it came to Katay—he was drawn horizontally, while all the others were drawn vertically.

Koretsky would have been happy to continue looking at the pictures while talking with his children, but it was time to go to the editorial office in the city. He reluctantly picked up his cap and turned to go, but just then Petro, pale and looking worried, appeared on the threshold.

"What's wrong, Petro?" Koretsky asked in surprise.

"Haven't you heard anything, Yevhen Petrovych?"

"No, I haven't . . . What is it?"

"They're beating up Jews in the city . . ."

"That can't be true!"

"I've just come back from the city. Hooligans are walking around with clubs, with cudgels. They're breaking into stores, dragging out whatever is in them, or smashing things to bits and pieces . . . When they come across Jews, they beat them mercilessly . . . I myself saw one that was bludgeoned to death."

"What about the police?"

"The police . . . In the city they're saying that permission has been granted to beat up the Jews for three days . . . The police are following the hooligans around, watching what they're doing . . . and laughing."

Koretsky looked very troubled . . . It was an obvious provocation . . .

"But there are bad things happening here, as well," Petro continued. "A few of those hooligans have rushed here, to us . . . They've gathered at Semenyuta's home . . . And there are others with them: Karpenko, and Starostenko, and Valyushny . . ."

"Really? Valyushny? But he . . ."

"Oh, those days are long gone! Now he shouts with the rest of them: 'The democrats want to tear the land away from us and give it to the Jews—but we won't let that happen!' They're walking up and down the streets, carrying a white banner. The police commissary arrived and went to meet them: 'Well, fellows, which company is winning: the red one or the black one?' 'The black one, Your Excellency!' 'Who is the main instigator here?' And they all said: 'Koretsky, the teacher!' 'Well, fellows, teach him a lesson!' 'We'll teach him so well, Your Excellency, that he'll be pushing up daisies!' 'No, why do that—we don't want anything bad happening: just give him a good thrashing!' 'Oh, we know what to do: he won't be speaking at rallies anymore— he won't be talking at all!' 'Well, do as you know best! Stand firm . . . Hurrah!' and then they all shouted: 'Hurrah!' He drove off, and they went to the tavern and started drinking . . . We have to hurry, Yevhen Petrovych, because they might be here soon . . ."

"Yevhen, what's going on?" a trembling voice asked, and Koretsky saw Talya's ashen face and her wide, staring eyes in front of him.

Koretsky was also momentarily stunned, but he quickly regained his self-control. After remaining silent for a moment he said: "Talya, you must take the children and get away from here."

"And what about you, Yevhen? What about you?"

"I'll remain here."

"But just think about it, Yevhen: they'll kill you!"

"No, they won't . . . I have to stay here to stop them, to persuade them, to calm them down . . . to protect the school . . . But you must go!"

"No, if that's how matters stand, I should be here as well. I'm staying!"

"But have you forgotten about the children, Talya? The men may terrify them so badly, that they'll be scarred for the rest of their lives," Koretsky said, as he pointed at Lida who was calmly playing with the dog, and at Volodko who was listening in on their conversation.

Talya glanced at the children and bowed her head . . .

"But what about you! Come with us!" she said, seizing his hand.

"I can't, sweetheart," Koretsky replied softly as he gently freed his hand. "Don't waste any time . . . take pity on the children! Go to Petro's home . . . Take Khymka with you—she can carry Lida . . . And Petro will see to it that you get there safely . . ."

"We must tell the others in our group," Petro said. "I stopped in at a few homes on the way here, but as luck would have it, neither Yakiw nor Panas were in . . . Vasyl and Dmytro are in the city, and Ivan has gone off somewhere . . . I have to go to a few more homes . . ."

"But first of all, take my family to your place . . ."

The children were ready, and they could have been on their way. But Talya hesitated once again.

"Yevhen! What will happen to you?"

"Nothing will happen . . . I'll talk to them, and everything will be fine . . . Go!"

He kissed his wife, his children—who did not understand what was going on—and led them out of the house into the orchard. They did not go by way of the street, but turned to go through the ravine.

Koretsky stood at the gate and watched them go. He waited until they crossed the ravine once, again in a second place, and then disappeared in the gardens beyond the willows—and it was only then that he turned around and went back to the house.

There was no one there because that morning old man Tereshko had asked for permission to attend to some matter at home.

Koretsky went into the classroom, circled it silently, returned to his room, walked through it, touched the shelves with the books . . . crossed over to Talya's room, looked at the children's beds, tried the bolts on the windows . . .

And then he came to his senses: why was he walking around? Instead of walking around and looking at things, he ought to be thinking about what he should do next.

He went back to his room and sat down at the table. He had tried to reassure Talya, but he himself was uneasy. He hoped that he would be able to dissuade them from harming him but . . .

If his students, the comrades from his group were here, it might be possible to repulse the assailants: there most certainly could not be that many of them . . . But they were not here . . . and he had nothing with which to defend himself—and it was not possible to defend oneself with bare hands.

No, if he was to subdue them, it would have to be by talking to them . . . not just by talking, but by drawing attention to everything that he had done thus far in his life, by reminding them about what he had done and what he was still doing . . . After all, the community had thanked him more than once . . .

Yes, the community . . . But he would be dealing not with the community, but with pillagers, thugs—with habitual hooligans or people who had been driven to become hooligans after hearing the lies that the land had already been given to the Jews . . .

And he would be facing thugs who were drunk . . . Of what consequence was his life and all that he had already accomplished to people like that?

Nevertheless, it was not possible to sit without doing anything: he must do something, prepare himself to fight!

Prepare himself to fight . . . against whom? Against the very people with whom he wanted to join forces to defend their right to live like human beings?

No, it was not possible! How could it be possible that these people among whom he had lived for nine years, for whom he had worked untiringly, that these people who knew him intimately and who were aware of his unfailing dedication to them—that these same people would come to beat him up? It was inhuman, unthinkable, unfathomable. It simply could not be!

But in his heart he knew that it could be; he was sure that the moment was drawing near . . .

A commotion could be heard out in the street . . . Muted at first, it kept growing louder and louder . . .

He got up and walked over to the window . . .

The din was increasing in volume, and he could hear numerous voices, but he could not see anyone beyond the bend in the street.

Koretsky walked out to the veranda and from there he at once saw a mob about fifty feet away.

At the head of this mob a tall, scrawny man with a dishevelled blond beard—bareheaded, with his clothing askew, and obviously drunk—was yelling and striding purposefully. He was shaking his fists and shouting over and over again: "I'll kill him! I'll kill him!"

It was Hawrylo—Koretsky recognized him. Next to him walked a sturdy young man in a jacket and a cap slung down on the nape of his neck—it was Mykhaylo-the-firstborn, a thug and a drunkard. They were followed by a group of older and younger men—about a dozen in all—who also were obviously tipsy. Some of them carried cudgels, and above them, flapping on a stick, was a white banner with an inscription that Koretsky could not make out. Behind them, a little farther back, there were another twenty or so men, and still farther back and fleshing out the sides there were children who were curious about this unusual event.

The entire crowd was yelling, milling about, and approaching the school quite quickly.

Koretsky stepped down from the veranda and stood on the ground.

"There he is! He's standing right there!" voices could be heard. The crowd moved forward a trifle more slowly and halted a few feet from Koretsky. The noise died down.

"Greetings, my good people!" Koretsky said. "What's the good news you're about to tell me?"

They all remained silent—no one had the courage to respond. Suddenly, a voice spoke up from the centre of the crowd. "We want to tell you: don't raise a ruckus!"

"Don't raise a ruckus! I'll kill you!" Hawrylo shouted, and he waved his fists threateningly at Koretsky.

"Who is raising a ruckus?" Koretsky asked. "I'm standing quietly by my house, and you've come to me with fists clenched, holding cudgels . . . So who is raising a ruckus?"

The crowd fell silent again, and Koretsky continued speaking: "Perhaps I've wronged someone? Then tell me, my good people! Every man makes mistakes: and if I have wronged someone—tell me. Let's start with you, Demyd," he turned to the young man with a dark beard who was holding a cudgel. "Have you something to say to me? But first, how is your arm? Does it still hurt? Can you use it to do what you need to do?"

Demyd flushed and replied with some embarrassment: "Well, yes . . . thanks to you . . . after you healed it, I can do everything again . . . May God grant you good health!"

"God be praised! And what about you, Semen, is Semenyuta still exacting those fifties from you?"

"No, everything is fine now . . . Thank you for taking the trouble to help me in the city back then—there no longer are any demands being made on me . . ."

"So then, tell me, my good people, whom have I ever wronged, and how did I do it?" Koretsky asked once again.

"You haven't . . . You haven't wronged us . . . Thank you! You've always helped us . . . And we thank you for that . . ." individual voices in the crowd murmured.

"Perhaps I didn't teach your children as I should have? Perhaps I taught them to steal, to drink, to disrespect their parents?"

"No, we thank you for teaching our children . . . The children are just fine . . . You did a good job of nurturing our children."

"Why are you listening to him?" Hawrylo shouted as he moved forward threateningly.

But others stopped him: "Stop, stop screaming! Let the man speak! We have time enough to do what we came to do if . . ."

"What's there to say!" Semen cried angrily. "No wrongs were committed! You haven't wronged us in any way! We've been led astray, and that's all there is to it . . . With that manifesto!"

"With the manifesto?" Koretsky interrupted him. "It's a fine manifesto that the tsar has given us, and there's no need to be angry with one another or to fight—we should be uniting like brothers. The manifesto says that no one is to be mistreated, that those elected by the people must introduce a better order . . ."

"And what about the land? Isn't it you, the damned democrats that have come up with the idea of giving the peasants' land to the Jews?" a voice screamed, and Koretsky saw Valyushny's face directly in front of him, all twisted with rage.

"The land to the Jews! The land to the Jews!" Hawrylo shouted, waving his fists.

"My good people . . ." Koretsky started to say.

"Beat him up, beat up the liar!" Mykhaylo-the-firstborn screamed, and mustering all his strength, he struck Koretsky on the temple.

Koretsky swayed, but he grabbed hold of the picket fence for support and managed to stay on his feet.

At that very moment, however, a shower of fists fell on his head, his face, and his back.

He raised his hands to protect his head, and suddenly he saw Demyd before him; his face was contorted by a venomous beastliness and he was holding a cudgel high up in the air.

Koretsky saw the cudgel flash through the air and come at his head—and he instantly lost consciousness.

IV

The sun was beating down mercilessly on his head when he awoke. But there was no sun shining above him—and yet his head was burning as if it were being seared by a summer sun. He wanted to touch his head, but realized that it was painful to move his hand. He finally managed to raise it and to feel his head; something wet and sticky had congealed on his forehead. He looked at his hand—it was covered with blood.

He struggled to understand where he was, and what was wrong with him.

The sky above him was covered with grey clouds. They were moving slowly, crowding together and then crawling apart— nauseously and disgustingly. He stared at them and could not comprehend from where they had come.

Finally he concluded that he was not indoors, but out in the yard. Near him, off to one side, he saw a picket fence; he groped around and realized that he was lying on the ground. Surprised, he quickly tried to get up, but his head pounded so badly that he fell back again and remained lying down for some time. Then he slowly raised himself and sat up, leaning against the pickets.

He glanced over at the school and saw broken windows. And he instantly recalled everything: the drunken crowd, the fists, the cudgel in Demyd's hand . . . and then, there must have been a pogrom . . .

He sat for some time, and then he forced himself to stand up. His head was throbbing, and he saw the world darkly, through a fog. Slowly, hanging on to the railing, he made his way up the stairs to the veranda and walked through it into his room.

On the threshold there were jagged shards from lamps that had been flung to the floor, leaving a reeking puddle of kerosene. A shelf, smashed into pieces, lay abandoned in the middle of the room, and instead of books, piles of torn, crumpled, trampled paper were heaped everywhere.

The desk, left with a single leg, tilted sorrowfully to the floor, and everything that had been on it—documents, an inkstand, a framed photograph, a bust—was lying shattered on the floor; white plaster fragments of Shevchenko's bust had been trampled into the black puddle from the inkstand.

The entire room was strewn with a jumble of pieces of wood, scraps of paper, drinking glasses, stuffing from a ripped mattress, and other things so badly smashed, ruined, and trampled, that Koretsky could not make out what they were. It looked as if a terrible, immense iron flail had thrashed the entire room to a pulp.

The books were especially badly vandalized—Koretsky could not see a single one that had been left intact—just wads of paper and broken spines. Throughout the room were scattered large pages from an illustrated edition of Dante, and on a pile of broken vials from the school apothecary lay a segment of the book: *The History of Culture*—he recognized it by its pictures.

Stepping over this rubbish he came up to the door of the other room and right there, in the doorway, he saw the frame from the large picture of Raphael's Madonna: it had been torn from the wall and flung down so forcefully that one end was jammed against the threshold, while the other had been punctured by a large boot. The boot had severed the heads of the Madonna and the Child, and left behind only their mutilated, headless bodies. Koretsky picked up the picture, looked at it, and then unthingly placed it on top of the pile of rubbish.

Then he stepped into the other room.

At first glance, it looked like snow. When he took a closer look, he saw that it was the white down from ripped pillows. The down covered the entire wooden floor as well as a pile of debris that lay heaped on the floor.

The two iron beds of the children were broken and twisted, scrunched up like cripples in the middle of the room, while chunks of the mattresses, chopped by an axe, were scattered throughout the room. On one of the pieces, the doll that Lida had brought him yesterday was lying askew, minus a head and with outstretched arms; fragments from its head were lying by the wall: someone must have smashed the doll against the wall and then tossed it aside. The chest of drawers was toppled over on the floor: its back was smashed in, and the emptied drawers were lying beside it. The armoire was also empty, and its doors had been yanked out; scraps of torn clothing were scattered here and there throughout the room.

He glanced around the kitchen as he walked through it—there was a heap of broken crockery in it.

He went out into the orchard.

From the windows, white swaths of feathers were blowing in the air. And farther on . . .

Farther on there was no orchard at all. The flowerbeds had been trampled, and the gouged soil glistened darkly. A large number of young trees, yanked out of the ground, mournfully exposed their tender torn rootlets, interlaced with soil, to the coolness of the autumn sky. Only the trunks of the larger trees were left standing; they had tufts of smaller branches at the top, but all the lower branches had been broken off or smashed with cudgels, and piles of branches with either green or yellow withered leaves were expiring around the base of every tree.

Only the stately oaks and the linden tree stood untouched; but under them, all that remained of the table was the stand that used to anchor it, and the bench was chopped in half. The same bench on which yesterday evening, under a star-lit sky, he and Talya had wept with happiness that there would be no more tyranny and suffering, no more violence and blood . . .

He walked farther on and passed through the gate. The path ran downwards, winding its way over the steep sides of the ravine.

Stepping carefully Koretsky walked along this path. On it he saw a knife and fork; a little farther down gleamed the cover from the samovar.

"They must have carried it down here . . ." Koretsky thought to himself.

At the very bottom of the path he found one more thing that had been lost: Talya's azure kerchief.

He halted, picked it up, looked at it, and tried to recall something . . .

Talya . . . There was something that he had to do . . . Something with respect to Talya . . . But what was it exactly? He raised his hand to his forehead, but then, feeling the blood there, lowered it . . .

Talya . . . Talya . . .

Oh, yes! He had to find out what had happened to Talya, to the children . . .

He moved forward swiftly, clambering upwards along the steep path. He quickly made his way to the top and stood by the abandoned brick factory, but the pounding in his head began once again, and a feeling of weakness overcame him. He was scared that he would fall down, but he did not want to lie out in the open, so he went into a dark shed.

Swaying unsteadily on his feet, he made his way into its farthest corner, the spot where he had once hidden from the rain with his wife and children; he collapsed on some straw and lost consciousness.

* * *

Two familiar voices: "Well, he isn't here," one of them said, and Koretsky had no trouble identifying Valyushny.

"Oh, may the devil take his father! We really blew that one!" the other one responded. It was Mykhaylo-the-firstborn. "He's fled! We should have gone back right then and there to check if he was still warm, or if he had croaked already."

"But we had to take all that stuff home," Valyushny countered.

"We started taking away all that junk, and forgot what we were supposed to be doing . . . I took his watch—and that was enough for me: I'm not going to be hauling home all sorts of garbage."

"But that Zakharko! That Zakharko!" Valyushny roared with laughter.

"Ha-ha-ha!" Mykhaylo joined in. "He dropped his banner and grabbed the samovar!"

"And off he ran . . . ha-ha-ha! Through the gardens!" Valyushny could not stop laughing. "And the water was still gushing out of it!"

"Well, my friend—we really gave that teacher a good thrashing! We may not have finished him off, but we sure let him have it. And our fellows got something out of it as well . . . His jacket fits me like a glove . . . And how is his cap on you?"

"It's a good fit," Valyushny said.

"It's a good cap," Mykhaylo said approvingly. "It should last another ten years . . . But someone took the money out of his wallet . . . only the devil knows who! I found the wallet, but some son-of-a-bitch had already taken the money out of it . . . Because the teacher had to have had some money . . . Well, my friend, let's be on our way! We'll root around some more . . . Oh, if only we could find him: I most certainly would give him a good pat on the head with this iron rod."

"It makes a good weapon . . ."

"Let's go!"

They left. Their footsteps gradually faded away.

Koretsky understood that they were looking for him. But he no longer felt any fear, or had a desire to flee, or to defend himself. He felt a crushing indifference . . . and a great weariness . . . Sleep was overpowering him . . . He shut his eyes and instantly fell asleep.

When he awoke, it was completely dark. Staring out into the darkness, he was able to discern in the clouded heavens only a scrap of lighter sky that was visible through the door at the other end of the shed. He raised his head and then stood up—he felt stronger now. His head was not throbbing as badly. He could walk now. But where was he to go?

And then all at once he recalled everything. He did not know where Talya and the children were, or what had happened to them. Fear for their safety overwhelmed him. He rushed out of the shed into the open air.

He glanced across the ravine at the school: not a single window was lit in it. She was not at home—she still had to be at Petro's place. He glanced over at the spot where he thought Petro's house should be, but it was dark over there as well. Could he possibly have slept so long that it was now the dead of night? He wanted to look at his watch, but could not find it. Then he recalled that Mykhaylo had bragged about having his watch. So that was how things were: they were trying to find him, and they might kill him . . . he had to be careful . . . But all the same he had to go to Petro's home to find out about Talya and the children.

Suddenly he noticed that on the other side of the ravine, by the school, there seemed to be something . . . like a man on horseback . . . He was riding around the orchard, turning this way and that way. And then another man on horseback appeared, and after the two of them met up, they turned around and vanished in the darkness.

He tried to figure out what was going on, but could not. And then his thoughts were cut off abruptly by a sound—a mournful, hopeless sound . . . It penetrated the silence and trailed off in the air like a long drawn-out thread . . . It was coming from over there, from the school . . .

"A-oooo! A-oooo!"

There was so much sorrow and despair, so much pain in that howling, that it left you with a sinking feeling. Koretsky recognized the voice: it was Katay. Abandoned, all alone, he was lamenting in the ruined yard . . .

He was weeping . . . he felt sad . . . But as for those . . . those who had perpetrated the destruction . . .

Walking quickly, he headed straight for Petro's house. He came to the spot where the ravine made a turn, climbed downwards and then clambered up again right into Petro's garden. He crawled over the fence and, stumbling through some dry cornstalks, came to the threshing floor, and from there he went through the gate into the yard.

There was no light in the house. The dog barked and lunged at Koretsky, but then he recognized him and, falling silent, began to fawn on him.

"Who's walking around out there?" Petro's voice drifted in softly to him, and a dark figure stepped away from the house and moved forward to meet Koretsky.

"It's me, Petro."

Petro rushed up to him, seized his hand and, without saying a word, led him back to the barn by the threshing floor. They went inside, and Petro closed the door and silently led Koretsky through the darkness into the farthest corner.

"Sit down here!" Petro whispered as he tugged at Koretsky. They both sat down on some sheaves.

And then, leaning in closely to Koretsky's ear, Petro said in a hushed voice: "Orders have been given for your arrest. Kozaks on horseback are riding around the village and looking everywhere for you . . . They've been at my place already, at

Yakiw's, and at Panas's . . . They're saying; if we catch him, he won't get away alive. . . ."

Koretsky now knew who the riders by the school had been.

"And where is my wife, Natalya Mykolayivna, and the children—where are they?"

"Don't worry . . . They're alive and well . . ."

"But where are they?"

"I drove them . . . to Hayky . . ."

Hayky was the manor of Talya's wealthy kozak father; it bordered the large village of Hrabivka.

"We thought," Petro continued whispering, "that even though they were not bothering Natalya Mykolayivna here, it nevertheless would be better for her to be farther away from Ladynka. At first she did not want to leave—she was very concerned about you . . . she wanted to go looking for you . . . But I convinced her . . . If she went looking for you, the kozaks would be right on her heels . . . And, to tell the truth, I told her a little white lie: I said that you hadn't been touched . . . that you were in the forest now . . . She believed me . . . She wrote you a note . . . I've just come back from taking her there . . ."

"Thank you, Petro! Were the children badly frightened by the kozaks?"

"No, they weren't . . . Lida didn't understand who they were, and after they left Volodko said: 'Well, I'll show them, when I grow up!'"

"They didn't bother Natalya Mykolayivna at all?"

"No, not at all. They probably didn't realize who she was, and they didn't ask any questions . . . Were you beaten badly, Yevhen Petrovych?"

"A little . . . I was hit very hard on the head . . . However, it's nothing . . . What about the school?"

"Everything there was destroyed . . . By the time that I finished driving Natalya Mykolayivna, and then rushed to some of the comrades . . . by the time that we dashed here and there— we ran up to the school, and found that the horde had already been through it . . . Only old man Tereshko was there, and he was weeping as he walked through the rooms . . . We rushed about trying to find you—you were nowhere to be found . . . We tried to do it in such a way that we wouldn't be seen, so that we could find you and hide you, or maybe take you to a doctor . . . You weren't anywhere around . . . Where were you?"

"At the brick factory . . . in a small shed . . ."

"So that's where you were! But when we saw Mykhaylo and Valyushyn come from that direction, we concluded that you weren't there . . . and so we didn't go there . . . I found some papers in the school and I gave them to Natalya Mykolayivna."

"What about the letter from her?"

"Here it is . . . But we must not strike a light here, because the kozaks might see it: they're still riding up and down the streets . . ."

"That's true . . ."

"You have to get away from Ladynka, Yevhen Petrovych; you must go someplace else."

Koretsky pondered the matter . . .

"There's nowhere for me to go, but to Kyiv . . . Because there I can find the most secure place to hide . . . How late is it already?"

"It will soon be midnight."

"So, the train has gone."

"You must not go into the city now . . ."

"Of course not! I'll go to Horobeyka, and catch the train there. It's about twenty *versts from here, isn't it?"

"Yes, about that . . . Maybe even a bit more . . . Can you walk that far?"

"Yes, I can."

"Because it's easier to spot you, if you're riding . . ."

"Of course . . . And I don't want to go on the morning train, because it would be easy for them to see me . . ."

"You'll wait for the evening train?"

"Yes. But not here . . . It will be better if I go into the forest to your apiary."

"Yes, it's safer there . . ."

"I'll spend the night and the day in the hut, and in the evening I'll get on the train."

"Do you want to go right away?"

"Yes, at once . . . But if you could at least give me a cap, Petro, because I have nothing of my own with me . . ."

"I'll be right back . . ."

Petro left, and Koretsky stayed behind to wait for him in the dark barn.

There was no doubt that it would be best for him to go to the apiary. Petro had already taken the bees away for the winter, so no one would be going there, and even if someone did show up, he could always hide in the forest . . . And from the apiary to the station in Horobeyka it was also at least three versts closer . . .

Petro came back, bringing with him a cap and an overcoat. The coat fit Koretsky very well, but he found it painful to put on the cap, because his head was still throbbing painfully.

"And here's a little something for you to eat . . . Go ahead and eat it!"

"No, I'll eat it later . . . in the apiary . . . and I can even eat as I walk . . . But now there's no reason for me to wait around here: it will be better if I leave as quickly as possible."

"Then let's go—I'm going with you."

"But why?"

"I want to make sure that you make your way safely to the hut . . . Once we get there, there's less danger, but who knows what can happen along the way . . ."

"But you might get into trouble as well—is that what you want?"

"Nothing will happen . . . I'm going!"

"Well, fine—it will be more pleasant for me. We'll go through the ravine?"

"Yes, we're less likely to be spotted in the ravine."

They came out of the barn and looked around—there was no one to be seen anywhere. They once again went through the garden, then down to the ravine.

Petro walked ahead, carrying the bundle, and Koretsky followed him. They walked in silence, because it was dangerous to speak.

Up above them the sky was cloudy, with only a few patches where it was clear, and in those patches the stars glimmered sadly. The dark sides of the ravine rose up steeply, and it was pitch-black in its depths. It would have been difficult for anyone to catch sight of them.

They made every effort to walk as quietly as possible, and they were advancing slowly.

Suddenly Koretsky shuddered.

"A-ooo! A-ooo!" the wailing sound echoed through the darkness.

And all the time that they were making their way through the ravine, the howls of the lamenting dog drifted through the air, leaving them with a feeling of hopelessness, and making them want to howl along with Katay . . .

They walked for half an hour through the ravine. As they went farther, the ravine became less deep; its sides became lower and, finally it ended as a narrow trench in the steppe. The two men glanced all around the field. At first, Koretsky did not see anything, but Petro touched his arm and silently pointed to the right.

There, in the distance, a large mound loomed in the darkness. After peering more intently in the dim light from the few stars, Koretsky made out something tall on the mound.

"Kozaks on horseback," Petro whispered.

Yes! They were trying to catch him even at night.

They had to turn back.

They turned around and plunged once again into the darkness of the ravine.

"To the willows," Petro whispered.

Koretsky knew the way. The ravine branched out into a field, but willows grew in clumps there, and all sorts of shrubbery was scattered over about one-and-a-half versts—so it was easier to hide in them and move farther away from the village, and then proceed into the forest by way of another path.

Once again they walked, quietly, carefully, stealthily. When they got to the fork in the ravine, they turned into it. It was more difficult to walk here, because the path was not well trodden, and bushes kept getting in their way. They had to go even more slowly, so that they would not make a rustling or a thumping noise.

Just as they were approaching the end of the ravine, they suddenly heard voices above them.

Two kozaks, riding above the ravine, were drawing quite close to them.

Koretsky and Petro fell to the ground and lay very quietly, without moving a muscle.

"How much longer are we going to be riding around?" A voice speaking Russian could be heard right above them.

"The devil only knows . . . He must have fled . . ."

"Should we ride through the ravine?"

"Oh, the devil take it! We'll break the horses' legs . . . Give me a light, my friend!"

A match was struck, a light flared, and there was the smell of tobacco . . .

Then there was the pattering of horses' hooves once again, as they slowly moved away at a walking pace.

Koretsky and Petro stayed where they were until the voices and the sound of the horses' hooves faded and then died away completely.

They waited for another quarter of an hour, and then Petro poked Koretsky.

"Stay here!"

And he quietly crawled upwards. Koretsky saw his dark figure move through the ravine, and finally he could see Petro's head poking up above the bank. He peered for a long time into the distance—and then he made his way back just as cautiously.

"There's no one to be seen now—let's go!"

And, still trying to make as little noise as possible, they came out of the ravine into the field. Koretsky looked all around—there was nobody anywhere—unless someone had purposely concealed himself. Hunched over and dropping at times to the ground, they wound their way in and out among the clumps of bushes and the willows for about a verst—until they reached an open field.

There was no way of guaranteeing that here, on the path to the forest, they would not meet up with some kozaks, but there was no other way of getting into the forest. They walked swiftly through the field.

And still following them, the distant howling of the dog echoed all around them—like a mournful lament on the ruins of the destroyed school . . .

V

When the wind blew on the trees they rustled sadly and gloomily, and then, growing more subdued, they whispered mournfully as if complaining about someone. At times, the wind drove the rain down in a fine, impenetrable sheet, but when it died down the raindrops pattered on the leaves and on the hut with a monotonous, irritating dripping sound, and it seemed that they would never stop falling.

Huddled on some straw, Koretsky looked out into the darkness and listened to the steady pattering of the wearisome autumn rain. It was cold, damp, and hopelessly depressing. So hopelessly depressing that you no longer felt like complaining, or even shouting with pain; you just wanted to huddle even more closely, curl up like an old, ailing dog in this rain, shut your eyes to avoid seeing anything, anything at all—and to die.

Nine years of work! Of dedicated, unceasing work, the kind of work that all of the joys and pains connected with it became their personal joys and pains. Even their love, their matrimonial matters were so tightly bound to this work, intertwined with it, that it all combined to make one complete whole—sometimes bitter and hard to bear, but at the same time so beautiful, so gilded with the radiance of their joyous hopes!

And it had all perished!

All by himself at first, and then together with his wife, he had raised a generation of young people who were illuminated by the light of knowledge and by civic consciousness. With their actions, with their own lives, he and his wife had always strived to be true to what they were teaching the people; whenever it was at all possible they had tried to help everyone, whoever needed their assistance, and they did so not only because their idealistic sense of duty told them that it was the right thing to do, but because they thoroughly enjoyed immersing themselves in the national sea and soothing the aches and pains of its people; because they loved these people who had been kept in the dark and oppressed by a hard fate—and they endeavoured to demonstrate this love in every possible way . . .

Perhaps they had done badly? Not done enough?

Who could say . . . But they had spared no effort, done everything that they could . . . And it had seemed that their work was not in vain. It had seemed that they were already creating around themselves a promising circle of people who were living new, better, and more meaningful lives . . . It had seemed that the broader community also understood them and demonstrated good will towards them . . . even quite recently, when he had been in prison, the community had resolved to make every effort to obtain his release and to have him returned to its school.

But all it had taken was a bit of nonsense—a trumped-up absurdity that someone wanted to take the land that should belong to the peasants and give it to the Jews—to have everything change, to have the fear of losing their land befog the peasants' heads, to make them lose their sense of what was right and what was wrong. And that very same Semen or Demyd who, probably more than twenty times, had received sincere, brotherly assistance from him, both in words and in deeds—that same Demyd had raised a cudgel over his head with the very arm that Koretsky had healed for him so that he could engage in honest labour.

Could there possibly be a situation that was more terrible, more hopeless?

And was that true only of Demyd? There was already news— Petro had told him about it—that there had been pogroms in Kyiv and in other cities. How much suffering, how much titanic work and struggling, how many incredible sacrifices had been made in the name of love of freedom and of one's nation, and now—just when the first ray of liberty and of hope for a better life had finally flashed, those same people in whose name all the previous struggles had been undertaken, responded to this ray with pogroms, by killing their defenders and their allies, and by obediently walking on a tether behind those who had always led them around in a heavy yoke.

Like a yoked ox, the subjugated people had clearly demonstrated now that not only had they been serfs from time immemorial, but that they were fated to remain slaves without hope forever.

And he recalled the words:

*And the sun will rise
And incinerate the defiled earth—

And only when the mighty sun consumed this defiled earth in flames, when it destroyed the brood of eternally servile serfs and gave birth to a new, assertive race—only then would it be possible to expect anything better. But the sun—it would not come, and it would not incinerate the earth, and things would continue to be as they had always been: there would be a serf and there would be a lord, and there would be blood, and pogroms, and chains!

If what he had just lived through had not happened, if he had remained in prison, or even if he had been sent to Siberia to do penal servitude of the hardest kind—that would have been easier to bear than what he was experiencing now. And even if he had died there, he would still have died happy in the belief that the day would come when the sun of freedom and of true humanity would shine over his corpse.

But now—how could he believe in that now?

To die, just to die—and not to know or feel anything!

The monotonous rain pattered annoyingly on the hut, the trees complained mournfully, as if softly sobbing, and the dark, impenetrable night oppressed his soul. He huddled, curled himself up ever more tightly and grew insensible from the unceasing, immeasurable, numbing, and hopeless pain . . .

He did not sleep, but he also was not fully conscious.

When he regained control of his senses, the grey light of a gloomy morning was already peeking through the cracks in the hut. He got up and walked out of the hut on unsteady feet.

It was no longer raining, but the earth, the forest, and the sky were all wet, grey, swaddled in clouds and fog.

He was shivering from the cold.

Somewhere deep within him something was aching dully and disgustingly, but now he knew what was causing that pain; his head also ached, it felt heavy and did not want to comprehend anything. He sat down on a stump by the hut and trembled involuntarily. The cold air was slowly reviving him. He went over to a little well to wash up. On the left side of his head his hair was matted with blood, and it had hardened to resemble the bark on a tree. He washed off the blood as best he could, and tidied himself up a bit. After he had finished, he returned to the hut and put on Petro's overcoat to warm up, but it did not help.

It was then that he remembered Talya's letter, and he pulled it out to read it. She had written that she and the children were well, and she begged him not to worry about them, and not to come and visit them at this time, but to go directly to Kyiv: she was sure that she was being watched, and that they would seize him if he came to see her. Because of that, she was going to Kyiv—it would be easier to see him there without putting others on his trail . . . She was happy that the pillagers-thugs had not hurt him (it was Petro who had told her this), and she encouraged him and tried to convince him that in a short while things would take a turn for the better . . .

"For the better!" Koretsky smiled bitterly. "Where does she get all this hope? Especially since the situation is so utterly hopeless!"

Better! When he could not even guarantee that the thugs would not go to her father's manor to pillage it and to smash the skulls of Talya and the children.

And as for him . . . he could not do anything, because even if he could go there and defend them with weapons, it would only make things even worse for them . . .

He groaned with heartfelt pain, and whimpered like Katay—over there, on the ruins . . . He was ready to slash himself . . . He felt like banging his head on an oak tree, smashing it into smithereens, so that it would stop thinking, so that his heart would stop aching . . .

He went back into the hut once again, crawled onto the straw in the far corner, drew his legs up to his chest, and lay there . . .

* * *

He could see that now it was lighter outside. He walked out of the hut. In the eastern sky, the sun was trying to break through the clouds. At first it appeared like a pale dull circle, then it grew smaller, dissolved, flashed once . . . twice . . . hid again, and then flashed anew and began to shine in a clear patch of azure sky.

He sat down in the sun and tried to warm up. The warmth permeated his body and, along with it, some of his strength started to return.

It was already noon when he heard footsteps—branches were cracking underfoot. The sound was drawing nearer, and it was possible to tell that it was only one man who was approaching. Finally a figure holding a bundle stepped into the glade, and Koretsky saw that it was Yakiw.

At first, the lad did not see his teacher, because Koretsky was sitting off to one side behind the hut, and so he called out softly: "Yevhen Petrovych!"

"I'm here," Koretsky responded.

Yakiw had already caught sight of him.

"I've brought you some lunch . . ."

"Thank you! Sit down!"

Yakiw placed the bundle by the hut and sat down beside Koretsky on a pile of wet straw.

The teacher peered intently into Yakiw's pale face and noticed that his lips were twitching nervously; and then, all at once, tears started rolling down the young man's face, one large teardrop after another.

"Yakiw, what's wrong?" Koretsky asked. "What's happened?"

"It's nothing, nothing," Yakiw replied, scarcely able to speak. "It's nothing . . ."

"But why are you crying?"

"I was in the school . . ."

And, leaning his elbows on his knees, he clutched his head and wept quietly, silently . . .

And Koretsky felt something roll into his throat, and his lips also began to tremble, and a hot tear—his first tear—rolled down over his face to the cold ground.

They sat together, the teacher and the student, and they wept silently . . .

Then they stopped crying. And both of them seemed a bit embarrassed at this unexpected outburst of tears, and for some time they sat without speaking.

Yakiw was the first to say something—he talked about what was happening in Ladynka.

The pillagers had rejoiced yesterday, drinking and carousing all night long, but today they had calmed down and did not crawl out of their yards. He had run into Valyushny out on the street—and the latter had turned away, lowered his head, and quickly walked away: he was ashamed to look Yakiw in the face.

There were also reports of pogroms in neighbouring villages. In Soltykiv the villagers had gone pillaging and had slain a doctor with an axe—because he was a democrat; and they had almost killed a teacher. Then they went off to pillage the lord; they wanted to kill him, but he managed to flee before they got there.

After that, the villagers went to the neighbouring village of Horobeyko and, together with those villagers, they pillaged the lord there. They were saying: "All the lords are against the tsar: we'll kill them all, to the very last one, and then the land will be ours."

And the lords rushed to see the Governor, to ask him to send kozaks to help them.

The kozaks had already departed from Ladynka. Petro had heard them talking among themselves out in the street: they were saying that the teacher must have fled on the train. Maybe they had already been sent over there, where the lords were being destroyed; and maybe they might rush back to Ladynka again, but you could breathe easier for at least a couple of days.

Their entire group was greatly saddened. They were planning to come here today—they wanted to at least see their teacher.

As Koretsky listened to him, the sincerity in his voice made his heart feel lighter, as if the unceasing pain in the depths of his soul was being lulled to sleep by what he was hearing.

"I brought you some lunch," Yakiw reminded him as he pointed at the bundle.

"I still have the food that Petro gave me," Koretsky said with a faint smile.

"You mean to say that you haven't eaten anything? For the second day? But you'll grow weak!"

"I didn't feel like eating . . ."

"Let's have something to eat right now, because I haven't had any lunch either, and they'll bring us more food later in the afternoon."

He began bustling about, spreading a cloth and setting the food out on it . . .

Koretsky realized that he was hungry as well, and he started to eat.

After they had eaten, Yakiw asked Koretsky if the wound on his head hurt, and he suggested that he might want to lie down and rest: after all, he had not slept during the past night, and he would have to travel on the train to Kyiv all night.

Koretsky truly did feel overcome by weariness. He lay down on the straw and quickly fell into a deep, untroubled sleep . . .

When he awoke, he glanced up at the sky through the door—it was growing late.

"Yakiw!" he called out.

"We're over here!" Yakiw responded outside the hut.

Koretsky walked out and saw Petro and Panas with Yakiw.

They had come a short while ago, and they were expecting other comrades to arrive quite soon. And indeed, a little while later, Ivan Petrenko came, and he even had his wife with him—a cheerful, fair-haired young woman who was also Koretsky's former pupil. They sat in a group and recounted what they knew about what had happened yesterday in the village. More comrades kept coming, singly, and in pairs: they had to be careful not to alert the pillagers about their meeting.

Gradually, most of the group gathered together . . . Six of them did not show up: two of them were not in the village just then, and one did not come because they had neglected to inform him about the meeting; but as for the three others . . . no one knew why they had not come . . . And they did not want to think about them just then . . .

They stood and sat in a group, crowding around Koretsky—and almost all of them had young, sincere faces; there were only five older bearded men, and among them was Panas, one of the group's most ardent supporters . . .

Petro was speaking with Koretsky, and as he spoke, his serious, somewhat prematurely old face seemed to grow even older from the sorrow that was settling on him.

"And so you're leaving us, Yevhen Petrovych, you're going away from us, and we're remaining here . . . Like orphans . . . We have only ourselves to blame—we didn't look after you as we should have, we didn't help you . . . It happened so fast, that before we knew what was going on, it was all over . . . Do not be angry with us for that, Yevhen Petrovych!"

"I'm not angry." Koretsky said quietly and sincerely. "I can see that there was no other way that it could have happened."

"But maybe there was another way," Yakiw responded, "If we had been better . . ."

"Well, you can't turn the clock back!" Panas sighed. "But we don't want you to think, Yevhen Petrovych, that just because things happened as they did, that we have changed, become different . . . No, now that you have shown us the way, even if a wagon were to roll over us, we would not depart from that path: we will try to attain our goal . . ."

"But you must teach us," Petro picked up on his words, "how to go on without you, how to stay together as a group, and what we should be doing . . ."

"Tell us everything that we should be doing! How to fight against the Black Hundreds!" all the comrades started speaking at once . . .

"And tell us where you will be, tell us so that we will know how to reach you, if the need should arise . . ."

And a long conversation unfolded about what to do and how to do it. They had to stick together at all times, never have a falling out, and always continue going down the same road that they had been on up to now . . . They must not let anyone sway them from that road—and they must always keep in mind that until such time that there was true freedom, it was not possible to do anything for the common good . . . They must spread these ideas, this knowledge everywhere . . .

This period of pogroms—it would pass, as all fumes pass away . . . And when these fumes dissipated, heads that were cleared of them would once again be able to understand what was right. Koretsky explained the laws that were included in the manifesto, told them how to fight for these rights so that they would all be enacted . . . He told them how they could contact him in Kyiv . . .

They crowded tightly around him and listened intently to catch his every word. They felt guilty and they wanted to atone for the wrongdoing by working even more fervently and with more dedication for the cause about which he was telling them. They believed in him; and the eyes of these few dozen people, who had gathered covertly in the middle of a forest to be with their hounded teacher, shone with great grief, faith and hope.

Twilight was descending when they began to leave . . . They exchanged kisses of farewell, not knowing when or if they would ever see their teacher again . . . And they left one or two at a time, so that hostile eyes would not spot them . . .

Koretsky silently watched them, as they walked away and vanished among the trees, and he felt that the warm waves of the familiar feelings of hope and power were rekindling a fire within him.

Only Yakiw remained with him—they were to go together to the train station. They kindled a small fire out of some brushwood, and in the light that it cast, Koretsky wrote a few words to his wife. He advised her to stay at her father's home— at least until this period of their lives was over. He had about a hundred *karbovantsi, and this sum would tide him over for the next while . . . If things changed in such a way that they would ask her to return to her teaching position, and if she was sure that it was safe to go back to Ladynka, then perhaps it might be best for her to do so. He kissed her and the children, included some sincere and tender words, and tried to renew her faith in a better life . . .

The brushwood finished burning and the fire died out. He gave the letter to Yakiw, and they set out on their long trek.

They walked seven versts through the forest and field without any problems. And then they saw the lights of the train station twinkling in the darkness. Koretsky stayed some distance behind, while Yakiw went on ahead to buy a ticket.

Just as he came back with the ticket, they heard a rumbling noise: the train was approaching. Its two huge, fiery eyes were piercing the darkness: they shone, came closer, and suddenly a lengthy dragon, shooting off fire and smoke, burst out of the darkness and, clanging and groaning, screeched to a stop at the station.

Koretsky shook Yakiw's hand and, avoiding the station, jumped into the last coach. There happened to be a vacant seat right by the window in the corner behind the door. Koretsky

216 | Borys Hrinchenko

glanced out the window and, a little way off in the distance, he saw a dark figure—it was Yakiw.

The train blew its whistle and started moving. The young man's figure and the station lights flashed past Koretsky's eyes, and the train plunged into the darkness of the autumn night.

"But this train will carry me into a brighter day . . . into a brighter day of realized hopes," Koretsky thought.

He no longer felt that dull, hopeless, disgusting pain. Everything that had happened seemed like just a fleeting moment in an event of far-reaching importance, the conclusion of which could never be in doubt . . .

And even though this moment was painful, they had to live through it in order to be tempered like the strongest steel . . .

The train was rushing powerfully forward, penetrating the darkness . . .

Why I Was Arrested
(1906)

As told by M. F. Dyachenko

I'm a peasant farmer, descended from generations of peasant farmers, and I'm registered under the name of Mykola Dyachenko in the records kept by my church in the village of Ivanytske in the Romen district.

Our village is not poor but neither is it wealthy; however, when it comes to being ignorant and uninformed, there is none that can claim to be its equal.

The peasants living in it are peaceful, humble, and submissive: they doff their caps before everyone who wears sparkling buttons; they respect a priest, regardless of what he is like, as if he were their father or mother; and they greet a district police officer as if he were the governor himself. And that is probably why every police henchman abuses our peasants to his heart's content.

It used to be that when the district police officer arrived to look into some matter he would keep all the men out in the freezing cold with their caps off for two hours or more and, in addition, publically curse every one individually or even punch out the teeth of a few of them. And while this was happening, the peasants would not utter so much as a single word, even though there were among them a good number of grey-haired men so advanced in years that the police officer could have been their grandson.

My heart ached back then when I witnessed that kind of brutality, and later on it ached even more when I observed the arbitrariness of the rapacious hordes of profiteers and government officials, because from a young age I had the opportunity to read many good books and from them I learned that not all countries look upon their peasants as being cattle, as they are viewed in our land. And that is precisely why I've been made out to be a criminal, why I was severely punished, and why my family has been left without a crust of bread.

They say that my uncle, M. F. Dyachenko, a deputy to the *National Duma, sent a formal inquiry to the Minister to find out why the Governor of Poltava had arrested me and given an order that I be evicted from Poltava—but in my view, it's pointless to trouble the Governor! Even though he boasted that he would arrest Christ Himself if He were to come to the province of Poltava to instruct the people, when it came to my case, he just washed his hands of the whole affair like Pontius Pilate, and I was punished by voluntary "*okhranyteli"—Mykola Semenovsky, the priest in Ivanytsky, and Yakushev, the administrator of Prince Levin's estate, and even they did not really know why they were punishing me.

I've already mentioned that our village was unenlightened, and that is why the priest, for the six years prior to the unprecedented "freedom" of *October 17, ruled the roost in accordance with his own wishes. Young, ignorant, hot-headed, unmerciful towards peasants, and a money-grubber on par with the best of them, he descended like a dark cloud on Ivanytske and went on the attack from the moment that he arrived

The temporary living quarters assigned to the priest by the community did not appeal to him and so, without any hesitation whatsoever, he wilfully settled in the district school . . . and lived in it for five years. We travelled to the district administrator, complained to the government, cursed and swore, and the younger men even wanted to forcefully throw the priest and all his belongings out of the school, but they didn't do it because the district administrator and the district police officer were on the priest's side.

And during all that time the children froze in a cold, abandoned hovel that used to be the village office; it was dark as a dungeon and as narrow and crowded as the road to the heavenly kingdom. The children had problems with their eyes; they were dropping dead like flies, and those who did survive learned very poorly because they were crammed in so tightly that they had to take turns sitting and standing.

After the district administration refused to help us, we suffered in silence because we were accustomed to respecting a priest. But when the peasants realized that the priest was not respecting himself—that he was selling the whiskey that he demanded from the peasants for officiating at baptisms, chasing his wife around the village square with a cudgel, behaving improperly with his female servants, and giving rise to shameful things being said about him and his wife—they stopped even doffing their caps before him.

And then we found out that the priest had stooped to stealing money that belonged to the church by forging the signatures of the people in charge. Well, in our view this was completely unacceptable, because we didn't think that it behooved a spiritual person to indulge in falsifying signatures. It's true that he paid back the money as soon as he was found out, but in our minds the blow against our church remained just the same! And that's when our patience gave out and we sent a complaint to the archbishop in which we begged him to remove from our village this money-grubber clothed in a cassock.

I admit that I was deeply involved in pursuing this matter and that I even took it upon myself to deliver the complaint to the proper authorities, and it was because of this that the priest conceived a deep hatred towards me—may God prevent anything like it! He continually cursed me and called me a "socialist," but, if truth be known, I didn't really know back then what a socialist was.

Nevertheless, the priest had to move out of the school on the order of the archbishop and there was an investigation into his behaviour. But don't we all know how an investigation is conducted when it comes to a priest? You take a turkey to the church provost, and that's the end of the investigation! In our case, the provost did not even hold a meeting; he just asked a few questions of the people whom the priest had invited to his home, then he had some tea, enjoyed a tasty dinner, and the case was closed.

Because of that investigation, we once again sent a complaint by telegram from the entire community to the archbishop but, unfortunately for us, the archbishop died and he must have taken the complaint with him to God, because our case grew cold. After all that had happened our priest became vindictively cruel and even in church he instructed people not to follow the "advice of the impious," and he would look directly at me when he said that. It was at that time that he struck up a friendship with Yakushev, the administrator of Prince Levin's estate and became related to him through a marriage between their families. From that time on the two of them supported one another.

And Yakushev, God forbid he should hear me, was an experienced extortionist without a shred of conscience, and the prison had been pining for him for a long time already. It is said that an enemy is a tainted witness, so I'll keep quiet about what I know about him, and instead I'll just recall a few deeds of this gentleman that were described back in 1903 by a correspondent to the *St. Petersburg Gazette.*

From these observations we can find out that on Prince Levin's estate that is administered by Yakushev, workers were fed meat from sick cattle that finally had to be slaughtered, and given meat for cooking that stank so badly and was swarming with so many maggots that even dogs didn't want to eat it.

All of the above is true, because even now we have a butcher who used to be called to the manor every time that an ox was close to collapsing while hard at work, and the lord's drudges would curse him soundly if the beast actually dropped dead before he managed to get there. We complained to the district administrator about that, but are you going to receive any justice when he's a friend of Yakushev?

It's true that there was one time that a new district police officer, accompanied by a doctor, rushed to the manor and dragged up from the cellar 40 *poods of meat that was so spoiled that it was nauseating to even look at it. They poured wagon-grease on it, buried it in the ground, and the district police officer wrote up a report and then . . . he had a tasty dinner at Yakushev's home, and that was the end of that.

In our parts that rotten meat was not soon forgotten, and I have to admit that I tormented Yakushev about it for more than a year. As soon as he would begin to jeer at us, I would immediately remind him about the meat, and that would make him ease up . . . but only after he gritted his teeth. And so it was still possible to live in the village, because back then all sorts of "freedoms" had not yet had time to see the light of day, and people were not sentenced to prison without cause.

But then they brought trouble down upon us by sending a guard to Ivanytske. Lord, how terribly he abused the people and how he stuck like a little puppy to Yakushev, trying to ingratiate himself with the man. He spent the days and the nights in the manor, played the master in the village as if he were an authority of some kind, and arrested people without any reason at all other than to impose his will.

The guard was a wretched fellow, a police hanger-on from Romen, but the ignorant people were not aware of that and at first they did not argue with him. And so this guard, in accordance with the wishes of the lord and the administrator came up with "a political matter" just to defame me.

In actual fact it was a trumped-up denunciation, and because they feared that they would be punished for making it, the lord's associates got Savluchynsky, a minor who worked for Yakushev as a drudge for two *karbovantsi a month, to do it for them.

This precocious spy had been expelled from his first year in a district high school and then from a city school in his third year; his dream was to eventually become a government official, and that's why he eagerly agreed to write the denunciation.

Upon receiving the denunciation, a few gendarmes, a procurator, and an investigating judge rushed into the village, searched my home and raised a scandalous hullaballoo, but that's where the matter ended.

The priest was hissing with anger and he publically shouted at the gendarmes: "Why are you pussyfooting around with this peasant? Lock him up and throw away the key!"

"We don't have the right to do that! Our search didn't turn up anything!"

And so I remained in the village like a cataract on the eyes of the lord and Yakushev, and it's hard to believe how closely they watched me.

Whenever I went to church, the priest would read the riot act while keeping his eyes on me, and they say that for several days afterwards he would continue to spread ill-founded rumours about me.

One time it so happened that my neighbour asked me to be a godfather, and so at the christening I put down 30 *kopiyky on the table for the priest, but I did not give him the bottle of whiskey that he expected, and from that time on, the priest branded me a "*Tolstoyan."

Actually, I still don't know: should I, as an Orthodox Christian, be paying for sacraments with whiskey? I really don't think so, for it isn't fitting for a priest to resell that whiskey as he was often prone to do. But, be that as it may, the upshot of this incident was to finger me as a member of the Tolstoyan movement.

All this happened towards the end of 1905, just before that "freedom" came, but I had no idea how dangerous it would be to be identified with all sorts of "subversive" labels after October 17, and so I continued standing up for my community.

It was at that time that Yakushev placed his daughter as the teacher in our school. Oh my God, how she abused the children and the peasantry, how she railed at them, and beat them until they were bloody, and pulled them by the hair. And, to make matters even worse, she taught very badly.

I couldn't tolerate the situation, and I began saying to others that we were paying to have our children tortured and crippled, and the community was just about to write to the district council with a request to have Yakushev's daughter removed from our school when those "freedoms" came.

The people were buzzing like bees in the spring sunshine as they discussed the manifesto from all angles, and then they finally elected me and *uncle Maksym to go to see the tsar, to thank him for the "freedoms," and, in addition—as the saying goes: if you're giving honey to a Gypsy, give it with a spoon—they instructed us to ask him to give the peasantry equal status with the other classes in society.

And so we set out and ended up staying a month in that Petersburg, but we only managed to meet with Lord Hurko, the man who was rumoured to have prattled a lot of nonsense in the Duma about the peasants and the land.

He treated us shabbily and shouted at us: "What other kinds of freedom do you still need? What kind of 'equal treatment' are you asking for? You, the peasantry, have been rooting around in the soil up to this time, so keep on rooting around in it forever!"

Obviously, Lord Hurko was comparing us to pigs, but it was pointless for us to argue with him, for the matter did not have the sweet smell of honey about it: that was the time when "the conquering of Russia" began.

We came home with nothing, but the powers that be were already waiting for me: they immediately took me away and locked me up in a jail in Romen.

It turns out that while I was in Petersburg, the priest, Yakushev, and the district police officer, in league with the guard, took advantage of the shifting new direction of Russian politics, and once again fabricated some kind of accusation against me. They were supported by several ignorant peasants such as Petro Yaroshenko, Fed Hnatkiw, and Naumenko who would sell Christ to gain favour with the lords, and so I was packed into a jail cell.

I sat in the Romen jail for three months without having any kind of an accusation brought against me, and in the meantime uncle Maksym finally managed to get to see the tsar because he had been elected as a deputy to the Duma from the province of Poltava. That news did not make life any easier for me or the others, because we knew all too well that we would be kept behind bars for a long time, that there was no one to review our cases because the bureaucratic workers, as the saying goes, have no time to either drink or eat for they are kept busy signing documents to send prisoners up north into Siberia, "where there is neither illness, nor sorrow, nor sighing."

And so we went on a hunger strike to draw the attention of the overworked authorities to our plight. We suffered for three days, but finally they "took mercy" upon us and gave us the real verdict (once again without any kind of accusation); as part of it, the Lord Governor exiled me from the province of Poltava for a period of two years, but that was to have been expected.

Sitting on cushioned sofas, travelling in carriages with springs, washing down tasty dinners with expensive wines, was it possible for him to understand that he was utterly destroying a family when he sent its sole worker into exile, especially a worker who had done nothing wrong?

And so now I'm wandering beyond the provincial borders of Poltava without a job and with the "seal of Cain" also known as "a court certificate," and back home I have an old mother, a wife, and four little children—and who is to feed them? Will it be Lord Hurko with his "food rationing committee," and his "land exploitation commissions?"

I place my only hope on amnesty, because even though uncle Maksym asked the Minister about me, the Minster, as we've already seen in the case of the people's fighter A. Shcherbakov, is unable to do anything and his word isn't worth so much as a plugged nickel, because after the police pogrom we were now placed in "a general-governor's yoke."

The minister asks the governor, the governor asks the provincial police officer, the provincial police officer asks either the district administrator, who is a friend of Yakushev, or the district police officer who wants to become Yakushev's son-in-law, the district police officer asks the village policeman whom our village has labelled a torturer, the village policeman consults with the priest at whom even the chickens are laughing in our village, and the reply, going back along the same route, would get to uncle Maksym and the Duma only if the Duma lasted that long.

So would it not be better if the Duma would put the question directly to Fr. Mykola Semenovsky, the priest in Ivanytse and to administrator Yakushev—what do you think?

I listened to the sad story of Mykola Fedorovych Dyachenko, looked at his gloomy, thoughtful face, called to mind the Duma with its "parliamentary" procedures, and could not come up with a response . . .

The Gracious Manifesto
(1906)

Evening was falling. The last sheaves of golden rays emerged from behind the cloud that had spread over the rosy western horizon, and the bright, pellucid azure blue heavens, viewed against the splendour of the wondrous reddish sky, seemed even brighter. Over the large valleys of the Kuban steppe, a land of murmuring, turbid mountain streams, light shadows had already fallen, and full-throated birds were falling silent as they prepared to rest after their daytime cares. Just a few more minutes, and nocturnal darkness would replace the brief southern evening and reign over an earth exhausted from the heat.

It was exactly at that time that my brother and I were returning from a neighbouring village in the same manner that most dejected owners of old motorcycles return from a distant journey—that is, we rode for three *versts, and then measured the remaining six with our feet while dragging our defunct machines behind us. I can't say that such travels really appealed to us and, taking into consideration the fact that the first brilliant stars of the southern country were already beginning to twinkle and we still had quite a distance to go, it is understandable how happy we were to hear behind us the rumbling of the ubiquitous Caucasian cart and a hearty ringing voice: "May the devil take you, you villains! Where the heck do you think you're turning— may your heads be turned right off your necks!"

"A fellow countryman!" my brother cried, and we halted abruptly on a slope and stared with great hope at the steep shiny path that wound behind us like a snake and hid itself somewhere at the bottom of the valley.

A short while later there appeared a pair of bullocks harnessed to a cart that was spread with fragrant steppe grass. In it sat a typical Ukrainian peasant woman wearing a kerchief and a nice new bodice. Next to her sat a tall man with long, distinctive whiskers, and wise, mocking eyes; his straw hat and white shirt were clearly delineated against the grey background of the darkening sky.

"Good health to you, *uncle. Would you give us a lift to Uspenke?"

The man, swishing his whip lightly, stopped next to us.

"But you have your own horses!" he responded in a somewhat bantering tone. "After all, it's more convenient for you to hurry along to the village on motorcycles, isn't it?"

"It would be more convenient if these demoniacal horses were in sound health, but they're restive: inevitably when you're halfway to where you want to go you have to lead them there by their reins."

"Oh, that's really unfortunate! Well, if that's the case, sit down as quickly as you can on my cart, and put your horses on it as well: praise God, the cart is a good one—there will be enough room for all of us!"

We thanked him, settled in the spot that he was pointing at, and then asked him: "Where is God taking you?"

"Huh! Would to God that I didn't have to talk about it! This is the third time that we're making the same trip to get our own money!" The man flung a light coat over his shoulders and settled in more comfortably. "You see, the way the world is now you almost have to take what belongs to you by ripping it out with your claws!"

"Are you engaged in trading?"

"No, not at all! This is the tenth year that we've been in the pottery business."

"Oh, and is there a good profit in that?"

"Well, we'd have no reason to complain, if only we received the money owning to us from the shopkeeper who takes in our pots; but by the time you buy some ordinary lead, some red lead, and this and that—and there goes all your profit!"

"That's really something to go on about!" the woman butted in unexpectedly into the conversation. "We work from morning to night, we never stop, and in ten years we've barely managed to scrape up enough money for a pair of bullocks and a house. If only God would see to it more quickly that we get some land, we'd abandon the potter's trade at once."

"Are you really expecting to get some land?" I asked curiously. "Are you expecting it from the *Duma?"

"Oh, no! The Duma hasn't had time to think about that, and, with the kind of respect that it gets from the lords, most likely it never will! There's a lot of foam there, but very little beer!" the man spoke up. "We have no one at all on whom to pin our hopes!"

"Well, on what is your wife pinning her hopes?"

"On sheer nonsense! The day before yesterday we received, for the tenth time, a document from the authorities, and in it was written: 'Wait!' . . . and so she's waiting."

"Oh, you're always like that, Karpo!" the woman interrupted him. "It's written quite plainly in that document, that not too far from here, in the Caucusus, they'll soon be giving away free land, and so they won't pass us by . . ."

"I've heard about that many a time already: they made my father happy for fifteen years with those kinds of promises, and now it's already the twentieth year that they've been making me happy!"

"But who promised you the land?" I asked the man in astonishment.

"Oh, that was a long time ago! If I try to recall everything in the way that it happened, there won't be time to finish my story."

"Why not? We're still quite far from the village, and otherwise we'll just be dozing for almost a whole hour."

The man thought about it for a moment.

"Our peasant life isn't all that interesting! One day is like another, and one person resembles another. We have the same grief, the same joys: if we have land—we say glory to God! If there is no land—we live in poverty! And as far as who got the worst of it, well, it has to be us, the peasants of Poltava . . ."

A mountain cart was coming towards us and the ungreased wheels loudly spun out their unending monotonous song.

The slim figure of a mountain man emerged out of the grey fog and then vanished somewhere behind us in the darkened steppe.

"Why are you complaining so bitterly about the fate of Ukrainians?" I asked the man; my curiosity was piqued.

"Well, you see, after the freedom that was proclaimed in
*1861, many people in Ukraine were left without any precious
land at all, and so they had to feed themselves by working on
the large estates of the *Muscovite lords. All the former court
people, the *Mykolayivski soldiers, and the greater part of the
'defenders,' did not have their own farms and were forced to
subsist on the kindness of the lords. My father was the son of a
soldier and he subjugated the Hungarians for *Mykola I—maybe
you've heard about that?"

"Yes, I have, I have!"

"And so my father had to trample their fields, destroy their
villages, and orphan their children only God knows why. And as
soon as they had subjugated the Hungarians, our soldiers were
sent to Sevastopol to new tortures, and it's impossible to relate
what horrors they experienced there.

"And it was only towards the end of the war that my father
got lucky: a bullet crushed his leg, and he came home, and
even though he was crippled, at least he came home. And being
crippled wasn't all that bad: instead of walking on two legs, he
walked on three. Within a year my father married a widow, and
before long they had their own little army in their home, one
that was happy and constantly hungry. There was an unending
racket, crying, fighting: 'Daddy, I want to eat!' 'Mommy, give
me some milk!'

"My father didn't worry about that, he just worked, because
he was a good shoemaker, and he couldn't handle all the work
that he was getting. And then came that freedom that took away
almost all the land from the Mykolayivski soldiers. The village
farms immediately shrank, orders in the smaller trades were
drastically reduced, and my father's former profit was no more.
He became very sorrowful and because of his great sorrow he
started going to the tavern. But finally our Merciful Lord looked
down upon us and did not allow us to die a hungry death: in 1868
the Gracious Manifesto came out . . ."

"Which one?" I asked in surprise.

"But haven't you heard anything about the Gracious
Manifesto?" The man pulled his pipe out of his pocket and began
tamping it and packing it with tobacco.

"It's the first that I've heard of it!"

The woman suddenly turned her thoughtful face towards us and said: "Why would you know about that manifesto, when it was for the peasants? Do you have the same worries as we do?" "It's not up to you, wife, to clap your tongue!" the peasant interrupted her. "They have to know everything, because this matter applies to them as well."

He lit his pipe and did not speak for a moment.

"Back then, you see, a war had just taken place in the Caucusus, and the people who had lived in the mountains had resettled by the thousands in Turkey, and so the authorities began asking our peasants to settle there. And the Gracious Manifesto promised to give all the Mykolayivski soldiers parcels of land and to register them as *kozaks if they went to the Caucusus. Permission was also granted to use your own money to buy land in Kuban where it was being sold at ridiculously low prices—from two to three *karbovantsi for a *desyatyna.

"My father was overjoyed—he immediately started selling off some of his belongings and packing the rest of them to take with him to the Kuban steppe. The neighbours all made fun of us, as if we were the most stupid people in the entire village . . . You'd go out in the street—the children would tease us as being little kozak children; my father would head for the tavern—and there he'd inevitably end up quarrelling or fighting because of that manifesto.

"But it was our in-law Tereshko Zuda who tormented him the most. He'd lean on our fence and start badgering him. 'Are you going, in-law?'

"'Yes we're going, we're going!'

"My father would keep on bustling around the yard.

"'Are you packing up your poverty and taking it with you, or are you leaving it here?'

"'Let it stay here with you, in-law! I'm not stingy and I won't regret leaving it behind.'

"'But why would you regret leaving it? The devil knows you have more than enough!'

"'Let me be, I beg you! Why are you bothering me?'

"'I feel sorry for a person, and so I bother him.'

"The in-law would go home for an hour or so, and then he'd come right back again. 'And will you register as a kozak?'

"'Yes, I will!'

"'And you say they're going to give you some land?'

"'Yes, they will, because they've promised to do so.'

"'That's strange. And who promised you that?'

"My father would start to grow angry. 'The tsar promised it, that's who! I served faithfully and honourably for ten years, and that's no joking matter! So now that the Gracious Manifesto has come out, they'll give us something!'

"The in-law would just laugh. 'Open up your pocket a little wider! Let's hope that everything goes according to that manifesto, for once they start setting their sights and taking aim, you'll see that they won't hit the mark that the tsar wanted them to hit. After all, back in sixty-one we all got a manifesto about *free labour and I, a former servant at a court, and a literate one at that, now have to sell my work to householders because I don't have my own land, and when I look at our people, I don't see any free labour.'

"Then my father would ask: 'Well, who is stopping you from going to the Kuban if things are so tight for you here?'

"And the in-law would reply: 'My mind won't let me! If it weren't for my mind I'd wander off just to find out for how much they're selling a scoop of misery now. But my mind tells me that in Kuban and beyond Kuban, and everywhere, it is equally difficult for all people who don't have their own land or who have small plots of land, because all of us have enough greedy masters for whom we have to work—so where am I to try to find free labour there?'

"My father started to think and walked around gloomily like a dark cloud for a few days, and then he up and says to my mother: 'That literate soundbox Tereshko has become very smart! He reads all sorts of books and then he starts singing services for the dead: it's bad for him here, and it's bad for him everywhere, and there's no salvation for him anywhere. That's enough listening to his nonsense, it's time to live according to one's own mind.'

"And he once again started doing his own thing. We sold off everything that we could and departed for Kuban . . . Oh, it was so sad to leave that happy land, the green groves, the fragrant orchards, the quiet, clear streams . . ."

"And where exactly are you from?" I asked the man.

"From Kruty Berih below Poltava—do you perhaps know that place?"

"Why wouldn't I? I lived in Poltava for the past five years."

"Really?" the man rejoiced. "Well, what's it like there now? Is it nice?"

"It's nice, very nice, but very crowded!"

"That's it. O Merciful God! If it weren't for the diabolical crowding I'd go back there at once."

"Sure, that's what you say," the taciturn woman spoke up. "It always seems better there, where we aren't!"

"A lot you know!" the man interrupted her. "You see, she's from these parts," he explained, "so she doesn't care about Poltava."

"Well you said your father fled from there, so it couldn't have been all that good there," the woman couldn't refrain from getting in a dig.

"And have you found anything better here? Oh, sure you have! We're almost reduced to being beggars!"

"Why didn't you register as a kozak?" I asked in an attempt to end the quarrel.

"Oh, the devil take them! We actually travelled all the way to Laba where new kozak divisions were being formed under General Zassa, and for two nights we stood watch with all our belongings in the middle of the steppe, and then we escaped. It seems that all the riff-raff from right across Russia had gathered there: drunkards, robbers, murderers—we were robbed on the first night. My father thought and thought about it and then took off for Dagestan, where unoccupied lands were being sold. But we were too late, because all the land had been already taken.

"Well, we returned to Kuban, and began pestering the authorities with requests: we passed them on to the *otamans, to the ministers, and in the tsar's name—and we received the same reply from all of them: 'Wait!' It was very difficult for us, very hard indeed. Whatever we earned went for food, and so we didn't have enough clothing; if you bought some clothes, you had to go hungry.

"There was nothing that we could do—we had to become hoarders. And this, if you don't know it, is also a form of serfdom. We lived on the lord's land, we worked the land, but we didn't have any profit from our work, because we had to pay the lord annually for everything: for the house—ten karbovantsi; for a horse—three karbovantsi; for a cow—two karbovantsi; for a pig—one-and-a-half karbovantsi; for chickens—fifty *kopiyky; for the land—a third of the harvest, a third of our garden produce, our straw, our chaff, our watermelons—a third of everything that God lets us grow. And then you still had to go to the manor and work off a day for the lord.

"My father grew worried and walked around like an autumn cloud. And then that winter there was some kind of a plague and all my brothers and sisters died—my father's pride and joy. My deceased father often used to say: 'My workers will grow up and they'll feed us even if we don't have any land.' The eldest son was about nineteen and they were getting ready to see him get married, but fate did not let him live long enough to have a wedding. And not too long after the children died we saw my mother off on the long road to God to look for justice there.

"And so just the two of us—my father and I—were left to await for the blessed land that had been promised to us by the Gracious Manifesto. Whenever Sunday or some feast day came along, my father would shuffle off to the village office to see if a document had arrived. But that document never did arrive. And if there ever was one, it always said the same thing; 'Wait!'

"My father waited and waited, and then he grew tired of waiting and he up and died. Eh, I thought, there's no use relying on the Gracious Manifesto! If I can't have any land, I'd better work at some trade. And so I got married and began making pottery with my father-in-law. I've been doing that for ten years now and I'm not complaining about my fate: praise God we have our own house, we have enough to eat, we don't bow before anyone for a crust of bread, and there's no point thinking about the land any more.

"Not long ago everyone was talking about it—about the land that's like a mother to us—when the Duma assembled, and the wife said: 'Maybe they will give us some after all . . .'

"But I recalled the Gracious Manifesto, and I thundered at her: 'Don't jabber nonsense like that! You're getting your hopes up for no reason at all!

"And what do you suppose? I was right: that Duma is long gone, and the land seems to have slipped even farther away from us . . .

"No wonder my late father said as he was dying: 'When a manifesto comes out, my son, trust it, but don't rely on it, because every Gracious Manifesto can be executed very ungraciously. Manifestos alone cannot dry a person's tears, and they can't suddenly change an old way of living and set out on a new path. Throw a stone into some mud, and maybe the mud will splatter a bit, but only a few steps away from it, everything will remain the same as it always was.'

"Yes, that's the way it is! But just look, while we were talking we made it all the way to your Uspenke!" he said as he turned to us and reined in the bullocks where we had to get off.

"Thank you, uncle, for a most enjoyable trip! Have a safe journey!"

"Thank you," he replied. "And I offer you my sincerest wishes: may you always encounter travellers with the simplest of carts if you should ever again wander off somewhere on your motorcycles!"

We laughed and turned to go to our home. The cart and the bullocks quickly disappeared in the darkness of the night, and behind us only the wheels creaked for a few more moments before an enchanting stillness covered everything with its mysterious blanket.

In a Village
(1907)

One warm sunny morning I was approaching Horodyshche, a village I had not seen for more than two years. A shallow, pleasant little ravine overgrown with thick luxuriant grass and fragrant field flowers wound its way through the forest together with a cheerful babbling brook that ran alongside my path. Full-throated birds were warbling in the summery air, calling out to one another in the branches and chirping in the green grass. There was not a cloud in the sky. The playful wind had died down; the rustling leaves had fallen silent. And my thoughts were soaring one after the other . . .

What had transpired during these past few years in our peaceful village, in this cheerful nook? Had it been touched by the waves of uprisings that were now rolling over the entire country, or was it still drowsing as it had formerly drowsed without being aware of the impending disaster?

For many years the peasants had lived as if in a safe haven: they rented some land, ploughed, sowed, paid their taxes, and had no idea that things could be any different. And truly, could it have been any different in this remote spot where the nearest large city was forty *versts away, and where representatives to the *Duma were elected on the basis of their height and the beard that they sported: "so that the tsar can't say that we don't have any proper people here."

The landscape spread before me in its entirety as if it were on the palm of my hand: a large valley surrounded by mountains covered with forests, lush green meadows, a meandering narrow river, small orchards, and a cheerful village nestled among clusters of trees. On the far side of the village the narrow fields of the peasants stretched all the way to the foothills flanked by expansively flung seigniorial leas, seigniorial pastures, and seigniorial forests.

All this land was contracted out to dukes who in turn leased it to the peasants for a tidy sum, but during the past few years the peasants had begun demanding that the manor lady either sell or lease her land directly to the community.

As I approached the boundary I saw a group of herders with village horses, cows, and geese on the seigniorial pasture.

"Is it possible that the peasants have acquired some land?" I wondered as I directed my footsteps to the three men who were sucking on their pipes with gusto as they lay right on the boundary.

"Well, what a surprise!" one of the men shouted. "Hello there! Do you recognize an old comrade?"

"Yes, I do, I do, but I don't recognize the seigniorial land. Why is the entire village grazing its animals on seigniorial land? Has the manor lady taken pity on you?"

"Oh, may she be struck dead! All she does is cause people to fall into sin! That blood-sucking spider of ours, that bug-eyed Odamenko, got frightened and backed away from signing a contract for the land, and so the lady became furious and won't lease us anything. We were offering her 80 *karbovantsi for the pastureland, but she leased it to Shestopal for 70 rather than let us have it . . . So now we're herding the animals on land that doesn't belong to us—after all, we can't let the animals die!"

"What about your own pastureland?"

"Ours has been barren for a long time already. And there's no grass anywhere, that's the problem! No one will lease the seigniorial island to the peasants, and the lady doesn't send anyone here—we simply don't know what else to do! And then there was a rumour that the lady was selling her land. Well, we thought, now we'll perish like the *Swede at Poltava! Someone may buy it and then stop us from renting it to grow our grain. We rushed to the lady to buy it ourselves. We agreed on a price of 240 karbovantsi each and went to her with the deposit. But that old dog Odamenko had been there already, and so the lady said to us: 'Give me all the money and an additional 300 karbovantsi for a *desyatyna!' What a wicked person!

"When our proxies came back and told us everything, we all shouted: 'If that's the case, we'll just mow the grass without paying anything!'

"And so now both the men and the women mow and reap wherever they want to—but what will come of that we really don't know! Rumour has it that the police commissary is threatening to come here with some guards."

"Are you saying that you have guards here as well?"

"No, thank the Lord we don't have any here, but at Prince Shcherbatov's place in Terny as many as 50 men have been hired as guards!"

"And so have things settled down in Terny?"

"Not at all, things are a lot worse now! One time a drunkard was going down the street, and he provoked a guard, and that guard stabbed him in the stomach . . . The people called in the village chief and complained to him, but he didn't even want to listen to them."

"Well then, you should have complained about that guard!"

"That's not something we sinners can do! The way things are happening in the village, you really have to watch your step. A brother will denounce a brother, a father will report on a son, and heaven only knows how many spies there are now! In our village, for example, Petro Tsorulyk and Odamenko act like Judases towards their fellow peasants. As soon as one of them hears something he rushes to inform the village magistrate. And if you dare to say a word to him about it, he says: 'Shut up or I'll denounce you, and then you'll find out where bedbugs are fed!'"

"Well, you shouldn't talk to those henchmen and then everything would be fine!"

"No it wouldn't be! There's no harmony among us: this one does that, and that one does something different. These mow the seigniorial grass, and those run to tell the magistrate! You'll see that soon enough for yourself!"

I bade farewell to the man and walked on.

Before long I came to the huge island—70 desyatyny in size—overgrown with tall lush grass. And, in actual fact, scythes and sickles were flashing here and there, and peasants were carrying off the grass in large sheaves.

On the other side of the island, a meadow abutted the village closely and only a small dam set apart the seigniorial land that encircled it like a snake: there was no way to walk or to ride out—you could barely take a step out of the village, and you were already on someone else's land, and then you were facing an appearance in court and a fine. It was a difficult situation for the peasants and there was nowhere for them to appeal. And so it was no wonder that they listened so attentively to any bit of news that happened to fly into this remote spot.

I had not yet had time to rest up after my journey when the men in the village gathered around me with their persistent questions: "Well, what's the Duma doing? Will we be getting some land?"

* * *

"How can you not be ashamed?" I asked them after a while. "Are you saying that you still don't know anything at all about what's happening in God's world? Can't you subscribe to a decent newspaper of some kind? You could read it and pass it on to others—but the way things are now, it's as if you're living in a dungeon."

"Oh sure, reading will do us a lot of good! Even if we subscribed to a hundred newspapers, no one will believe what's written in them."

"But you'll believe what's in them!"

"What good is that? We studied in school, but others say: all books are the work of the Antichrist! Even the gospel has been held up to ridicule by being rewritten in the peasants' language!"

"What utter ignorance! But where in the world did you get hold of that gospel?"

"The teacher sent us two of them! Everything in them is said so well and it's so easy to understand that you could listen to it forever. But that doesn't sit well with some fools. They shout: we must close the school, because heaven only knows where all this literacy will lead us!"

"Well, the school won't be closed! It won't happen here like it did in Kurmany!" another man interjected.

"In Kurmany?" I exclaimed in astonishment. "In such a large village? How could that have happened?"

"It just happened! The older men demanded it. They said that it was the root of all evil: that it gave rise to the riots, and that we're not getting any land because of it, and that the strikes were caused by it. People were better off when there was no literacy!"

"And there are many people in our village as well who are sharpening their teeth against the school!" a young man with a blond beard added.

"I don't understand!" I interrupted them. "In what way has the school ever harmed you? You haven't had any riots or any strikes. You live peacefully . . . so how is the school to blame?"

"Ask them," the blond man spoke up again. "They say that literacy will not lead to anything good, that life was better without it. But just look at them: they live like sheep, they don't understand anything, and anyone who wants to can lead them around by the nose. Do you remember Ulyana Tsorulykhova?"

"Ulyana? Of course I remember her!" And I called to mind a slovenly, dissolute young woman who was insolent and half-witted.

"Well, she's the one who runs the entire village now!"

I was truly astonished. "What in the world is going on? How did that happen?"

"Here's how! She woke up once with a hangover and began to prattle that the Mother of God had come to her and taught her how to cast spells, and so the people started flocking to her. She spits, whispers some nonsense—and lo and behold, there's a *palyanytsya. She got up one morning and said: 'The Mother of God told me that our woman secretary is a witch!' or 'You don't know who stole Babak's linen cloth, but the Mother of God told me that it was Mykyta!'"

"And do the people believe her?"

"What do you suppose? More than they believe a book! And when she begins to babble about the Duma, we all roar with laughter!"

"If that's the case, why don't you put her to shame?"

"Oh, the devil take her! If you mess with carrion it will only stink worse!"

"I can see that things are in a bad way here. There's neither light nor enlightenment. If only you'd inform yourselves about some matters and then pass that information on to others!"

"You can't expect sinners like us to do that!" a taciturn man from the reserve soldiers spoke up. "We were hoping you'd bring us some good news, but it's obvious that you also haven't seen the light as yet!"

I could sense that the peasants were left feeling dissatisfied when they walked away from me. And they had every reason to feel that way. They had hoped that I would tell them an enjoyable fairytale about the Duma and the land, but instead, they had heard only the truth.

The next day I left for the neighbouring village of Ivanytske to see my relatives. I saw there the same hunger for land, and I heard the same ideas. And a few among them stated sadly: "We have no freedom. If there is no freedom, having land will be of little help!"

But that desire for freedom or the personal longing for mitigation from all sorts of unwritten "liberties" and "constitutions" was voiced very fearfully, as if some terrifying event had occurred in the village.

I soon found out that the people truly were terrified. During the widespread unrest someone had incited them to organize some form of self-defence. The younger men eagerly embraced the idea and began arming themselves—forging spears, and procuring revolvers. But many of those who joined the association were more interested in thievery than in anything else.

It didn't take these fellows long to begin making things hot for everyone. First of all the lord's property was set on fire—seven times!—and the last time the fire gobbled up even the stable and not a single horse was rescued. After that, the association began harassing wealthier peasants: relieving them of their money and breaking into their storage bins.

Before long the association began preying on everyone: wherever there was a storage bin in an isolated spot or wherever there was flour or grain that wasn't under lock and key, that's where the young fellows would get to work. In December they broke into the home of the cantor's wife and made off with 1,000 karbovantsi; 500 karbovantsi were later recovered, but the other 500 vanished without a trace. Shortly afterwards the church was robbed and there was evidence that the robbers belonged to the "self-defence" association.

As time went by, the members of the association grew lazy, began drinking heavily, and treated other people badly. But then one day the police unexpectedly came rushing in along with some *kozaks and the district police officer, and a round of arrests was begun. All this happened when one of the peasants was celebrating a wedding at which the association was enjoying itself wholeheartedly. Everyone was already inebriated when the house was surrounded by kozaks, and the following day many of the guests had to sober up behind bars. They arrested the bridegroom Semen Senko, his best men, Klym, Prokop, and Andriy Senko, along with Khvedot Senko, Mykola Dyachenko, Ilko Svyrydiv, Ivan Kovalenko, Vasyl Hawrysh, and Trokhym Hursky.

The guards looked after the arrested men so well that not long afterwards Vasyl Hawrysh gave up his soul to God. The rest of the detainees were sent to a jail in Romen where they were still waiting to go to trial.

After this happened, things were quiet in the village for a while, but on the eve of the Epiphany there was an unfortunate incident. More than a 150 peasants went out on the seigniorial fields where beets were stored in heaps covered with earth and began to take matters into their own hands. The lord's guards rushed up and began shooting; five of the peasants were wounded and the rest ran off in all directions. The lord gave every guard 15 karbovantsi and dropped the matter for the time being.

And then spies began cropping up in the village and once again there was a big mess: the names of the peasants who stole some beets were revealed along with the names of all those who had burned the lord's hayricks and made threats against him, and more than 150 men were detained in jail. The word was out that it was Khvedot Lykhno and Mykhaylo Zaparynny who were spying, and it did seem likely that this rumour might be true because Zaparynny had grown very lazy, drank heavily, and threatened his enemies, who—without warning—were taken away one after the other!

"That's freedom for you!" the villagers were saying. "We wish to God that we had never seen it. Now you have to be careful even about your walls, because the devil will pull them down to find out if they can speak!"

"Give something to a government official or a police officer, and you'll come out a winner," one man boasted to me. "I've shaken out more than one fiver for them myself! Someone told them that I had given money to buy weapons, and so they came after me: 'Give us something if you want to be left alone, or else we'll write a report and you'll be sent off to a place where you'll be feeding bedbugs!' And so I spat on it all and gave them what they wanted! I'm telling you exactly how it is: there's no point in living in a village now. Our only hope lies with our Duma—our Duma-mother. Well, tell me, how is it doing? Will it be giving us anything at all?"

On the fourth day I left the village feeling deeply grieved by this spiritually broken nook, and on the fifth day a government official was already conducting an investigation there and "instilling loyal thoughts" in the peasants.

To See the Sovereign
(1908)

Three of us were riding in the sleigh: a stout, well-to-do merchant with a ruddy mug resembling a copper pot, a broad, varicoloured nose, and a woollen fur-lined coat with a huge collar; a sallow peasant in a shabby sheepskin coat; and I.

The wind was growing stronger by the minute. It was sweeping up huge heaps of dry, stinging snow, swirling it wrathfully and ferociously around us, flinging it upwards with a savage wailing, and tearing over the expansive steppe in wild pursuit of someone unknown. White butterflies, whirling through the air, were blinding our eyes, blanketing the sleigh, and causing the horses to stray from the road. By now, however, we were very close to the train station and so the blizzard did not concern us in the least.

Only the coachman, old and capricious, was out of sorts and kept muttering angrily under his breath: "What diabolical weather! I simply can't wait to kill my hangover with a drink, but the horses are moving as if they were on their way to a cemetery!"

"Don't get upset, you'll still have time to tie one on," the merchant said as he pulled a large red handkerchief approaching the size of a tablecloth out of his pocket.

"Oh, if only I had the wherewithal to do that," the coachman said as he turned towards us. "But my earnings nowadays have dwindled to nothing. The cost of bread, hay, and all sorts of provisions is constantly going up and up—you can barely afford to buy enough food for yourself and your horses."

"You're right!" the man in the shabby sheepskin coat affirmed. "And there's absolutely no hope left for those of us who aren't from these parts. You have to rent a place to live, feed your family, provide clothing—and where is a fellow to get all that money?"

"Truer words were never spoken, my friend!" the old coachman started in again. "The Christmas holidays are over, but as to when they ended I really can't say. There's not a crumb left in the house, and there's nowhere to borrow any money—so if you don't make a trip to the station, you won't have even a crust of bread."

"That's why you have to rid yourself of a hang-over the next day," the merchant spoke up. "You don't have anything to eat, but there's always enough money to drink."

"It's not like that at all," the old man laughed. "Yesterday I got drunk for the first time in a long time, and I didn't do it on my own money; I was called over to my son-in-law's place for a discussion."

"Well, you can talk all you want to, but don't drop the reins because you might run over someone."

The old man turned back to the horses and began to shout: "He-e-ey, you there! Watch where you're going!"

A figure, caught in the blizzard's blinding snow, turned aside from the road and stopped abruptly in a snowdrift. It didn't seem likely that the grimy old cap and tattered grey military greatcoat with its turned-down collar were doing much to warm the scrawny, sickly person that we caught a glimpse of beside the sleigh.

From under the cap peered a youthful face with large, gentle eyes that seemed thoughtful and a trifle frightened. But his lips smiled like those of a child as he hastily whipped off his cap and began saying hurriedly: "How do you do! How do you do! How do you do!"

"Hello, hello, young fellow," our coachman responded. "You'd better get a move on or you'll miss the train . . ."

I turned around and saw that the traveller bowed a few more times to us before he got back on the road.

"Who is this strange person?" the well-to-do merchant asked. "Is he in his cups, or is he drunk without having had any whiskey—it looks as if he's not all there."

"Huh!" the old coachman responded. "Aren't there a good number of fellows walking around like that now? He grows lazy and feeds on easily earned bread by begging! And he furtively sneaks looks at what other people have to see if there's something

that he can profit from . . . Oh, I have no pity for them! One
*khakhol like that stole a brand new horse-collar from my shed."

We all remained silent for a few moments.

"No, no, don't say things like that!" the shabby sheepskin
coat entered into the conversation. "He's not that kind of a man
at all! He's been living in our village for two weeks now and he
hasn't harmed a soul. He walks around in rags, eats whatever
he's given, gives out coins to the children, and smiles ever so
kindly at everyone—just like that *God's fool that they write
about in books."

"I've seen those God's fools!" the merchant spoke up once
again. "He pretends to be a fool to entertain gullible old women,
and they feed him in return. Never fear, if you provoke him
when you're with him one on one, he'll give you a lot more than
you ever bargained for."

"Well, you didn't get that one right!" the peasant in the
sheepskin coat continued. "He's had all sorts of things happen to
him in our village, but he minds his own business. The forester
brought him in from the forest by the Mykolayiv Road. He said
he went out in the evening to see to his cattle, and that's when he
saw a strange person trudging about under the windows. And so
the forester asked him: 'What do you want?'

"'Who? I?'

"'Yes, you!'

"He just smiled and didn't respond.

"The forester grew frightened. 'Why did you come here, and
where are you going?'

"'To see the sovereign,' he said and he walked on into the
porch.

"The forester cuffed him on the ear, and the fellow sat
down in the snow and began to whimper like a little child. The
forester's wife came out of the house and the children ran out
as well, and they could all see that this man was not in his right
mind. They let him into the house, and in the morning they took
him into the village."

"What does that mean: 'To see the sovereign?'" the merchant
was curious to know.

"God only knows!" the peasant replied. "He's trying to save
his soul, and so he says all sorts of things, and sometimes you

can't figure out what he's saying. We didn't ask him too much because we didn't want to offend him—he's like a little child: at times he just sits and sits, and then he begins to weep."

The horses trotted up to the train station, and I went into the waiting room to warm up.

This station, like all Russian train stations, was much too small, much too cold, and much too drab. As in every such station all the workers—beginning with the stationmaster and his assistants and ending with the lowliest servant—received a paltry salary and had to look for other sources of income.

The stationmaster oversaw the passengers. For his efforts he always received a *karbovanets from the railroad, "as much as possible" from the conductors, and perhaps even something from those who hopped on board the train without a ticket. Together with his assistants, he made a profit on kerosene and hard coal because whenever workers loaded freight cars they never forgot about their superiors.

At the station it was always cold and dark, but in the neighbouring villages the priests, for a trifling outlay of money, had good fuel and inexpensive kerosene.

The servants, however, did not have the same access to such "sinless" income, and that is why they had to resort to various sinful deeds. Sacks of wheat frequently disappeared at the station, and occasionally some merchandise vanished from freight cars, and whenever that happened, a gendarme would gleefully rub his hands as he wrote up a report that unfailingly ended with the same words: "Measures have been taken to investigate the matter."

These words were absolutely true, because it is said that in every instance the gendarme did in fact take his own "measures" along with his share of the profit.

There was only one time that some unexpected turbulence stirred up this quiet corner for several days—but soon afterwards it quickly settled down again. In the vicinity of the station there was an outbreak of robberies and murders; an investigator was sent out, but all the clues had been completely obliterated as the most daring hothead among the servants at the station had taken off for parts unknown, and there was nothing that could be pinned on the ones who remained. After this incident the gendarme was recalled and peace and quiet once again reigned at the station.

When I entered the waiting room, the stationmaster's assistant, a bug-eyed man with a reddish beard and attired in a red beret and a greatcoat with shiny buttons, was just finishing a business deal with the local miller-manufacturer. They were arguing heatedly and barely stopped to say hello to me.

"Well, judge for yourself!" the miller was shouting, and his saliva was flying. "I gave them plenty of spirits to seal a deal with them to ensure that they would give me two freight cars for my flour, but they sold the cars off to Borysenko!"

"Don't talk nonsense!" the offended red beret screamed. "Borysenko ordered two freight cars earlier on, and am I to blame that they just happened to arrive today? Maybe yours will also show up soon!"

"Go and tell that story to your uncle's wife! The day before yesterday when you were enjoying my wine, you said that you'd definitely have the cars for me today, but Borysenko must have come along and stuffed a fiver in your teeth, and so he ended up getting the freight cars."

"You're a real pig!" the assistant flared up. "You just won't believe me that we're expecting your freight cars to come along any minute now . . ."

I don't know what the miller would have said in response, because just then the stationmaster walked into the waiting room and gave an order to start issuing tickets. Seizing the opportunity to continue vociferating his endless complaints, the miller-manufacturer ran up to the stationmaster and stuck to him like a burr on a sheep, while I went into the ticket office to watch the people as they bought their tickets.

The assistant was still in a vile mood, and so the ticket buyers had to listen to volleys of abusive words because there wasn't enough change in the cash register, because the ink bottle had overturned on the table, and because the miller had spoken harshly to him. The coarse grey peasant cloaks and tattered overcoats listened meekly to the assistant's abusive language as, one after the other, they walked up docilely to the open wicket.

Among the ticket buyers I spotted the unknown man whom we had met on the road. Seen from up close, the man appeared to be about twenty-five and he had the typical soldier's face on which the main tenets of the military catechism seemed to be permanently reflected:

"Yes, sir!" and "At your command, sir!"

He had a cleanly shaved chin, neatly trimmed whiskers, and his thick hair was cut closely in a brush cut, but it was his eyes that were his most outstanding feature: when he gazed aimlessly into the distance they were like the sad, mournful eyes of a beaten old nag, but when he raised them to look at us they changed at once to become like the carefree and cheerful eyes of an innocent little child.

He was clutching his cap in his hands, but it was difficult to say whether he was doing this because of a natural or acquired servility, or simply without thinking.

"Where are you heading?" the stationmaster's assistant asked when the stranger leaned into the wicket.

"I?"

"Yes!"

"I'm going . . . far away."

"And where is it that you're going?"

"Who, I?"

"Yes!"

The man laughed: "Where am I going? I am going to Russia."

"And to what place should I issue a ticket?"

"To what place . . . a ticket?"

"Yes! Why do you keep on asking things over and over again?" the assistant was losing his temper.

"A ticket . . . well, let it be to Rostov."

"That will be three rubles and eighty kopiyky."

The man stood and waited with an indifferent look on his face.

"Give me the money, you gaper!"

"Who? I?"

"Yes, you of course!"

"I don't have any money!"

The assistant remained silent for a moment . . .

The unusual traveller was also silent.

But it must be that the noble greatcoat with its shiny buttons perceived something that was rather special in the tattered ignoble greatcoat, because the assistant appeared to soften and he asked more gently: "And whom are you going to see there?"

"Who? I?"

"Yes!"

The man hesitated for a moment . . .

Then his face suddenly lit up with a childish smile and his pale cheeks took on a reddish glow.

"I'm going to see the sovereign!"

"The sovereign?"

"Yes."

The assistant looked long and hard at the pale, sickly face, and then said: "They won't let you see him."

The man just tittered strangely and said confidently: "Yes, they will: there's a certain word that I know!"

"Ah-h-h! Well, that's another matter! But here's how things are, my good man—I can't give you a ticket unless you pay for it: the authorities wouldn't forgive me if I were to do that!"

"He'll pay for it!"

"Who?"

"The sovereign will pay for it!"

The assistant smiled and then calmly began saying again that the man had to pay for the ticket right then and there.

For a moment the traveller's face vanished from the wicket, but the grey military greatcoat did not go away from the ticket booth.

And then the man once again leaned into the open wicket.

"Take a look in your office records: maybe the money has come already."

"From whom?"

"From the sovereign!"

The assistant replied seriously once more: "No, it's not there; I've already looked."

The traveller just stared at him incredulously.

"From where have you come?"

"Who? I?

"Yes, you of course!"

"From Pyatyhorsky."

"And why were you there?"

"Huh?"

"Why were you there?"

"Who? I?"

"Yes!"

"I was being treated!"

The man bent his head and pointed at a spot where there might have been a serious wound.

"And where were you wounded?"

"Who? I?"

"Yes!"

"In *Port Arthur."

"And why did you end up in Pyatyhorsk?"

"My father lived there . . . I'm not from these parts."

"And where is your father now?"

"My father?"

"Yes."

"He went back home . . . to Kharkiv!"

The stationmaster's assistant thought for a moment.

"Listen, my good man, you can get on the train without a ticket and you'll be taken where you want to go."

The man from Port Arthur looked at him silently, as if the assistant wasn't talking to him.

"Get on the train. Go on, get on it! The sovereign has given orders that you be taken there without a ticket. I'm not fooling you."

The man shuffled his feet a few times, glanced once more at the wicket, and walked away.

"There you have it!" the assistant turned to me. "They cripple a man in a war, make him lose his mind, treat him for whatever they can, and then send him, deranged as he is, on his way . . . And you should be aware that more than a dozen of them have come through here from the Pyatyhorsk hospital: this one is off to see the sovereign and that one's heading to see God, but not one of them is going home. For does an unfortunate fellow like that actually have a home to go to?

"Just stop and think how every one of them is going off to see someone, be it even to see the sovereign! Take this cripple: where has he been? Through which villages has he wandered? What has he been eating? And why is he going in exactly the opposite direction from Pyatyhorsk?

"And what about the police? Oh, they know how to catch vagabonds without passports, they know how to detain every dangerous person, but they do not want to have anything to do with these unfortunate madmen who are roaming around train stations as they look for roads that lead 'to the sovereign.'"

"And why do you suppose this chap from Port Arthur is going to see the sovereign?" he added.

"Well, why?"

"You should ask him: it's either to lay a complaint, or to get a reward."

With these words he stepped out of the ticket booth. The people were already going out on the platform because the train was approaching the station. We also made our way closer to the tracks, but the deranged man was nowhere to be seen in the crowd.

As was usually the case, there were many passengers even though not many tickets had been issued, but the station had a special platform for those who hopped on board trains without tickets.

When a train came in, the conductors would stand beside the coaches and begin shouting as loud as they could: "Where do you think you're going? Where's your ticket? You don't have one? Get out of here!"

And then they would quietly add: "Hop on board on the other side. Why are you pushing your way here in front of the authorities?"

And the astonished passenger would board the train from the other side. There were a lot of people there, but no one asked for tickets on that side. There was only a weary conductor who was saying to everyone: "Take your seats quickly, or the train will leave without you!"

Before long the second bell rang, and I was ready to get on board when an unusual scene attracted my attention. The unfortunate man from Port Arthur was trying to board the first coach, but a well-heeled, corpulent conductor was shoving him away while screaming at him at the top of his lungs so that the stationmaster could hear him: "Where do you think you're going? Show me your ticket! You don't have one? Get a ticket before you come here!"

The madman was clutching his cap on his chest and waving his free hand around as if he was pleading with the conductor to let him get on; he was even bowing down low before him.

All the travellers turned their attention to this scene. And this made the conductor even angrier. "I'm telling you, you can't travel without a ticket! Go get a ticket!"

The assistant stationmaster was hurrying to come to the assistance of the unfortunate soldier from Port Arthur, and he was shouting as he ran: "Let him get on, let him board the train!"

But just then the third bell rang, the people began jostling to get on board, and a blaring whistle drowned out everything.

The train started moving.

I was standing on the steps of a coach and staring with inexpressible grief at a spot up ahead where an old grey military greatcoat showed up darkly. The conductor must not have heard the assistant's words and probably thought that he was being reprimanded for letting a passenger get on the train without a ticket, because he was roughly shoving the madman away as the latter tried desperately to grab onto the coach.

A moment later the madman flew a few *arshyns away from the train, while the conductor jumped up on the steps of the coach and rode off.

Curious people from all the coaches were looking out at the platform where a small grey figure was sitting hunched over in great grief.

When our wagon drew up alongside him, I could clearly see how tightly the demented man was clasping his cap to his chest as he stretched out his other hand to us and cried out like a little child as copious tears rolled down his face.

The station had long since been lost to view, but my heart still ached fiercely, and it seemed to me that the wheels of the indifferent train were pounding out the words: "How many, how many are there, these men from Port Arthur?"

The Hunger Strike
(1906)

"This situation, you know, does not fit in with our plans at
all. If times were different—it would not matter in the least!
We would simply spit at it. There would be a few, or even a
few dozen who would drop dead—forgive me for putting it that
way—and our problems would be over. It would be of no great
consequence! But now . . . The government, you see, wants to
borrow money from European banks, and so we have to be very
vigilant. As you can see, I am speaking very frankly with you.
After all, if only one or two dropped dead, it would be possible
to cover up the matter. But there are eighteen of them, and they
are all threatening to commit mass suicide, and your son is the
mainstay in this affair. He has—it must be admitted—some
kind of power within him. It is unfortunate that he did not direct
this power into proper channels: he could have attained great
heights. But now . . . he will only make it to the highest . . . tee-
hee-hee . . ."

He notices that she is deeply upset. "But that's not the point.
I summoned you here to tell you that your son's condition is
very precarious. Very precarious indeed. Our prison doctor
says that your son could die at any moment—perhaps as soon as
today or tomorrow. And that is very awkward for us, because,
as I stated earlier, that could trigger a mass suicide. It is some
kind of a devilish solidarity. I have had this position, God be
praised, for a long time, but I have never before seen such like-
mindedness. Well, sometimes it does happen that the prisoners
want something or other, and so they shout, smash windows,
and, at times, threaten to do even more; but the experienced eye
can see that it is all just idle talk, and certain individuals can be
spotted in that 'mass' movement, and you know ahead of time
what has to be done, and what the result will be. But in this
case—the devil only knows what your son has inspired them to

do. They are all of one mind! If you attack one of them, you will knock all of them down. I am telling you this very frankly."

After a pause he continues: "I feel sorry, so sorry for your son. He is a very talented young man; in fact, I would not hesitate to call him a genius. Do not think that I am saying this just because you are his mother—no, I swear on my honour, that is not the case at all. I am speaking seriously. But now we must tackle the matter at hand. I have been so bold as to approach you, because I know you to be a wise and sensible woman, and I think you can help me. Let me draw your attention to the fact that I am talking to you not as a functionary, but as a person who, like you, has a heart and a soul. I am asking you to wield your influence over your son . . . Use your maternal logic to make it clear to him that what he is doing is utterly insane. I am appealing to you in the name of humanity . . ."

"Excuse me for interrupting. What is the reason for this hunger strike?"

"You see . . . Something unfortunate happened here . . . A female political prisoner who suffered from neurasthenia hanged herself . . . That kind of thing does happen occasionally in the chronology of a prison. And because it happened at a time when I was in charge, the political prisoners are demanding that I be discharged . . . and that's all there is to it."

She, looking straight at him: "And is there any truth in what is being said in the city, that you, supposedly . . . raped that girl, and she hanged herself and left a note for her colleagues?"

He, raising his hands: "O my God, my God! What vileness, what malice! How could you ever consider me capable of such a loathsome deed? After all, I am an intelligent person, I have a wife, children . . . Oh, just think to what lengths human baseness will go!"

"Yes . . . Well, be that as it may. Let us return to the matter at hand. So, you are attempting to use the ploy of exploiting my maternal influence? Well, this tactic has been used before in your 'criminal chronology,' so you have not come up with anything new. And exactly what, according to you, am I to say to my son?"

"What? Well, actually, nothing extraordinary. Just tell him that most of his comrades have begun eating, and that he is torturing himself in vain. By doing so, you will help not only him, but also all the poor youths who are emulating him by staying on a hunger strike.

"You and I are both adults, and we understand that no hunger strikes, no self-motivated actions, no individual acts will accomplish anything or change anything. We are talking about an entire regime here! It is not to be taken lightly, is it? There is a huge governmental apparatus, a colossal machine—and standing in opposition to it there are the lachrymose protests of some youngsters. It goes without saying that the machine will crush them. It will crush them without even taking note of them. But how much grief that will cause fathers and mothers! I am not trying to convince you or to agitate you; I am simply saying what I think. In the historical epoch in which we are living, the protests of your son, or of his comrades, or of hundreds, or even of thousands of analogous youths—will be of no consequence, absolutely none.

"Let us take the present, concrete case as an example. They want my dismissal. And I would leave, I would be happy to leave, because, to tell the truth, I am sick and tired of being viewed by people as an ogre of some kind. But I won't be allowed to leave; they will force me to stay, because I must uphold the prestige of the authorities.

"Let us say, however, that I did leave—what good would that do? There are ten candidates who are more than ready and willing to take my place. In what way will they be any better than I am? They won't be. I even dare say that they will be far worse. Because I have done some reading, I have seen a thing or two, but as for those fellows—well, you yourself know what they are like: ignoramuses, failures.

"Things did not go well for him in the regiment, or he got caught stealing, or something else happened—well, he won't be tried for it, because the honour of the uniform must be maintained. And so he has to leave the regiment. But where is he to go? There is nowhere for him to go except to join the gendarmes. And so that kind of person—a person lacking in intelligence, with a sullied reputation, and bitter about his failure—comes here. And he takes it out on the wretched political prisoners. Is that not the case?

"As you can see, I am speaking frankly to you. And here you have these eighteen young people who have been on a hunger strike for nine days in order to replace a more or less 'palatable' gendarme with another one who is of a lower sort. Is this a reasonable thing to do?"

She was aware that the logic of this clever man was confusing her. She herself had said more than once: "Beware of Greeks bearing gifts." And she knew that you should never listen to anything that was said from "over there." In this instance, however, the game was overly subtle, the net was very diaphanous, and it was imperceptibly entangling her.

She swiftly said her good-byes and left, saying that she would give him her decision the following day.

She thought about it all night. She did not sleep. And she was aware that over there, her son, exhausted by his nine-day hunger strike also was not sleeping . . . There could be no question that she would gladly give her soul to ease his suffering. But how was she to do it? Was she to go and say the things that the clever gendarme had told her to say?

She paced the room agitatedly, not knowing what to do, not knowing what to tell her son the next day. At one moment, it seemed to her that she should go there and strengthen his resolve, that she should be like a *Spartan woman, like the mother of the *Gracchi; and the very next moment she ridiculed herself for being ready to sacrifice her son's life simply for appearance's sake.

It was with an aching head that she began her day, and even though it is said that the morning is always wiser than the evening, even the morning did not help her. She walked around in a distracted daze, unable to decide what she would say. One moment she felt that she should say one thing, and the very next moment it seemed to her that she should say something entirely different.

The time came for her to go. She got dressed and went. And she still did not know what she would say. But as she walked past the display window of a patisserie, she stopped and stood still for a moment, and then she stepped inside and ordered three sandwiches spread thickly with butter. She put in her order mechanically, and when it was given to her, she drew back with a start. All at once it seemed to her that it was the gendarme who was passing the food to her.

She took the sandwiches and rushed out of the shop.

"I'm despicable," she whispered to herself, and she glanced around to see if there happened to be a dog running by so that she could toss the sandwiches to it. Up ahead, a dog did show up, but instead of throwing the sandwiches to it, she tucked them into her muff. A small corner of the paper wrapping protruded from it, and she shoved it farther in.

She arrived at the prison.

The colonel greeted her politely, but not overly familiarly. His eyes rested knowingly on her muff, and his lips twitched sardonically.

He gave an order to take the lady to cell No. 7. In response to the startled look of the superintendent—as long as the prison had been in existence, private citizens had never been taken to the cells—he repeated his order.

They walked down the corridor. There were locked doors on either side of it . . .

A guard greeted them with an amazed look on his face. Then he understood that "this is how things are to be done," and he paced up and down at some distance from the cell with an exaggerated indifference.

Now they were in front of the door.

On it there was a huge lock hanging on an immense latch, as if a hundred elephants were being kept under guard behind that door.

Her heart contracted in pain . . .

With an accustomed gesture, the superintendent unlocked the lock, flung the door open widely, admitted her into the room, and closed the door once again. Then he quietly took up a position near the door and listened.

. . . She had imagined that he would fling himself into her arms with a despairing cry: "Mother!" But he only raised his head from the pillow and, as if she had just been there no more that a half hour ago, said: "Ah, is it you?" And then he let his head fall back on the pillow once again.

In that single moment, she saw a terrifying face, impossibly emaciated. His eyes blazed for a moment like those of an insane person, and then they instantly dimmed.

All the words that she had been prepared to say about the sanctity of the deed, about the great future of their native land, about the debts that we owe to our nation—all that got stuck in her throat and instantly became superfluous. She saw before her a skeleton that was ever so dear to her, and with a heart-stricken wail she fell to her knees beside the bed.

Later they sat side by side, and he did all the talking. He was obviously tense, and his words got muddled, but he did talk. And the sole topic of his conversation was—food. It was in vain that she tried to steer the conversation in another direction, he could talk about nothing else. Not about his father, or his sister, or the latest revolutionary news—or about anything else.

"I sense, mother, that I will collapse very soon . . . I will not be able to endure it any longer . . . and I will become . . . either I will become despicable in the eyes of my comrades, or I will smash my head against this wall . . . I cannot go on, mother . . . My comrades are stronger than I am, because they were raised by parents who were workers, peasants . . . You were the one who raised me, but you did not instil in me the Spartan ability to withstand hunger and thirst. You gave me only shattered nerves—and now I feel that I am about to lose my mind . . .

"And they, they . . . those devils have drained all my strength. Do you know what they do? Every day they place the most excellent fare on my table, tasty roast meat, fresh bread . . . borshch . . . Oh, how wonderful it all smells! Mother, I can't stand it any longer. I gnaw at my fingers, cover my mouth, my nose, but that aroma insinuates itself everywhere, it permeates the entire room; my clothes are saturated with it, my hair, everything. And at night, when I am alone, and no one can see me, when the entire prison is sleeping, both the tormented and their tormentors—my suffering becomes intolerable. Because the food remains here, they do not take it away, they just continually replace it . . . No one can see . . . no one will know . . .

"O mother, mother, if only you knew how wonderful it smells! Yesterday there was a goose stuffed with apples . . . The apples were so nicely roasted . . . the gravy . . . the soft, white bread . . . Oh, I can't, I can't . . . They knew that you would be coming, and so they did not leave any food here today . . . You must come every day . . .

"You know, mother, even the chimneys wail here . . . I swear to God it's true! Oh, how they wail! And dogs howl . . . Even though their howls do not reach us here, I can still hear them. And at times like that I feel an overwhelming need to weep, I feel like weeping bitterly . . ."

And he truly did begin to cry. Tears gushed suddenly from his eyes, and he looked as if he was just a little boy, a very little boy.

Oh, if only he were the way that the gendarme had depicted him: strong, influential, unshakeable, then she could have talked to him about the sanctity of truth and justice on this earth, about the splendour of great deeds, about the glory that would be his among future generations, and other things like that. But here, in this instance—what could be said about truth and justice to this innocuous, defeated being, and, moreover, did that truth and justice truly exist? Some say that there is only social justice; others say that it is an individual matter, or perhaps even less significant. Which one should she talk about here? And was it even necessary to talk about truth and justice! Why not talk about a goose stuffed with apples?

With eyes that were blazing just like his, she leaned in closely to him and whispered: "Listen! Is there any sense to take on so much suffering for such a foolish, insignificant fact like the dismissal of some gendarme? Why, there are already hundreds waiting to take his place, and they might even be worse . . . After all, he is, one could say, an intelligent man, he has done some reading, but as for the majority of his brethren—who are they? Unsuccessful officers, dissolute blokes, completely ignorant men . . . And twenty of them are already waiting for his spot . . .

"And as for you—you're torturing yourself because of that? You know that you have great talents concealed within you, that you can do much for your native land . . . Are you not capable of setting yourself more worthy goals? You're so talented, so intelligent . . . Why would you want to die in this mire without having accomplished anything, when you could be sitting at the very heights . . .

"Listen! No one can see us . . . no one can hear us . . . Look what I brought you . . . Their food, the food brought by the gendarmes will remain untouched, but you will boost your strength, a strength that you need not only for yourself, but also for your comrades."

And, shielding his face with her mantilla, she raised a piece of bread, thickly spread with butter, to his mouth.

And he took of the fruit . . . and ate thereof . . .

At that moment the door opened, and two of his comrades from a neighbouring cell appeared on the threshold . . .

And one of them spat harshly: "Scumbag!"

In a Free Country
(1906)

I found myself quite by chance in a foreign country.

I ended up far away from the usual forms of oppression to which I was accustomed, far away from the indigenous poverty, from all the phenomena, antagonisms, and other things that were intelligible to me. I found myself, as I was informed, "in a free country . . ."

In a free one!

But it is possible that we do not understand the word "freedom." We associate that word with endless other words, and concepts, and hopes, up to and including "personal happiness." But that is just like associating the word "priest" with the concepts of "holy," "sincere," "honest," and so on. And while we have already pulled priests down from their pedestals, freedom still remains enthroned.

But the time has come! The time has come to look with sober eyes at this impostor—the worst of all impostors—that is so ingratiating and delightful at first glance.

It is time that it was understood—not by those who are being deceived, they will realize the truth soon enough, but by those who are doing the deceiving, who are deceiving themselves—it is time that it was understood that the word "freedom" is quite possibly the most naked of words, even though it holds forth the promise of luxurious garments; it is the most famished of words, even though it sets out to feed everyone; it is the most impoverished of words, even though it appears to encompass the entire world.

Let us do away with all romanticism—and let us wrest freedom . . . from freedom! Do not hang jingling baubles on a sacred tree, and do not attire yourselves in the clothing of shamans as you wail like jackals before the idol of freedom. Let us have more realism and understanding! It is not for poets that we are striving to attain freedom, for poets have no need of freedom.

And so I found myself in a "free country . . ."

I went to the post office to mail a letter. Ahead of me stood a soldier of the "free country"—he wanted to send a telegram.

The functionary counted the number of words and then requested payment.

The soldier blushed furiously . . .

A beet-red flush flooded his kind, naïve face. Someone must have told him that soldiers' telegrams were sent free of charge, and he had believed it.

The functionary rudely flung a few insulting words at him.

The soldier grew even more embarrassed. He picked up the telegram with his large, reddened hands and shifted awkwardly from one foot to another.

And I recalled that people flushed just as helplessly in my servile country. Back there, a person, driven to distraction by the circumstances of his life, stands just as despairingly before an official benefactor, all the while kneading his cap in his hands; and the eternal parable about the poor man is illustrated in the same way—the poor man from whom his very last lamb is taken to feed a rich man's guests, the eternal disproportion in taxation, both moral and material.

And just when will you, my poor soldier, finally stop paying taxes? Taxes for eating, and for being alive, and for breathing, and for gazing at the moon at night and at the sun during the day? When will you stop paying taxes with the blood of your sons, as you send them off to die for those who do not have any right at all to lord it over you? When will you stop paying taxes with the bodies of your daughters whom you cherish and lovingly raise only to have a putrid buyer take advantage of their virtuous young flesh?

Alas, O soldier, O soldier! I will not forgive you for flushing. I wanted to see you proud and free, I wanted to admire an expression of human dignity on your face, I wanted to have the right, after returning home, to say to my wretched brethren: "That is how people are supposed to live!"

But you, O soldier, have turned out to be just like the one that I saw back there, at home. Crippled, with a hole in his chest where his heart should have been, he sat in the sun and hoarsely croaked away his final days. And every morning he prayed for the Tsar, and every evening he once again prayed for the Tsar. "Our Father the Tsar has been feeding me for nothing for thirty years already!"

"You old fool!" I wanted to shout at him. "And for how many hundreds of years have you been feeding the Tsar for nothing?"

And so it seems that you, O soldiers, are all alike. A cripple like that one back home will weave a tale that there exists some kind of divine order, that there is something higher than a human being, and you believe that, and are afraid to kick down the prison that has been erected.

Do not be afraid! Topple it boldly! It is you yourselves who have built it. And if you learn how to scatter all those delusions, you will see that the bricks of that prison are the bones of your brothers, the cement is comprised of their blood and their sweat, and the uppermost embellishments on it resemble the trophies that savage leaders hang around their necks, trophies made out of the teeth and the skulls of their conquered enemies.

So unite more quickly, O you proletarians of all countries! And so that you are able to unite, first of all create a country, your own country. It is not the proletarian who does not have a country—it is the bourgeois. To a bourgeois it is all the same where he trades or in what language he signs a promissory note, and his international coat is sold for the same price both in London and in Brussels. But the proletarian has no time to learn European languages; his only wish is to learn his own language well enough so that he can bring the light of knowledge into his home.

Create your own country, so that eventually the proletarians of all countries can unite. Win over adherents and people of like minds, for there are more of them than it might seem at first glance. All those who are pitied, who are given work, who are benevolently given a place to spend the night, who are graciously given something to eat. All who have lived for at least a day on such benevolence, all who have eaten at least a crust of bread that was graciously given to them, all who have crossed another's threshold while begging—all of these are yours. Just learn how to find the way to their hearts, learn how to make the strings of their being resonate; do not revile them with disdainful words, do not stand apart like members of a sect—and your ranks will grow in numbers.

Your new allies will bring you the gift of their insulted diginity, their flaming cheeks, along with their words of gratitude. And they will bring the bitterness of the times when they were unemployed, and the coldness of strangers, and the heights that could not be scaled. They will add new notes to your songs, they will join their hands with yours—and it is then that the long-anticipated day will fly down more swiftly to the earth!

The Three
(A Sketch Based on Life in *Halychyna)
(1908)

Three youths were sitting in a coffee house in Lviv. Their faces were pale—it was clear that they did not find life easy in these times. Their heads were tilted in the same direction—they were listening as one of them read. And they were so intent on what was being read that they forgot where they were; they forgot that they were surrounded by hundreds of people, and that the waiters were watching all the guests to ensure that no one ran off without paying; they forgot that this was a public place, and that revealing your soul in it was as improper as sticking out your tongue . . .

They listened as a nervous, slightly hushed voice read:

There is a new station on our nation's torturous path to its historic Golgotha, a new bloody sacrifice has been placed by our peasantry on the altar of freedom. Beastly in their anger, the Pharisees are ceaselessly shouting: "Crucify him! Crucify him!" And all sorts of Pontius Pilates are washing their hands of the innocently spilled blood.

The more news that becomes available about the Koropets murder, the clearer it becomes as to what was done in the village of Koropets "in the name of the law"—the more one's blood freezes in one's veins, and it is impossible to explain how something like this could have happened in a constitutional country in Central Europe, and even more so, under a government based on a national parliament that is elected through a general vote!

The village of Koropets lies in a district where, after long years of feudal servitude, the peasants finally began to fully appreciate their rights as citizens and to recognize the political oppression and economic exploitation they had endured. From distant times, the people in Koropets have engaged in industry and trade, while at the same time becoming renowned for their love of freedom, and their discipline in organizational life. In the village there is a *Prosvita reading room where almost the entire community gathers with the exception of the insignificant pro-*Muscovite faction that is grouped around the reading room of the Kachkovsky Society. In addition, our people have a savings bank and a store, and also an Agricultural Union that is very well organized.

All the elements that are hostile to our nation have grouped themselves around the local lord, Count Stanislav-Henrik Baden, who is running against us in the elections to the regional parliament. Foremost in his campaign were manor personnel who worked ceaselessly to organize all kinds of patriotic manifestations to make fervent Poles out of those Ukrainians of the Latin rite who did not know how to speak Polish. Working alongside them were Polish priests and all manner of Poles—male and female teachers, the district doctor. The police precinct also fulfilled its mandate. And as a result a Polish public reading room came into existence and even a small bank was founded to undermine our institutions. It was inevitable, of course, that additional support was also garnered from the camps of so-called khruny, betrayers of their own nation; among them, for example, was the current reeve, Mykhaylo Melnychuk, who placed himself at the service of the manor.

Poland grew and strengthened, and there were growing numbers of provocations and all sorts of abuses perpetrated against our people; but at the same time, our peasants were also becoming more organized. The leader of the community in its fight with the local Polish powers was Marko, the son of Vasyl Kahanets. It was not because of his wealth that he rose to this position in the community—for he had only a cottage, a quarter of a *morg of land for a garden, and two morgs of fields—but because of his intellect and his love for his people. He had led the community for several years; everyone respected and obeyed him, while he, in turn, defended and instructed the citizens every step of the way with an incomparable self-sacrifice that, in the final analysis, sealed his death . . .

Preparations were being made for the elections to the regional parliament. The manor and the riding in which the local lord, Count Baden, was the candidate, made every effort to thwart the Ukrainian national cause, and the first step was to falsify the electoral lists so blatantly, that the peasants, under the leadership of Marko Kahanets, filed no fewer than seventy-five complaints. At a meeting, the community council decided to set up a committee comprised of five of its members to look into the complaints.

The secretary was not present at the meeting, and so the reeve stated that the resolution would be recorded at a later date in the official record book. The next day, however, a rumour swept through the village that the reeve did not want to have the resolution recorded in the minutes, and that meant that the entire matter of the resolution would come to nothing: the manor's faithful adherents, who did not even have the right to vote, would elect the representative, while honest people and householders with legal status would be denied that right.

Marko Kahanets went to see the reeve, and the latter confirmed the rumour, basing his argument on the fact that the resolution supposedly was within the jurisdiction of the county head. It was in vain that Marko tried to convince the reeve otherwise by showing him the relevant paragraphs in *A Compendium of Administrative Laws*; the reeve, aware that he had the backing of the manor on this point, stubbornly stood his ground. It was decided that a telegram should be sent to the county office with a prepaid response—and that was done. But the county office did not reply on the same day, and so

Marko decided to drop the matter of the complaints until the following day.

The next day, Marko walked out of his house and, after meeting up with a neighbour, they decided to go to the community office to find out what was happening with the complaints. Marko's wife, aware of the manor people's hostility and police threats, had not wanted him to leave the house. Marko had tried to convince his wife that he had nothing to fear because he had done nothing wrong, and that was why he intended to go; but his wife, instinctively feeling that something was not right, went with her husband. Along the way they met Marko's sister Yustyna and a few other villagers who were also curious about the response from the county office. And so, in all, about eight to ten people set out, but they were walking separately, and not in a single group.

A wide stream called the Koropchyk flows at the end of the square. It is spanned by a long, wide bridge, and just beyond it stands the chapel of St. Jan, and the village office behind the chapel is reached by turning left from the main bridge onto a smaller bridge that conceals the street below it. A barrier divides this smaller bridge into two halves; the half that is closer to the large bridge leads to the public square, while the other half leads directly to the office by way of a narrow path enclosed by a balustrade.

And so, when the people were approaching the smaller bridge that led to the office, two policemen came out and swiftly approached the group.

The senior officer halted three steps away from them, and addressed Marko and his neighbour: "I am arresting you in the name of the law. Please step into the council building."

The arrested men did not protest, and the policemen began leading them away.

Marko's brother Ivan was also among those gathered there, and he shouted: "My friends! Let's go with them!" And everyone started moving in the direction of the building.

Outside the building, more men and women who were curious about the charges had already gathered. When the policemen reached this group, they abandoned the arrested men, pushed their way past the people and made their way to the office door.

Turning to face the crowd, they took up positions by the door, and a third policeman walked out of the office and issued an order: "In the name of the law, I ask you to disperse, or I will begin to shoot."

To avoid a confrontation with the police, the peasants turned around and began to make their way back to the road. The police followed them. Marko was in the middle of the group and his wife, his brother Ivan, and his sister were with him. The people were walking calmly, but they obviously could not disperse until they got past the narrow path with the balustrade that led to the road, and then from the road—over the large bridge and back into the village . . .

Suddenly, one policeman rushed into the midst of the crowd, and, for no reason at all, struck Marko on the head with the butt of his rifle.

Marko shouted: "Help! Help me!"

His wife and sister grabbed hold of him so that he would not fall.

The policeman waited until the other two policemen reached him after forcing their way through the crowd, and then the three of them jumped over the balustrade on the little path and, running ahead of the people, once again shouted at them to disperse.

"Where are we to go, if you're standing in the way?" the villagers asked. "Why have you blocked our path?"

But the policemen just stood in a row and pointed their bayonets at them. "In the name of the law, we ask you to disperse or we will begin shooting."

At that moment the situation looked like this. Marko was among those who were in the lead; his sister, who was holding his hand, was ahead of him, his wife was clasping his neck on the right hand side, and his brother was gripping his right shoulder. Upon hearing the shout from the policemen, the people up front, including Marko, halted, but those behind them had not heard anything, and so they continued pressing forward—and then something terrible happened. As they let the other people go past them, all three policemen simultaneously attacked Marko, and only Marko. One stabbed him with his bayonet on the right side of his chest, right between the hands of his wife and sister . . .

"My friends . . . the blood is gushing out of me . . ." the unfortunate victim groaned, and just then the senior policeman stuck his bayonet into Marko's stomach, once, twice, and a third time . . . Marko took two steps, and dropped dead . . .

The policemen wiped the blood from their bayonets with handkerchiefs . . . Nothing else happened, no one else was assaulted, no one was arrested—the policemen had killed their enemy and that was it. And all because Marko had taken part in many political processes in which he always won out over the policemen, because Marko had stood up for the community.

Then two of the policemen went away and only the senior one remained (it was a very dangerous situation for the police); he wanted to shoot another enlightened Ukrainian—Mykyta Vasylok, but a group of Jews surrounded him to protect him. And when the dead man's brother and a couple of other men wanted to carry Marko's body to his house, the policeman forbade them to do so—and the body lay on the road. The policeman stripped the coat off the dead man, undid his shirt, tore off a piece of it near the collar, took a bandage out of his bag, and staunched one of the wounds on the corpse.

The local priest ran out of his house and prayed over the dead man. Some of the people fell to their knees, others raised their arms to the heavens as they prayed, and all of them were weeping; but the policeman did not show any respect even at this moment, and he shouted: "In the name of the law, please disperse!"

And the body of the national martyr lay out on the road for about four hours.

Three days later the funeral was held. Almost six thousand local people and strangers gathered to pay their final respects to the fighter for national freedom.

* * *

They continued reading.

On a simple sleigh there was a platform covered with dark rugs, adorned with pine and little crosses. The coffin was swathed with coverlets; at its midpoint there was a wreath of flowers, and at the head—a martyr's wreath of thorns. Four horses adorned with ribbons pulled the sleigh, and youths, dressed alike in white caps and wool coats, and draped with national banners, rode on the horses.

A peasant honour guard, attired in neat wool coats and fur caps, accompanied its leader on his final journey. At the four corners of this solemn procession, men carried national flags, and three peasants draped in national banners flanked both sides. A peasant carrying a cross headed the honour guard, and five priests walked behind it.

In the first row behind the coffin walked the deceased man's brother, his widow, and his sister-mourner who had thrust her chest out towards the bayonets, and they were followed by an immense throng comprised of representatives from hundreds of neighbouring villages.

And when the procession neared the spot where the murder occurred, a great weeping and wailing shook the people like a storm: "Here, it was right here that he was slain!"

At this point the reading abruptly ended, as if someone had cut a thread.

The three fell silent. The mindlessness of the crime, and the harshness of the conditions of life that could result in such misfortunes, oppressed all of them alike.

The youthful heads were bowed . . . Should they shout? Should they cry?

And all the while the coffee house hummed with its own odious, humdrum noise; the smoke from cigars and from cigarettes hung heavily like a grey cloud, and all the voices seemed to be mired in it, unable to reach the ceiling. Somewhere in a corner, an invisible orchestra, engulfed by the smoke, played sadly, and a shattered, ruined tenor wailed a tender romantic song.

The three remained silent . . .

And then there was a heavy sigh, and the voice that had been reading, whispered: "O Lord! Whose curse has bound us to this nation from time immemorial?"

Facing the Door
(1908)

The viceroy's door.

The bailiff has already passed through it to inform him of the next name, and then he will open it again.

And in these few moments—there are a thousand, a million emotions.

To begin with, he did not know what to do with his hands. And yet, never before had he found himself lacking in dexterity. His heart was pounding so loudly that he was sure that everyone could hear it. Indeed, it seemed to him that everyone was staring at him, and that they could even see what he had in his pocket. Another moment—and they would all be shouting: "Sound the alarm! Grab him, hold him, hang on to him!"

And despite himself, the blood drained from his face, and all his muscles tensed, ready to do battle, to fight back, maybe to lacerate them with his teeth, or maybe . . . after meekly bowing his head, to give himself up without protest—it was a lost cause in any event.

But at the same moment that he was thinking these thoughts, he was trying to convince himself that, in actual fact, no one was paying the slightest attention to him. He was just a young man who probably had come with a personal request, or who had been sent on someone else's behalf. And if he looked a bit pale and appeared to be slightly nervous, that was quite understandable: such important officials are not approached on a daily basis.

No, no one could see the storm raging within him, the frenzied pressure of his thoughts, the irrational tension of all his nerves, of his entire organism. No one could know that every moment a thousand thoughts were careening through his brain, and that it seemed this furious kaleidoscope would be endless;

one moment his chest felt as if it were constricted into a single insignificant cell in which even the small chunk of flesh that was his heart felt cramped; and in the next moment it expanded so greatly that the whole world could fit into it—and there would still be room left over.

I am bearing an illegal intention on behalf of my nation, and that is why I am trembling so intensely. All of my ancestors were law-abiding to the very depths of their souls, they licked the lord's boots that kicked their faces and smashed them into a bloody pulp. At times when a knife should have been plunged into a chest, the most daring among them gathered petitions. And thus we were the *Orpheuses among wild beasts, but we did not have a charmed lyre.

An unlawful idea conceived by a new generation has been entrusted wholly to me. My people have commanded me to go covertly to commit a bloody deed—but the servile opportunism of generations weighs heavily upon me. And this is what weakens me, makes my hands shake, divests my movements of confidence, and drains the colour from my face.

The situation is different in other nations . . . There, the forbidden thought has always lived alongside the permitted thought, and there have always been fighters who came forward to do what I am doing now. But in our case there is no one who has gone before me.

I am the first to approach that door with a pistol in my hand.

As I stepped into a streetcar with Miss Olya, some boor ahead of us took the last seat.

"My God!" Miss Olya said to me. "You're so useless!"

I'm useless—because I wasn't able to grab the last available seat on a streetcar. But what if she had known that at that time I already had "his" portrait, and that I had spent entire days and nights looking at it; that during the day I went out into the fields to learn how to shoot a *Browning, and that at night horrible nightmares suffocated me, and when I awoke I bit my hand to stop myself from crying out loudly and awakening the entire household . . .

*O gentle world, O land so dear,
O my beloved Ukraine!
Why are you so sorely plundered?
Why are you perishing, Mother?

That's what I wrote on a blotter in the library. Even now the blotter is lying there on a table. Perhaps some fervent Pole will read it—but he won't know that it was I who wrote it.

I! There's already something special in that word. Yesterday it was only a student's microscopic I, but today it has matured significantly because I now have a pistol in my pocket . . . A small object, to be sure, but it makes me feel as if I'm discovering a great new law of nature, as if I'm getting to know one of its most treasured secrets. Probably everyone who is the first to take on a deed like this feels the same way.

And in this instance—I am the first!

A sturdy door blocks the road to my nation's happiness. Armed people are always standing by that door, guarding it. I kill the leader of those people, the cowardly guards flee in all directions, and I kick open the iron portal and shout: *"We will light a fire and set every soul aflame. . . so that on the renewed earth there will be no executioner and no enemy, so that human beings will inhabit the earth!"

Oh what naïve thoughts! For both the history and the civilization of a nation have their own ironclad laws and is it possible that you, a young man, can overturn them? You won't overturn anything except your own life, and the life of your family, the lives of those who are nearest and dearest to you . . .

What am I doing? Into what kind of an abyss am I thrusting myself, my dear mother, my sisters? And will life become easier for anyone because of this? No, not for anyone, not in any way. I'll only be placing an incalculably dreadful burden on my dear mother, on her frail shoulders.

O my dear mother! A while back, we were talking about exploits, about great deeds, and because I was already nursing my idea within me, I asked you what you would say if your son went to his Golgotha—and you replied: "I would be proud of him!"

Those were noble words—but how bitterly you will weep because of them!

And O my sisters . . . my dear beloved sisters . . . Will I not be depriving you of your mundane human happiness? Will I not be standing in your way like a silent apparition, like a high threshold, like a dark curtain that has curtained off your peace of mind?

Oh! It's the bailiff . . .

He's coming . . .

The bailiff is coming . . . the door is opening . . .

I hear my name—I'm being called . . .

I'm going!

Mother—farewell!

It Had To Be Thus
(1908)

He will come today!

Oh, why does he keep coming? It would be better if he did not!

But I have to admit that he brings with himself a great and unusual idea.

Everything that has transpired passes before my eyes. As if it had happened just yesterday . . .

Warsaw . . . A conspiratorial meeting . . . Comrade M., "a technician," is preparing a bomb. He says that it will be "like a candy."

"But, my precious young lady, you must keep foremost in mind three things: vigilance, vigilance, and more vigilance. If you remember this, all will be well."

And on that day . . . My heart feels so cold, empty, and expansive, ever so expansive . . . The whole world could fit in it—but there is no room there for tyrants.

I am standing . . . Near my breast there is the coldness of the metal projectile, and in my thoughts—a prayer . . .

"O my native land! Our insurgents placed their noble hearts on the altar of your freedom. With their shackled legs they traced bloody roads throughout Siberia, the Orenburg Steppe, and the shores of the distant Northern Sea. They raised monuments to themselves that were not made by human hands; they created for you, O my native land, the glory of an eternal revolutionary, of a pioneer of free thought, of a person ready to die for you.

Oh, yes, yes! Those who are ready to die for you have not become extinct, and as long as you are bound in chains, as long as you are trampled by a conqueror, as long as you are a slave in your own land, the insurgent spirit will not die away. We will always rise up! In masses, and individually! We will fight for freedom! For our own free native land!"

And these thoughts emboldened me, made me feel warmer, and the cold metal of the bomb nestled even more closely on my breast. It was a joyful feeling to be going to one's death—as long as it was a life for a life.

"We will embrace, O tyrant! I will kiss you with the kiss of death, I will entangle you like a *Medusa, and we will tumble together deep into the abyss. And the news will be carried from the royal capital to all corners of the earth: 'The tyrant has died!'"

And with this shout: "The tyrant has died," I threw the bomb.

But the tyrant did not die.

The girl's hand was shaky, and the tyrant remained alive, and she also remained alive.

She was ashamed to face her comrades when they were spiriting her across the border.

"I'm fleeing without having accomplished anything . . . I'm so ashamed . . ."

Her comrades comforted her, saying that something like that could have happened to anyone, that she had demonstrated her bravery . . . and so on, and so forth . . .

Krakow at last! Only an hour or two by train from Warsaw—but it is as if you are entering another world. Here, her native language is spoken everywhere; no one hauls you off to the police station for saying a word in your native tongue; no one persecutes you just because you are a Pole.

With tears in her eyes she listens to the lilting Krakow accent.

"Pol kurnik-a-a-a," a little boy unaffectedly warbles a child's song as he plays.

The Mariacki tower . . . Sukiennice . . . Wawel, the eternal Wawel—all this is so dear to one's heart, bound up with every nerve, sprinkled into one's very soul.

O Poland, Poland! When will your entire land be free?

But the living tyrant wanted to demonstrate that he was still living. He stretched his fingers across the border and groped with them, like an octopus. The Russian government was demanding that she be handed over.

278 | Hnat Khotkevych

But that effort could be laughingly dismissed. It turns out that those who are all-powerful over there, where you are, O tyrant, have no power at all beyond the narrow strip that is called a border.

For official reasons, "for the sake of national decorum," a trial was held. But it was more like a judicial farce. Or it would be better to call it—a poster. They flung it out into public view only to write on it in bold letters, yet one more time, a curse directed at the autocratic regime, to shout once again to the whole world: "Death to tyrants!"

And the trial was turned into a triumph. They feted the girl who was guilty of the assassination attempt as a national heroine, greeted her with applause, flocked to meet her, escorted her everywhere, and threw flowers at her feet. And when the eloquent lawyer compellingly cried out: "Whosoever rises up against the enemy of his people—that person is not a murderer, but a hero!" the courtroom shook with applause, and the court unanimously pronounced a verdict of acquittal.

She was borne away on the shoulders of the crowd. She was smiling, but she did not feel happy. Her heart was filled with anguish: "All of this is undeserved, but I must accept it . . . And after all, it is a sign of freedom from tyrants, an indicator that there is still a place where the Polish language can resound freely and where tyrants do not hold sway . . ."

And not long after this, in *Lviv, a city that was far away and unfamiliar to her, a shot rang out—a young student killed a Polish tyrant.

She had not yet had time to think through this incident, but everyone around her was already buzzing unanimously.

"What? The Ukrainians? Those who are obligated to us in every possible way? Those who under *Russian occupation do not have even one-hundredth of the freedoms that we have given them? Oh, it's the *haydamaka blood in their veins— they cannot exist without their consecrated weapons. Butchers and murderers from time immemorial. And that young *Gonta should be punished in the same way as the old one was. The gallows are not punishment enough for him."

These comments and others similar to them resounded at all the crossroads, in all the coffee houses, in theatres, and at public and private gatherings.

But as for her, she could not make up her mind about the matter, and so, uncertain as to how to react, she did not react at all. On the one hand, she did not want to think that Poland—the Poland that was so dear to her heart, the holy and great martyr Poland—could give birth to tyrants, that from one and the same root could grow both insurgents and Polish *Skalons. But on the other hand . . . it was all too glaringly disturbing to read, in the same newspaper, about the weeping in Poznan and the royal kingdom, and then, right next to it, tirades saturated with a deep hatred for Ukrainians, demands for the gallows for that youth, that terrorist.

And that was when he came. Who he is—she still does not know. Most probably, he is a Ukrainian, but maybe . . . maybe he is a Pole after all . . . She only knows that he has turned her soul inside out.

It was late in the evening when he had come to see her the first time. She was surprised, and even slightly frightened.

"What is it that you want, sir?"

He sat down without responding. His eyes were fixed on her face. But she quickly recovered her self-assurance and looked straight at him.

"My conscience is clear, and I can look everyone directly in the face," her eyes seemed to say.

But after some time, she felt that something was taking hold of her, gaining control of her. She felt like lowering her eyes before his searing, steely gaze and it was with great difficulty that she stayed the course.

"Did you, my young lady, read the paper?"

"Yes, I did."

"And did you, my young lady, read about the trial of the young student who shot to death the tyrant in Lviv? And did you, my young lady, read how the people shouted: 'Hang him! Hang him! His blood is on us and on our children!' And did you, my young lady, read how they smashed the windows of the Ukrainians to uphold Poland's honour, threw ink bottles at the windows of a Ukrainian bookstore, incarcerated people for praising his deed, and confiscated newspapers for citing passages from *Mickiewicz? Did you read that? Well, did you? Did you? And did you, my young lady, read that the newspaper in which your deed was compared to his was confiscated?"

"I read all that, but . . ."

"And did your face not flush in shame? And did you not feel like shouting? And did the spirit of protest not move you to act? How is it that back there, in Warsaw, you were capable of perceiving the tyranny of tyrants, but here—you are not? Does the border smooth things over? How is it that you were capable of standing up for the oppressed when you were there, but now that you are here, you calmly read newspaper articles about the ignominy, the greatest shame perpetrated by your own native land—and remain silent?"

"What am I to do?"

"Protest!" he shouted furiously.

"Against what? There is no tyranny here. There is freedom here . . . a constitution . . . Surely you heard, sir, what was said at my trial?"

"Rea-ea-lly? There are no tyrants here? Only Russians and Germans can be tyrants? A Pole, even if he is a tyrant, can't be called that? So then, what should he be called? *'Stańczyk'? *'Narodowy democrat'? Or how does it suit my young lady to call him? No! A tyrant must be called a tyrant, and tyranny must be called tyranny throughout the world and throughout all ages. The essence of the concept is the same for all nations and for all eras. And a tyrant is a tyrant, be he a Russian, or a German, or a Pole. Do not be a hypocrite!"

"But a Pole cannot be a tyrant!"

"He can't be? You're saying that he can't be? That's perfect! Poland is a *Matka Boska, a Madonna forever radiant, grieving, in a wreath of thorns, with tears in her eyes! But come up to her from behind, and you will see how your Madonna keeps the Ukrainian peasants under control with whips, and how she winks encouragingly at the Austrian police to run up more swiftly with their bayonets. Look at the hands of your Madonna, and you will see that they are covered with blood. Look under her feet, and you will be seized with terror, because those holy feet are trampling corpses.

"In order to attain a Polish mandate from the Austrian parliament, Ukrainian peasants are slaughtered in the villages; in order to maintain the power of the nobility, the entire country is being sacrificed economically to a foreign tribe; in order to strengthen the landed gentry, they are forcing landless Ukrainian peasants from their native land that is soaked with their blood, and replacing them with Poles that they are bringing in from Podhale.

"Oh, none of this is tyranny! And those who are doing this are not tyrants. It is Skalon who is a tyrant! But it was the enemy, a conqueror, an autocratic tyrant of millions that installed Skalon in Warsaw against the will of the people; and our tyrant, the Polish viceroy, sat on the throne on behalf of the party, in a constitutional country. The administrative apparatus used Skalon to their advantage, and the viceroy of Halychyna himself took advantage of the Austrian administrational apparatus.

"It was not the government that forced a political straw man on us, it was the party that put forward his candidacy—that is, it was you and I, and we are all to blame for what happened. Because governments maintain their power by cannons, whereas parties are kept alive by the lifeblood of the people. To take away the power of a government, it is necessary to have a revolution, but to take away the power of a party it is only necessary to stop giving the organization the lifeblood that it requires to stay alive. And if we have a party that creates tyrants, that means that we ourselves are no different, for we permit such things to happen!"

He rose to his feet and waved his arms about, and his cape undulated like the widespread wings of a gigantic bird.

"Skalon . . . Skalon set out against his enemies, but we are setting out against a brotherly nation with whom we have lived on the same land for 800 years. Is this not the worst of all tyrannies? Oh, it is a disgrace, an everlasting disgrace!"

He covered his face in a gesture of inexpressible grief.

"No! We must cleanse our name! So that it truly will be spotless. So that our *Matka Polska will not be a lying, theatrical Madonna, but a veritable one. It is only then that we will remove her wreath of thorns. When she shatters the chains that she has placed on others, the chains that bind her will fall away as well. When she stops inciting the police to go after those who are weaker, she herself will not be gobbled up by those who are stronger. If she grants others freedom, she will gain it for herself."

And all of what he said was like nothing that she had ever heard anyone ever say before. It was something terrifying. She had not been as terrified when she had gone to her attack position and stood there with a bomb as she was now, standing face to face with this person who had such great love . . .

Everything that is great—is terrifying. A great sea, and great mountains, and great hatred, and great love.

After he left, she collapsed on her bed and lay there like a stone. And when she got up—her comrades found it hard to recognize her.

"What has happened to you? Are you ill? Do you long to be in prison? Do you regret that Skalon is not in the kingdom of shadows?"

She did not respond, because a furious thought stirred in her heart: "You're—tyrants! We're—tyrants! The Russians are fighting for the freedom of everyone, but as for us—we're only fighting for our own freedom. And wherever we get it, we ourselves become tyrants. "

These thoughts were terrible, and they seared her worse than blazing flames.

A few days later, the stranger came again. And she had known that he would come. She silently opened the door, and he walked in without speaking and sat down.

They sat there . . . On the Mariacki tower the hourly bugle-call resounded mournfully, and a hundred years were exhaled in those sounds, and they echoed and sank into eternity.

"We remained true to ourselves," he started speaking in a sepulchral voice. "We stood our ground to the end, and . . . we sentenced that student to death on the gallows . . . I thought . . . I kept hoping that the good genius of my people would awaken, would say its word of goodness and of justice . . . but there you have it . . ."

Suddenly he leapt to his feet.

"You! You—you Polish heroine! Why aren't you protesting against your laurels? Why don't you fling your freedom in the face of those who gave it to you at the cost of the gallows for your brother? Why don't you go into the public square and shout: 'Hey, fellow countrymen! How can it be that for one and the same deed you place one person on a pedestal, and drag another one off to the gallows? If that's the case, do you have two logics, two truths, two faces? Show me then: what is your justice like, what is your true face like? Or are both of them, perhaps, mendacious?'"

She was trembling uncontrollably. And he, like an implacable god, continued flinging his thunderbolts at her, reaching into the very depths of her soul.

"You will live, study, talk with friends, and go to the theatre, while he, your comrade, your co-worker, your fellow traveller on the road to liberation will be hanged . . . Go ahead and enjoy yourself! Take delight in your triumph! Live freely in a free country, among free and grateful people. Lie to one another and justify yourselves to one another: the people before you, and you before them. But you should know that even if you killed ten Skalons, your nation would not stop being a nation of tyrants, until people with power similar to yours turn to healing their own sores. Because tyranny is a sickness. All of you want to cure the Russian government of it, but you yourselves are chronically ill with it."

"What am I to do?" she cried as she wrung her hands in despair. Her faith was weakened; the white gown of the Holy Mother was stained, and from under the mask smeared on the Madonna peered the face of a gossipy, lying hypocrite.

He glanced at her and said curtly: "If you yourself don't know what to do, I'll tell you. But not just now. First, we'll see what they do to him."

Never before had she waited so impatiently for the newspapers as she did after that day. Not even when she had been reading about herself.

The verdict was sent to the Kaiser for his confirmation—the matter was now no longer in Polish hands.

The newspaper augurs tried to read the future in entrails: would the Kaiser confirm the verdict, or not? If he confirms it, that means that we are still powerful, and that the right of oppression will still remain with us for a long time to come. If he does not confirm it, it means that something is amiss in the governmental apparatus, something needs to be greased; one has to figure out which way the wind is blowing, and remedy the situation, remedy it, remedy it!

The Kaiser did not confirm the verdict, and the death penalty was commuted to twenty years in prison.

On that day he came to her again.

"Twenty years in prison . . . So that means he'll go to prison as a young man, and he'll come out as a broken old man of forty. And during that time, you will marry a Russian ex-terrorist, and you will beget many little terrorists."

"Tell me, once and for all: what is it that you want me to do?" she asked, and she clenched her fists malevolently.

He stared at her for a long moment.

Now she was able to withstand his gaze.

Empathically, firmly, as if hammering out every word, he finally said: "Go . . . and do . . . what he did!"

She blanched.

"What? You want me to . . . me . . . a Polish woman?"

"Precisely because you are a Polish woman. And precisely because of who you are. I would gladly do it myself, but if I did it, the deed would not mean anything, however, if you do it . . . well! If you do it, the deed could be an important turning point in our history, it could have an impact on our national psychology, reorder the structure of Polish life, sweep away some parties from this world, and give rise to others to take their place. Oh, you have no idea, no idea at all, of the power that you now hold in your hands!

"Your deed there, in Warsaw, was only child's play in comparison to this one. I know of no other instance in history when so many threads came together in one person's hands, and female hands at that. And even if I were to perish, I will force you, yes, I will force you to do it! Do you hear me? I will force you! For I am—a pathfinder. In a vast desert I find deposits of precious metals that can enrich our nation."

She stood motionless. All this was beyond her.

A small lamp niggardly lit the room, and the marks of her triumphs looked down at her: dried wreaths, various decorations of honour. Just like the ones an actress in a provincial theatre might have.

And he, the tyrant, was rushing about the room. He noticed where the young woman's attention was focussed.

"Aha! You're looking at the marks of your heroic deed? In your opinion, was it truly heroic? The way I see it—it was no such thing. But then again, it really doesn't matter. It's just that a sacrifice is always greater than a heroic deed, because a heroic deed inevitably feeds one's pride, but a sacrifice does no such thing. Heroes are honoured, even fake ones, while those who sacrifice themselves may be spat upon. And I'm calling upon you for that kind of a sacrifice. And you must do it! You must! And you will do it! You will!"

And he darted about in front of her. Thin, tall. The metallic ring in his voice was replaced by an accusatory tone that was brimming with tears.

"Say that you will do it. Say that truly *jeszcze Polska nie zginela . . . Say that Poles still do exist, and that great noble deeds have not yet perished in their midst."

He, this damned demon, was himself boundlessly agitated, and when he ran out of the room he left behind a sea of emotions in her heart. A desire to fight, and a hesitation, and an awareness of her petty "heroism without a sacrifice." Now she hated herself. She had thought that she was standing on a pedestal of some kind, but he had come along, torn down the decorations from it, and it had turned out to be nothing more than a stand for slop pails.

"Heroism had perished . . . The era of heroes has passed, and the heroic has become ridiculous. There remains only one heroic act to be done in this world, and I must do it or . . . or else I must stop living."

But then something tore at her heart and shouted: "Come to your senses! What are you doing?" And an even more decisive response resounded: "I cannot do otherwise . . . I cannot . . ."

The entire world became odious to her, and she could not look people in the face. It was as if an abyss had opened up and was yawning at her feet, separating her from her fellow countrymen, from those who up to now had been so dear to her. When she sat down to eat, she could not swallow a morsel of food, because she kept thinking about that one who was incarcerated in a Stanislav prison, who was doing penance for her. He appeared to her in dreams . . . saying: "How fortunate it is to be a child of a privileged nation. It is only my brethren who do not enjoy any privileges anywhere in the world, and that is why I have been sentenced to twenty years in prison."

"And I am there with you!" she shouted in her sleep.

And when she awoke in the morning, she always saw a bouquet of beautiful flowers: an admirer sent them to her every day. And these flowers—that until just recently had brought her such joy—now painfully pierced her heart and made it ache.

"Everything is for me, it's all for me . . . But all he gets is a bowl of watery prison soup and the right to see his mother once a month . . ."

She listened to her heart and walked around as if condemned to death.

Her friends grew alarmed and sent a doctor to see her, but she did not want to talk to him. And then there came the day when she vanished from Krakow.

* * *

In the large waiting room of the viceroy in Lviv, there were, as always, a great many petitioners. When she gave the guard her name, he looked her over curiously. He was a *Galician Pole whose family went back for centuries, and that is why the concept of some kind of an armed protest was completely foreign to him, and so he looked at this girl as he would have looked at the Tsarivna Numitara-Khataba who, after six and a half years, rose from her grave.

"Is it you? Is it really you?" he asked her with a guileless naiveté.

She just smiled painfully. The civil servant was both pleased and a trifle disappointed. This heroine seemed to him to be much too . . . ordinary. She had neither a star on her forehead, nor horns on the back of her head.

The viceroy, upon hearing her name, gave an order that she be allowed to jump the queue.

"Ah . . . my dear compatriot!" and he shook her hand as if she was an old friend. "I'm very happy to see you, my young lady. And I assume that you'll greet me a little differently than you greeted my colleague in Warsaw, tee-hee-hee!"

And he laughed, and once again reached out to shake her hand, and it was only then that he noticed the pistol that she was holding.

He blanched . . . and his lips trembled.

"But why? Why?" he asked weakly.

She groaned as she raised the Browning and fired almost without aiming . . .

The viceroy toppled to the floor . . .

* * *

The entire country shuddered. Even if a volcano had erupted in Stry, a suburb of Lviv, it would not have had a greater impact. No one knew what to think, what to make of the situation. Even the age-old reason that was always given—Prussian intrigues—could not be applied in this instance.

Once again the windows of Ukrainian buildings were smashed, and a few high school girls were beaten up for speaking Ukrainian out in the street. But the news that it was a Polish woman who had pulled the trigger prevented the Poles from venting all their anger on the Ukrainians.

There was total consternation.

Finally, one perspicacious person came to the fore with a single word, and the entire country sighed with relief.

"She's insane . . ."

"Well, of course! Why didn't we think of that sooner . . ."

"If that wasn't the case, it would be beyond belief . . ."

"Her triumph went to her head, and so, well . . ."

A professor of surgery at the University of Lviv wrote a treatise: "Unusual Forms of Insanity," and in the preface he stated: "Even though I am a surgeon, in a time of national need, if I were told to crow like a rooster from a professor's chair, I would do so."

In no year that had ended in the number 00 did people await the end of the world with the same impatience as they now awaited the trial. The number of monthly newspaper subscriptions rose dramatically. *The New Age* promised that it would be published daily, and that in every issue there would be a bonus of a Madagascar or Polynesian lottery.

And in the meantime, the young female criminal was rigorously interrogated in psychiatric hospitals. The most eminent local psychiatrists unfastened the linen flaps of their tomes and pored over them ten times over—but they still could not find any signs of insanity, even a temporary one. Finally they settled on other tactics, and began to plead with her, to adjure her by the names of all the Polish kings, up to and including *Sienkiewicz, that she, of her own accord, manifest some signs—no matter how small—of insanity.

"You are killing us in the opinion of all of Europe! We are losing the sympathy of the entire civilized world," one psychiatrist said.

"Perhaps you're thinking that, after what you have done, the conditions in which you are to live will be miserable? Well, we vow to you, by all the stars above, that we will give you whatever you want; we will give you a furnished apartment fit for a queen; you will have everything that you desire," a second one said.

"Or, if you so wish, we will make it possible for you to escape, and we guarantee that no one will come after you," a third one said.

But it was all in vain; she did not agree to any of their proposals.

Finally, the day of the trial arrived.

Admission tickets to the room were being sold at fantastic prices. A reporter from the Ukrainian newspaper *The Deed* was beaten to death at the gate, while another one from *The Polish Word* was greeted with cries of hurrah!

Four adjoining streets were jammed with people, and in the courtroom itself something quite out of the ordinary was happening. Half a dozen ladies fainted, and some very helpful bachelors carried them out after first carefully searching their purses with the specific purpose of finding their admission tickets that they could then give to their acquaintances that were still standing out in the street. But the ladies who fainted were not entirely lacking in sense, and before their fainting spells, they had hidden their admission tickets in the peasant fashion—in their stockings.

The trial began!

Everyone was seated. The police endeavoured to quiet things down. At long last, the room did grow quiet.

The usual opening statements. The indictment, written, as was the Polish fashion, in a literary manner. In it there were both powerful epithets and colourful descriptions of the deed itself, a deed that was eventually put into verse form by *Kasprowicz; but—strangely enough—it was discovered later that this document was simply a copy of an earlier, analogous indictment. The man who did the copying was so caught up in his task, that in some instances he retained words in it that grammatically could not be used for a female. In the haste with which it was done, no one caught these phrases, and they were later read out at the trial.

The trial proceeded. The witnesses—who viewed themselves as very important personages, and who took inordinate pleasure in the fact that they were appearing before such an august gathering—distinguished themselves. And that is why every witness spoke as long as possible. And because they all had rehearsed their statements on their own in front of a mirror, and then had a trial run before the chairman of the court, the speeches of these witnesses took on a finely crafted format that charmed the ear. During the entire procedure, the stenographers doodled on their documents, because they had prepared everything well ahead of time.

The procurator's speech was the epitome of oratory art. He scaled the heights of pathos—and raised himself up on his toes; in the most compelling passages he tugged at his hair, even though he differed from *Bismark only in that he had four strands of hair on his head instead of three. He said that *Lucheni was a saint in comparison to such an unheard-of transgressor.

"And she is Polish! A Polish woman, yes indeed! It is a crime that could have been committed by a haydamaka, a man who already has an inclination for slaughter in his blood and who supplies enough butchers for the entire world, for his nation is unsuited for culture, so unsuited that even a nation like Poland, experienced as it is in cultural propaganda, was unable to bring its influence to bear upon it in the course of the past five hundred years. Please tally up all the noble acts that flowed down upon the *Rusyns by the authority of the Poles during this time, and you will have a figure that is utterly incredible. For starters, I shall just go back to the time of *Casimir the Great."

And the procurator, forgetting all about the topic that he was supposed to be addressing, spent almost an hour elaborating the topic that is the favourite one of all Galician Polish procurators, until finally the presiding judge sent him a note via a bailiff. The procurator then came to his senses and changed the direction of his presentation.

"And so, as I have said, if this deed had been done by a representative of that criminal, that murderous element of our society, it would be understandable. It could even be forgivable, if you want to put it that way. Even desired . . . I misspoke myself. But it was a Polish woman who did it. A Polish woman, yes indeed!"

And he thumped the pulpit.

The defence lawyer "who had been appointed" spoke briefly, disposing of his speech in a few cursory words. He asked that, "keeping in mind the previous meritorious service of the accused," the punishment be lessened by at least half—that is, to hang her on a hangman's rope that was only half the length of the usual one.

Finally the accused had her chance to give her final statement. The courtroom grew so still that a fly could be heard.

"Yes, I am a Polish woman! And now, I am more Polish than I have ever been throughout my entire life. And perhaps even more so than any of the people that I know. Because my comrades give their lives to lessen the pain of their native land, while I am giving mine in order to lessen, at least partially, a bit of its exultation. An exultation that is built on violence, on brutal oppression.

"I would prefer to see my Poland in a wreath of thorns than in a policeman's uniform with a cudgel of violence in his hand.

Because a wreath of thorns can be removed in battle, but a policeman's uniform grows into the skin and eats its way into the heart. I want to see my Poland as an innocent martyr before whom all knees would be bent, all heads would be bowed, and not as a tawdry actress who, on stage, dons a wreath of thorns, but who, at home, slaps her little sister on the cheek with her slippers.

"And as for you, my Galician brethren, you do not love your native land. You have besmirched its sacred national relics, spat on its national hymns, made a mockery of its national holidays and turned them into a farce. You recall the name of *Kościuszko, without comprehending that if he rose up from the dead, he would direct his very first salvos at you, he would shoot all of you, all the internal enemies, and only then would he turn his attention to the external ones.

"You have shamed the Polish name before the entire world! A Pole was a synonym for a fighter, for a son of the revolution, because he did not ask in which country barricades had been erected, he just asked if they had been erected. Because he spread the Great Volodymyr Road with corpses. That Pole is not your brother. Your brother is a chauvinist, a rank, putrid boil on the Polish organism, a foul, stinking tapeworm that sucks out the lifeblood of our nation, and its daring, and its spirit of protest, and its honour!

"But with my deed, I am reinstating my nation's honour! With a single shot I am undoing your work that goes back six generations, your work of ruining its national spirit, your work of inciting disunity. And after my deed, my martyred country will once again stand in a white wreath, and it will look once again with clear eyes at the entire world, and it will once again be a sister to all who suffer.

"I have plucked my country from the camp of the oppressors. I have turned it back onto its rightful, its only path—the path of doing battle with the enemy. I have strengthened it with the power of a brotherly nation that has been freed from under the Polish yoke! I have broken, O my brethren, the Polish yoke! It would be better for us to be bound in chains, than to forge them.

"And now, kill me, kill me at once, if you do not agree with me! Hang me and bury me as fast as you can! Because if you do not, I will stand with a threatening mien before each and every one of you, and I will curse you. In the name of the pure garments of my own dear Mother. For her stolen wreath of thorns! For shaping and constructing the Polish yoke!"

In view of the murmurs of sympathy that were beginning to spread among the listeners, the presiding judge, disregarding a thousand-year judicial tradition, ordered that the mouth of the accused be forcibly shut, and in the newspapers the following day it was noted that the voices that were heard in the courtroom were the voices of Ukrainian haydamaky, because no Pole would lower himself so far as to give credence to even the slightest portion of the lies of the insane woman, whom only chance had prevented from being in *Kulparkiv. Moreover, even her first deed had been nothing more than a manifestation of her mania for killing, for killing anyone at all, whoever happened to be around; and it was only servile friends of questionable nearness who had trumpeted that deed of hers to the world as a highly commendable political step.

No additional questions were put forward.

The jury unanimously voted "guilty," because even though there was one who opposed the verdict, he was offered a position in the Hofflinger Candy Factory, and so his voice echoed the voices of the other voters.

The Kaiser confirmed the verdict.

On the Road
(1907)

No matter where Kyrylo was, no matter what he did, he was invariably surrounded by a dense and distinctive atmosphere that obscured many objects around him as if they simply did not exist. It was a feverish, anxious atmosphere, filled with danger and struggle, a perpetual swinging between misfortune and triumph, the blossoming of hope and then utter despair, a feeling of power followed by ennervation, and an infinitely long road on which so many had already perished . . .

It was a road that seemed to have no end in sight—a long line of sacrificial victims, the loss of the most noble and the dearest, the scent of blood and the dance of death, a searing, hostile breath that feverishly tracked you, and the eternal "you must" that hounded you to build anew—that was the aura that always emanated from Kyrylo, like the fragrance of a flower.

It had estranged him from his family; former habits and the imperatives of a young life had vanished in it; and even his own surname had disappeared. "Kyrylo," "Comrade Kyrylo"—had he ever been called anything else?

The beauty of nature, the allurement of women, the charms of music and of the written word—all rolled by like waves on a distant sea, alien and invisible. Nature was reduced to either day or night, winter or summer—a convenient or inconvenient time for work; a woman was either a friend or a foe; a song was only something that summoned you to battle.

And it was as if his twenty-three years, doubled by the shadows on his emaciated face, by the furrow on his brow, had given up their inalienable rights and had desiccated his youthfulness . . .

Tall, slim, and fair; blue eyes that were slightly weary; a dark shirt, a wide belt—that is how he looked when he arrived in the city.

Kyrylo went to a secret location and gave the password. Good! Now he only had to wait for a letter.

But in the meantime he was led to a place on the outskirts of the city where he could stay in relative safety.

They walked for a long time down stiflingly hot streets thick with dust until the sun set and the silhouettes of poplars and roofs showed up darkly against a golden sky that resembled the background of a Byzantine icon. The comrade was talking nervously, as if he wanted to reassure not only Kyrylo but also himself that the case was interesting; at the same time, however, his faded figure and shabby overcoat exuded an aura of guilt and hopelessness.

A landlady met them at the apartment and showed them the room. It was now time to say good night. As soon as the letter came, he could get to work at once.

Kyrylo was left alone, and he watched indifferently as the night—black, dense, and warm—enveloped the orchard. He sat on the threshold and smoked. It was so calm, so quiet. The red tip of his cigarette glowed like a flower of good fortune; in the darkness it was possible to think more clearly than one could ever think when there was light. He thought about why he had come and what he had to do, and the black spider of anxiety began to weave its web.

Unexpectedly, something suddenly interrupted the dark silence . . . something vibrant, happy, and carefree. It darted about on the leaves, awakened the air, jolted the ground, and breathed damply into one's face. It rushed by with a rustle, washed the earth, and vanished. And then the moon swam out into the sky. Kyrylo walked out into the orchard and simultaneously took in the trees, heavy-laden with water like sponges, the silvery laughter of the wet leaves, the whispering of the raindrops among the branches, the embraces of the shadows with their greenish glow and the deep, dark blue sky that was clear and calm. Nature sighed deeply, and Kyrylo also sighed.

Was it possible that he had never before seen this?

It felt strange, but there was also a renewed sense of pleasure to have cold raindrops tickle him, to have a green light wash over him, to have a heart that was as calm as the sky . . .

He could not fall asleep for a long time.

The next day he woke up late—and his very first thought was about the letter. He hurried to the landlady's quarters and opened the door.

"Good morning! Has anyone brought me a letter?"

"Oh!"

High-pitched, utterly feminine, and sharply clear, this "oh" blended into a lightning flash with a pink body and the patter of feet. A door slammed, and the room was left empty.

The landlady walked into the porch from outdoors. No, the letter had not come.

It was odd that he accepted this response with such indifference.

He picked up his cap.

The day was brilliant, summery. To the right, the smoke-blackened city huddled with its roofs and the chimneys of its factories; to the left, green meadows and garlands of sinuating forests spread before him. To the right? Or to the left? He hesitated a moment—and set out for the meadows.

Nothing had actually changed in the short time since his arrival, but for some reason his eyes saw things differently, and his thoughts were not his usual ones. It was as if he had dropped something and did not want to pick it up, as if something had been washed off of him by yesterday's rain—perhaps that was why he felt so light-hearted. It was pleasant to walk along the well-trodden path, to feel the resilient muscles of his legs at work. One, two! To raise your face to the sun and the wind, and to wander aimlessly, without thinking about obligations, people, work. To walk through the field, to bathe your body in the golden waves, and your eyes in the azure. Like a wild animal. There was something new in all that, and something shamefully sweet. He returned only towards evening, weary, blackened like a gypsy by the sun, and with his hands full of flowers.

The landlady's daughter served him his supper. This was the "oh" that had been startled in the morning. Young, fair, with a delicate figure, snub-nosed and blue-eyed.

Kyrylo stretched out his hand.

"Did I frighten you this morning?"

She burst out laughing and pouted with pink lips that were full and moist.

And once again Kyrylo felt something strange stir within him; he was attracted by the line of her lips and by their rosy dampness.

Well, naturally, she had been frightened; she had been tidying up, she wasn't dressed, and she hadn't expected anyone to open the door.

He begged her forgiveness, for he could not have known that in this home there was such a . . .

"Such a what?"

"Well, such a, such a . . . Miss Olena . . ."

"Olena?"

"Haven't I guessed right? Isn't her name Olena?"

"Ha-ha! But perhaps it isn't Olena?"

"Well, then it's Natalka."

"Oh sure! Ha-ha!"

"I still haven't guessed? Well then, it must be: Barbara, Nastya, Oksana, Mariya . . ."

No, no, he would never guess, but, for her part, she knows he is Petro.

"But no, that's not right . . ."

"It's Petro, Petro, Petro . . ."

The landlady called out from the other room.

"Ustya, where have you disappeared to?"

Aha, so now the truth has come out. In honour of his first meeting with Miss Ustya, he is giving her these flowers.

"These weeds?"

Well, if they're weeds, he'll take them back.

But Ustya had already grabbed the flowers and run out of the room.

The letter did not come on the second day either. Kyrylo was angry. The swine! The loathsome creatures! He was wasting precious time, and they were sitting around with their arms folded. And this was called working for the party! The devil only knew what was going on!

He paced the house with long, light strides, as if his anger was tearing him away from the ground, and fanned the flame of that anger in order to blow it into a conflagration. But, at the same time, springs somewhere deep inside him bubbled up and extinguished the flames. He caught himself being insincere, and felt an aimless sense of discouragement shadowing him like a swiftly flowing cloud. And this renewed his anger. He had to go into the city and find out what was happening. He quickly got dressed, stepped out into the street and . . . turned off into the fields.

But as soon as the greenery that rolled in luxuriant waves through the meadows and the forest filled his eyes, as soon as the sky lowered itself and gently touched his face like downy fluff, as soon as the golden liquid of the air filled his chest, he was enveloped by a sweet languor, like a person who had arisen from his death bed, and everything that had motivated his life up to now—the passion for his work, the fire of danger, the fumes of blood and battle— tumbled into an abyss . . .

He felt as if he had been born only yesterday, on the same day as youthful nature. And he did not have the strength, nor did he want to stop to ponder what was happening to him; he shook off all his thoughts and doubts just as geese shake the water from their wings after they have swum across a river.

He roamed through the rye and looked all around with fresh eyes . . . no, not with fresh ones, but with eyes that had been sleeping for a long time under the weight of his inert eyelids. He watched as bluish spikes of young rye rustled, overflowed, and beat in waves against the dark forest.

And the forest itself was receding into the distance. The pine trees, their tall trunks lined up in rows, were on the move. On their tips, yellow like pineapples, dark crowns perched like shaggy Caucasian fur caps. They had come from far away, crossing rivers, violet-shadowed paths, and deep swamps, and they had dirtied their legs, for their trunks appeared grey half way up, as if caked with mud. They kept on walking and then, farther on, vanished into the grey-blue mist.

When Kyrylo stepped into the forest, his feet glided over the ground as if he were walking on a parquet floor, branches contorted themselves whimsically above his head like balls of coiled yellow snakes, shaggy boughs swayed like armchairs where the sun could rest, and small twigs and budding pine branches spread out against the sky like expensive embroidery on azure silk. And the sun flamed behind them as if it were behind a Chinese screen.

Beyond the forest the meadows lay dreaming, like still waters under a mat of duckweed. The shadows of flying clouds wandered over them, and, like greyhounds, they bounded in, sniffed, and vanished in expanses of mignonettes.

He came across small ponds that sparkled and trembled like the scales of a silver fish cast out of the water onto a grassy bank. And larger ponds—with walls of blue reeds, with white-faced water lilies, with swampy banks, dark and shiny like the wet spines of hippopotami, and with the warm odour of water and slime.

And everything was so healthy, whole, and carefree, and everything was singing praises to the solitude . . .

*   *   *

Kyrylo no longer asked the landlady about the letter. But one day, as he was preparing to go out, she handed it to him.

Aha! Was it for him? Well, that's fine, that's fine . . .

He took it mechanically and, without even looking at it, stashed it in his pocket. What was she saying? Someone had come to see him and had not found him in? Was it Miss Ustya who had arranged such a pretty bouquet? What was that? He had asked him to come in today without fail? Well, that's fine, that's fine . . . What wonderful flowers—and what good taste Miss Ustya has.

Now he lay for days on end on the riverbank, gazing up at the sky. He was intrigued by the clouds—this turbulent, heavenly population that he was watching; it was perpetually animated, perpetually in motion. At times there were upheavals up there, national uprisings. The incensed masses, black with anger, sped along, threatening, roaring, with the thunder of rifles, with fiery bombs, with red flags. The heavenly wars went on and on, corpses fell, and new ranks continued trampling over their chests. And it was impossible to say who had won.

At other times, it was peaceful, and the heavenly inhabitants strolled about as if on boulevards. The happy throngs—tender girls, grand women, rosy-cheeked children—flowed along joyfully and easily in white and blue veils, and there was joy and laughter everywhere.

Sometimes pale clouds appeared, lank and transparent, as if they were tubercular patients strolling about in a spa by a blue sea.

Or sheep grazed—whole flocks of white lambs—and the golden sun was their shepherd.

Kyrylo watched the creative processes transpiring in the sky. Someone unknown, a great master, was moulding animals, people, birds, buildings, towers, entire cities out of the grey masses and freeing them to spread over the sky. But all of it was molten and, without time to harden, lost its form.

Animals changed into towers, mountains arose out of people, and birds out of cities; buildings took on human forms, and these in turn changed into cliffs that surrounded deep lakes brimming with water. Magnificent temples toppled, snow melted on the Alps, and splendid roses lost their pink petals.

But the unknown master was becoming frenzied—he created dragons, winged horses, griffins and crocodiles, but these too lived for only a moment before they transformed themselves into something new. And then, completely drained and in despair, he stirred everything together into a grey chaos while he himself dissolved into sadness.

The shadows and their lives were also interesting. Kyrylo watched them closely as they shrank under bushes, the trunks of trees, the bank of a river. They found it cramped and painful. And only when the sun became weary and began to descend from its pinnacle of glory, did the shadows slowly and carefully straighten out their crooked limbs, begin to grow, and crawl out ever farther and farther. Towards evening, they stretched out full length and lay down in the valleys—endlessly tall, black poplars, windmills with slender wings, pointed bell towers, and the chimneys of factories—an entire city of *Cyclopes, black, silent, and vile.

Kyrylo did not hear any reproaches. He greedily imbibed the beauty of nature and its peacefulness as someone thirsty drinks water without giving it a second thought. As something that was his due. Something that had been lost, and now had been found again. Sometimes, from far away, as from under the ground, an echo of familiar signals reached him, but it was so faint, so weak, that it perished at once. And he did not want to listen to it. But, because of that, he was tortured at night. In his dreams it seemed to him that he had to do something, he absolutely had to do something—but he could not. He did not have the power. He mustered all his strength, strained his will, sweated profusely—but he could not. Yet he had to . . . It was painful.

He woke up feeling shattered, exhausted, but the first ray of the sun that reached out to him through the windowpane absorbed that nightmare into itself and returned his strength to him.

Now Kyrylo no longer walked alone; Miss Ustya knew some wonderful crannies, oases of flowers.

She walked ahead of him, fresh and pure, with a blinding figure, and she laughed happily and warmly like the sun. In the forest she would sit down on a limb and swing her legs, her strong, young legs. Like a nymph.

"Don't look at me."

"But I want to."

"But I don't want you to."

"I don't care."

"I'll cover my face."

"And I'll uncover it."

"Just you dare."

"I've already dared."

"Oh!"

And once again that "oh," high-pitched, ticklishly feminine, and silvery clear.

He held her hands, and she closed her eyes, hid her face, and laughter poured from her throat like forest nuts into a crystal vase.

They exchanged words, empty and meaningless, just to hear each other's voices, and the words stuck to them like burrs that are difficult to pull off one's clothing.

On the riverbank she took off her shoes and waded in the shallow water. The water made it possible to look at her feet, ever so pale, like little wreaths of narcissi. Light clouds floated over the azure water and vanished, and she seemed like one of them—pink, transparent, gilded by the sun.

Kyrylo filled his lungs and let loose a shout that sped like an arrow over the bank: "U-u-ustya!"

The tall bank and its ravines, the forest wall, and all of the hills pursed their lips like Kyrylo had done and echoed in reply: "U-u-ustya!"

And Ustya laughed.

Together, like two birches growing from a single trunk, they appeared first here, then there; they gathered flowers, dug out mushrooms from beneath fallen leaves, bathed in both the sun and the shade, or, holding hands, sped down hills into succulent valleys. And he could not distinguish her from the rustling of the forest, the flight of the clouds, the fragrance, the grass. She was so naïve, and yet so clever; she knew so little and so much, like the ant that builds splendid palaces, but lives in dark cells.

They lay in the tall grass amid a sea of flowers, and gazed all around. There, at the lowest level, yellow lady slippers and tiny cinquefoils were like grains of golden sand, and above them rose tall veronicas, some greyish-blue, and some dark blue. Red pompoms of clover stuck their brushes out like porcupines from three-leafed saucers, and fragrant wild thyme wove a heliotropic rug down the side of the hill. Trefoils opened wide their little umbrellas. Among their white tents fluttered the wings of blue butterflies. Occasionally a beetle settled on a parasol and caught the sun in the green mirror of its wings. Ustya would hold her breath so as not to frighten it.

Gloomy yarrow scattered piles of stars, bright yellow but sad, like golden tassels on the black sides of a coffin, and next to it a chicory plant bent its grey and knotty stem over which blue flowers, faded and uncombed, sparsely clambered. From the grass, a camomile's eye peeked out at Kyrylo. Tiny harebells, so delicate and so tender that they themselves wondered how they existed in this world, dispersed themselves all over the meadow and sowed sorrow. The unapproachable poison ivy, heavy with seeds like a bee with pollen, whispered in a housewifely manner in its resting place.

And over there, a shaggy cornflower extended its petals in all directions, as if trying to fill the wide expanse with their bluish-pink hues. Farther away, horse sorrel, scorched by the sun, smouldered darkly like a funeral torch, and verbascum stood in a dignified manner like the golden seven-pronged candelabra in ancient temples. Kyrylo showed Ustya the valleys where spurge secretly rolled milk up its succulent and raw stems, like the teats of a cow, from its dark piney roots to its round yellow rosette. On hillocks grey wormwood grew like a jungle and intoxicated the air with it bitter perfume, thick and stifling.

And here and there pussy's toes reached to the sun, dry, soulless, soft, like velvet, and among them the field mint gathered together every pair of leaves into its belt of heliotropes. It seemed to Ustya and Kyrylo that the naïve clove pink blushed in the grass like children's faces, while above them the worried broom grass bent its branches and wept with yellow tears. Thistles, so blue that they were almost steely, occupied huge expanses by themselves. They looked like an abandoned fire that was dying with a final azure smoke. And over there, covering the meadows, yellow dandelions shone like stars in the sky, bindweed twirled on one leg, milfoil clung tightly to the ground, wild roses waved their grey branches, and whitish-pink, reddish-blue and hot yellow flowers perched like butterflies on the sweet peas. This was an orgy of flowers and grasses, an intoxicated dream of the sun, a riot of colours, perfumes, shapes . . .

Ustya was lying face down upon the ground and chewing on a stem; Kyrylo bent a bush of sweet calamus towards himself and pressed his hot face into it. And then, without words, without any conspiring, their eyes met like four of the most beautiful flowers, and their lips reached out to one another. And, together with the sweet dampness, the taste of the bitter grass blended into one . . .

* * *

It was after one of these days that something happened. In the middle of the night, when he was alone in his own room, someone flung a word at him: "Traitor."

Loudly and clearly.

A traitor? Who?

Kyrylo glanced around, but the shadows were lying quietly, and the patterns of the undistinguished wallpaper shone calmly in the light of the lamp.

He sat up on the bed and unconsciously grabbed at the pocket where the unread letter still lay. But he did not take it out. A hostility, an aversion began to growl within him like a provoked dog, and his hand back fell impotently. He felt weary, and he sat quietly and listened as the word echoed in his empty breast—in his breast, from which the blood had suddenly receded, and the cold had rushed in as into a crack. Then he immediately felt hot; a searing wave rose up from somewhere below and flooded that emptiness, struck his head, and chased Kyrylo from the bed.

The devil take it! He had the right. He had the right to a full life—the right that goes with being twenty years old . . . The right to a life that would never again be repeated. Who would forbid it? Who could? Who could extinguish the "I," rub out the colours, ruin the fragrance . . . even if that were necessary for the good of thousands of others? Others, whom he does not even know. The devil take it! He would not give them everything . . . he had the right to leave himself something as well.

Everything within him was churning and chasing him around the room, from wall to wall, from corner to corner.

Traitor! Just let them say this to his face! Then they would see . . .

But this had been said to his face! That "other" that lived within him, that genuine and implacable "I." The "I" that burned brightly within him . . . that consumed in flames everything personal, impure, bestial. But the "first I" struggled, fought, wanted to live, shouted about its rights and tugged at him.

The two were reconciled by exhaustion. Colourless and muddy, it was lying dreamily somewhere in his depths, like a fog under the water, waiting for the chance to reach out with its sticky embrace . . .

*   *   *

What was happening in the world? Did he know? He did not even want to know. He did not read the newspapers, there were no letters, and no one came to see him. At first, someone had dropped by now and again but, after never finding Kyrylo at home, had stopped coming.

In the evenings, when the city was glowing peacefully and sighing gently after its exhausting day, he took Ustya by the hand and went there.

They wandered through the dark, canal-like streets, huddling closely and stopping under a window to listen to some music. They hid in the shadows and caught the sounds. Ustya liked happy tunes; she sang along quietly and beat her heels in time to the rhythm, and the sounds flared like flames within Kyrylo and blossomed like flowers at sunrise. They floated on the waves of light that poured out from the window and gave birth to a longing. For something beautiful and unknown, so distant and yet so near . . .

One time something black and unkempt blocked the light and tore through the music.

"Ah!"

"Ah!"

"Is it you?"

"Yes."

The black figure nodded its beard and its big straw hat, and shaking Kyrylo's hand, asked him how he had come to be here.

The figure embraced him lightly around the waist, and led him away. Leaned over and pleaded.

It was not possible? Nonsense. Their cottage in the country was not far from here. He would see his wife and the life they now led; they would recall old times. Two years . . . yes indeed, it was two years since they had seen one another . . .

Kyrylo's hand lay in the other's hand, and a friendly warmth caressed him, but he felt a disinclination. Ah! Once again the newspapers . . . and those endless conversations . . . once again the black apparition that needed the sacrifice of blood and of strength.

No, he could not.

He remembered that "bandit," fiery, brave, and loving, who thundered at meetings, calling others forth to battle; and his wife, so small, so active, who only recently had still been at the hub of things. "Comrade Mariya." By what miracle were they still enjoying freedom?

No, he did not want to end up among them.

He was begged, coerced, and by morning he was already at their cottage.

They were met by "Comrade Mariya" in a housecoat that she hastily fastened on her bare neck. How fat and flaccid she had become, like a well-fed goose! She was so happy to see him, but, oh dear, the house was such a mess!

She pressed his hand, and then rushed up to the table; unread newspapers swiftly tumbled in their wrappers into a cloud of dust.

Weren't they read here?

Ivan laughed good-naturedly, and immediately changed into a loose-fitting shirt.

Rows of cabbages and a forest of corn peeked in through the windows, and, somewhere nearby, a setting hen clucked in the same housewifely fashion as "Comrade Mariya."

Tea was waiting for them on the balcony.

While they were having their tea, Ivan, somewhat hurriedly and in a high-pitched voice, started a conversation about current events. Mariya pursed her lips and, with an expression of obstinate pain, stubbornly stirred her tea.

Everything was being said much too loudly, as if the words were falling into an empty barrel where they grew out of all proportion. And there was something futile and insincere about them, as if one sick person were consoling another one on a death bed.

Everyone—Mariya, who was stubbornly stirring her tea, Kyrylo, with a hostility born of his weariness, and Ivan, who was loudly spouting all the right words—everyone felt as if somewhere not far away, in the next room, there was a corpse that should be forgotten, but which one could not forget. And that was the only reason why the conversation was taking place.

Even the setting hen clucked about this at their feet, but no one paid any attention to her. It was only after the chicks clambered up their legs, and from there onto the table where they rolled about like little yellow balls among the glasses, that Ivan's words dissolved into a smile and tumbled down over his black beard.

"Cheep, cheep, cheep . . ." Ivan tenderly chattered as he blinked his eyes happily and he wove a little yellow ball into his black bandit's beard.

"Cheep, cheep, cheep . . ." Mariya puckered her lips and lovingly cuddled a yellow tuft of soft feathers against her rosy neck.

The atmosphere lightened; chairs moved freely, the conversation immediately became animated, and switched to the topic of the different breeds of chickens.

They invited Kyrylo to have a look at their small farm.

The cow was called "Hashka;" she had a wonderful udder, and licked everyone's hands. Ducklings, grey and round like little lumps of soil, rolled around under their feet; trim chickens, lifting their pointed tails immodestly, dug about in the manure and laid eggs punctually, much to the delight of their mistress. Maybe he would like to examine the eggs? A red steer spread its legs and stared dully at the fence, but he was of good pedigree: it was truly worthwhile to listen to his biography. A pig was rooting in the yard.

"Don't be afraid, bend over . . . Scratch it . . . go ahead, scratch it . . . between its legs, because it really likes that. Oh, you dear little boar! He's a pure-bred Berkshire . . ."

"But Ivan—he's a Yorkshire . . ."

"Hmm . . . it's strange . . . you're always getting things mixed up . . ."

Suddenly their eyes fell on the garden, on the blue sea of cabbages.

"Marusya, do you see that?

"Oh, God . . . the pigs are in the garden . . . Run, head them off . . ."

A stick cracked, and a body leapt up . . . "Sooey! Hey there!" Feet thumped, shirts flashed amid the greenery. "Sooey! Get! Open the gate! Here, piggy . . . Here, piggy!"

A solid, bristly creature tore through the air like a bullet, and bumped against his legs. Then there was a gust of warm, human steam, the whistle of rapid breathing, flushed faces flashed by— and it was only then that Kyrylo saw how much energy the chase had cost them.

All that was happening was far removed from anything that Kyrylo had feared when he was travelling to the cottage. There was no need to have any worries here.

Why then, instead of enjoying peace of mind, was there something unpleasant and irritating stirring in his chest? A sharp question jabbing him, goading him? Something unexpectedly disagreeable?

On weekdays, Ivan went to work and returned home late, at dinnertime. He railed against the current county council in which he served, and made fun in a bad-tempered way of those liberals who so readily changed their sheep's clothing for that of a wolf. He gathered up all the dirt of contemporary relationships, the filthy and bloody scum of life—and one sensed he derived an evil pleasure in that. It was better this way. Let it be thus. Wonderful!

He brought them the latest news. Between spoonfuls of borshch he passed on information about deaths by execution. Eight had been hung. Three had been sentenced to death. All were young—they had scarcely begun to live. The words were washed down with the borshch, and, during the entr'acte, they found out that people were being shot like wild game in the villages. And everything was stated calmly, even coldly, as if these were facts from the Middle Ages that could be recalled but could not be fathomed.

At times, Mariya was interested in the details—the legs that had been torn off by a bomb, the children who had been crippled, the location of a deathly wound, but all of this was immediately pushed aside by the concern that the pie was overdone. Forgetting about the legs that had been torn off, the dead children, and the young people who had been hung, she ran to the kitchen to scold the help.

After dinner, they always lay down to have a nap. To sleep— and after dinner! Perhaps they even snored—the fiery orator Ivan and . . . "Comrade Mariya!"

Kyrylo would run out of the house to avoid hearing it.

Kyrylo also slept—well, not during the day, of course—but during the nights his dreams made him suffer. In those persistent dreams he felt there was something he had to do; he simply had to; it was painful. . . He had to, but he lacked the strength, and did not know what needed to be done . . .

In the evenings, a curly-haired student, exiled from someplace, came to their home from a neighbouring cottage. She always brought along a book under her arm, and a fantastic, other-worldly enthusiasm on her face.

They greeted her joyfully—Mariya with kisses, and Ivan with smiles that cascaded in waves down his black beard.

It was as if they had been waiting all day for her arrival. They at once sat down at the table and read by lamplight in the small room that was like an island in the sea of night. *Huysmans' *Against the Grain* and *The Knapsack*, in which love festered like a wound and the "I" bloomed like a splendid poisonous flower; an orgy of the spirit and the body, supernatural instincts, and that protest of everything against everything . . . Or else they argued.

Then their faces flamed; the tips of Mariya's ears reddened and her eyes blazed; Ivan paced the room with an inspired look, and amazed everyone with examples of the finest oratory; the student listened with rapturous enthusiasm like a queen in an underground kingdom.

And the further that Ivan's thought or his imagination was removed from the terror and suffering that enveloped reality, the more eagerly all three of them fastened on to his words as if they were hurrying to sail with closed eyes over the depths where the pieces of a ship that had just been wrecked now rested.

The readings finished late in the evening. Ivan would walk the student home, and when he returned, would find his wife sitting by the lamp. Stopping her ears with her hands, she would be feverishly finishing the book, and the pages rustled in the silence as if the wind were turning them.

It was time to go to bed, but they could not agree who would take the book for the night.

"You'll finish reading it tomorrow, because I have to go to work in the morning," Ivan protested.

"You only care about yourself . . ."

"And what about you?"

And there would be a scene.

Now no one raised painful, burning issues, as on the first day when Kyrylo had arrived at the cottage. The houseguest had already received the honour that was due him, and what more could be expected?

But something, by way of a contrast, arose uninvited and spoke out. Something indistinct, depressing, alarming—and it was only occasionally that it seemed to Kyrylo that he was just about to catch it, that he was just about to figure out what it was that he had to do . . .

Every time that Ivan, waking up after dinner with puffy eyes, a pale face, and ruffled hair, yawned deliciously over and over again, Kyrylo, shrinking from the sight, fled from the house in order not to see it . . .

After all, would it not be the same tomorrow—work, the calves, symbolism, and cabbages? Puffy eyes and yawning?

He had had his fill of such "peacefulness." He felt stifled by that atmosphere, and he did not even stop to think when he flung the words out at them: "How can you? You . . . This stinks!"

He was very upset; his words came out with difficulty, as if from under a pile of dirt where they had lain for a long time.

"How can you . . . when all around . . ."

Those words, so short and understandable to both of them, were painful, and they did not strike only Ivan. They tore through all obstacles and burst out like rockets.

How could he! Ivan shrugged his shoulders. But what was he supposed to do? Amid general ruination, apathy, exhaustion? He was no hero . . . and who had the right to demand heroism from him! He had worked whenever it had been possible to work . . . No one had the right . . . there could be no doubt about that, no one had the right to reproach him . . .

They raised their voices, and both of them shouted. Angrily, crossly. And in each man it was his own pain, his own shame that was shouting, his own ennervation . . . It was the need to wound himself, to lash out at the other who was shouting . . .

They parted angrily, and both of them were very upset.

Kyrylo wandered for a long time until he finally cooled off a bit. Was he justified? Had he not offended Ivan needlessly? No, it was necessary to re-examine the whole matter once again calmly, without anger. He must see Ivan right away. The poor man would most certainly be suffering after such a terrible scene.

He must go back there! It was quite close by . . . He could already see the white walls, the fence, the blue cabbages . . . And there . . .

He saw Ivan and Mariya. Bending over at the waist, they were weeding the garden.

On the green lowland, flooded by the evening sun, only their rounded rumps could be seen among the cabbages, a big black one and a smaller blue one neatly lined up and pressed staunchly together like an emblem of peace. And there was something so revolting in that picture, so disgusting, that Kyrylo shuddered.

He did not go into the garden, but went straight to his room. And the first thing he did was to put his hand into his pocket and pull out the letter. All worn, crumpled, and grey. He tore open the envelope and scanned the creased paper. No, it was not too late yet.

He had finally found what it was that he must do! And while he was deciphering the mangled letter in the dull light, Mariya's voice drifted in from the balcony.

"Come and have some tea! Today we're having a pie!"

"A pie-ie-ie . . ." Ivan's bass voice rang out; he was in a good mood, as if nothing at all had transpired.

But Kyrylo did not answer.

He was girding himself for the road ahead.

The Unknown One
Étude
(1907)

. . . Why? And from where is this longing coming? Life has been left behind out there, beyond these stone bastions, and here, within these damp cold walls, death has locked itself in with me. I do not fear it. I called it to a just cause and it came, took its victim, and then, like a grateful dog, remained at my feet. It is with me now. Well, go ahead and stare at my shadow from the dark corners, lie in wait for me with your bloodthirsty eyes . . . This is your reward.

But I am still alive. I can feel the hard prison mattress beneath me; I can see my body stretched out on the cot, my big feet shod in shoes, my hands with which I . . .

A lamp glimmers in the corner, and a hostile silence, grey and damp, hovers over it. But I do not want to see that . . . I do not want to . . . I'll shut my eyes. Fiery circles. They dance and scatter sparks . . . And now . . . now the river of life is flowing.

For does it really matter that they have locked me in this cold dungeon when the entire beautiful world, all the colours, all the bustle of life, are right here within me, in my head, in my heart . . .

Oh, how I would like to draw up brimming handfuls of that golden liquid. How I would like to pick up a pen, dip it in the azure of the sky, in the murmuring water, in the blood of my own heart, and write down everything; write down, for the very last time, what I have seen, what I have felt. Oh, for a scrap of paper, just a scrap of paper . . . Hey there, guards! It's not permitted? What? For a human being who is about to die? Ha-ha-ha! Well, that's that!

Perhaps it's better this way. I'll lie here and, without ink, without paper, and without words, I'll thread the strings of my thoughts like a coral necklace. For thoughts are swift and light, like birds, and words are like a snare in which one catches them; you catch one and the rest dart up and flutter away . . .

This will be my literary creation, better perhaps than those that people have read; this will be a story for a single reader, for the most grateful and sensitive reader. And this will be the thread that unites death with life, and, while it is unwinding, I am still alive.

How quickly have all the voices echoed forth . . . How quickly has the stream of life rushed into this tomb . . . Oh, what a crowd! No, I cannot do it this way. Stop. Let me catch you. Aha!

They were all so serious, so pale and decisive when they asked: "Who will take the deed upon himself?"

"I will."

The "I will" burst forth from my chest like stinging ice. And instantly a wall arose between me and my companions, between me and life. A lock clicked, and decisiveness was secured in my heart. Embraces and kisses, and within a few hours I was already on my way, that "unknown one" who . . . and so on. I was without a name, without a lineage, without a clan, and it was only my friend that everyone would have been able to recognize. He had a short name: *Browning.

It was an exceptionally cold morning when I arrived. Yes, it was cold. A fierce foe from the north, clear and sharp as a sword, had arisen and, gleaming with an icy eye, was blowing billows of smoke over the sky and chasing their dark shadows over the snow. The sun was looking on helplessly, indecisively. It was even afraid to blink. The trampled snow, compressed and unresisting, stuck closely to the ground. People and horses were fleeing as if pursued by a ferocious enemy, the billowing smoke was fleeing, and even the steaming breath of people and animals was fleeing.

I felt no fear. It was all very interesting. I looked closely at the city, now as familiar to me as a grave, the city in which the buildings huddled in a single mass like sheep when it is cold; men turned grey from the frost, but women's faces bloomed like poppies.

I began my wanderings on that very first day. I blended in with the crowd and walked. Grey, alien, unknown. Down unknown streets. I remained silent, even though I needed to ask questions, even though I needed to know a great deal. Where does he live? When does he leave the house, and where does he go? When he eats, goes to sleep, all of his habits. What is he like? But slowly. Not all at once. I didn't have a plan. Where? How? When? Actually I had a thousand plans that spun around and died away in my brain like sheaves of sparks from a threshing machine in a dark field . . .

There was only the certainty, firm like a rock: he will be mine. And I found the building where he lived. Yellow, huge, cold. A state sentry box and a state sentry who rubbed his hands to keep them warm and crunched back and forth over the snow like a dog on a leash.

"Aha!"

Had I said that?

No, I had only thought it.

I sat down on the boulevard across from the building, and the dwelling with its rows of cold, dark windows eyed me with hostility. I wanted to topple the walls with my eyes, to see the man because of whom villages were going up in smoke, and people, hunted down like animals, were being bled to death. Because he, those villages, the people, the Browning, and I, were links in a single chain. And the longer I sat across from the building, the more fiercely the icy block of courage seared my heart.

"It has to be done."

Had I said that?

No, I had only thought it.

And once again people and the stream of life surround me. How azure-blue the sky is today, how clear and lofty! And the golden laughter of the sun! Hot steaming breath billows from horses, people rush about, and the frost is striking fires. And it is amusing to see, as if at a masquerade, milk-white whiskers stuck on youthful faces . . . and horses white and shaggy like lambs. Ting-a-ling . . . Little bells sow transparent sounds, and sleighs sail behind the swift legs of horses.

A girl is running towards me. Her cheeks are blazing, her eyes are burning, and she catches my glance with a warmth and a devotion that only those who meet for a moment before parting

forever are capable of. An instantaneous romance—short and
sweet, like a shooting star. I am grateful to you. You threw a
flower into my heart, and I caught it, and perhaps I'll carry it to
the grave. To the grave? What grave?
Ah, yes, that's right . . .
And now, grey, alien, and unknown, I'm among people
every day. I'm absorbing everything that I need to know, just
as the earth soaks up raindrops during a drought. From where?
Here, there, from the air. Because everyone knew him, because
he was odious to everyone, harmful to everyone, and everyone
growled at him just like a timorous dog who is too scared to bite.
He sometimes goes for a walk in the morning. Aha! But not
alone, his guards are with him. At twelve o'clock he receives
visitors, but strangers are frisked. I already knew that he had
a daughter, a beloved daughter, and that he loved the theatre
even more. I knew his habit of stroking his beard, and his other
habit—hiding his fist behind his back. Finally, I even knew when
he ate, went to sleep, got up. I knew everything that I needed to
know and even things that were superfluous. It was as if I were
preparing to write his biography or his obituary.
I still had not seen him, but the theatre interested me. I
stopped in front of the billboards, read the posters, and tried to
guess what attractions Fifi held, who Cecilia was, and which one
of them was prettier. I even attended the theatre; I saw Fifi, I saw
Cecilia—but he wasn't there.
And once again I wandered. Alone, grey, and unknown, like
a distant and pale shadow.
Finally, I did catch sight of him. Once . . . I remember . . .
It was snowing that morning. An even, thick, and warm
snow. Tiny snowy beings that died in the sky and fell to the
ground to their eternal rest in a quiet cemetery. Rows of houses,
rows of trees receded like white shadows into the distance and
dissolved in a fog. A white flood. All the sounds came from
below, as from under water. The cathedral bell rang hollowly;
the submerged bell sobbed mournfully for a long time. Slush-
slush, slush-slush—feet splashed by at a measured pace. It was
as if something huge was chewing under the water, chewing and
swallowing the sounds. And everything that moved in the fog
became a shadow and vanished forever.

Suddenly, something wild and bizarre broke into this silence. A *kozak, hunched over the neck of his horse and breathing heavily in unison with it, dashed by at breakneck speed. And then horses, black and sleek, pulled a carriage past me at a gallop, and in the clear glass, as in a frame, were reflected a handsome, waxen profile, frowning eyebrows, and a white beard. And while I was still gazing at this image, everything vanished, dissolved, and became a shadow . . .

What? A shadow? Yes . . . a shadow . . .

Mother!

Shh . . . quiet . . . I'm the unknown one . . . Ha-ha-ha!

Will anyone hear the voice shouting in my heart, in the depths of my heart? Will anyone know that you are my mother, and that I'm your son? Mother, don't cry . . . Your son will meet death with a pure heart and with his head held high. Because all the blood, innocently spilled, is seething in his heart, because all the tears of his people have poured into it, and the anger of his nation has flared up in flames. Kill me, executioner. You are killing my nation . . .

. . . Never before had I thought that the earth was so lovely, that a patch of sky, a tree, laughter, a human voice could bring such deep joy, and that they are as vital to people as the air. So does an impoverished rich man reach down, pick up from the ground and kiss the scrap of bread that he used to throw to dogs. Right now I can see—and it makes my heart rejoice—the flames of the lanterns burning in the thawing ruts, while the snow is dark, as if blackened by smoke. The eaves are dripping, and every drop hums and sparkles with fire in its flight. The unpolished windows in the stores gleam like pearls, and a silvery aureole hovers over the city as over a saint. A saint or a martyr.

And I walked—I could not remain indoors—and my thoughts, covetous and inalienable, were always following him, step by step. I could see him. He is having breakfast; his wide chest is draped with a serviette, and his soft white beard tumbles down over it. His eyes are smiling at his daughter and at the pink radishes that he also likes. Delicately picking up the white stem of a radish with his waxen fingers, he is pleased that everything is so nice, so clean, so tasty, that it is warm and quiet in the house, that his beautiful daughter is beside him, and that he himself is handsome and dignified. He rests for a moment . . . A fish is served—and he inhales the fragrant steam and places a large portion on his plate. If only he doesn't choke on a stupid fish bone! I'm so afraid . . .

And here is the office. He is scowling and reading attentively, and frowns gather around his eyes and twitch angrily. A bell rings, an official runs in, and how sorely he tries the patience of the one in command! How I hope that there is no unfortunate incident . . . I'm so frightened . . . I'm frightened that there might be an accident, sudden death, for everything is possible . . . Well, praise the Lord, the day has ended without a mishap . . .

A bedroom. A soft, green light falls gently on a ponderous body, on a white beard, and on a noble, elderly profile. Sleep does not come at once; his thoughts hover, and his eyes see something over there, in the shadows . . . perhaps, me? Go to sleep. Good night . . . perhaps until tomorrow?

I'm becoming more and more accustomed to him. I feel that he is growing into me like a root grows into the ground, that he is becoming dearer to me. I do not separate myself from him. I can't. Something secret, mystical is concealing itself in our bond, as if one of us is the shadow of the other: while one of us is still alive, the other must also live. And the Browning is concealing two bullets—one for him, and the other for me.

I dreamt of him last night: a handsome, majestic, elderly man with a waxen face. And during the day uneasiness hissed in my chest. Something irritated me, something sucked at my heart, something was missing. Now I know what it was. The desire to hear his voice was beating fitfully within me. I had to hear it.

And time dragged on.

. . . I met up with her once again. The one who had cast a flower into my heart. She glanced at me with such a friendly, tenderly curious eye, that the flower came to life and emitted a fragrance. And instantly it was springtime; the sun, the joy, and the laughter all revived . . . I felt an urge to seize in my embrace a stern-faced man coming towards me and to press him to my heart: my brother!

I saw you, my dear mother, mending your dark clothing by lamplight . . . so good and so poor . . . so dear and so poor . . .

and I listened to the din of life as if it were music. Happy and free once again, a son of the earth once again, no longer the anger of a nation . . . And the hateful profile disappeared from my sight . . .

What? It vanished? Away with everything that is crowding into my heart! I am the unknown one . . .

Now I am here, amidst these walls, like an animal in a trap. It is you, O blind eye, who is watching me through the hole in the door . . . it is you who has reminded me . . . But how? To perish in here . . . in this sack . . . when there is freedom out there . . . work . . . friends . . . Where? Ha-ha! The window is high? Yes, it's high . . . What about digging my way out? Under the walls? That's impossible. Smash my head against the wall?

Alone . . . all alone . . . how tedious . . . how tedious . . .

But perhaps?

No . . .

*   *   *

How strange, how extraordinarily strange. I can hear—somewhere up above bells are ringing. The frozen trees, the tiny twigs, are covered with ice. With glistening ice, with transparent glass. And the wind, the old bell ringer, having gathered together a thousand threads, is shaking the branches and ringing them over and over again . . . Ting-a-ling . . . ting-a-ling . . . And flaming sparks—green, red, blue—leap over the branches . . .

Where have I heard this? And when did I hear it? Back then, when I was still little? When, when did I hear it? Ah, yes, it was not so long ago . . . three or four days ago . . . Ting-a-ling . . . Ting-a-ling . . .

*   *   *

I burn with shame at the very thought of it. Once . . . yes, once—and never again.

Once I glanced around because I felt the cold slimy trace of strange eyes on my back. Something was following me. An overcoat. I turned and walked back. It was there. I walked more quietly. It was still there. I stood by a tree. It seemed to have stopped. Should I look back? No. I walked on more quickly. It seemed to be racing after me. But maybe it was my heart? Who could tell . . .

This was making me angry. I screwed up my courage, turned around, and came face to face with him. Our eyes met. Mine were indifferent, innocent, calm, but his were evil and sharp as needles. With laughter in the corners. Well, fine. What next? You're clever, but I'm no less clever.

I tensed my nerves like a ship's rigging in a storm, and walked on. He seemed to be lagging behind. Should I look back? No. I whistle. Indifferently. What am I whistling? Could it be the *Marseillaise*? More likely—a waltz. Why continue walking? Would it not be better to stay alone at home and not draw attention to oneself?

He seemed to be lagging behind. I looked around. There was no one there. So it's safe. I went to the left, into an alley . . . and bumped right into him, into his sharp, cold look—a look like a bayonet . . . Aha! You're in pursuit! You've already found the one you need and now, calling for help, you're going after him. Aha! You're out to catch him . . .

And suddenly coldness arose from below and, like mercury, rolled upwards to my heart, to my throat, to the tips of my fingers. It pressed on my brain and pushed it out of my skull. Should I shoot? Run away? Where to? Over the fence? It didn't matter, as long as I got away . . .

And I became light, weightless, and I sped blindly, like a scrap of soiled paper in a storm, through strangers' gardens, over fences, over the deep snow, and something was pursuing me, whistling, yelling, and stretching out its arms . . .

It was my fear.

And only after the danger had passed, when my brain had settled again in my skull, and the blood coursed through my body, did I recall my vileness . . . I remembered that while fleeing I had thrown away my Browning . . . yes, thrown it away heedlessly, like something hostile, something dangerous . . .

I had to go back! A burning shame made me go back over the fences, through strangers' gardens, over the deep snow, back to find it, no matter what kind of danger lurked there, even if death itself was there . . .

I still feel revulsion . . . at the recollection . . . and the knowledge that a despicable, frightened animal dwells within me . . . sears my heart . . .

. . . The waxen profile, and the white beard . . . It was as if he were rebelling within me, as if he were very angry that he had flown out, together with my brain, for even a moment. He was growing larger in my chest; he was taking over my brain, oppressing me, stifling me, and I wanted to get rid of him ever so badly.

"Aha, you thought I was yours, but now—you are mine," he teased me, laughing malevolently.

After all, what was he to me? And in what did our bond exist?

I was the anger of the people and their retribution, the breath from the lips of truth, the fire from the black cloud of human injustice, the arrow from its bow . . .

. . . It was as if I had known. I gulped the air so greedily, my chest breathed so freely, my eyes stared so intensely—all as if for the last time.

Hoarfrost . . . hoarfrost covered everything, and night descended, quiet, sensitive, and profound. Trees blossomed with cold flowers, white and filmy like bridesmaids. A poplar, veiled, slender and trembling, stood like a betrothed on her way to her marriage. She waited: a young man would come, take her hand and lead her away. Lead her among the wedding guests, into the azure silence, amid the fires.

And the sky was dark and clear, and fragrant, as if made of violets. And the wedding guests were there. All the stars came, even the tiniest ones that do not come out on damp nights; they huddled together in heaps, stood in rows, sat by themselves, pale, quiet, modest and splendid, glittering and shameless, changing their colour every minute. From distant streets flowed the music of human hubbub, and little bells sped along, clean and naked like after a bath . . .

That was the wedding night, my wedding night . . . A flower bloomed in my heart and a familiar face lured my eyes, who knows from where . . . from the variable stars, from the blossoms on the trees . . . The first and final night . . . It was as if I had known.

There must have been something interesting at the theatre because people were flocking there. Happy, animated, and buzzing like swarms of bees flying into a hive. The cold light laughed shamelessly, and the door slammed rhythmically. Sleighs were continuously floating by, horses were breathing, whistling, snorting, and flinging the snow around.

"Do you want a ticket? Here it is . . ."

And I'm caught up in the crowd.

A feather boa tickles my cheeks . . . the warm scent of perfume . . . a cold, angry look . . . a growl: pardon! Before my eyes there is a grey overcoat, and, behind me, someone is breathing down my neck . . .

Why have all these details impressed themselves on my brain? Why do these memories stick in it like thorns, when the main event—the end and the beginning and the middle part all taken altogether—seems to have been swallowed by my memory. I only remember that I began to tremble. Because the oppressive profile, the waxen profile exited from me . . . and took its place not far from me.

He was stroking his beard and hiding his fist behind his back. And I heard his voice. Now that voice, sticky, drawling, lives in my ears; it has plastered itself over my brain . . .

Did I shoot? There was no sound. A deathly silence. The frowning eyebrows lifted upwards like wings, chased his sorrowful eyes, meek and startled like those of a puppy, from his forehead, and became a shadow . . .

The great anger that lived within me flew out and did its deed. And a cold wind immediately blew into my empty breast, straight into the searing wound . . . Just for a moment. Then there was nothing.

I don't know what came next . . . a moment or eternity . . .

* * *

. . . The cold floor dug into my cheek, I saw a boot, big and wet, before my eyes, and a weight was thrust upon me . . . knees, hands, until I could not breathe. All at once there was an uproar, shouting . . . Footsteps on the stairs, doors slamming, and a thin wailing sound, like that of a fly. Then frost, fresh air . . . and crowds of people everywhere, all strangers to me. Not people, but mannequins from a store . . .

And then?

Then . . . a wolf's lair, and both of us are in it: my death and I. Well, keep on waiting, keep your bloodthirsty eyes on me . . . from over there, from the dark corners . . . You've earned your reward . . .

What? Are they coming already? And are you approaching as well from the dark corners? I must remain calm . . . I must remain calm . . . So calm, that my heart will become a block of ice, my forehead will be chained in pride, the grey morning itself will shudder, and the hearts of the executioners will smoulder with fear . . .

I go without regret—it had to be done.

How beautiful my road is . . . my final, short journey. The morning is splendid, white and hazy, like a funeral shroud.

Clink . . . clink . . . rattle the rifles slung on their backs, and the men carrying them trample their own grey stares under their feet.

Already? So soon? It has happened. There is no need . . . I'll do it myself . . . so that my eyes can see . . . And my own final breath . . .

Mother! It is you in the snowdrifts . . . You're swimming in the snowdrifts like a grey shadow of suffering in order to seize my final breath in your warm palms . . . a sigh, dedicated to others, but not to you? Don't listen, mother, and don't look . . .

Ping!

*   *   *

Ping!

Did I just imagine that I heard it? Am I still alive?

I touch the walls . . . Yes, the walls are cold, hard . . . and I see my feet shod in my shoes . . . I can raise myself, get up, fill my chest full of air . . .

Is the window high? Yes, it's high . . . What about digging my way out? What? It's impossible?

But perhaps . . ?

Why?

(1907)

He was moving swiftly, as if being pursued, as if fleeing from Tartars. Every time that he took a step, every time that he yanked his foot out of the deep snow, the wind rushed up, swirled around him, howled, and completely covered up his footprint, and once gain everything became smooth and devoid of all markings, like the sea when it is calm. A white, boundless ocean, and he was out on it all alone, like a rickety boat struggling against the looming darkness.

The dark clouds, which during the day had sped over the sky like black flocks of huge wild birds, were now massed together and spreading over the horizon in a large silent carpet, as opaque as a blind man's eye. They had already covered every last bright spot in the sky, and it was impossible to see anything. Occasionally, a dried-up weed, sticking out of the snow, creaked mournfully, as if complaining about its fate, or a lone leaf tore itself away from a branch and began fleeing to warmer, more temperate climes, or a stump crept out of a small mound like an animal out of its den, and then once again there was only whiteness, and once again there was nothing, only the wind blowing, and the frost chattering its teeth.

He is walking. He does not need to see the road, because his heart tells him where his village is. Let the night remove every last bit of light from the sky, let the entire world change into a cave, he would still find his way to his home, to his wife, to his children; he would celebrate Christmas Eve with them.

He has enough strength. Back there, in that odious, cramped, stuffy, dark hole, he had lain for days on end, for many a sleepless night, thinking about work. He had rested. And he has no fear of animals. He feels that he could wrestle a bear to the ground.

But he does not want to meet up with anyone. He is fleeing through the fields like a dog that has lost its way and is afraid of coming across strange hounds. If only he can avoid seeing anyone until tomorrow, so that he can spend a few, just a few hours with his wife and small children in his own house, like a true man and a master of his home!

And then? The border isn't far away. He will cross over to the other side, and then—only his name will be left behind. He will manage one way or another.

All he has to do is to get to the river, to the clear ice—and he will fly over it like a bird . . .

He tucks his hands into his sleeves, draws his head into his shoulders, and continues treading, trampling the white snow determinedly, angrily, despairingly.

The wind is jostling him, pushing him into deep white pits, piling up heaps of snow, but he does not pay attention to any of that—he keeps on going—he has to get there!

Here is the mound. From it, you could usually see for hundreds of *versts—versts that are sprinkled with villages and farmsteads, spread with grass, ruffled with meadows, belted with rivers, bedecked with flowers.

But now there is snow everywhere, darkness everywhere.

You could take a step, and it could be game over. You could tumble into veritable obscurity.

He presses himself closely to the top of the mound that has had its white fur cap blown off by the wind, and he listens, he listens intently . . . It's the wind . . .

But somewhere far away, very far away, there are sounds of life. The barking of dogs. That means there is a village . . . But where? To the right, beyond the river—so there are at least ten versts left to go . . .

And renewed strength surges through his body, renewed desire fires up his breast. He is awash in a deathly sweat, but he walks on, he keeps on going. And when, a long way up ahead, he sees the first light in the village, he flies towards it with the eagerness of a child.

The light floods his heart with brightness. It is his native village, the one that he had vainly tried to catch a glimpse of for so many months through the iron prison bars, the village from which he had been forcibly torn away, leaving his wife and children abandoned.

In another moment he would be with them. He would sit down to the *Holy Supper in his own warm, neat house like a man, like a householder. And tomorrow? Tomorrow let come what may. He could not remain any longer in that filth, in captivity, in that hellhole . . .

But he will not go through the village. He will enter it from the fields, like a wandering mongrel that fears village dogs. On this day, or for even two days, he does not want to meet up with people . . .

He keeps on going . . .

Now he is in his own yard, in the porch, in his house.

His wife was stunned when she saw him.

"How did you get here?"

"Just as you see."

"Did they free you?"

"May God free them of their sins at the Last Judgement in the same way that they freed me."

"You escaped?"

"Of course I escaped . . ."

And her face that had momentarily brightened with joy clouded over again with a new sorrow.

"What will happen now?"

"I don't know . . . If you have some food prepared, give it to me, because I'm dying of hunger."

His wife rushed over to the oven, opened the damper, and the scent of borshch and cabbage rolls wafted through the room.

"So you haven't eaten yet?"

"No, we haven't. It didn't seem right to eat by ourselves."

"And the children?"

"They were waiting for the *first star to appear, and then they got it in their heads that daddy was coming. They waited and waited, and then fell asleep."

He walked up to the bed and smiled.

"My, but they've grown, the poor dears. Mariyka looks like you, and little Pavlo is such a *kozak—it's incredible."

"He takes after his father," his wife said.

He stroked the children's round little heads, sighed, and fell deep into thought.

"Give me some decent clothes, so that the children don't see me in this 'uniform'."

"Oh, I'd forgotten that they dressed you up in such fancy clothing there."

She opened the trunk and passed him some clothes.

He washed up, combed himself, put on the fresh clothing, and he looked like a different man. And then he rolled up the prisoner's garb and threw the bundle in the stove. He added some kindling wood, lit it—and it caught fire and burned.

"Oh my, just look at the smoke and the stench from it. Tfu! It's really crackling."

From the mouth of the stove there poured forth such a thick dark cloud of smoke that it seemed as if the house was on fire, and the sizzling noise woke up the children.

They rubbed their sleepy eyes with their plump little fists and stared at their father in amazement.

"Daddy?" the boy who was older asked.

"Yes, it's daddy, my children, it's daddy," and he lifted them out of the bed.

The boy sat down by his father on the bench, and the little girl perched on his knees.

They began to eat.

"Where were you for such a long time, daddy?" the boy asked.

"I was far away, my son, may you never have to set foot there yourself!"

Then the little girl asked: "Who cooked for you there?"

And then they started talking in a rush of words.

"Mother cried for you every day."

"And I did too."

"We have some small piglets."

"They're ever so white!"

"And the reeve said, that you'd never come back to us," they babbled with happy, cheerful voices.

"The reeve, my children, is a fool. Don't listen to what he says. If daddy goes away someplace, he'll always come back to you. Eat your borshch, children, because if you don't finish it, you won't get any *kutya."

"We don't want any kutya."

"Oh! Why is that?"

"Because the kutya is bitter."

"How can it be bitter? Kutya has honey in it, it's sweet."

"But mother said that the kutya would be bitter this year."

"Mother just frightened you by saying that, my children; eat it. The kuytya is sweet."

They fell silent and ate. The wife gazed at her husband as at an icon . . . He had not lost much weight, but he had aged, and he no longer had an air of freshness about him. Only his eyes still shone just as they used to shine. When he looked at you, it felt as if hot embers were being strewn on you.

A year ago, when he talked about freedom at the meeting, sparks like lightning flashes flew from those eyes, clouds hung over his brows, and his voice roared like thunder. He was handsome and terrifying, so terrifying that they had taken him away and locked him up like a wild animal.

"Why are you looking at me like that?" he asked, feeling her warm gaze upon him.

"Because it seems strange to have you here with us. It's as if I'm in a dream. It's a strange Christmas Eve supper."

"A strange one . . . Strange things are happening now in this world, and there's no end to the strangeness . . . If only you could see the people who are rotting alive in prisons, if you could hear the kind of tortures that they have to endure, you would pray to them as you pray to the holy martyrs."

And he began to talk passionately about what he had heard and seen. The small room was gradually filled with people who had been murdered, tortured, who had died an agonizing death while having only one desire: freedom. Shrieks and groans made their way into the room from all corners, and a mighty blast of anger and revenge rocked the house, like a storm shakes a tree in the forest.

Chests heaved ever higher, hearts beat ever faster. The children's pupils widened, as if they wanted to reflect in them the whole world with everything in it that they had not seen and could not see.

Suddenly: "Mother, someone is coming!" the boy said and he clutched his father's arm.

Quiet . . .

"You just imagined it, my child," the mother said.

"Someone was walking down the street."

"Cover the window, so that evil eyes can't look in."

"It would be better if you sat in the corner; no one can see you there."

He obeyed her and moved over, but he was still uneasy. Something alarming, unknown was prowling near the house. They did not *cast the kutya up at the ceiling, the children did not *cluck in the hay; they extinguished the lamp and sat in the dark.

He told them about his captivity, how he had suffered and grieved, until he had finally reached the point that either he would break out of that tomb, or die by his own hand. Today, because of the Holy Supper, they had been guarded less strictly, the guards had more to drink than they usually did, and so now he was here, beside her.

"You've lost weight, my poor dear, you look disheartened," he said, stroking her face with his hand, and her heart with his voice. "Don't worry; it will all work out somehow."

And she responded not with words, but with tears.

"I'll celebrate the holiday beyond the border. And once I'm there—they can search for the wind in the fields. I'll find work on an estate, or in a factory—I'll manage one way or another. In the spring you'll go to our Mykhaylo—have him rent the field out to someone. Today everyone needs land, and they'll pay for it, and Mykhaylo will see to it that we're treated fairly. You'll tell him to sow wheat on the dried-up pond, and rye on the middle field, it will grow like bullrushes. Don't sell the cattle. God willing, a new law will come into being, and I'll return, and you know how difficult it is to be without any cattle."

They talked, and time kept passing by. And then the night passed by. The wind calmed down, the stars tumbled out over the heavens like sheep out of a pen.

Trees, silvered by hoarfrost, could be seen through the window, and the well-travelled road that went down the length of the village looked like an embroidered linen cloth that had

328 | Bohdan Lepky

been washed and spread out to dry. Cottages with snow on their thatched roofs stood alongside the road and gazed with their lit windows at a church in a linden grove on a hillock. Smoke swirled out of a few of them. They bore a striking resemblance to householders in white fur caps smoking their pipes as they made their way to the church for an evening Divine Service.

There were the sounds of someone running from one yard to another, of a gate creaking, of dogs barking. Over here the neighbours were returning home after taking the Holy Supper to the priest, over there Ivan was on his way home after visiting Sofiya, and then there was Mykyta Hrim, the village's most notorious drunkard who was on his way home from the tavern, but he could not find his cottage. He toppled over in front of the blacksmith shop and began carolling. At the other end of the village, people were singing . . .

* * *

"Someone is coming! Do you hear?"

"Yes, I do. Look out the window, maybe you'll recognize someone."

She stuck her head in the window.

"It's the county policeman and a few other men. O Christ our God!"

"Don't shout. Did you lock the door?"

"Yes, I did. O our Holy longsuffering Mother, look down on us and on our children."

"Stop wailing. If they come, tell them that you don't let men into your house at night. Do you understand?"

"Yes, I do. Oh, my wretched fate. Why are you punishing me so cruelly? Alas, O fate!"

"I'm telling you, don't shout, because you'll wake the children. Go to the door, you can hear them knocking on it."

Someone struck the door three times with a cane, in the manner of matchmakers.

The wife forced herself to speak: "Who's there?"

"It's me, the county policeman, open up!"

"I'm alone in the house, and I don't let men come in at night," she replied.

Laughter resounded outside the door.

"Just look what kind of a saint she is! And what about the one who has been sitting with you all evening, is he not a man?"

She did not respond.

"Don't open the door," her husband prompted her. "Let them break it down."

Hundreds of thoughts raced through his head.

"I'm ordering you to open the door in the name of the law!" the policeman said in a serious official tone.

"And I'm telling you, my good people, that I don't let men into my house at night. Come during the day, and stop scaring my children at this hour."

"We're not just any men, we're officials, do you understand that, you stupid woman? And if you don't let us in willingly, we'll use force to enter your house, because a community cannot shelter a convict . . ."

She felt as if she had been struck with a sledgehammer.

"A convict!"

"Just you try and do that," the man who had been offended spoke up. "I'll greet you like thieves that try to break into someone else's house at night.

"Ah, we greet you with the holidays, Sydir. You see, we're saying that we want to have a talk with you, but your wife doesn't want to let us in! We've come on official business. Let us in!"

"Don't let them in, don't!" she begged, hanging on to him.

"Well, what am I to do? Am I going to crawl out through the chimney, or what? You can see that they've surrounded the house. I have to go out."

"Well?" the policeman insisted. "Are you going to let us in, or aren't you?"

"First of all, send your people away."

There was the sound of whispering by the door, and the crunching of feet on the snow. A few men could be heard walking across the yard, opening the gate, and then closing it.

Sydir tied up his coat and put on his cap.

"Don't go. Listen to me. Don't go!" his wife pleaded, clinging to his feet. "Don't go!"

He gently pushed her aside and opened the door . . .

They stood silently for a minute.

One man was in the doorway, and the other was on the path leading to the house. Sydir—a proud, broad-shouldered man with sparks flashing in his eyes, and the policeman—scrunched up and looking diffident as if he is guilty—scrawling on the snow with his cane.

"So, have you come to get me, as you'd come to get a murderer?" Sydir asked haughtily, and he waited for a reply.

The policeman remained silent.

"Just like Judas betrayed Christ, you want to give me up to the authorities, me, who was your voice and your lips, who wanted to gain freedom and land for you and your children! And is that why you've come together as a group to hunt me down as you'd hunt down a wild animal?"

Anger was distending his chest.

"Tell me, have I ever harmed anyone in the slightest in the community!"

Grief surged into his throat and choked him so hard that he was unable to speak.

The policeman replied cordially.

"No one is saying anything like that. Every child will testify to the fact that you were an upright householder and a good neighbour."

"Then what do you want with me? Why are you attacking me in the dark of the night?"

"Because that's the law, Sydir, that's the law. You know that it's not permitted to shelter an escapee, that severe punishment is meted out for that."

"And as to why he has escaped—you're not interested in finding out why?"

"That's another matter. We're not to blame for that."

"Then who is to blame—am I?"

"You're not to blame as well. Only Holy God knows who is to blame."

"God? You're fools. Instead of helping me, instead of everyone standing up for me, as I stood up for all of you, you hounded me like hunting dogs, you vile creatures!"

"Don't be angry with us, Sydir. You know that we're not doing this of our own free will. The authorities tell us what to do."

"Let the authorities say whatever they want to, but here's what I'm going to say to you. Go home and have a good night's sleep, and by tomorrow I'll no longer be present in the village. All right?"

The policeman remained silent; he was scared to reply.

"Well, how about it? Tell me."

"It can't be done that way."

"It can't be?"

"No. The people know, and they'll inform the authorities, and there will be trouble. Get dressed and come with us to the village office; if Merciful God helped you escape once, then maybe He will help you a second time. Get dressed!"

"Sure, Holy God is supposed to help me, but you won't, even though I endured so much suffering for you, you vile, miserable slaves. Get out of my yard. I'll do as I have said. Get out, because it's all the same to me now—get out!"

And he raised his powerful fists just like Moses in the icon when he raised the tablets with the commandments.

The policeman glanced at him with his sly, slanted eyes, grasped what was happening, and without a second thought, rammed his head into Sydir's chest and simultaneously tried to grip him as hard as he could.

Sydir yelped, tottered, but quickly regained his balance, and like a drummer striking a drum, swung his powerful hand and struck the policeman's back. And, just as from a drum there comes a loud sound, so from the policeman's chest there issued a dull, deep sound—huuu! He doubled over, like a man who dove headfirst from a riverbank into a river, and his nose dug into the snow.

"My back! Oh, my back! He's broken my back," he shrieked as he rolled over the ground.

"Beat him up, beat him, oh, my back, oh, oh, oh . . ."

Several male bodies fused to form a single monstrous entity that spun, roared, and groaned through the yard, swinging its fists, kneeling on its numerous legs, tearing swatches out of the dishevelled hair of its heads, and spitting out curses and blood.

The policeman struggled to assist, but with every attempt he collapsed even lower, and cried out more pitifully: "My back! Oh, my back! Beat him as long as he's breathing! Oh, my back!"

And the monstrosity, whirling through the yard as if it had lost its mind, gone mad, was leaving behind a trail of groans, blood, swatches of hair, and torn pieces of clothing.

Fluttering after it like a seagull on the waves, a woman with her clothing in total disarray was pleading wildly with bloodless lips: "Leave him alone! You'll kill him! Leave him alone! What are you doing, people? Leave him alone!"

The children had awakened inside the house and were screaming.

The monstrosity rolled from the threshold to the gate, and then fell apart, like a chopped up snake.

A few men, bloodied and gasping for breath, stood over a heap of human flesh.

"My goodness, but he's strong—like a wild animal."

"He grew strong like that in prison."

"He sure gave us a good drubbing!"

"Just look where my teeth are!"

"He bit off my finger!"

"Oh-h-h-h-h!"

"Oh, my back! I can't stand it!" the dying policeman groaned.

* * *

Stars blazed in the sky. A bell rang out in the church. Softly at first, as if someone was lightly tapping on the gates of paradise, and then more loudly, as if silver bullets were ricocheting off the domes of the church, and then even more loudly and more frequently, until the pure sounds soared over the village, over the fields, over the meadows, announcing to the world the joyous news that Christ was born.

Under Dark Clouds
(A Sketch)
(1907)

A May evening was approaching the village quietly and imperceptibly. A flaming sun was setting behind a hillock and its parting rays flickered on the crosses of the village church. A pleasant coolness and a gentle, charmingly enigmatic aura permeated the air.

Human voices died away, and the alluring sounds of a spring night intensified: May beetles buzzed over orchards and somewhere far off in the distance frogs were croaking, nightingales were singing . . .

On the horizon, a full moon was rising serenely and grandly. Somewhere, youths and maidens were breaking into song. The evening was becoming so delightful, so cheerful . . .

But not everywhere . . .

At some distance from the village, a cemetery trailed down the steep slope of a hill until it reached a pond. Dark, weather-beaten crosses, flooded by the pale rays of the moon, stood gloomily in it.

Here and there, some of the crosses were crumbling and falling into ruin. The graves were overgrown with prickly shrubs, tall weeds, and wild flowers.

Down below by the pond, silent willows, bowed deep in thought and trembling lightly, were reflected in the silvery ripples. The many diverse nocturnal sounds scarcely penetrated there. Only screech owls, calling out dolefully, occasionally disturbed the deathly silence. Everything was sleeping, enveloped in a quiet sadness.

But it only seemed that way . . .

At the very edge of the cemetery a recently-placed grey stone cross stood all by itself. On the fresh grave beneath it, young grass was growing and bright-hued flowers were blooming. In the midst of the prevailing silence and somnolence, it was only by this flower-bedecked grave that life was shaking violently in the painful embrace of sorrow and grief.

An elderly mother was kneeling by the grave and, as she bent down low over the flowers, scalding tears from her faded eyes were falling like sparkling dew upon them. The poor woman was sobbing softly . . .

After a while she raised herself, clasped her hands prayerfully and, gazing intently at the starry heavens, pleaded with the Highest One to grant her son, her one and only hapless son, a better fate at least in the next world. And there were moments when it seemed to the poor woman that the bright heavens heeded her fervent prayers, and at those times her aching heart, sinking into oblivion, found some peace, felt a soothing relief.

But the stone cross still stood before her . . .

And once again, the pale image of the youthful suicide floated out of the mist—and once again her heart cramped painfully with unutterable grief, and once again she wept inconsolably and pleaded with the heavens to take her up there as well, to take her to her son.

It was now late in the evening. A resplendent moon had ascended high in the sky and was joyfully illuminating the village scattered haphazardly over the hillocks. In the moon's glow the white cottages stood out vividly amidst the dark, fragrant orchards.

It was quiet in the village. The lights in the cottages had long since been extinguished. People, exhausted by their hard work, were now resting; it was only youths who were still calling out to one another in the streets. Every so often, dogs that had been alarmed by rustling sounds of one kind or another raised an angry ruckus, and in the enchanted orchards the amorous songs of the nightingales rang out.

It was at this hour that the weeping mother, leaning on a walking stick, slowly made her way home from the cemetery to the village, accompanied by inconsolable grief and pursued by silent anguish.

* * *

The grave with its stone cross and colourful flowers marked the end of the sorrowful story of one young life. It began in the comfortable home of a well-to-do farmer. Its childhood years passed by like rolling waves moving with the tide. Warmed by the unstinting love of a father and a mother, this young life unfolded like a spring flower in the warm rays of the sun. The poor flower! Little did it think that before long that same sun would scorch it with its fire of kindness.

Both the father and the caring mother boundlessly loved and indulged their only son, their only hope and joy. They wanted him "to get ahead in the world," and so they sent him away to study in a high school. The gifted boy flung himself with an unquenchable thirst at the healing fountain of "the living water" and drank avidly of it. The parents could not take enough delight in the diligence of their beloved son.

But in his keen mind there soon arose the eternal questions: "Who am I? Why am I living in this infinite world? Is there another world beyond the tomb?"

And these burning questions clung tenaciously to the youth like evil spectres. He wanted to forget about it all, to flee somewhere far away . . . But is it possible to flee from one's shadow? It will chase you everywhere until the sun finally sets.

And yet, all around him, people were calmly shouldering the squalid burden of daily life and for them everything in the world seemed so clear, the goal in life so easy to comprehend.

Troubled to the depths of his being, the youth turned to his father and mother for consolation. He spoke eloquently and passionately to them about his painful and ever-recurring questions and tried to get a comforting answer from them.

But the elderly parents, unable to comprehend his thoughts, were alarmed by what he was saying, and they advised the poor fellow to do his best to "get ahead" and assured him that everything in the world comes from God, and that it was not up to people to judge what is good and what is bad; they talked of the evils of sin and the terrible punishment sinners would endure in the next world . . .

And afterwards, when the father was alone, he would throw up his hands in despair because he simply could not understand what had happened to his Sashko.

"If only he doesn't end up with the *Stundists! Nothing seems to please him, nothing seems quite right to him!" the father worried. But then he would immediately console himself: "Many things happen in a lifetime! It will all pass—and everything will be just fine."

And the mother wept softly and prayed fervently that her child would have a good fate.

The unfortunate Sashko felt even worse after these conversations. "Get ahead!" Oh, if only they knew how disgusting it was for him to look at these envious people among whom he was to "get ahead."

"A sin!" But how was he to to find a person without a sin?

And the poor youth gazed with anguish at the gulf that was growing between him and his parents, and he felt so sad, so pained that he could cry. He felt sorry for his father and mother. They loved him so much, admired him so greatly, and had vested all their hopes and dreams in him. They worked tirelessly for him, possibly even taking advantage of others and sacrificing their honour in the process, and they did all this to make "a man" of their son, a gentleman.

And what about him? Could he respond in kind to their love and affection? Was it possible for him to bind his life with theirs in the way that they had done? Oh, if only it were possible for others to understand how painful and difficult it is to know that you are loved boundlessly, that someone lives only for you— and, instead of feeling genuine gratefulness, to have only cold disdain in your heart! Oh, what a distressing situation it was! But whose fault was it?

A few years went by in this way. Not having received any words of advice from his parents or from people that he knew, the young man began to search for answers ever more fervently in the writings of "great dead men." And not long afterwards, the pink flame of a goal in life started flickering before his sorrowful eyes.

And as that flame began to burn more and more brightly, it filled his young heart with an ardent desire to fight for what he believed, with passionate hopes and the joy of being alive. And in the youth's visions of the future everything seemed so splendid, so full of beauty and power . . .

It was at this time that, just like a spring thunderbolt in the middle of winter, a stormy tumult arose and the luckless nation awoke under its powerful impact; trembling with joy, all who lived and breathed gathered under a new flag. Young Sashko was completely caught up in these enthralling waves. He forgot about everything: his own life, his father and his mother. Only the great goal of the liberating struggle blazed before the young man, and he soared towards it with his entire being, and there was no abyss that could have stopped him. Oh, how he lived, how he believed!

But all too soon the new songs began to fall silent.

Black snakes crawled out of their dens and with the sepulchral coldness of "pacification" they killed the splendid blossoming of this new life. With an insane ferocity these black victors buried everything that hindered them from leading a vegetative existence in this world. They understood that the sun could not be extinguished, and so, falling into an even greater frenzy, they covered it with clouds.

Under the dark clouds that hovered so gloomily over the country, *Oleksander's life disintegrated: in his penultimate year in school he was expelled for "free thinking."

* * *

Dawn was breaking. A warm breeze was blowing. Light clouds floated in the sky. Gradually the crosses in the village cemetery and the willows by the pond emerged out of the darkness.

It was still cold, but the air was already buzzing with the victorious songs of spring. Raging streamlets raced down the hills; in drier spots the grass was turning green; by the pond the willows were budding . . .

A youthful, alluring power was trembling everywhere, trying to free itself from a cold embrace.

It was also trying to free itself in the heart of a young man who was standing motionless, as if petrified, under the willows by the pond. Tall, thin, and pale, he lowered his head that was exhausted from his thoughts, and nervously clutched a pistol in his right hand.

"Why am I waiting? Why am I hesitating? I can't go on living—that's completely understandable!"

Sashko had said this to himself several times now, but he was still standing and staring into an invisible distance, and the same painful thoughts kept penetrating his mind of their own volition.

"To live at home—that would be to forego my spiritual development, all my beloved dreams; to listen, day in and day out, to my father's reproaches, to quarrel with him and to watch my mother weep over my fate? Oh, no, never! That's not possible! Poor mother! And I also feel sorry for you, father . . . After all, is it their fault that they cannot understand in what I have vested my happiness, what I cannot live without? The poor dears! What will happen to them after my sudden, unexpected death? But then, I'm not to blame that I am no longer able to live in this world!"

And in his mind's eye he saw the evening when he had come home from the city after being expelled from school. It was only a day after it had happened. Seeing from afar his native village and his father's house illuminated by the rays of the setting sun, he had stopped and thought for a long, long time: was it right to disturb the tranquility of this home, of this village? And there were moments when he pulled out his pistol with a trembling hand, but then he at once put it back again. The sun had already set behind the mountain peak; a pleasant breeze was blowing from the west, and pink clouds were rushing across the sky.

"No, it's better that I keep on going and tell them everything, just the way that it is: maybe they'll understand; and if they don't, then . . ." and he had continued on his way.

The old folks were in their comfortable home and, as was their custom, they were talking about their son. He would finish his studies, become a gentleman, and he would not have to bend his back under the weight of heavy toil as they had done . . . They had not worked and saved in vain—at least they had a son who would thank them . . . And it would bring them so much joy to look upon his good fortune—that was what they had been living for . . .

Rumours were circulating about all kinds of "riots" in schools, but God willing, they would all come to an end; and after all, would Sashko actually want to ruin both them and himself?

At that moment the dogs raised an angry ruckus out in the yard, and the elderly couple had not yet had the time to look out the window when . . .

What was this?! An apparition?! Sashko, looking pale and distraught, walked into the house. They both blanched and flung themselves at him.

Calm and decisive words: "They've expelled me from school, and they won't take me back . . ."

"My dear ones," Sashko thought as he stood under the willows, "if only you could comprehend who our enemies are, who has so cruelly ruined my life and, along with it, yours as well!"

And tears welled in his eyes: he could almost see his father standing before him, his eyes flaming with furious anger, his grey eyebrows tensed in a grim frown, his hands shaking: "Get out of here!" he had shouted and groaned. "We lived only for you, slaving away and denying ourselves! And you? You? You villain! Get out of here! I never want to see you again!"

His mother seemed to have collapsed at first, but then she embraced him and would not let him out of the house.

And when she was alone with him, she reproached him and wept, and simply could not understand what he was saying.

"Am I to live at home and to see, every day, those tears, that grievous sorrow? Oh, no, no, no! It's better to flee to the ends of the earth! But who will welcome me anywhere, of what use am I to anyone? It's the same all over as it is here. Oh, you damned ones . . . How wonderful the world would be without you!" And he clutched the pistol tightly in his hand, and his tearstained eyes flared . . .

It was growing lighter by the pond . . . In the village the roosters had long since crowed. Here and there fires had already been lit in cottages.

Sashko could feel his body shaking, and this seemed to awaken him from slumber.

He fearfully asked himself: "But why am I waiting? People will wake up soon, someone may come here . . . Am I really so faint-hearted? Oh, how shameful!"

At that moment he saw the old church watchman start to walk down towards the pond.

"Oh . . . he's coming here! Farwell, world! Oh, alas . . . how I long to live . . . And over there . . . what's waiting for me there? Oh, this is being cowardly! It's so shameful!" the youth whispered through pale lips as he pressed the pistol to his forehead . . .

His widely opened eyes no longer saw anything, and in his brain thoughts were replaced by frenzied apparitions.

The trigger clicked loudly and the watchman shuddered with apprehension when he heard the shot.

He walked swiftly to the pond and then recoiled in horror when he spotted the body all splattered with blood lying under the willows.

"O Lord, it's Sashko Dolenko!" the old man said and, leaning over the deceased, he carefully looked him over.

Then he doffed his cap, crossed himself piously, and muttered: "O my God! What has he done? Has he committed suicide? There's no one else nearby . . . O Lord! I've lived for a long time on God's earth but never before have I seen such a misfortune. What could have happened?!"

And he rushed off to see the elderly Dolenkos.

It was quiet, very quiet around the deceased: only the rustling of the branches of the reinvigorated willows and the splashing of the indifferent waves against the bank. And then the sun came out and benevolently cast its rays on the bloodstained face of the suicide.

* * *

An autumn day hovers over the village. Clouds have covered the sky; a fine rain is drizzling.

The houses have turned dark; the leaves have fallen from the trees.

At the cemetery the crosses have taken on an even gloomier appearance, and the leafless willows are imbued with even deeper sorrow.

It is only on the grave with the grey stone cross that the yellow immortelles and varicoloured asters are still blooming.

And even though some of them have wilted, and even though the ones that are still blooming are being set upon by the cold and battered by the rain—that does not matter at all: they cheerfully lift their beautiful little heads to the heavens.

And the immortelles whisper to the asters: "Let the clouds cover the sky . . . Let the rain fall thick and fast, and let the wind howl. Let them! The long-awaited time will come! Summer will come and the clouds will vanish, for the sun will rise. It matters not that we will wither and fade away . . . The time will come!"

The flower-bedecked grave is not as lonely now as it was in the springtime.

Just a short distance from it, another grave, recently heaped up, looms darkly: it is the mother who has found her eternal rest beside her ill-fated son.

And the dark clouds scowl ever more gloomily as they cover the earth with oppressive sorrow.

When the Acacia Trees Were in Bloom
(1907)

I

The acacia trees were blooming luxuriantly. Their branches, covered in white blossoms, peered through the windows. It was still early. The sun was blazing. It looked as if it might rain. The acacia trees emitted a strong fragrance. It was oppressively hot in the house. The fragrance of the acacias was irritating.

Mr. Vitold Dynovsky, a pharmacist, felt very uneasy. He was waiting for the doctor, but the doctor, for whatever reason, was taking his time—he was nowhere in sight.

There was no one in the pharmacy. It was unbearably hot. Today there was a market in the town, and wagons rumbled past the shop one after the other, raising clouds of dust.

Mr. Vitold closed the door so that less dust would drift inside. And there still was no sign of the doctor.

The sound of footsteps could be heard through the wall. The pharmacist's son Vitya was walking in the adjoining room, pacing the floor from one corner to the other.

"He's been pacing for such a long time. He didn't undress or lie down all night. He just keeps walking and walking . . ."

And as he listened to his son's pacing, Mr. Vitold grew even more agitated: why wasn't the doctor coming? He feared for Vitya, and he was half-expecting that another misfortune, a new grief, would befall him at any moment.

Vitya had returned from Warsaw in a strange mood. Mr. Vitold could see that he was not well, that his heart ached, that terrible thoughts had taken hold of him.

And Mr. Vitold's heart also began to ache and troubling, foreboding thoughts crept one after the other into his head. They seared the elderly pharmacist's heart, shrouding it in sorrow and dread.

And Vitya continued pacing and pacing and pacing . . .

And every footstep painfully wounded the father's heart and reverberated in it with a scalding pain.

Now Mr. Vitold began pacing in the pharmacy. His footsteps rattled the small bottles on the shelves.

The pharmacist paused and listened . . . Yes . . . Vitya was still walking and walking . . .

"Over there, in that corner, his footsteps can't be heard for a moment. That's the spot where he turns around . . . But over here, at this end, they can be heard clearly. Now they can't be heard again. Yes . . . yes . . . he's turning around."

As he listened to his son's footsteps, he tried to chase away his frenzied thoughts, but it was hard to rid himself of them . . .

Oh, how disturbing they were!

The doctor finally arrived, tall and woeful looking. He had a long stride and he did not seem to be in full control of his movements. This created the impression that it was difficult for him to carry his own wasted, lanky body, that something was pressing down on him, something heavy, reproachful. And the look on his face was always so sad, so pensive: it seemed that he could see right into his patients' hearts and that he knew, without anything being said, what was hurting them and what they needed. That was probably why patients loved Dr. Stanislav Markevych so dearly and preferred to go to him than to the stout Dr. Vitvitsky with his cold, indifferent eyes.

"Good day, Mr. Vitold."

"Good health to you, doctor. Do sit down. Forgive me for troubling you."

"That's fine; I'm a doctor, and everyone has the right to trouble me. So, who is ill at your place?"

The doctor slowly lowered himself into an armchair.

"But who could be ill at my place, doctor? Vitya has come home . . ."

"He has?" Dr. Markevych asked somewhat indifferently as he set about lighting a cigarette in a long holder.

"It's been three days now since he's come back from Warsaw. I noticed at once that he was ill, that his heart was troubled."

"His heart? That's just as I expected . . ."

"You expected it?"

They both fell silent for a few moments.

Mr. Vitold understood what the doctor was saying . . .

"You see, Mr. Vitold, I know your Vitya very well. He has a good, sensitive heart. He always was the nervous type."

The doctor seemed to be speaking half-heartedly, sadly, drawing out every word in an enervated manner.

"And now, Dr. Stanislav, he has come home very ill. He has completed his training to be a pharmacist, he has taken his last exam, but he's ill, very, very ill . . . His heart is broken. I can see that he doesn't have the strength to live. You know, Dr. Stanislav, why he finds it so hard to live . . ."

The doctor looked up at Mr. Vitold and remained silent for a moment.

Then he said even more sadly than before: "I know . . . Well yes, of course I know . . . So you're afraid that after the death of your . . ." The doctor's voice trembled. "After the death of your daughter Zosya . . . Vitya no longer has the will to live?"

"Yes, that's what I fear . . . Have a look at him, ask him what's wrong. You have the right to do that, you're in a better position to ask him, because you're a doctor."

Mr. Vitold's eyes were pleading.

"He likes you. You know how to. . ."

"Fine, I'll look in on Vitya. Is he there, in his room?"

"Yes. Just don't tell him that I sent for you."

The doctor walked out.

The pharmacist heard him knock on Vitya's door and greet him in a loud voice, but after that he could not hear anything. They were speaking quietly. Only Vitya raised his voice from time to time.

A young married woman came into the pharmacy and, sobbing bitterly, handed Mr. Vitold a prescription that she untied from her kerchief. The woman spoke of her husband who had injured himself a year ago when he was working for the lord, and now it looked as if he might die; that he had not been accepted into the hospital because it was overcrowded with patients . . .

The young woman wept and talked on and on through her tears about her grief, but this grief was foreign to Mr. Vitold and it did not pierce his heart with a sharp pain because his heart was already aching from his own, more personal anguish.

He set to work preparing the prescription for the young woman.

II

Upon hearing the doctor's voice, Vitya halted in the middle of the room, looked at him in astonishment, and then walked up to greet him.

"Good health to you, my dear Vitya."

"Doctor . . . good health to you too . . ."

Vitya extended his hand to Dr. Markevych and, enveloped in his sadness, remained standing close to him. His eyes were filled with weariness, and sorrow, and grief. His curly blond hair fell uncombed onto his pale forehead. His entire small, lean figure reflected the anguish of an afflicted heart.

He did not say anything for a few moments, and then eyeing Dr. Markevych closely and coldly, he asked: "Did father send you to see me? Have you come to heal me?"

The doctor, without replying, crossed the room, sat down on the bed, and looked directly at Vitya with the same cold look. Their eyes met. Vitya found it hard to withstand the doctor's self-assured gaze: he was peering right into his heart, stirring it up—a heart that was broken and heavily burdened.

"Why have you come?" Vitya asked once more, and it was evident that he was becoming upset. "Have you come to hear my confession, or what? Why are you doing that . . . why are you looking at me like that, doctor?"

The doctor was silent for a moment, and then he asked softly: "Does your heart ache?" And he patted the spot next to him on the bed.

Vitya sat down. He felt that an unknown power was drawing him to the doctor, to this good, kind Dr. Markevych, in whom he had more than once confided his secrets and his worries from the time that he was a child. It seemed to Vitya that even if he refrained from saying anything, the doctor would know what was in his heart and would understand . . .

And he felt he had to tell him what was burdening him, oppressing his heart like a stone; he had to tell him, because it was weighing so heavily upon him . . . because his heart was dying from grief—a grief that was inexpressibly distressing, as cold as death itself . . ."

"Yes. It aches. . . It aches so terribly, so terribly, Dr. Stanislav!"

They fell silent again for a moment.

"What am I to do, my dear Dr. Stanislav?"

The doctor did not respond. He kept his eyes fastened on Vitya, and his look—warm and gentle, but penetrating—pierced Vitya's heart.

"I can't go on living! I don't have the strength to go on living like this!"

And Vitya, in a distressed voice, began expressing his grief in an unending stream, all the while dropping his head to his knees, and then raising it abruptly.

"In my heart, something terrible is stirring . . . such an implacable grief . . . Ahh! Doctor! You once claimed that you understand the human heart, that you could have become a good psychiatrist, so tell me, is it possible to live with such a heart? But tell me honestly, not like a doctor, but like a friend."

"What kind of a heart?"

"One that is crippled, defeated. You were planning to be a psychiatrist, Dr. Stanislav, so why do you need to ask me questions? You know what is in my heart, I can see by your eyes that you know. You don't know? Well, then, maybe I'll tell you all about it . . ."

Vitya fell silent, collecting his thoughts. The pain in his eyes revealed how difficult it was for him to irritate the wounds in his heart with words.

"When I recall . . . when my sister Zosya stands before me with that daring look on her face, with her disdain for death, something whispers to me, reproaches me, sears my heart with harsh words: 'But you couldn't do that, you wouldn't have the courage' . . . and then I don't know . . . I don't know what to do, where to get the strength to go on living, for I . . . for I could not have done that. It's true, I sense that I care too much about myself to do what my sister Zosya did, to draw a lot and go to meet a certain death. And I am seared by flames of shame, and my heart weeps, but still . . . Well, tell me, my good, kind sir, is it not senseless to die like that? She went, missed the target, and shot herself. Are there no other paths that can be taken?"

"It would seem that other paths cannot be found."

"But what came of it? For what did she die? The man that she shot at is still alive, but Zosya's bravery, her disdain for death fired up our brother's heart . . . and the poor lad . . . our Stas was sentenced to do hard labour. And my father and I have been left orphaned. Our hearts have been broken."

Vitya stopped abruptly.

"But what am I saying? What am I saying, doctor? I'm thinking only about myself, caring only about myself . . . I'm ashamed of myself, Dr. Stanislav, and this shame has split my heart in two! No, into more, many more tiny fragments . . . And every little fragment hurts differently, unlike any of the others— it has its own pain, sears me with its own distinctive fire! Every tiny fragment of my heart, doctor! Do you understand? There is such an intolerable ache in my heart. I . . . I cannot find a way out, I do not know how to save myself!

"Doctor, dear doctor, heal me so that my heart will not ache, so that there will not be so many little fragments, so much pain, so much suffering!"

Vitya leaned his head on Dr. Markevych's shoulder and wept: quietly, and then more loudly. And at that moment he felt truly wretched, desperate.

"Do you know how to heal me, Dr. Stanislav?" he asked through his tears.

"Yes, I do. But you must not carry on like this. You must be calm, and listen to me."

"And I'll get better?"

"Yes, you will."

"I'll get better . . . Ha, ha . . . But I have no right to be healthy, I have no right to live!"

Vitya stood up and, as if seeing phantoms, hesitantly brushed them aside with a listless movement of his weary hands.

The doctor approached Vitya, embraced him, and took hold of Vitya's hands with which he had covered his face.

"What is it? Are you imagining things?"

"It's nothing. Now there's nothing . . . it's gone. Truly, am I not a miserable useless wretch? A gutless creature? No, no! I shouldn't go on living, I shouldn't!"

"Yes, you should," the doctor said confidently.

"What for?"

"For your father, for your native land."

"Of what benefit am I to them? Does my native land need people like me? Ha, ha . . ."

Vitya once again began pacing the room.

Dr. Stanislav stood deep in thought. And then he suddenly stepped up to Vitya as if he wanted to tell him something, but he lost his nerve and stopped himself.

"Ahh . . ." Vitya groaned in a weary, exhausted voice. "How it aches, how painfully my heart aches . . ."

It was then that Dr. Stanislav came nearer, placed his hand on his shoulder, and spoke softly to him.

"Vitya, do you know what I'm going to tell you?"

"What?"

"That my heart also aches, just like yours, and that I, just like you . . ."

Vitya turned to face the doctor.

They were standing by an open window, and the sun's rays fell on both of them. The doctor noticed that a joyful flame instantly sparked in Vitya's eyes.

"Your heart also aches? Of course, it's true that the hearts of many people ache now. It's just as difficult for many others to live as it is for me." He was speaking very quickly, as if clipping his words.

But a moment later that flame went out. And once again sorrow, and weariness, and grief were reflected on his face.

"Vitya, I should . . . I want to tell you something . . ."

"What?" Vitya responded almost indifferently.

The doctor was quick to catch this tone of voice and the fact that his eyes were enveloped in sadness.

"No, I've already . . . I'll talk to you about it some other time."

Vitya, hunched over, his head drooping, was pacing the floor. To look at him was to see the living embodiment of the sorrow that had entered the room.

Dr. Stanislav pressed his hand firmly in farewell.

"Look at me, Vitya, I'm just like you, but I'm living . . . I'm enduring it. Well, that's enough. I'll write you a prescription to calm you down."

Vitya accompanied him to the door.

"Come more often. We'll grieve and bemoan our fate together."

"I will. Thank you . . ."

Vitya sat down on the bed and thought for a long time.

He thought about the fact that he was weak, superfluous, useless. "But the doctor said that he was like that as well."

And Vitya felt a little better, because he now believed that he was not alone in his sorrow, in his helplessness, and he imagined that there were hundreds, thousands of others just like he . . . many, many crippled souls . . .

He lay down and thought some more; he thought about the doctor, and about his brother.

And as for Stas, his brother, and Zosya—most likely they too felt like that, but they knew how to hide their feelings, to save themselves through their fervour.

And that was why Zosya had gone to her death, and Stas had gone to do hard labour.

Exhausted by his thoughts, his pain, and his despair, Vitya fell into a sound sleep. And he awoke only when the sun was setting.

III

Vitya got out of bed, picked up his violin, and began to adjust the strings. He felt stronger after his nap. He no longer felt the sharp, terrible pain in his heart.

He had not played for a long time, and the strings were badly loosened.

As the setting sun was going to its rest, it flooded the orchard with its last warm rays. Stillness and gentle peacefulness crept in with the evening hours. And a tender, comforting tranquility permeated the heart. And simultaneously there arose a desire to share one's grief with someone, to cry softly, quietly.

Vitya played the sad melody of a folk song. The strings sang, and the violin spoke gently and tenderly to the soul. Vitya played and, along with the melody, something precious, comforting, surfaced in his heart. Memories of the past came to life.

Earlier, Mr. Vitold had glanced in through the door several times, but seeing that Vitya was still sleeping, he had softly closed it again. Now he heard Vitya playing, and he entered his room hesitantly with the filled prescription in his hand.

Vitya saw his father, but he continued playing. The more he played, the more clearly and sadly the violin sang. The melody sobbed, grieved, and melded with the chords of the evening stillness and the fragrance of the acacia trees.

He finished playing but continued to hold the violin in his hands, moving his fingers over the strings. He was thinking. It was as if he had forgotten about his father who was standing beside him, forgotten about everything, everything.

"My dear Vitya, here's your medicine. You have to take it three times a day."

"Aha! Three times a day? Well, let's have it . . . I'll take it."

Mr. Vitold poured out a dose and passed it to him. Vitya drank it and grimaced—the medicine was bitter.

His father took the spoon and turned around to go, but then he stopped, apparently wanting to say something.

Vitya was standing near the window with his back to his father.

"Listen, my dear Vitya," Mr. Vitold addressed his son cautiously.

"What is it, father?" Vitya turned around.

"Are you feeling better, more at peace?"

"Yes, I am, father, but don't ask me any questions . . . I want to think. I don't want to say anything. I'll just play, and play some more . . . I feel good when I play."

"Well, I just . . ."

"No, no, father dear, please don't be annoyed, don't be offended."

Vitya was standing close to his father.

"Why are there tears in your eyes? I'll tell you everything in good time, everything. I'll just spend some time thinking. I need to think . . . We'll go on living one way or another. We are being told that we must live! Well, you can go now. There's no need to look at me so mournfully!"

Mr. Vitold started to leave again, but then he turned around and asked: "You don't want to talk to the doctor either? He's asking if he can come in to see you."

Vitya thought for a moment and then put his violin down on the table.

"Please ask him to come in."

Vitya sat down on a stool by the window and waited for Dr. Markevych.

The doctor walked in hesitantly, with a troubled look on his face.

"I feel better, Dr. Stanislav!"

"That's very good. Would you like to go for a walk with me in the forest or by the river?"

"No. I prefer to stay in the house."

"Well then, I'll have a talk with you here."

Vitya glanced up at him with startled eyes.

"Don't look so worried. I won't talk to you as a doctor. You must remain calm, Vitya. I told you that my heart also ached: and that was the truth."

"I believed you."

"Your heart aches for your sister. You should know that it was your sister that I . . ."

Vitya shuddered.

"My heart aches for Zosya, because . . . I loved her. None of you knew that. She was my wife in everything but name."

"Zosya? At seventeen?"

"Yes, yes! Stay calm."

Dr. Markevych clasped Vitya's hand in his.

"Forgive me: I loved her, I loved her dearly . . ."

The doctor's voice trembled.

"But I couldn't hold her back. She told me that she would never be anyone's slave, that she wanted to be free. And that's why she wouldn't marry me, and she remained free to the end of her life."

Dr. Stanislav dropped Vitya's hand and stood before him, forlorn and vulnerable.

"But didn't you know that she was going to her death?"

Vitya asked the question in a choked, hoarse voice.

"Yes, I knew. Zosya and I were in the same organization, and we drew lots for the assignment. The lot fell to Zosya, and she travelled to Warsaw to carry it out. I pleaded with her to let me take her place; I kissed her feet . . . O Vitya, my dear Vitya," the doctor groaned.

And that groan attested to the intense suffering in his heart.

"But Zosya wanted to stay free, and she said that, if she died, I should quit the organization."

Vitya involuntarily glanced up at the doctor and stared at him in terror and despair.

"She said that if she died, my work in the organization would be tainted, because I would want to avenge her death. And I vowed that I would honour her wish. And now I curse myself! If only one had known how burdensome it was going to be, how very painful!"

The doctor nervously walked over to another corner.

It had grown darker, and in the dim light his tall, shadowy figure melded with the twilight and imbued the room with a mood that was heavy, gloomy.

Vitya felt a sharp hatred flare up in his heart, it was growing stronger and surging into his throat, simultaneously burning and choking it.

"Dr. Stanislav."

Vitya walked up to him decisively and whispered: "I'll do it for you and for myself."

"But you mustn't."

"Why not?"

"We have to honour Zosya's memory."

"But didn't Stas revenge himself for Zosya's death and didn't he go to do hard labour because of that? But I, the worthless wretch that I am, sit around, pining away, thinking . . . It's a shame, a shame!"

"No, it's not a shame. A sacrifice, my dear Vitya, should be as pure as a sunbeam."

Vitya fell silent, sat down on the bed, and let his head sink to his knees.

Warm air, saturated with the strong fragrance of the blossoming acacia trees, streamed in from the orchard. This fragrance irritated both of them, and neither of them wanted to go on living.

They sat like that for a long time.

Finally the doctor rose to his feet and, in parting, said: "I must go to see my patients, to bring people back to life. We all must live. We are orphans, my dear Vitya, and life is equally difficult for both of us, but Zosya told me to live for her, to keep her memory alive. We must go on living, my dear Vitya, there is nothing else that we can do! You have your violin, you have your father . . . but I have neither a violin, nor a father. I have no one. A star flashed and then it disappeared, died away, leaving behind a luminous trail. We must live, my dear Vitya. Goodbye for now . . ."

He left, and a moment later he could be heard talking with Mr. Vitold in the pharmacy.

But Vitya seemed to have been turned into stone: his heart was in the cold grip of fear, and despair, and impotence, and he had no desire to live. He felt utterly depressed.

IV

For a long time that night, the pharmacist did not lie down to sleep. The light was still on in Vitya's room, but he did not come out. More than once Mr. Vitold went up to the door and cautiously opened it.

Vitya was sitting at the table, writing something and occasionally leaning back in his chair. It was evident that he was thinking hard about what he was writing.

It was one o'clock when Mr. Vitold, still very concerned about his son, began to undress. He said his prayers, turned off the light and, sighing heavily, got into bed.

He slept right next to the thin wall that separated him from Vitya's room. Through this wall almost every little sound could be heard.

The pharmacist held his breath and listened. A foreboding did not let him fall asleep.

He heard Vitya get up from the table and walk about the room. Then he leaned out the window, probably checking to see

354 | Leonid Pakharevsky

if his father's light was still on. He went to the door, came back, stood by the table, shuffled some papers, and went out the door once again, gently opening it and shutting it behind him. He walked stealthily down the corridor and stopped momentarily at his father's door.

Mr. Vitold wanted to call out to him, to ask him to come in, but he was seized with fear and stayed silent and still. He remembered that Stas had also wandered through the house at night, and in the morning they could not find him anywhere, and he had never come home again. After remembering this, he was even more alarmed.

Meanwhile, Vitya quietly opened the door to the pharmacy and walked in.

An even more terrible thought seized Mr. Vitold. He quickly leapt out of bed, threw on his robe, and ran barefoot to the pharmacy. He came to a stop in the doorway.

Vitya had lit a candle and, standing with his back to his father, was trying to open the door to the cupboard where poisons were kept.

But the cupboard was locked, and Mr. Vitold always kept the keys in his pocket.

Vitya was trying to tear the door off its hinges.

Mr. Vitold ran up to him and grabbed his hand from behind his back.

The candle fell, and the room plunged into darkness.

"My dearest Vitya! What were you going to do?" the pharmacist cried in terror.

"Nothing, nothing . . ." Vitya responded in a whisper.

"Did you intend to poison yourself? You too? You dared to think to abandon me as well? But what about me? What would I do then?"

Vitya collapsed against his father's chest and huddled closely to him.

"Oh father, my dear father . . ." and that was all that could be heard, for he was sobbing loudly, wailing.

As Mr. Vitold embraced his son's neck, he felt that he was holding his only salvation in his arms. He caressed the dear head with its soft curly hair, kissed it, and wept over it with old fatherly tears.

"It's so hard for me, I don't have the strength to live. Why didn't you let me go there . . . to join Zosya?"

"My dear Vitya, you mustn't! After all, I'm living . . . Live for me, my dear one, my beloved son . . . The two of us will be together . . ."

And both Vitya and Mr. Vitold wept unrestrainedly in the dark pharmacy.

A dark, sultry night reigned.

A light breeze drifted in occasionally, carrying with it the fragrance of the acacia trees. And both the wind and the scent of the blossoms spread a comforting tranquility over the land.

This nocturnal peacefulness peered through windows at weary, aggrieved people and whispered softly about better times to come, about brightly resplendent days on earth, and exhorted them to live!

Plantations
(1925)

Chapter One

The manor yard is large—a few *desyatyny in size, and there is no fence in sight. The buildings, huddling closely to one another, enclose the yard in a circle of red brick. There are only two gates. The one for the cattle and the farm workers is between the mill and the barn for the oxen, and the other that serves as the visitors' entrance is located between the manor office and the building housing its employees.

The main gate politely permits the young lords and ladies of the manor to walk through it and allows a carriage to drive into the manor yard.

The enclosed circle of buildings is broken in one spot by a colourful splash of aesthetically laid out trees and flowers, and behind them, forming a white background, rises a manor house built in a modern architectural style.

If one were to go from the cattle barns with their ammoniacal fragrances across the yard to that manor house, one's eyes would alight on the heavy, skilfully carved door of the front entrance and the copper tablet affixed to it:

FELIX FELIXOVYCH RAMP

CHIEF ADMINISTRATOR OF THE STAROSTYN ESTATE OF THE

COUNTESS VOZNYAKOVA-DONCHYTS

No icon has ever experienced from a human hand the kind of respect shown to this tablet.

And that is why its brilliance blinds the eye and focuses one's attention on the thick black letters:

FELIX FELIXOVYCH RAMP

The eye quickly fastens itself upon these three words and the petitioner's hand presses the button of the electric doorbell. The icon-door is opened by a fairly old and self-important footman in a long frockcoat and a collar as white as snow. The petitioner's knees begin to quake and his tongue ties itself into a hopeful knot. The knot has every intention of leaping into his windpipe, but his brain, like a broken gramophone, is pounding, and he is only able to stammer: "Is he . . . Is he . . . Is he . . ."

Suddenly, the liveried footman, having given the visitor a quick once-over and assessed his social standing, states abruptly: "My good sir, you should come back in a week . . . The lord is not at home . . ."

And even though the lord's voice can be heard quite clearly within the manor rooms, the footman once again emphatically states with an inexorable firmness: "No, he is not at home . . . In a week . . ."

After these words are spoken, it is not fitting for the visitor to remain in the vestibule, and that is why the elderly lackey in the frock coat starts to shut the door as if there already was no one there. He steps on the visitor's tattered shoes and uses other diplomatic tactics that he has learned during his long service as a footman to forcibly shove the visitor out the door.

Finding himself out on the veranda, the nameless visitor once again reads the inscription on the copper tablet, the knot in his tongue gives up its attempt to leap into his windpipe, and his hand, that up to now has been trembling uncertainly, clenches itself into a firm fist, and his tongue, freeing itself from the powerful knot, begins to function formally: "To hell with you!"

His feet carry him resolutely out of the manor yard.

Ramp is a foreigner, but his nationality is not known. His surname would seem to indicate that he is German, but there is nothing German about him. His impeccable knowledge of the English language could have given the impression that he is an Englishman—if it were not for his swarthy complexion and his dark, provocatively aggressive eyes that reminded one of a Rumanian Gypsy. His habit of always holding a long-handled whip or having it tucked in the leggings of his lacquered boots during official conversations emphasized his resemblance to those swarthy experts of horse breeding.

His character traits also gave rise to certain thoughts about his lineage. Ramp knew how to take advantage of any situation and this seemed to confirm the fact that the genealogical branch from which he sprang was linked to a family tree in the benign seclusion of a Gypsy tent.

Ramp lived alone in a luxuriously appointed apartment. And he never talked about his kinfolk, even though questions about his parents were often posed to him.

Every Sunday guests arrived at the white mansion either to play cards or to go hunting, and Ramp treated all the neighbouring landowners and the senior employees of the estates and sugar refineries with ironic familiarity and an unconcealed disdain in the depths of his dark eyes.

Ladies were often present in the company. Ramp addressed pleasantries to them, but the sardonic twist of his mouth belied his words.

In his struggle with the semi-proletarianized peasantry, Ramp held as tractable armaments tens of thousands of desyatyny of land with two sugar refineries on them. The countess had no need to worry about her income: it flowed into her delicate hands in a golden stream through the navigable rivers of the banks.

It seems that the countess who owned the estates and the sugar refineries had made a deliberate choice to stay forever in foreign spas instead of returning to Starostyn.

Two years prior to the 1905 Revolution she had put in an appearance in Starostyn; she had stayed there for only a few days, but this brief visit was remembered for a long time on all the estates.

It was on a fine spring day that the countess, accompanied by Ramp, had gone from her mansion to the sugar refinery and then from there to the manor.

Everyone noticed that the countess was unhappy and disturbed about something.

They were wont to recall that in the evening the countess
had summoned Ramp to her mansion and, without mincing any
words, had shouted hysterically: "I'm not at all pleased with you,
Mr. Ramp . . . You don't know how to run things . . . Under your
supervision, even the refinery isn't working! And yet you keep
writing to me that it's turning a huge profit!"

During the exchange, Ramp had kept his whip in the leggings
of his boots, but upon hearing these words he swung it once and
sliced through a silk couch right down to its springs. He did not
say a word, but his eyes were blazing ferociously, and his hand
was snapping the whip handle into fragments.

The eyes of the countess froze and then rolled out of sight as
she slid weakly onto the carpet.

The chambermaid brought some water and cologne before
she was curtly ordered to leave the room.

When the countess regained consciousness, Ramp, acting
as if nothing had happened, said politely: "You, my illustrious
lady, are exhausted. You need to rest, and I'll take the liberty of
focussing your attention on . . ."

And Ramp spoke to the countess in a whisper for a long
time.

The chambermaid could not hear the whispered words, and
so they remained a secret.

The next day the countess went abroad after sending the
main office a letter in which she gave Ramp permission to take a
yearly stipend out of the income of the estate as a reward for his
excellent administration of her estates and the sugar refineries.

And a month later, a package containing documentation
arrived in Ramp's name, and on the carved door there appeared
an additional tablet:

FELIX FELIXOVYCH RAMP

TRUSTEE IN ALL THE BUSINESS MATTERS OF THE

COUNTESS VOZNYAKOVA-DONCHYTS

Chapter Two

The estate of the Countess Voznyakova-Donchyts stretched in a wide swath from Domashiv to Krasnopil, encompassing hundreds of square kilometres of the Domashiv and Krasnopil districts. Dozens of small villages along with two sugar refineries were scattered over this expanse, and in the centre of it, like a diamond, lay the main Starostyn manor with the mansion of the countess and the largest sugar refinery in the district . . . And that was why the entire group of properties was known as the Starostyn Estate and was under the direct control of the main administrative office located in Starostyn.

In the vast expanse of the Starostyn Estate only a small handful of land belonged to the peasants and to the petty impoverished nobility.

And over time the lands held by the petty nobility kept shrinking because the estate of the countess gobbled them up as it rounded out its holdings.

The impoverished nobility ended up on farmsteads, lost its distinctive class characteristics, and gradually began working the land. And if the grandfathers still flaunted their tattered courtly uniforms and their completely useless credentials, their young descendants walked behind a plough and, on their way home from the fields, cheerfully whistled and sang the songs of peasant youths . . .

The great railway that linked two seas traversed the length of the Starostyn properties, and on it, as if flowing through a giant artery, the lifeblood of industry came and went.

From distant Chile, it brought saltpetre; from Moscow, manufactured wares; from the Don, coal; from New York, machines; from Germany, kainite; from Podillya, superphosphate; from Sweden, whitefish meal . . .

All these varied materials were digested in the industrial stomach of the estate and of the sugar refineries, and in their stead Starostyn flung onto the world market sugar, wheat, and fattened oxen.

And the sugar, the wheat, and the oxen were miraculously transformed on the stock exchanges of Moscow, New York, London, Berlin, and Odessa into *karbovantsi, francs, dollars, sterling, and marks. The iron artery brought nutrition to the industry and took away the products of its life processes. It took away more than it brought in, because to everything was added the labour of thousands of semi-proletarianized peasants, the riches extracted from the earth, and the energy of the sun that was harnessed by the green networks of the plantations.

From early spring to late autumn, hundreds of thousands of workdays were swallowed up by the beet plantations on the Starostyn Estate. Entire armies of diggers and hoers of beets, unable to devote their labour to their own niggardly plots of land, moved out onto the plantations. And while the older peasants busied themselves on their small parcels of land, the younger ones spent the entire year working off the two months of forced labour on the lord's plantations.

From the age of seven, children picked cockleburs, the primordial saboteur of sugar beets. As soon as they learned to handle a hoe, they went out on the fields to loosen the soil, to get rid of weeds, and in the fall, when whole families took over strips of land to dig out the beets by the *berkovets, these most tender youngsters spent days on end out in the fine autumn rain picking over the cold wet beets with their chapped hands and cutting off the stalks.

Babies were born out on the plantations; mothers snatched a bit of time from their work with the beets to nurse their infants; and the children, as they grew up, devoted their strength to the same plantations.

And the sugar, refined by the cracked, roughened hands of people who had only a crust of bread and a small onion for breakfast, painstakingly bypassed their small villages so that it could be used to feed pigs in faraway, enigmatic England.

Long before the laborious production work on the expansive beet plantations begins, the production apparatus stirs and comes to life. Before the arrival of spring, the railway casts out yellow sacks of superphosphate, jute spheres filled with whitefish meal, machines, and other material for the Starostyn Estate.

Dignified oxen pull large carts weighed down with fertilizer to the small villages that are the smallest units of the production organism.

In the main Starostyn manor, weapons are being prepared to conquer the thousands of desyatynas of *chornozem.

Machine shops shriek with tension, hammers in the smithy ring out cheerfully, planes in the carpentry shop smooth wood to a silken finish, and a circular saw wails as it gnaws its way into a piece of wood.

In the spring the sugar refineries are glumly silent. Only their tall smokestacks draw attention to them as they look down over their domains. The refineries are repairing their bodies that had been tattered in the manufacturing process.

At the outset of spring, the main administration's attention is not directed at them; all activities are diverted from the iron organisms of the refineries to the dove-coloured expanses of the fields.

It is only at the beginning of autumn, when the final berkovets of beets is delivered, and the festivities move onto the street where the sugar refineries proudly puff on their smokestacks as they digest the sweet pulp of the sugar beets.

In late autumn the plantations become deserted. The diggers' silhouettes are no longer seen in the weary autumn drizzle, carts creak infrequently here and there as the few remaining sugar beets are gathered up, and later only flocks of crows disturb the grey mist of the darkened expanses.

Near the sugar refineries grow dark sausage-like mounds from which beets are taken in pushcarts for processing. The tracks for the pushcarts stretch from the refineries to stifling holding pits and then still farther on to long barns where oxen, resembling grey giants, are being fattened for slaughter.

In the autumn the old, exhausted, and worn-out oxen are weeded out and sent to be fattened.

Only the young oxen are left on the estate to gain strength for the hard labour in the spring.

The fattening-up process presents the oxen with their final resting place. They have now been reduced to waste material that must bring in profit not by means of their labour but with their meat.

From early spring they pulled heavy ploughs, scrapers, harrows. In the summer they hauled heavy loads from one manor to another, and in the fall they made innumerable trips with grain from countless threshing machines. In the late autumn these same oxen with the large twisted horns pulled heavy carts loaded with beets from the plantations to the sugar refineries. They struggled belly-deep in the swampy chornozem roads, strained their muscles and cracked their hooves.

These horned animals are renowned for their strength, patience and submissiveness. And now, exhausted by their hard labour, they enter long stables in which cement troughs are filled with leftovers from the warm beets in order to close the circle of their productive mission.

The sugar-beet pulp returns their strength to them, they quickly put on layers of fat, and soon after Christmas the central office draws up contracts with businessmen in larger centres to whom they sell hundreds of fattened oxen.

The slaughterhouse is the final stop for these oxen on their path in the manufacturing process.

Chapter Three

To the Novo-Slobidsky
Agricultural Institute

From the Chief Administrator
of the Starostyn Estate
March 3, 1905
No. 273—68

On behalf of the Chief Administrator we are requesting that you send us a student who has completed his studies at the Institute and is prepared to undertake a practicum on the Starostyn Estate.

Administrator SARANCHUK

With a flourish befitting an accomplished accountant, the office administrator, Illya Matviyovych Saranchuk, officially stamped his own signature and passed the document to a junior clerk.

"Illya Matviyovych, you're being summoned by Felix Felixovych!" a young courier announced at the door of Ramp's office.

Saranchuk leapt to his feet and, bowing obsequiously, walked through the open door of the office.

Ramp was rifling through some papers as he sat at his desk and, without lifting his head, he asked: "Have you written to the Institute?"

"Yes, I have, Felix Felixovych. I'll be sending the letter to the post office right away . . ."

"Have the postman wait for a moment, I'll send a letter as well . . ."

Notwithstanding the important position that Saranchuk occupied, Ramp addressed him using the informal "you," in the same way that he spoke to all his subordinates.

Ovsiy Omelyanovych!
Send me a serious student, someone who knows how:
1. to speak English, 2. to ride horseback, 3. to play cards
well. It wouldn't hurt if he was also a good hunter and
marksman.
I'll send a stupid and clumsy student packing.

Ramp

Ramp wrote out the address on the envelope:

Ovsiy Omelyanovych Virny,
Pro-Rector,
The Novo-Slobidsky Agricultural Institute.

Ramp and Virny had been friends when they attended the Institute as students; but after graduating, Virny had immersed himself in further studies while Ramp had travelled over three-quarters of the globe and undertaken three-quarters of all possible professions.

In Crimea he had sprayed insecticides on fruit trees and packed fruit in the orchards of Chebukhtayiv; in the Caucuses he had been in charge of shipping corn across the border; in Switzerland he had bought up watches in bulk; in Cairo he had owned a ladies' dress shop; in Brazil he had looked after herds of horses; in Canada he had been a member of a Doukhobor colony; and in one of the equatorial republics of South America he had held a position of great influence as a confidant of the president.

It was not known what he did in London and Petersburg, but the recommendation of Prince Musnytsky—who had noted in a letter to the Countess that Ramp was his best friend—was proof that the members of the upper classes considered him to be one of their own.

It seems that Virny was the only person whom Ramp implicitly trusted and whom he did not treat with a concealed disdain.

After sending the letter Ramp once again immersed himself in his papers, but then his attention was diverted by shouts and a hubbub in the office.

"But I . . . want to see him!" a shout rang out.

There was a response in a quiet voice, and then there was another outcry: "Well, the devil take him! Let me go!"

And then a troubled-looking Saranchuk ran into the office and said in a trembling voice: "Felix Felixovych! That . . . Khved, who you said should be fired . . . he's come here, he's drunk . . . and he's swearing . . ."

"Well, so what? Chase him out, and that's the end of it!"

"He has a knife! He's waving it around! He's saying: 'I'll slaughter him!' It's you he's talking about! . . . Don't go out there . . . We've phoned for the guards . . ."

Cool flames ignited in Ramp's eyes, and under his trimmed moustache there appeared an even deeper sneer of disdain, and it was difficult to say if it was directed at that Khved who had come to wave a knife around in the main administrative office, or at the cowardly little man whose fear had made him lose his aplomb as an administrator.

"You fools! 'We've phoned for the guards!'" Ramp mimicked Saranchuk. "A drunkard comes, and they called in the guards!"

In five strides Ramp was in the outer office.

Khved was cursing and swearing frenziedly beyond the grating that separated the official section of the office from the waiting room.

Khved spotted Ramp. "Ha, you Gypsy snout! So, you're firing me, are you?" and a colourful curse filled the air.

The accountant ran up to Ramp and whispered obsequiously: "He's drunk, and he's got a knife!"

Ramp, ignoring everyone, walked up to the grated door. The doorknob crashed to the tiled floor and in an instant the chief administrator was standing face-to-face with the fired stableman.

At first Khved appeared to be dumbstruck, but he quickly regained his senses and, raising his knife, lunged at Ramp. That was his last conscious movement in the office. A moment later he was lying on the floor, and the knife, fashioned from a scythe and used to cut the stalks off beets, clanked on the tiles.

It was not the first time that Ramp's training in Brazilian boxing had stood him in good stead.

"S-s-scoundrel!" Ramp hissed in revulsion and, opening the door to an outer office shouted at someone: "Take him away, and call a doctor for me!"

Ramp had miscalculated the strength of his blow and had sprained a finger.

While the doctor from the sugar refinery was assiduously examining the administrator's hand, the unconscious Khved was lying on a bare bench in the small room of the office guard.

Khved, a landless peasant, worked in the lord's stable, but when Herod, Ramp's favourite stallion, had somehow or other wounded his leg, Ramp had personally flayed Khved with his Gypsy whip and given orders to fire him.

Khved's patience snapped. It is a well-known fact that long-suffering is correlated with one's position in society—the lower that position, the more one suffers.

Khved had long harboured protests, but had not had the nerve to express them. His courage was drained by work and depression, so he had to bolster it with whiskey . . .

Yukhym sprinkled the unconscious Khved with water, and the latter opened his eyes.

The effects of the alcohol dissipated, and Khved grew terrified of what he had done. The spectre of hunger, poverty, and jail arose before his eyes . . . Pressing his face against the grimy bench he wept soundlessly . . .

Yukhym bent his grey head over him and whispered to him: "You're a fool, Khved, a fool . . . What made you rise up against a lord, especially in full view of others? A lord must be beaten up when he's alone . . . so that no one will see . . . with a brick, so he doesn't have time to pull out his revolver . . . And what do you suppose will happen now?" Yukhym continued. "You'll be put in jail, or maybe something even worse will happen . . ."

Half an hour later, two guards led Khved away to the sugar refinery.

Chapter Four

Among all the properties of the Starostyn Estate, the Zelenets manor was probably the smallest.

And it was for this reason that Ramp placed Yosyf Matviyovych Varlamenko as the land-steward there—let him not strut around so proudly if he wants to get a good wage managing a larger property.

As Yosyf Matviyovych strode heavily down the orchard paths that were still damp from the recent snowfall he was thinking that the fiscal year had ended two weeks ago, but he still had not prepared his yearly report.

Saranchuk was phoning him on a daily basis, demanding the report, and informing him that Ramp was becoming angry . . . But in the office he had three idiots and that was that . . .

The path through the orchard led from the steward's building to the main administration office. Yosyf Matviyovych strode down this path several times a day, and when the office door was closed behind him by the office boy Syuska, his voice could be heard going on and on through the dust-laden windows: "Rumble . . . rumble . . . Blah . . . blah . . . blah . . . Rumble . . . rumble . . ."

The employees were bent over massive volumes, entering thousands of numbers and clacking on their abacuses as they counted up the *kopiyky and karbovantsi that had passed through their hands in the past year's production process.

The office was calculating the annual balance sheet.

After glancing over the rows of carefully entered numbers, Varlamenko went to his adjacent office and let his thoughts fly over the work of the entire year.

It had been necessary to reseed the beets, the wheat had been flattened, a plague had taken its toll on the oxen, neighbouring estates had greatly raised the cost of hiring workers . . . The hopes of seeing a profit margin were in vain.

The agitated Varlamenko went out on the office porch, looked beyond a pond at the field where harrowers were working, and spotted Ramp's familiar carriage.

"Damn it! It's the devil himself that's bringing him here!" Varlamenko said out loud as he went up to the gate to meet Ramp's carriage.

"Yosyf Matviyovych!" the chief administrator shouted as he got down from the carriage. "The devil only knows what's going on! You still haven't submitted your yearly report! Aren't you aware of the orders from the main administration?"

Nervously clutching his heavy walking stick, Yosyf Matviyovych walked up to Ramp. "I don't think that there's a need to shout about this matter throughout the entire yard, Felix Felixovych!" he observed in a restrained manner.

Ramp's whip twirled more swiftly. "I demand that my orders be treated attentively!"

Varlamenko could not restrain himself. He empathically spat at Ramp's feet and went back into the office without saying another word.

The chief administrator instantly jerked back sharply as if he intended to strike Varlamenko, but he controlled himself. Agitatedly swishing his whip, he stepped into the carriage and gave an order to depart.

When Varlemenko was seated at his desk, he overheard a conversation between the junior clerks. Comically copying the Ramp's voice and mannerisms, one of them was saying:

> They mowed the large meadow in Starostyn, and on
> the next day it rained. And it also rained on the third

day and on the fourth one, and Ramp is holed up in his apartment growing more and more nervous.

"Mykhaylo," he shouts at the lackey, "step outside and see if it's raining!"

"It's raining, sir!" Mykhaylo says when he comes back in.

Ramp sends the lackey outdoors half a dozen times to see if it's still raining, and then he finally he grabs his *Browning from the table, opens the window, and begins shooting at the sky—bang, bang, bang—saying: "If you're going to be assuming the role of a god, then go ahead and act like one! The devil take you!"

The clerks roared with laughter.

"Most certainly nothing came of that because of the absence of the addressee!" Varlamenko thought as he smiled.

Ramp's brief but temperamental exchange with Varlamenko did not have the most pleasant outcome for Ramp.

Chapter Five

"It's magical! It's truly extraordinary!" exclaimed a sharp-nosed youth wearing a student's peaked cap as he walked out into the yard with Ramp from behind the flowerbeds.

Ramp was talking in a hushed voice with his young co-conversationalist, and a look of slick satisfaction was spreading over his face.

It was obvious that he liked the student.

"No, just pay attention to this!" And Ramp said a few words in English. "That's just the point!"

"That's marvellous! Truly marvellous!"

They went to the barn where they examined the remarkable horses that had more diplomas than the most highly educated person in the world. Ramp, with the proud look of a father who is showing off his talented children to the world, talked about every horse in great detail.

As they came out of the barn they met Varlamenko, and Ramp introduced the student to him.

"This is our intern—Avgust Petrovych Volner!"

They exchanged a few words about the work that needed to be done on the plantations. The time to do the weeding was approaching, and so the entire administration was working intensively.

Soon afterwards Varlamenko rode out of the yard in his buggy—he had to take advantage of the holiday to ensure that the girl labourers would begin working on Monday.

"Aha, I forgot to tell you, Avgust Petrovych, that today I'll be having guests—Colonel Voznesensky and his daughter . . ."

A shadow flitted momentarily over Volner's face, and then he inquired: "And just who is this colonel?"

"Vasyl Pavlovych Voznesensky is a gendarme colonel. He's supposed to trade his hunting dog for my Laska!"

"Is he from Domashiv?"

"Yes . . . about twenty versts from here . . ."

In the evening, before the sun had set, a lacquered carriage drove into the yard.

Two armed gendarmes stood on the steps of the carriage on both sides, and half a dozen men mounted on horses were riding behind it. A sturdy man, clinking his spurs, stepped to the ground and assisted a young blond woman out of the carriage.

Before they could take a couple of steps, Ramp rushed outdoors to meet his guests and conduct them into his home.

"Today you'll find it somewhat more cheerful at our place, Nina Vasylivna; there's a partner with whom you can play dominoes!"

"Who is it?" Voznesensky inquired.

"It's our new intern, a most wonderful young man!"

"But who, exactly, is he?" Voznesensky was always interested in new people.

"Who is he?" Ramp burst out laughing. "He's a completely trustworthy person and, I think, he does not bear the slightest resemblance to your type of clients, Colonel!"

"I, of course, am not at all interested in him from that point of view . . ." the colonel observed with a smile.

"He's of German-English ancestry, and his properties are in Bessarabia, but he's interested in sugar refining . . . He says that he'll liquidate his properties over there and buy something suitable in our parts," Ramp explained in order to satisfy the colonel's curiosity.

Volner made a favourable impression on the guests. Within the hour Voznesensky was saying to Ramp: "He's a nice chap, a decent, well-bred youth!"

"Would he make a suitable son-in-law?" Ramp asked with a side-long glance.

"Well now, that's going too far too fast!" the gendarme skirted the question.

More guests arrived. After a noisy supper they all dispersed in various directions. The majority of them seated themselves at the card tables, but Volner, after offering Nina Vasylivna his arm, went out into the orchard. There, as they strolled down the damp lanes, he told her about Bessarabia, about his trip to London last year, about his amusing professors . . .

Nina Vasylivna was laughing in a ringing voice and, shying away from the shrubbery, pressed more closely to Volner.

When the colonel's carriage, accompanied by the horsemen, rolled out of the yard later that night, or rather, in the wee hours of the morning, Nina Vasylivna said to her father: "This Volner is a most pleasant person . . . He's so cheerful and polite. His granny is living in London now! He travelled there to see her last year."

"Yes . . . He's a fine young man . . . well-bred."

"And it's ever so nice on their estate in Bessarabia! They grow grapes!"

Voznesnsky did not continue the conversation with his daughter. He was thinking about something rather unpleasant— yesterday a proclamation had been found in Starostyn and brought to him . . . He had his suspicions, but he had to look into them first . . .

Chapter Six

Khved was not prosecuted.

When Ramp found out that he had already been held in jail for two weeks, he said rather unwillingly: "Give him a cuff on the ear, and let him go!"

They cuffed Khved, but not only on the ear . . . One eye was swollen shut, and only a small slit marked its place.

The beets had already sprouted and they stretched in green strings all the way to the horizon against the black background of the plantations.

The day bent over the earth with its blue belly and stared mockingly at Khved with its widely opened eye.

To avoid being noticed, Khved walked along the outskirts of the fields on his way home.

Khved's wife Motrya was busy in the yard washing clothes, and a grimy child was crawling about at her feet.

Upon seeing Khved, his wife straightened up from the washing trough and looked intently at him. No cry of joy flew from her lips, and as soon as Khved drew nearer, her pale lips stirred: "You were beaten?"

Khved went into the house without replying, and his wife sobbed silently in the yard, wiping her eyes with a soiled apron. The child was tugging at her skirt and pattering undecipherable words. A short while later, his wife wiped her face and once again began rinsing the clothes.

In the house Khved sat down at the table and chewed on a crust of bread sprinkled with salt. When his wife came in, he put down the bread, wiped his mouth and said: "They're not prosecuting me."

Motrya was nervously kneading her apron and looking at the corner where the wine-cask was kept.

"What are we going to do?" She was thinking her bitter maternal thoughts . . .

"I'll go away to look for some work . . . No one nearby will hire me . . ."

"And what about us?"

Khved did not respond. He rose from the table, lay down on the floor, and tucked an ancient sheepskin coat under his head.

Motrya had worked from childhood on the plantations. When she was still little, she cut the stalks off beets, and after growing up she wielded a hoe. In the autumn she dug beets on a strip of land with her parents. Just like her grandparents and great grandparents. But now Motrya was worried that she would no longer be permitted to do this . . .

She was sure that the foremen had been instructed not to let her work . . .

After all, her husband . . .

Motrya's thoughts were interrupted by the rumbling of wheels by the gate; she saw a wagon stop out in the street, and the portly lord from the Zelenets manor stepped out of it.

Varlamenko had not even had the time to open the gate when Motrya ducked into the room.

"The lord from the Zelenets manor is here!" she shouted.

And when the door opened and Varlamenko walked in right after she said this, she did not know what to do next.

"Is Khved at home?"

Khved got up from the floor and smoothed down his tangled hair.

"I've come to see you about a certain matter, Khved . . ."

After saying this, Yosyf Matviyovych sank down heavily on a bench.

Khved was standing directly in front of him.

"The woman may leave now . . . This matter does not concern her . . ."

Motrya walked out as if someone had physically pushed her away.

Varlamenko spoke with Khved for a long time about the fact that Khved and his family were fated to swell from hunger, and then he finally said what he had come to say: "Despite everything, I'll give you a job . . . You'll be my coachman . . ."

Khved breathed deeply and sank down on a bench.

"The pay will be good . . . and you'll also receive some oats for the horses . . . There will be gifts on the holidays . . . And, in addition to everything else, if you agree to do one thing that I want you to do, I'll give you twenty karbovantsi . . . Do you understand?"

Khved did not understand anything, but nodded as if to say—of course I understand! It was unthinkable to risk losing such a job.

"Come on Sunday . . . and if you're hard up now, here's a karbovanets to buy the children some bread . . . But don't flap your tongue too much about this job . . . Just say that you were hired, and that's it."

When Khved showed Motrya the karbovanets, she was dumbstruck.

"What's it for?"

"On Sunday I'm taking on the job of coachman at the Zelenets manor . . . It's a down payment . . ."

Chapter Seven

"The devil only knows what this is!" Volner shouted as he crumpled a piece of paper and threw it on the floor. After pacing his expansive room a couple of times, he picked up the crumpled letter and read it once again:

Dear Avgust!

I regret having to trouble you, but I can no longer keep you uninformed about certain matters.

Borya and Kolya have failed their final exams and they've been kept back in the same class that they were in last year. It seems that they will have to be taken to their aunt in Irkutsk; they say it's easier to finish a classical high school there.

The tutor who was helping them turned out to be a dishonourable person who even walked away with their textbooks. They've gone to him several times—but he won't return them. The devil only knows what's going on! I feel very badly about the whole situation, especially about your textbooks—I was keeping them as a memento of your school years.

By the way, that blue-nosed character asked for your address—he probably wants to ask you for some money—but I didn't give it to him.

I haven't received anything from the estate for a long time now. It seems that all is not well there.

I kiss you heartily.

Your cousin Olya.

After reading the letter, Volner set fire to it with a match and then threw the ashes out the window.

"Berman and Kolodko are in jail, but they're trustworthy fellows, and they won't reveal anything. But the papers! What papers were taken?"

And Volner began examining in his mind's eye all the letters that he had written to his comrades during the past year.

"I don't think there was anything compromising in any of them," Volner reassured himself.

The provincial organization, taking advantage of the opportunity, had sent Volner here, to Starostyn, to gather together the remains of the routed forces . . . and he had been fortunate that Virny had been able to facilitate his placement here as a gentleman intern. It was convenient, but at the same time the position of an intern, and a privileged one at that, was not propitious for establishing ties with individual comrades. It was necessary to make use of intermediaries, but this complicated his work.

"If only they don't find me out for at least three or four months, it might still be possible to accomplish something."

As he was falling asleep, a humorous thought flashed through his mind about "cousin Olya," who most certainly was standing now in a cellar behind an underground safe and, while typesetting the next pamphlet, was singeing his rough beard as he bent over a candle . . .

In the mornings, Volner rides out into the fields, where thousands of girls, boys, and women move in compact lines down the rows of green beets; behind them walks the "barker"— the steward. It is he, this worthy man in high boots, who has control over hundreds of bent figures. It is his duty to bark at these figures, and for this duty he is paid slightly more than a common worker.

The workers leave their bags and their babies in swaddling clothes at the edge of the field in the care of children who are so young that they are not even able to pick beetles. Grimy little boys without any trousers and little girls who are no less grimy and who wear long dresses that trail to their heels look after the infants. They are active participants in the production process, and it does not matter at all that their entire vocabulary consists of only a couple dozen words, and even these words are childishly misspoken.

The entire administration, beginning with the barkers and all the way up to Ramp, is hard at work on the plantations. The land-stewards, dashing about on horseback and on carts, curse the barkers and the girls; the regional manager, driving by in his cabriolet with its lacquered sides sparkling in the sun, shouts at the stewards and the barkers to work harder, but he takes no notice of the bent figures.

It is Ramp, however, who is the driving force behind all this administrative energy. It is he who empowers the barkers through a vast hierarchy of employees who go about on foot and ride around in carts and cabriolets.

Ramp's two-horse phaeton energizes the administration the moment that it appears on the horizon.

The intern Volner often rides with Ramp. He enjoys a special position, unlike interns from small villages who have completed less-qualified schools and who begin their careers working as barkers. He is wearing gloves. The shiny student uniform that he is still wearing and his trousers with their silver stripes give him the appearance of an officer.

The carriage is swaying in the ruts, the well-fed horses are frisky, and a desultory conversation is being carried on in the phaeton.

"We'll finish the weeding in three days . . ."

"The Sharkiv manor will probably be late, because Ivanivka has snatched up all the girls . . ." Volner remarks.

They fall silent once again as they ride past fields of winter wheat that braids the ground with its green sprouts and dark fallow land that looks like a fallen dark-blue wing. Farther on there is a grove seemingly cut out of blue paper.

"Mykhaylo, turn around and head for home," Ramp says to the coachman.

They have travelled far enough today. The fried sun, tilting to one side, is dimmed by dark-blue smoke.

On the way back to Starostyn, Ramp began a circuitous conversation that he had been preparing from the time that

Volner had expressed a desire to transfer his wealth to the sugar refining regions.

"What are you hearing from home?"

"Nothing special . . . My trustee informs me that he has a buyer for my properties . . . I'll have to make a trip there quite soon . . . I've entrusted him to conduct the preliminary discussions . . ."

"Do you think that you'll realize a lot of money on the deal?"

"No, not all that much . . . two or three hundred thousand. It could have been more, but the vineyards haven't been kept up."

"You're a good partner to have."

"What kind of a partner?" Volner was confused.

"I'm looking for a partner . . . You see . . ." Ramp hesitated momentarily. "You see, it's still a secret, but I can tell you."

And leaning closer to Volner, Ramp, speaking confidentially in English so that the coachman would not understand, told him about his accomplishments.

The countess was a foolish woman. He had scared her with his threat to throw all her wealth down the drain with one stroke of his pen. The countess had been forced to give Ramp full control of her affairs, and he was not a fool to just stand by and do nothing . . .

In short, within a month, Starostyn with its sugar refineries and half of the entire estate would be his . . .

But he was not a cruel person . . . He did not want to reduce the countess to a beggar—he would leave her a couple of small villages and a few worthless items from her patrimonial inheritance . . .

"I'm sure you understand, Avgust Petrovych, that you will not err if you invest your money in a deal like this . . ."

"I'll be very pleased to become your partner in this matter!" Volner said, and he shook Ramp's hand fervently.

The sun was setting in a carroty-red haze when the phaeton of the chief administrator came to a stop in the yard of the Starostyn Estate.

Chapter Eight

Volner was sitting in his room and pondering the stupid position in which he found himself.

Having the position of a privileged person on an estate did not bring with it the advantages that his comrades had envisioned back there, in Novo-Slobidsky.

Volner was thoroughly fed up with pretending to be a pampered young lord who bragged about his fictitious wealth and a granny in London.

"What's the good of all this? The comrades at the sugar refinery look upon me as some kind of a suspicious character and conceal everything from me . . . They even viewed my 'official document' suspiciously, even though it should not have evoked any doubts . . .

"And, may the devil take it, nothing is working out with the gendarme . . . There's only the possibility of using Nina to some advantage . . ."

Volner had explicitly begun courting the colonel's daughter after he became convinced that he could not ferret any information out of the colonel.

What bothered Volner the most was the fact that, in his position, he could not conduct himself freely with the workers. In order to remain incognito, he had to behave at all times like a young lord.

Late at night, when everyone and everything was sleeping, Volner climbed through a window into the orchard and from there he went out into a field.

Somewhere behind him, dogs barked in the distance and a watchman made a rattling sound, but then all grew quiet once again.

The moon had not yet risen. At an appointed spot in a small ravine, two individuals were waiting for him.

Volner coughed and heard the same kind of cough in response.

"Have you been waiting long?"

"No, we just got here . . ."

All three of them moved closer in to one another and began talking in whispers.

If Ramp had seen this group, he would have been stunned. His intern, who would not shake hands with any employee below the rank of a steward, was now lying amiably alongside the lowly junior clerk Sulenko and the locksmith Yarovy from the sugar refinery, and they were saying things to him that even Ramp would not have dared to say.

"You haven't done a single thing to assist us in the two months that you've been here, Avgust. And your stay here could be considered almost inconsequential, if it weren't for one matter about which you can do something . . ."

"But I've told you that having to become an imposter has placed me in an idiotic situation!"

"There's no need to get all upset like a young lady. We understand that your position is a difficult one, but some advantages can be gained from it . . ."

From what Yarovy said, there was a very serious matter at hand. There was a spy at the sugar refinery—he had been hired under the pretence of being a worker . . .

"He's trying to ingratiate himself with us . . . Obviously Voznesensky must know something about us . . ."

Volner interrupted him.

"From what sources could Voznesensky have found out about you?"

"The devil only knows! But you must go after the daughter, because it isn't possible to find out anything from her papa . . ."

"We must find out everything as soon as possible . . . The village is restless and there may soon be arrests . . ."

"But what if Voznesensky also knows about me? What then? The daughter is sure to have instructions from her papa . . . Nevertheless," and Volner slapped his forehead, "we must hope for success. On Sunday I'll be in Domashiv at the home of the gendarme!"

"Someone should go with you . . . for contact purposes."

After coming to an agreement about all the details, Volner walked out of the ravine and went back to the manor.

It was the third year that these two comrades of his were working in the region of the Starostyn sugar refinery, but they had not been able to conduct any widespread action. It had been mostly propaganda work, but even that was not going very well after three men had been arrested for distributing propagandistic literature.

They had focussed mainly on spreading the word on an individual basis, attempting to prepare in this way a nucleus of enlightened people.

The provincial organization had longstanding ties with Starostyn and that is why it had sent Volner there, but this move had done little to further the cause. As he returned from the meeting, Volner planned how he would approach the gendarme's daughter.

"If only I don't betray myself in some way . . ."

* * *

These days Ramp was walking around in a cheerful mood. About a week ago a renowned lawyer from the provincial capital had departed after visiting him and assuring him that everything would be fine and that within a month Ramp would receive the documents that he wanted.

The feverish work on the plantations had ended, and the broad leaves of the beets were gleaming in the sun.

It was now the period that usually dragged on for two or three weeks before the mowing season began. Cheerful groups of guests came to the manor more frequently. Countless bottles of beer were drunk, card tables were brought out on the veranda in the evenings, and card games were played until morning. They rode out in groups to hunt and, when there was no wild game to be found, they shot the villagers' ducks, and if an old woman started to wail—they threw her a couple of coins and left her the duck as well.

Volner was gloomy.

They laughed at him and teased him for being in love with Nina, and in his heart he rejoiced that his sadness was being explained away in such a natural way.

But the real reason for his sorrow was his lack of success in Domashiv. The situation had turned out very unfavourably, and Volner had not found out anything.

Now he was looking for other ways and means. He had a goal to find out everything in the coming week, and in order to do this he had to come up with a plan to be on closer terms with Nina.

During the two days that the gendarme came with his daughter to celebrate a holiday, Volner began his attack.

It turned out that Nina's heart was not at all the fortress that Volner had imagined it to be, and on the very first evening the gate to it, figuratively speaking, was welcomingly opened to him. After that, it was necessary to step with the foot of a victor into the second fortress—the secret drawer of the gendarme.

Volner spent the entire next day hovering around Nina like a dove, readying himself to attack her in the evening like a hawk.

"Oh Avgust, how wonderful it is to be with you!" Nina mewed languorously when they found themselves alone in a dark lane of the park. "It seems to me that it's my dear departed mother who is caressing me!"

Nina's mother had died a long time ago, when Nina was just a little girl, and the colonel, having tasted family bliss once, was not tempted to try it a second time, preferring to remain a widower.

"I'm afraid, Nina, that the way things are going, I too may not be caressing you for much longer," Volner said in a sad tone.

"What are you saying, Avgust? You're alarming me!"

"Don't be alarmed, my dearest, be brave . . . You can help me . . ."

Volner sensed that even if the enemy had not gone away, the position in which that enemy found itself was very awkward.

"What? What? Tell me how!" Nina squeezed Volner's hand impatiently.

"Nina, my dearest love, just don't be alarmed . . . because I must tell you frankly—they want to kill me."

Nina pressed closely against him as if protecting Volner from an unseen enemy. "Who?"

"I don't know . . . Only yesterday I received an anonymous letter . . . They're demanding that I hand over five thousand to the revolutionaries for their odious activities, or else they'll kill me . . . You must understand that it's not the money that bothers me, but I can't give money to criminals . . ."

"My dearest, don't be afraid. I'll tell daddy, and he'll catch them—he'll destroy the villains!"

"No, anything but that!" Volner sprang up in terror. "If they find out that I told the gendarme, they'll kill me anyway . . . They know everything . . ."

Volner, to his own surprise, was displaying quite a talent as an actor and a diplomat, and the gendarme's daughter became the first victim of his wiles.

He convinced her that he could be saved only if he knew the names of all the people who were under suspicion in the district. This had to be done discreetly and without being observed by her papa, as her papa, because of his military training, could spoil everything.

"You understand, my little darling, that you're holding my life in these delicate little hands of yours, and if you let go of it, if you even drop a hint about our discussion . . . You must believe me, once I know the names, I'll handle the matter myself as best as I see fit . . ."

A long kiss sealed the obligation not to say anything . . .

"On Wednesday come to visit us as if by chance . . ."

In the evening of that day, Volner locked himself in his room, and spent a long time at his table scrawling with a pencil:

Volner!
You must place five thousand karbovantsi in the hollow of the old willow by the dam. The money is needed for revolutionary matters. If you don't do that—you'll die.

He looked at what he had written with satisfaction and smiled.

Then, picking up a pair of scissors, he cut out a crossed dagger and pistol from a scrap of cardboard, smeared the cut-out with ink, and stamped the note with it.

"Wonderful!" he praised himself.

"If the silly little fool blurts something out, I'll have some proof . . . a document!"

Chapter Nine

Khved had been working as a coachman in Zelenets since early spring. Varlamenko was pleased with him, but as yet he had not made any of the demands of him that he had alluded to in Khved's home. But as soon as they began hauling grain to the threshing machines, and the hay stood dreamily in dark green sheaves in hayricks near the manor, Yosyf Matviyovych decided that the moment had come.

Riding down the field with Khved in a cabriolet, he initiated a conversation.

"Well, Khved, there's a certain matter that you have to attend to . . . That's the reason that I hired you in the first place and pulled your family from the fangs of death . . ."

"Have I ever refused to do something? Just say the word, and it will be done in a flash!"

"The work, my friend, is very special . . ."

"I'll do whatever you say!"

"But will you set fire to the haystacks at Starostyn?"

Khved was dumbstruck.

"So that's what it's all about!" the thought flashed through his mind, and he was seized with terror.

"Why aren't you saying anything? Are you scared?"

"Ye-e-e-s, sca-a-a-red," Khved managed to say.

"Well, if you're scared you can go to the devil three times over and starve to death . . ." And after a moment of silence he added: "Tomorrow you'll harness the wagon and clear out of the estate!"

The lord spat on the boundary, and the coachman was staring past the horses into the distance. His head was void of all thoughts except for the one sharp thought about hunger that forced him to look for a way out.

"But what if I'm caught?" he managed to whisper with his dry lips.

"If you do it right, they won't catch you!"

Varlamenko knew that the deed was as good as done. Khved would agree, for what else could he do?

The steward thought: "If they catch Khved—may the devil take him—I'll support his family if he keeps his mouth shut, but if he says something—I can always talk my way out of it because there is no proof . . . And even more to the point, the matter can be explained very simply: Khved is angry with Ramp."

As they drove up to the Zelenets manor Khved said: "I'll burn down the devil of a Gypsy, and his hayricks, and his ox sheds." And his heart seethed with hatred.

"You should have said that long ago! And we'll do it in such a way that no one will ever find out about it."

After calling Khved into his study and locking the door behind him, Yosyf Matviyovych showed him the device that he had come up with—a little paper box with a candle stub in it, and some finely shredded paper around the stub. Khved would put the little box under the hayrick, light the stub, close the box, and scatter some straw on it. And he would not have to hurry to get away—the stub would burn until the flame reached the shredded paper, and then the fire would take over.

Khved was amazed at the device.

"And these can be placed under several hayricks at the same time?"

"Even under a hundred; and the best part is that you'll have time to get away . . ."

When he was alone, Varlamenko thought: "After everything burns down, Ramp, the devil's father will have you as a trustee! The countess will have you grabbed by the tail and flung straight to hell . . ."

Chapter Ten

Volner "unexpectedly" dropped in at Domashiv. Nina greeted him with an air of embarrassment and led him into the living room.

"Would you like a glass of tea, Mr. Volner?" she addressed him in the tone of a polite hostess.

"I won't refuse one . . ." Volner said.

At first it seemed to him that Nina was behaving as if there were other people nearby, but he soon convinced himself that there was no one in the neighbouring rooms.

Nina's flustered look when he greeted her troubled him.

Over tea Volner asked: "Why aren't you acting the way that you usually do?"

And he stroked her hand.

Nina jerked her hand away somewhat nervously, as if disgusted, tears glittered on her eyelashes and, lowering her head on the table, she began to wail.

Volner drew his chair up closer and embraced her waist.

Nina pushed his hand away.

"I don't understand what's going on!" Volner said in a choked voice and, lighting a cigarette, he sat down in an armchair and waited for a response.

Twilight was approaching. It was growing late, and Volner would have to leave the manor soon.

Today his comrades would be waiting for him in the valley and he was to pass them the information that he obtained from the gendarme's daughter.

Recently the atmosphere in Starostyn had been tense because many of the day workers had been paid a *hryvenyk less than they had expected. This shortfall had evoked a belligerent mood among the village youth and an outburst could be expected. And if this happened the gendarmes would first of all go after the suspicious elements in the factory.

"And I wouldn't be able to wriggle my way out of that," Yarovy had said.

Now, sitting in the colonel's home, Volner glanced at his watch and saw that it was already past nine, and shortly after ten his comrades would be waiting for him in the valley in the steppe.

"I'm demanding a response," Volner finally said after a short silence.

Nina wiped her tears and stood up by the table.

"You, sir, acted dishonourably . . . You fooled me and everyone else around you . . . But you should know that I found out that you're an imposter . . . Papa knows all about you, and you're going to be arrested today!"

At first Volner was dumbstruck, but he quickly regained his equanimity and listened to Nina with a disinterested air.

"So, your papa has gone to arrest me?" he asked when Nina fell silent. He had found out earlier from the servants that the colonel had driven off somewhere.

"Yes, but . . . you'll be arrested right here . . . I won't forgive you . . ."

Volner realized that he truly could be arrested here. After all, there were always two armed guards at the colonel's home. Obviously protestations of love would not help in this instance. He had to make some decisive moves.

Volner reached for his Browning in his pocket and, leaning towards Nina, said in a whisper: "Answer all my questions. If you call anyone I'll kill you on the spot and escape through the veranda."

He placed the hand that was holding the Browning on the table.

In the dusk of the summer evening it was impossible to see faces.

Nina leapt from her chair and stood tall.

"Sit down and be quiet!" Volner ordered as he pointed the Browning at her.

Nina groped for the chair and sat down.

"Where did your papa go?"

Nina, shuddering uncontrollably and tearing the sounds from the depths of her chest, said: "To Starostyn . . ."

"Will he be stopping in anywhere along the way?"

"In Vilshana . . ."

"So," Volner thought, "that means that he intends to make an unexpected arrival at Starostyn at night."

"Whom else is he going to arrest?"

"I don't know."

"What did he say to you?"

Nina suddenly burst into tears. She was defeated and destroyed. Her shoulders were shaking and she sobbed soundlessly.

Volner did not know what to do next. He could get on his horse and ride off—but then Nina could raise the alarm and he would be caught. There was only one way out—to try to gain some time by forcing Nina to accompany him to the outskirts of the town.

"Nina Vasylivna, you will accompany me out of the neighbourhood. When we go outdoors, do not call anyone, and do not talk . . . I have my Browning at the ready."

Nina walked like a mannequin beside Volner.

He untied his horse that was hobbled by the veranda, and, leading him by the reins, he held on to Nina's elbow with his free hand.

The wooden sidewalks of the county town creaked, and there was the scent of gillyflowers and fresh manure in the air. The town was sleeping.

When they were on the outskirts, Volner said: "Good-bye until our next happy meeting!"

And he jumped on his horse.

Nina just stood there without saying a word.

Volner gave his horse a sharp tug and vanished in the murky darkness.

Volner rode swiftly without sparing his horse. All along the way he could not stop thinking about Yarovy and Sulenko. Would the gendarme catch them at home, or would they fortuitously manage to escape being arrested?

It was almost midnight when Volner halted in the ravine about three versts from Starostyn.

He walked another verst to the appointed meeting spot but neither Yarovy nor Sulenko were there. So he sat down and waited.

The moon had not yet risen. The grass was damp with dew: a shaggy fog was rolling into the ravine.

About a quarter of an hour later, a figure walked up from down below and halted.

Volner instinctively grabbed his gun and froze.

The figure drew nearer and Volner recognized Sulenko.

"I'm over here," Volner said in a hushed voice.

Sulenko came up to him and bent over . . .

"Is it you, Avgust?"

"Yes, where's Yarovy?"

Sulenko looked disconcerted and then, without replying, asked another question.

"What did you find out at Domashiv?"

"They're going to arrest all of us today."

"And you as well?"

"And me as well . . ."

Sulenko sat down close to Volner and listened as he described his misadventure.

When Volner finished, Sulenko said: "Yarovy is nearby, in the ditch . . . The gendarmes are already at the estate . . . We barely managed to escape . . ."

"They're afraid of me," Volner thought, but he was not offended. "They're cautious fellows."

He had to tell Yarovy all over again what had transpired in Domashiv.

"What are we going to do?" Sulenko asked when the situation became clear.

"Dawn will be breaking soon, and we can't get very far away . . . It would be best to wait it out someplace . . ." Yarovy stopped to think for a moment, and then he added: "It would be best to hide in the hayricks . . . and the forest isn't too far from there . . ."

There was no other way out. They had to consider what they should do in their situation and they needed some time to do this. The comrades made their way to the hayricks through the dewy beet field.

The tall stacks of the lord's hay had been carried from the wet lowlands to a high even spot that could not be reached by the spring flood. The stacks, tall and long, like green cottages without any windows and doors, stood in rows, creating blocks and streets. Like a green village!

Volner, Sulenko, and Yarovy climbed up on one stack. From it, through the bluish mists of early morning, they could see the estate, the sugar refinery, and beyond them—the village of Starostyn spread in a ravine.

Before dawn broke, small silhouettes went from the village to the estate, and horse patrols galloped by herding to the pens the village cattle that they had impounded on the lord's fields.

Later, when the sun rose, the threshing machines began belching smoke in various fields, and the steward's cabriolet passed by.

Life on the estate awakened, thousands of arms waved in the air and there arose the din made by thousands of human voices, by machines and by animals.

There did not seem to be anyone who did not belong on the estate, and Volner began to have his doubts.

"Is it possible that we've created a panic over nothing?"

"The devil only knows! You may be right . . ." Yarovy responded without taking his eyes off the estate. "But the gendarmes did come—I saw them myself."

They fell silent.

"I'm hungry," Sulenko said to no one in particular.

Not more than half-an-hour after that, their doubts were dispersed.

A couple dozen men on horseback galloped over the dam that led from the sugar refinery to the estate, and a short time later a carriage drove by followed by two horseback riders.

Now all three stared intently at the estate.

"Gendarmes . . . the colonel's carriage . . ." Volner reported in a half-whisper.

"They must have searched the sugar refinery. Do you suppose they found our hectograph?" Yaroslav wondered.

"Where did you hide it?"

"Under the porch of the count's gazebo in the park . . ."

"Well, they won't find it there!"

The gendarmes rode into the manor yard, and the buildings blocked them from their view.

"But you fellows don't have anything they would want, do you?" Yarovy asked.

"I left my pistol at home—the barbarians will be sure to take it, but there's nothing else . . . just a dozen books . . ."

"Oh, you stupid scribbler! To forget your pistol," Yarovy chided Sulenko. "I don't keep anything in the house . . . Everything is in a safe hiding place."

All the literature was kept hidden in Volner's quarters, because his comrades thought that he was above suspicion.

The carriage drove away from the estate in the afternoon, and the horsemen followed it in ranks.

The search was over.

Had they found anything?

Yarovy did not take his eyes off the band of gendarmes until it was hidden behind an oak forest.

"And now, comrades, let's sleep—there's no point in coming out of hiding until nightfall."

Sulenko's proposition was accepted.

The sleepless night had exhausted the fugitives and they fell asleep on the fragrant hay.

Chapter Eleven

Felix Felixovych Ramp was getting ready to retire when he heard the sound of horses' hooves and voices out in the yard.

It was eleven o'clock in the evening. It was about an hour after the young men's songs and whistles had died down beyond the manor, and the barrel-organ rented especially for the workers had finished whining its pathetic songs.

Ramp opened the window. "Semen! Hey, Semen!"

Semen the watchman responded.

"Who is it?" Ramp asked.

"It's the colonel with some soldiers!"

Felix Felixovych hurriedly put on his silk jacket and his boots, and walked out into the yard. On the path beyond the flowerbed he was met by the colonel of the gendarmes.

"Felix Felixovych, forgive me, but I must search Volner's quarters!"

"What's this nonsense all about? What's the reason for it?" Ramp asked in astonishment.

"There's a reason," Voznesensky replied drily and he set out for Volner's living quarters with armed gendarmes.

Ramp shrugged and followed him.

The door to Volner's room was half-open, and when they lit a lamp and walked in with pistols at the ready, Ramp found the situation amusing.

"But there's no one there!"

"He's not there? Well, where is Volner?" Voznesensky glanced severely at Ramp.

"Volner left for Domashiv after lunch, and he hasn't come back yet."

"Why did he go there?"

"How would I know?" Ramp's tone changed from bemusement to arrogance.

The colonel turned around and nodded at the gendarmes: "Start the search!"

A thorough search of the room was begun.

They pulled out desk drawers and overturned the bed. They did not find anything in the bed, but they took a packet of letters from the desk.

They examined the bookcase most carefully. The books were in German and in English, and they set these aside as being completely innocuous.

Finally, one gendarme got lucky. "There's a political book here, Your Excellency!"

Voznesensky took the heavy volume and read the title: *Political Economy. A Textbook for Higher Institutions of Learning. Approved by the Ministry of Public Education for all Educational Institutions of the Russian Empire.*

"You fool! Put the book back where you found it."

This incident dispersed the heavy atmosphere between the colonel of the gendarmes and the chief administrator.

"Isn't it possible that Volner is just as guilty as that book?" Ramp asked with a smile.

"He has some history with us," the gendarme said a little obscurely, and ordered a stop to the search.

Then he went up to a young gentleman dressed in civilian attire who had been bustling about the room all that time and gave him a folded piece of paper.

"And now to the sugar refinery, to get those others . . . If the need arises, shoot!"

The gendarme and the spy walked out and the colonel went arm in arm with Ramp to the study.

When they were sitting in armchairs across from one another, the colonel began talking.

"It's a serious matter. Just between the two of us, Volner is a dangerous revolutionary. He lied about his wealth. I have accurate information. He's the son of the emigrant-anarchist Volnov and he changed his name to sound like a foreigner."

"That can't be!"

"It's true. He wanted to use my daughter to steal some documents, but my Nina has been brought up better than that . . . He has acquaintances here . . . They're being arrested right now, and then you'll see for yourself what ties he has with other people . . ."

Ramp, upset beyond measure, was racing around the room.

"Is it possible that I've been deceived?" and he slapped himself on the forehead.

"It sounds incredible, but it's a fact!" the gendarme smiled.

"Then send someone to Domashiv to hold him there."

"It's all been taken care of, you needn't worry . . ."

Dawn was already breaking when the colonel was informed that neither Yarovy nor Sulenko had been found, and that there was nothing of any interest in their living quarters.

"They've escaped, the wretches! Bring my carriage around!"

In the morning mist, the colonel rode off to the sugar refinery, and Ramp continued pacing his room for a long time until he finally fell asleep on the couch.

The gendarmes did not find anything in Sulenko's room except a pistol that they entered in the register as material evidence.

The colonel came back very upset. "They must have an entire circle of spies here—otherwise they could not have learned about the search."

Ramp was completely distraught. Forgetting about his guest, he continued pacing the room and it was only when the lackey announced that lunch was being served that he came out of his deep reverie.

When the colonel began getting ready to go home after lunch, he whispered to Ramp: "I'll leave two gendarmes to assist the night watchman . . ."

Ramp interrupted him: "There's no need. If anything happens, I'll take care of it myself . . ."

"Fine . . . That will even be better . . . I'm relying on you—but 'those' will not be afraid . . ."

Chapter Twelve

The village was stirring angrily. Ramp had declared that if anyone dared to approach him for that additional "hryvenyk" he would "punch him in the chops."

He had made this assertion to two youthful delegates who had come to talk to him about the shortfall in the money that had been paid out in wages.

After standing around for quite some time on the threshold of Ramp's office, the youths finally walked away.

"Riff-raff!" Ramp thought after he had sent the messengers packing. "They want to rip off everyone!"

That was what the administrator was thinking, but he knew full well that even though he had given instructions to tell the day-labourers that they would receive a daily wage of seventy kopiyky, only sixty had actually been paid out. In this way the estate had realized a profit of almost four thousand in just a matter of a few days.

The conversation with the messengers had occurred just prior to the search. While the search was being conducted, Ramp had forgotten about it, but now, after seeing off the gendarmes, he recalled it, and for some unexpected reason, this recollection disturbed him.

"The devil only knows what's wrong! Even such trivial matters are upsetting me. It appears that I'll have to tend to my nerves."

After getting dressed in his usual fashion, Ramp gave an order to saddle a horse so that he could ride out to the threshing machines.

By the nearest threshing machine people were milling around in the dust by the straw shaker, the grease-covered stoker was shoving firewood down the gullet of the steam engine, and on the top of the hayrick, a dozen youths were neatly piling the golden straw.

Without dismounting, Ramp called out to the foreman to approach him: "How are things going here? How's the work coming along?"

"Good . . . but the people seem to be agitated . . ."

394 | Oleksa Slisarenko

"How so?"

"They're threatening to take action . . ."

"Is it because of that hryvenyk?"

"Yes."

"How much are we getting for sixty sheaves?"

Ramp asked the last question to divert the foreman's attention from himself and his own uneasiness, but he did not listen to the reply before riding off to the next threshing machine.

Halfway there, Ramp stopped, looked back at the manor, and rushed off towards it.

When he got home, Ramp resolved to get a grip on himself. He went into the office and immersed himself in business documents, but his thoughts kept flying away from the carefully written lines, and the image of Volner in his white gloves kept twirling before his eyes. Now Volner smiled and made a witty remark.

Suddenly the telephone rang sharply. Ramp put the receiver to his ear.

"Who is it?"

A steward from a subsidiary manor was calling.

"The threshing machine workers are agitated . . . We should call for police protection . . ."

Ramp, unexpectedly even for himself, grew furious.

"You idiot, you hornless cow! Villain! Get out right now—I don't want hide or hair of you left in that manor! Who is agitated? Punch them in the mug, the worthless wretches!"

He slammed down the receiver and collapsed in an armchair. And then, overcome with disgust, and without looking at anyone, he stalked out of the office.

At home he drank some bromide and lay down to relax on a couch.

Chapter Thirteen

When the sun was setting, Volner and his two comrades climbed down to the ground and sat in the shade between two hayricks and waited for night to fall. The darkness was descending indolently. The comrades sat without speaking, and when they heard the crunching of stubble under boots somewhere beyond the hayricks, they held their breath.

Someone was drawing near to the haystacks, and before long, in the narrow space between two hayricks a human figure appeared and came to a halt. Then the figure went up to one of the hayricks and, bending over, made a rustling noise with something.

Suddenly a match flared and lit the person's face.

"Khved!" Yarovey exclaimed, unable to restrain himself. The figure stood stock still and the match went out.

Yarovy went up to Khved and grabbed him by the shoulder. Khved was trembling.

"Don't be afraid," Yarovy whispered softly into Khved's ear, and then he led him to where Sulenko and Volner were in the sheltered spot. "Don't be afraid, Khved, we won't report you . . . Did you want to start a fire?"

Sulenko knew Khved the best.

"Oh, fellows, just don't tell anyone!" But when Khved found out that none other than the gentleman intern was sitting next to him, he clammed up in fear.

It took Yarovy a long time to convince Khved that he had nothing to fear . . .

"Varlamenko sent me . . . He said: if you set fire to them, they'll think that it was the re ... vo ... lu ...tion ...aries," Khved said, striving to his utmost to get out the difficult word.

Khved did not know what to do now, and so he sat silently beside a hayrick while the others talked in whispers about what they should do.

"How many little burning devices do you have?" Sulenko asked.

"Five."

"Give them to us, we'll do everything ourselves . . . And you go home and don't say a single word to anyone about any of this!" Sulenko instructed him in a severe tone.

"But what if the lord asks me about them?" Khved asked uneasily.

"Say that you set the hayricks on fire . . ."

Khved silently paced about in one spot for a short while, and then went away.

Yarovy fixed the candles and shared his box of matches with his comrades.

An hour later, three figures were heading towards the village, bypassing the estate.

Chapter Fourteen

Night was fading in the east and rooster's voices were bursting out over Starostyn when a bell rang to sound an alarm.

The people must have been waiting for the sound of that bell, because all at once grey figures began emerging from yards. They clustered in groups and, after standing around for a while, they set out for the manor, joining up with other groups along the way. Over there, where the smokestack of the sugar refinery was wedged into the grey paper of the predawn sky, flaming tongues were leaping above the buildings on the estate and above the distant hayricks.

The ox barns and the hay were burning beyond the manor.

The crowds kept growing at the outskirts of the village, with more men, women, youths, and girls joining in. There were old men with bushy unkempt beards and pitchforks riding on their shoulders and adolescents who were chided for coming, but who were not chased away.

"But where's the intern?"

It's not easy to recognize the intern when he's wearing a peasant's coarse wool coat!

A mighty peasant force was running, not walking, through the fields, and it was trampling the beets with bare feet.

"Fellows, let's trample what belongs to the lord, because it's trampling us!"

It had been a long time since the plantations had seen peasant power manifest itself with straightened backs, and the beets were darkened by the dew.

There was a great hubbub in the manor yard.

The fire hose was making a smacking sound, flames were roaring above the ox barns, horses were neighing, and people, as if gone mad, rushed about the yard shouting and not listening to one another.

No one was paying any attention to the hayricks—as if to say: nothing can be done about that.

Ramp was racing around the yard with his whip and, seeing the throngs of villagers shouted: "Get to the hayricks at once!"

And when he saw that the people continued to stand there clustered in a crowd and not moving, he began swearing: "You stupid dolts! Villains! March off to the hayricks this instant!"

A youth in a torn cap and jacket stepped out from the crowd. His eyes were blazing.

"Beat him up, fellows!" and he lunged at Ramp with a pitchfork.

Ramp jumped back, grabbed his Browning, and before the youth knew what was happening, the administrator fired at him point-blank . . .

The youth appeared to take a step backwards and, falling to one knee, dropped his pitchfork.

Clutching at his chest with his left hand, he valiantly tried to pull something out of his jacket pocket with his right hand. A frenzied tautness tensed his figure, but suddenly it snapped, and the youth fell to the ground.

Someone in the crowd shrieked insanely, and Ramp, taking advantage of the temporary confusion, raced through the yard towards his house.

Pitchforks, axes, and hoes rose high above the heads of the villagers, and the throng rushed after Ramp.

They knocked the administrator off his feet by the flowerbeds, and he fell upside down under a trimmed acacia shrub.

"Put the Gypsy mug into a trunk!" a sharp-nosed old man shouted, and the crowd that had rushed forward to rip the administrator to shreds stopped in its tracks.

They bound Ramp's arms with a whip, and then they dragged in a trunk from someplace and threw some soil into it to cover the bottom.

"Get in, you disgusting creature!" the sharp-nosed old man ordered Ramp.

Powerful hands seized Ramp and flung him forcefully into the trunk.

Ramp was silent; he pressed his lips together tightly and glared fiercely at the people.

It was only when they were lowering the lid that he shouted: "Villains! Cattle! You . . ." but then he could no longer be heard over the crowd's roar.

The trunk was lifted above the heads of the people and it flowed with the crowd towards the dam. There the people stopped, gave the trunk a good swing, and flung it from the high dam into the water.

A terrified scream was heard from the trunk, and then there was dead silence. The trunk sank to the bottom.

The people stood without moving and watched as bubbles sprang up over the misty morning water of the pond.

Geese began to gaggle under the willows and then dove noisily into the water.

On the other side of the pond restrained voices sounded in the yard of the sugar refinery—workers, terrified by the events of that night, were running off in every possible direction . . .

Before dawn the plantations on the sloping fields were gleaming greyly in the morning dew, preparing to drink the sweet day.

The plantations, having sucked in human sweat and blood in the springtime were now greedily drinking the sunlight; they were becoming pregnant with sugar.

But what was this?

Uneasiness and alarm leapt through the crowd like an electric current: a man, waving his arms, was running from the manor.

It was the old man Yukhym, the office watchman.

"My good people! My good people! The soldiers are coming from Vilshanka!"

And when he ran up closer, he explained, catching his breath: "Saranchuk phoned for them . . . I overheard him . . . It's only six versts—they'll be here in a flash . . ."

The crowd stirred.

"Go back to your homes!" someone shouted from the middle of the crowd.

No one argued with this.

"Go home!" a few more voices shouted and then fell silent.

The people began bustling about and the mass that had been monolithic up to now began to disintegrate rapidly.

Small groups of two or three individuals were running off in all directions, leaving behind a silent, half-burned down estate.

Only two men walked towards the ravine in the opposite direction.

And the estate grew deserted and silent.

The scarlet circle of the sun rolled out over the steppe, seemed to stop for a moment, and then continued moving indifferently over the blue field, generously gifting life to the earth.

The smouldering logs of the former cattle pens were sending their blue smoke over the lonely corpse of a blond youth in a torn peasant jacket and new student trousers with silver stripes.

His rigid hand was near his jacket pocket out of which a revolver was pulled halfway out. His face was marked by a courageous ferocity that no one had ever seen when the intern was still alive . . .

Glossary

The glossary of selected terms and phrases, some familiar, and some obscure, is provided for the convenience of the reader who wishes to gain a fuller appreciation of the historical, social, and political contexts of the stories. For the convenience of the reader, the plurals of certain Ukrainian words in the stories are anglicized, i.e., the "s" ending is used.

1861   emancipation of the serfs in the parts of Ukraine controlled by the Russian Empire

And the sun will rise   from a poem by *Shevchenko

arshyn   about two feet

berkovets   weight equivalent to 400 pounds, or 181 kilograms

Bismark   Otto von Bismark (1815-98) German statesman and first chancellor (1871-90) of modern German Empire

Black Hundreds   organization of monarchist and ultranationalist landowners, bureaucrats, intellectuals, and clergy

Browning   pistol designed by John Browning (1885-1926)

Casimir the Great   Casimir III (1310-70) Polish king known for legal reforms and expanding the territory of Poland

cast the kutya   Ukrainian tradition: at the start of the Christmas Eve Supper the father casts a spoonful of *kutya up to the ceiling to divine prospects for the coming year

chornozem   rich, black soil [Russian: chernozem]

cluck in the hay   Ukrainian tradition: hay, symbolizing Christ's manger, is scattered under the Christmas Eve Supper table and children scramble for treats hidden in it

Cyclopes   [Class. Myth.] giants with a single round eye in the middle of their foreheads

desyatyna   [pl. desyatyny] land measure; 2.7 acres

Duma   Ukrainian regional and national parliaments

first star   Ukrainian tradition: the Christmas Eve Supper begins only after children see the first star in the heavens

free labour   unpaid labour required of peasantry by the nobility

Galician Pole   ethnic Pole in living in *Halychyna

God's fool   a strange, humble, perhaps mentally ill person; in old times respected for religiosity

Gonta   Ivan Gonta (?-1768) leader of a rebellion of kozaks against
             the Polish-Lithuanian Commonwealth
Gracchi   two Roman brothers circa 2nd c. BC; tribunes who used
             oratorical skills to push through radical social and
             economic legislation to redistribute land, relieve poverty
Halychyna   [Galicia] historical region in southwestern Ukraine
haydamaka   [pl. haydamaky] 18th c. freedom fighter in Western
             Ukraine; fought against Polish oppression, serfdom
Henya   endearing diminutive form of Yevhen
Hohol   Mykola Hohol (1809-52) [Russian: Nikolai Gogol]
             Ukrainian novelist who wrote in Russian; his novel *Taras
             Bulba*, was about a *kozak who led his sons into battle
             against Polish lords
Holy Supper Ukrainian Christmas Eve Supper that consists of
             twelve Lenten dishes
hryvenyk   former coin equivalent to about 3 pennies
Huysmans   Joris Karl Huysmans (1848-1907) Dutch novelist
Irkutsk   place of exile since the 18th century; capital of Eastern
             Siberia since 1822
Ivan the Terrible   Ivan IV (1530-1584) Grand Prince of Moscow;
             expanded the medieval state into an empire of which
             he became the first Tsar
Ivas   endearing diminutive of Ivan
jeszcze Polska nie zginela . . . opening line of Polish national anthem:
             Poland has not yet perished
karbovanets [pl. karbovantsi] dollar in pre-1966 Ukrainian currency
Kayala River   site of 1185 battle as described in *The Tale of Ihor's
             Campaign,* an epic poem written in the 12th c by an
             unknown author; based on traditional minstrelsy the
             unique work is renowned for its rich language, folk
             influences, and Christian motifs
Kasprowicz   Jan Kasprowicz (1860-1926) Polish poet, playwright, critic
khakhol   [pl. khakly; also khokhol, pl. khokhly] derogatory
             Russian term for a Ukrainian person
Kościuszko   Tadeus Kościuszko (1746-1817) Polish soldier; led an
             unsuccessful uprising against Russia in 1794
kopiyka   [pl. kopiyky] hundredth part of a ruble; penny
kozak   Ukrainian for "Cossack"; by this period the famous
             Zaporozhian Host that defended a free Ukraine had lost its
             independence and been incorporated into the Russian army

Kozak Council   gathering of free *kozaks to elect their own leaders, and democratically determine political and military issues

Kulparkiv   suburb of *Lviv where there is a psychiatric hospital

kutya   ancient ritual dish of boiled wheat, ground poppy seeds, and honey; the first of twelve Lenten dishes served at the Christmas Eve Supper

kvass   sour-sweet lightly fermented beverage made from malt, rye bread, etc.

Lermontov   Mykhayil Yurievych Lermontov (1814-41) leading Russian romantic poet and novelist

Lucheni   Luigi Lucheni (1873-1910) Italian anarchist; assassinated the Empress of Austria in 1898

Lviv   historical capital of *Halychyna and Western Ukraine; cultural intermediary between Western and Eastern Europe

Lyubov   formal for Lyuba

Matka Boska   Polish for Mother of God

Matka Polska   Polish motherland

Medusa   [Class. Myth.] beautiful maiden punished by the gods who turned her hair into hissing serpents; whoever looked at her turned into stone

Mickiewicz   Adam Mickiewicz (1798-1855) revered as the national poet of Poland

morg   land measurement; the equivalent of about one acre

Morituri te salutant [Latin]   Those who are about to die salute you; said by Roman gladiators upon entering an arena

Mukden   Russian base in China, captured by Japan in 1905

Muscovite   native or inhabitant of Moscow

Mykola I   [Russian: Nicholas I] (1796-1855) conservative Russian Tsar under whom the empire reached its greatest geographical extent

Mykolayivski soldiers   soldiers of *Mykola I

Narodowy democrat   reactionary Polish party

Narzan   Caucasian mineral water

National Duma   see Duma

Nekrasov   Nikolai Nekrasov (1821-78) renowned Russian poet

Nero   emperor of Rome, 54-68 AD, said to have "fiddled while Rome burned"

Novoingermanlanski   regiment in the Imperial Russian Army

October 17   Russian Tsar signed the October manifesto in 1905 granting basic political rights

O, gentle world . . . from a poem by Taras *Shevchenko

okhranyteli   agents of the Tsarist secret police

Oleksander   formal for Sashko

Orpheus   [Class. Myth.] poet who played his lyre so wonderfully
that wild beasts were spellbound

otaman   [also hetman] leader of a *kozak army

palyanytsya   [pl. palyanytsi] wheaten flatbread

perestroika   Russian term for reorientation, reformation

pood   weight equivalent to 40 pounds or 18.1 kilograms

Port Arthur   [now Lushun] city in northeastern China; captured by
Japan in the Russo-Japanese war, 1904-05

Potemkin   Russian battleship whose crew mutinied against their
Tsarist officers in 1905 in support of workers

Procrustean bed   [Class. Myth.] Procrustes stretched or amputated the
limbs of victims to make them fit his bed; an arbitrary
standard to which exact conformity is forced

Prosvita   Ukrainian organization for the promotion of education and
culture

Rachael   after the slaughter of male infants on Herod's orders in his
wish to kill the newborn Christ, Rachel's lamentation was
heard on high; symbolizes mothers who weep over the
deaths of their children

Russian occupation in this context refers to Russian imperial control of
eastern Ukraine from the mid-17th to early 20th c.

Rusyn   inhabitant of traditional Ukrainian lands; in this period
mostly used for Ukrainians in Austro-Hungarian Empire

Sha River   site of major battle in Russo-Japanese war in 1904

Shevchenko   Taras Shevchenko (1814-1861) his artistic talent bought him
out of slavery, but his inspired, visionary poetry in which he
championed the universal ideals of liberty and justice,
brought him exile and military penal servitude; revered as
the bard and castigating prophet of Ukraine, his profound
influence on its national and cultural life remains to this day

Sienkiewicz   Henryk Sienkiewicz (1846-1916) patriotic Polish writer;
father's family actively engaged in the revolutionary
struggle for Polish independence

Skalon   Georgi Skalon (1847-1914) governor of Warsaw who
introduced martial law leading to deadly protests; in 1906,
Polish Socialist Party member Wanda Krahelska bombed
his carriage, but he survived

Soma   endearing diminutive for Solomiya

Spartan   the Spartans of ancient Greece were renowned for their rigorous discipline, courage, and austerity

Stańczyk member of a reactionary Polish party

Stundists members of a Baptist sect that originated in Russia in the the mid-nineteenth century

Swede at Poltava Swedish-*kozak army was defeated by Russian forces at Poltava in 1709; reference to "a Swede a Poltava" means total defeat

Telin   an area in China

the blue sky from the poem "Autmun" written in 1883 by Ukrainian Romantic poet Yakiv Shchoholiv (1823-1898)

the great chain. . . from the long satyrical poem "Who Lives Well in Russia?" written in 1873-76 by *Nekrasov

Tolstoyan follower of ideas of Leo Tolstoy (1828-1910), acclaimed Russian writer of aristocratic descent who advocated a simple, religious life of manual labour

Tsushima strait between Korea and the Japanese island of Kyushu; Russian fleet was defeated there by the Japanese in 1905

uncle   term used by peasants when talking about or addressing an older man, not necessarily a relative

verst   land measure equivalent to .66 miles or 1.07 km.

We will light a fire . . . from a poem by *Shevchenko

Biographical Notes

Mykola Chernyavsky
(1868-1946)

Mykola Chernyavsky was born into a village priest's family in eastern Ukraine. He graduated from the Katerynoslav theological seminary in 1889, taught in a church school in Bakhmut from 1889-1901, worked as a statistician in Chernihiv and Kherson until 1919, and then returned to teaching. He embarked on his writing career in 1885 by publishing lyrical poetry that he wrote under the influence of *Shevchenko and Ukrainian folk poetry, and went on to write historical poems, sonnets, short stories, novellas, and memoirs. Under Soviet rule he became less active as a writer and translator, and ceased publishing in 1933. Even though he distanced himself from politics, he was accused of nationalism and persecuted by Soviet authorities. His works were prohibited until after Stalin's death, but even after his rehabilitation, not all his works were published.

Borys Hrinchenko
(1863-1910)

Hrinchenko, the son of an impoverished noble in Eastern Ukraine who forbade his children to speak Ukrainian, became a prominent Ukrainian writer, translator, ethnographer, linguist, community leader, and political activist. He wrote short stories, novellas, and plays that focussed on the plight of peasants in Ukraine; translated the works of Western European writers; established a publishing house in Russian-ruled Ukraine that published ethnographic materials and popular-educational books despite severe censorship; and compiled a four-volume dictionary of the Ukrainian language based on ethnographic records and literary works of the 19th century. In his articles and books he expounded his ideas, based on his many years of community work and political activity, about shaping "out of the Ukrainian nation one nationally conscious, enlightened community" that would eliminate the gap between the common people and the intelligentsia.

Pylyp Kapelhorodsky
(1882-1942)

Kapelhorodsky was born in 1882 into the large family of a landless former serf in a village in the province of Kharkiv. A gifted pupil, he obtained his schooling at crown expense by agreeing to enter a seminary in 1897, but he voluntarily left it in 1902 after being identified by police as a participant in revolutionary activities. Persecuted by the tsarist authorities for the revolutionary poetry that he began publishing in 1905, he was forced to go into exile in Kuban. After the October Revolution he returned to Ukraine where he worked for several newspapers. In addition to writing poetry, short stories, novels and novelettes, he was a prolific satirist and publicist. Accused of being a nationalist, he was arrested in March 1938, during the persecution of the Ukrainian intelligentsia. He was posthumously rehabilitated after the death of Stalin.

Hnat Khotkevych
(1877-1938)

Born in Eastern Ukraine, Khotkevych worked as a professional railroad engineer in Kharkiv. A man of many talents, he was also scholar, a highly popular writer of short stories, novels, and plays, and a prolific translator of Shakespeare, Moliere, Hugo and Schiller. In addition, he gained renown as a composer, a gifted bandura performer and teacher, a theatre director, an editor, and a civic figure. Forced to emigrate to Western Ukraine in 1906 after organizing and actively participating in a railroad strike, he returned to Kharkiv in 1912, and later participated in Soviet cultural life. One of the most widely read authors in Ukraine, an eight-volume collection of his works was published in 1928-32. Unfortunately, he was arrested during the Yezhov terror in Ukraine (1937-38) when the intelligentsia was decimated, and he perished under unknown circumstances. He was rehabilitated after Stalin's death, and a collection of some of his literary works was published in two volumes in 1966.

Mykhaylo Kotsyubynsky
(1864-1913)

One of the most talented Ukrainian writers, Kotsyubynsky was born in Western Ukraine. In 1882 he was expelled from a theological seminary for his Populist views and placed under police surveillance for the rest of his life. Unable to obtain a higher education, he read voraciously to satisfy his intellectual needs. In his short stories that he began publishing in 1890, there is a progression from a realistic, populist style to one that incorporates impressionistic techniques and devices. Drawing upon his interest in man's internal spiritual states, the horrors of the 1905 Revolution, and his perceptive observations of the people among whom he was living, be it in his own land or during his work-related expeditions to Bessarabia and Crimea, he explored both the dark side of human nature, and its optimistic, life-affirming traits. A number of his short stories draw on pagan demonology and folk legends, and are marked by a subtle psychological realism and a lyrical impressionism.

Bohdan Lepky
(1872-1941)

Lepky was born in western Ukraine. After studying at universities in Lviv, Vienna, and Cracow, he became a professor at Cracow University in Poland (1899-1914). He began publishing short stories in 1895 and poetry a few years later. During the First World War, he taught Ukrainians interned in German prisoner-of-war camps and worked for the Union of the Liberation of Ukraine. After the war he wrote historical novels and, from 1921-1926, instructed courses organized by the Association of Ukrainian Students in Berlin. In 1926 he returned to Cracow University and taught there until 1939. A man of many talents, he devoted his life to the promotion of Ukrainian culture. He published numerous articles on Ukrainian literature, compiled songbooks, primers, and poetry anthologies, and translated Ukrainian literature into Polish, and European literature into Ukrainian. He was also an accomplished artist who included among his works many portraits and historical paintings.

Yakiv Mamontov
(1888-1940)

Mamontov was born into a peasant family in a small village in the county of Sumy. His parents were determined to see that their son receive an education and they managed to send him to a high school near Kharkiv. At this school Mamontov displayed a great talent for drama, and it is in this field that he earned himself a prominent place in Ukrainian literature as a dramatist, a professor, a theatre historian, critic, and theoretician. In addition to writing his own plays that centred on the revolution, he adapted a number of *Shevchenko's works for the stage and wrote librettos for operas. Initially, he also wrote some poetry and prose, and the story in this book was the first one that he published. His plays were very popular and were frequently staged in the 1920s; in the 1930s, however, they were banned by Soviet censors. Fortunately, Mamontov was not arrested during Stalin's repression of intellectuals, and he continued writing and teaching in postsecondary schools in Kharkiv until his death in January 1940.

Leonid Pakharevsky
(1883-1938?)

Pakharevsky was born in a village near Kaniv in Eastern Ukraine. After graduating from Kyiv University and the Lysenko School of Music and Drama, he embarked on a promising career in the theatre as an actor, director, playwright, and critic. In 1905 he began publishing short stories in major journals and newspapers, and over the years his prose style evolved from populism to impressionism. Like a number of other authors, he stopped participating in the literary and cultural life of Ukraine during the Soviet period and traded in his career for a teaching position in a school for workers in Kyiv. It is generally assumed that despite his attempt to lower his profile, he suffered political persecution during the Soviet terror of the 1930s, and died in either 1938 or 1941.

Oleksa Slisarenko
(1891-1937)

Slisarenko is the pseudonym of Oleksa Snisar, a poet and prose writer who grew up in a small village in the province of Kharkiv. While attending high school in Kharkiv, he became an avid reader. He started his literary career as a poet, but in 1924 he introduced a new genre into Ukrainian prose when, under the influence of American and British authors, he began writing thrillers. In these prose works he focussed on the unpredictable reactions of people who were caught up in unusual situations in the period preceeding, during, and after the 1917 Revolution. His works, written at a furious rate, were uneven in quality, but they were very popular with Ukrainian readers. He was arrested in 1934 during Stalin's repression of intellectuals and sentenced to the Solovets Islands where he was executed in 1937. In the late 1950s he was posthumously rehabilitated and some of his works were republished.

Language
Lanterns
Publications

Other books available from

LANGUAGE LANTERNS PUBLICATIONS
www.languagelanterns.com

WOMEN'S VOICES IN UKRAINIAN LITERATURE

English translations of selected short fiction
by Ukrainian women authors

Translator: *Roma Franko*   Editor: *Sonia Morris*

Volume 1: The Spirit of the Times
Olena Pchilka (1861-1930), *Nataliya Kobrynska* (1855-1920)
Soft cover, 480 pp.; ISBN 0-9683899-0-2 (v.1) 1998

Volume II: In the Dark of the Night
Dniprova Chayka (1861-1927), *Lyubov Yanovska* (1861-1933)
Soft cover, 480 pp.; ISBN 0-9683899-1-0 (v.2) 1998

Volume III: But . . . The Lord Is Silent
Olha Kobylianska (1863-1942), *Yevheniya Yaroshynska* (1868-1904)
Soft cover, 480 pp.; ISBN 0-9683899-2-9 (v.3) 1999

Volume IV: From Heart to Heart
Hrytsko Hryhorenko (1867-1924), *Lesya Ukrainka* (1871-1913)
Soft cover, 480 pp.; ISBN 0-9683899-3-7 (v.4) 1999

Volume V: Warm the Children, O Sun
Stories about childhood and adolescence by several of the authors
Soft cover, 480 pp.; ISBN 0-9683899-4-5 (v.5) 2000

Volume VI: For a Crust of Bread
Stories about social values and marriage by several of the authors
Soft cover, 480 pp.; ISBN 0-9683899-5-3 (v.6) 2000

**Ukrainian Children's Literature
in English Translation**

Translator: *Roma Franko*   Editor: *Sonia Morris*

Once in a Strange, Faraway Forest
Yaroslav Stelmakh

Colour illustrations by
Anatoliy Vasylenko

A whimsical tale for children and their favourite adults

Soft cover, 96 pp.; ISBN 0-9683899-8-8   2001

Ukrainian Short Fiction in English

Translator: *Roma Franko*   Editor: *Sonia Morris*

Broken Wings
Anatoliy Dimarov

Transitions, choices, and turning points: coming of age
in Soviet Ukraine.

Soft cover, 320 pp.; ISBN 0-9683899-6-1   2001

Ukrainian Short Fiction in English

Translator: *Roma Franko*   Editor: *Sonia Morris*

A Hunger Most Cruel
Anatoliy Dimarov
Y evhen Hutsalo
Olena Zvychayna

The Human Face of the 1932-1933 Terror-Famine
in Soviet Ukraine

Soft cover, 288 pp.; ISBN 0-9683899-7-X   2002

Ukrainian Short Fiction in English

Translator: *Roma Franko*   **Editor:** *Sonia Morris*

Passion's Bitter Cup

Selected Prose Fiction by

Mykola Chernyavsky
Ivan Franko
Hnat Khotkevych
Yevhen Mandychevsky
Mykhaylo Mohylyansky
Stepan Vasylchenko
Volodymyr Vynnychenko
Sylvester Yarychevsky
Mykhaylo Zhuk

Soft cover, 352 pp.; ISBN 0-9735982-0-4   2004

Ukrainian Short Fiction in English

Translator: *Roma Franko*   **Editor:** *Sonia Morris*

Riddles of the Heart

Selected Prose Fiction by

Mykola Chernyavsky
Ivan Franko
Hnat Khotkevych
Mykhaylo Kotsyubynsky
Osyp Makovey
Mykhaylo Mohylyansky
Panas Myrny
Leonid Pakharenko
Valeriyan Pidmohylny
Stepan Vasylchenko
Volodymyr Vynnychenko

Soft cover, 352 pp.; ISBN 0-9735982-1-2   2004

Ukrainian Fiction in English

Translator: *Roma Franko*   **Editor:** *Sonia Morris*

Works by Ivan Franko (1856 – 1916)
Published on the 150th anniversary of the author's birth

Behind Decorum's Veil
For the Home Hearth: Dlya domashn'oho ohnyshcha
Pillars of Society: Osnovy suspil'nosti

Soft cover, 416 pp.; ISBN: 0-9683899-9-6   2006

Turbulent Times: A Trilogy

Volume I: Winds of Change
Hryts and the Young Lord: Hryts i panych
The Cutthroats: Rizuny
The Involuntary Hero: Heroy po nevoli
The Raging Tempest: Velykyy shum

Soft cover, 356 pp.; ISBN 0-9735982-2-0   2006

Volume II: Beacons in the Darkness
Unknown Waters: Ne spytavshy brodu
Lel and Polel: Lel' i Polel'

Soft cover, 416 pp.; ISBN 0-9735982-3-9   2006

Volume III: Fateful Crossroads
Fateful Crossroads: Perekhresni stezhky

Soft cover, 384 pp.; ISBN 0-9735982-4-7   2006

Ukrainian Short Fiction in English

Translator: *Roma Franko*   Editor: *Sonia Morris*

From Days Gone By
Selected Prose Fiction by

Yuriy Fedkovych
Ivan Franko
Borys Hrinchenko
Hnat Khotkevych
Oleksander Konysky
Panteleymon Kulish
Bohdan Lepky
Panas Myrny
Oleksa Storozhenko
Sydir Vorobkevych

Soft cover, 416 pp;   ISBN 978-0-9735982-5-4   2008

Ukrainian Short Fiction in English

Translator: *Roma Franko*   Editor: *Sonia Morris*

Down Country Lanes
Selected Prose Fiction by

Tymofey Bordulyak
Mykola Chernyavsky
Ivan Franko
Bohdan Lepky
Dmytro Markovych
Les Martovych
Stepan Vasylchenko
Volodymyr Vynnychenko

Soft cover, 416 pp;   ISBN 978-0-9735982-6-1   2008

Ukrainian Short Fiction in English

Translator: *Roma Franko*   **Editor:** *Sonia Morris*

Desperate Times: A Trilogy

The stories in this trilogy by a total of 18 authors explore the human side of the social, political and economic upheaval in Ukraine from the tumultuous opening days of the 20th century, through WWI, the 1917 Russian Revolution, and into the early 1920s under Soviet rule. The stories in this trilogy provide readers with a general sense of the historical progression from pre-revolutionary to post-revolutionary times.

Volume I: Brother against Brother
Selected Prose Fiction by

Mykola Chernyavsky
Borys Hrinchenko
Pylyp Kapelhorodsky
Hnat Khotkevych
Mykhaylo Kotsyubynsky
Bohdan Lepky
Yakiv Mamontov
Leonid Pakharevsky
Oleksa Slisarenko

Soft cover, 416 pp; ISBN 978-0-9735982-7-8   2010

Desperate Times: A Trilogy

Volume II: Between the Trenches
Selected Prose Fiction by

Borys Antonenko-Davydovych
Mykola Chernyavsky
Hryhoriy Epik
Vasyl Grendzha-Donsky
Hnat Khotkevych
Antin Krushelnytsky
Bohdan Lepky
Osyp Makovey
Dmytro Markovych
Oleksa Slisarenko
Stepan Vasylchenko
Volodymyr Vynnychenko

Soft cover, 416 pp; ISBN 978-0-9735982-8-5   2010

Volume III: Conflict and Chaos
Selected Prose Fiction by

Borys Antonenko-Davydovych
Hryhoriy Epik
Vasyl Grendzha-Donsky
Pylyp Kapelhorodsky
Antin Krushelnytsky
Bohdan Lepky
Valeriyan Pidmohylny
Oleksa Slisarenko
Stepan Vasylchenko

Soft cover, 416 pp; ISBN 978-0-9735982-9-2   2010